MW00980055

THE
PRISON
OF
POWER

A MAN-MADE TALE

G MICHAEL SMITH

INDIEOWL
PRESS

INDIE OWL
PRESS

4700 Millenia Blvd
Ste 175 #90776
Orlando, FL 32839

info@indieowlpress.com
IndieOwlPress.com

THE PRISON OF POWER: A MAN-MADE TALE

Illustrated by G Michael Smith

Cover art © Mila Supinskaya Glashchenko
Cover design & Interior layout/design by Vanessa Anderson
at NightOwlFreelance.com

Paperback ISBN-13: 978-1-949193-12-1
Hardcover ISBN-13: 978-1-949193-13-8

For Cheryl, who grabs my hand when I slip into the pit.

Michael Smith

"We still think of a powerful man as a born leader and a powerful woman as an anomaly."
— *Margaret Atwood*

THE BEGINNING

E've opened her eyes. The omni-present light stabbed like needles puncturing her face. The pain morphed, and she clutched her stomach as she rolled onto her back on the small cot. They had punched her there until she vomited. At that point, she stopped struggling. She did not want to, but she had no choice. She had used up all her strength. She had nothing left to fight with. They bent her over a waist-high beam and tied her down. She was naked; her legs spread wide. The sultry voice crooned over the speakers in the room, "Relax, you must accept it. This is what God intended for you. You are a vessel for the seed of man. Take solace in serving his will."

She slipped her hand between her legs. Everything down there hurt. She had to pee. Peeing would hurt. Not peeing would hurt more. She stood up and squatted over the hole. She relaxed the muscles to start the flow. A sharp pain made her clinch. The flow stopped. She relaxed again, prepared for the stinging she knew would come. She glanced down and saw her pee was pink. As her bladder emptied, she sighed. On her way back to her cot, she looked out of the cage that held her captive. She could hear the sounds of the others moving about. Across the aisle were cages. Overnight, one of the empty cages had gotten a new occupant. A pretty young girl with dark hair was sitting on the edge of her cot, staring straight at her. They made eye contact and, as if that had turned a switch, the girl stood and walked to the front of her cage.

Her fingers laced through the wire. She was wearing what Eve thought was a party dress. *Stupid bitch. That won't last long here,* she thought.

The girl glanced furtively down the aisles between the cages. "Where are we?" she asked. "Who are these people? What do they want?"

Eve sat down. "You will see soon enough. Word of advice—fight a little, but not too much. There are two things that get you killed in here: fighting too much and fighting too little." The girl in the cage opposite scrunched up her face in confusion. Eve lifted her tunic. She was naked underneath. She pointed to her legs and stomach. They were covered with green and black welts. "This happens when you fight too much."

"What about fighting too little?"

"Fighting too little means you must like what they do to you. Liking it is the worst sin. You are not allowed to like it, but you must endure it. Don't ever pretend you like it, or you won't survive. You will be branded as…God, what is the term they use…" Eve considered for another moment, "a succubus— an evil demon who tries to seduce men to her will. The previous occupant of your cell was one of those. She thought she could get special privileges by urging them on and pretending she liked it. She disappeared. I saw them take her away. They came to her cell with a wheelbarrow. She stood and tried to temp them with lewd actions and gestures. They stuck a cattle prod in her mouth and dumped her in the wheelbarrow. Then they all kneeled and prayed out loud. That was the last I saw of her."

"What did they pray?"

"Something like, and I'm paraphrasing here: *We thank you for revealing the evil hiding in this woman,* along with some other gibberish."

"What—"

"…do they do to the girls in here. Are you sure you want details?" said Eve.

The girl nodded slowly.

"They tie you up," she paused, "and spread you open." Eve stopped, as if explaining it was painful. "They rape you. Usually, three at a time. One for each orifice. You have to fight a little, but not too much. I used to fight, but now I just go limp and try to think of something pleasant. They finish and then return you to your cell. There are enough women here, so you have to go only once every couple of days. When a new girl arrives, those of us who have been here

2

awhile get a longer reprieve. You are going to be seen as a treat, and they all will want you over the next few days. Prepare yourself." Eve sat down on her cot. The girl slid down to the floor.

A bang echoed from the far end of the building, and the door opened. All the cells became silent. Eve looked up and saw three men with masks over their faces. They always wore masks, as if to protect themselves from the women who might recognize them. Eve did not fully understand it yet, but assumed it had something to do with fear. It seemed that men spent a great deal of energy hiding their fear of women from themselves. The men pushed an old-fashioned wheelchair they often used to restrain and transport their choice to the room at the far end of the aisle. As she predicted, they stopped in front of the new girl's cell.

"Stand up," one of them ordered.

The girl quickly got to her feet. "Don't hurt me. My mother has a lot of money. She can pay."

"Shut up and take a step back."

The girl stepped back.

The man opened the cage door, tossed a tunic on the floor, and shut the door again. "Strip and put that on."

"Take my clothes off?"

"That is what strip means," he laughed and turned to one of the other men, "this stupid little cunt is going to be fun."

The girl stood frozen. She stared, wide eyed, out at the men. "Strip and put the fucking tunic on!" shouted the man. The girl caught motion from the cage opposite and stared. It was Eve, gesturing and encouraging her to do what they had ordered.

One of the men turned and walked over to Eve's cell. She sat and looked at the floor. He simply banged the wire cage with his cattle prod and turned back. The girl slowly reached down and picked up the tunic. She held it against her as she slowly removed her clothes. She was about to slip the tunic over her bra and panties when the man shouted at her. "Everything off." He turned to the other men. "It looks like she is trying to hide something. I think we should search her. What do you boys think? She might have concealed something dangerous." The other two men nodded and opened the cage door. Two of the men entered and grabbed her arms. They held them out to the side while

3

the third man waved the arcing prod in front of her face. He took a knife from his pocket and pointed it between her breasts. With a flick of his wrist, he cut her bra in half and flicked it open with the end of the blade. She winced. He had nicked her skin and a bead of blood formed and ran down to settle in her navel. He did the same with her panties, and they hung between her clenched thighs. He stepped back. "Open your legs."

The girl moved her legs apart as tears started to flow down her face. "Please don't hurt me," she begged.

The men holding her arms started to walk her in a circular direction. She was now facing her cot. "Bend over," commanded the man behind her. The two men holding her pulled her arms down in encouragement. "Let go of her arms," ordered the man. "Now let's have a look at what this little twat might be hiding. Spread your cheeks." The girl was frozen in fear. The man grinned and slapped her buttocks hard. The girl started to cry. "I said, spread your cheeks." The girl reached behind her and pulled her cheeks open. "Lookie here, boys. She is a sweet one." The two men moved to stare at the naked girl standing bent over with everything exposed. He then shouted, "Stand up and put the tunic on. Maybe next time you will do what you are told without all this female bullshit."

The girl quickly grabbed the tunic and slipped it on. Her underwear lay where it had fallen. One of the men reached down and snatched it up. She moved like a zombie as they put her in the wheelchair and her arms were zip-tied to the arms of the chair. The three men wheeled the chair down the aisle.

A tear rolled down Eve's cheek as they passed her cell.

Nisheeta was thinking of her sister as she slipped into her gear. She had been a member of Fempol for five years. Next week she would write the officer's exam. It would mean a lot more credits and a bigger apartment. Eve would have a bedroom of her own. Nisheeta couldn't blame her for not coming home when home was just a sofa in the corner. Eve had not been to the apartment for over a month, and she was worried that something had happened. The longest time she had previously been absent was a couple of days. It would soon be five weeks. She needed to find out where she was. Her role as parent had been thrust upon her. Their parents were killed when Eve was very young. Nisheeta was ten years older than her sister. She knew her parenting skills left little to be desired and her role as policewoman made her a bit of a hard ass. That is what Eve often called her, usually followed by, *"You are not my mother"* and *"Go fuck yourself."*

She adjusted her helmet so her hair was not sticking out and looked around the change room. Everyone was almost ready when the sergeant entered.

"Okay, ladies, it is time. I know you have not been informed about this mission and believe me, there is a good reason. But it is time: We have received information about a male supremacist religious group operating right under our noses. Our informant tells us they are particularly nasty males who have been raping and killing women under the guise of religion. They have manipulated phrases from every religion that suggests women need to be suppressed and subjugated by men. They have made this their credo. They have been kidnapping young women and caging them in a large building just outside of the city. We think the area used is part of an organic farm. Some of the buildings are used to imprison women. The men running the farm are semi-autonomous, that is, there are no females in supervisory roles. I know that is an anomaly, but the men running the farm have always been trustworthy. Until now. As usual, the male of our species submits to his very base instincts. They fear women and feel they must hurt us to validate their own worth. They continue to provide reasons for us to keep them under control as well as protect ourselves. Our job today is to determine the truth of the matter. We have the entire farm under surveillance. Nothing gets in or out without our knowledge. This raid has to be kept secret to ensure we catch them all. I don't want any of them escaping, and I don't want any of their female prisoners hurt. Use your judgment when it comes to lethal force. Protect yourself at all cost."

All the officers stood and marched out to the vans waiting in the parking lot. There were three vehicles with 12 policewomen in each. Their job was to deploy and sweep the entire property. Each van would start at one of the three egress points. All the buildings would be swept. Nisheeta and fellow officers were in the third van. Their job was to enter the building believed to be where the female prisoners were being kept. A medical emergency truck would follow the van and be ready to provide emergency aid to any of the prisoners that were injured.

The farm was 45 minutes away. Nisheeta closed her eyes. Her nerves always seemed to calm just before a raid. She breathed deep and felt her body relax. The time to the location seemed to speed past. She felt the van slow to a stop, and she opened her eyes. The policewomen filed out of the van and concealed themselves behind it. It was 3 a.m. and the sky was overcast. The time had been well chosen, for the darkness was nearly absolute. None of the buildings had any exterior lights, which struck Nisheeta as odd. Why would these men want total darkness? There was no sound except for the croaking of frogs from a nearby pond. Suddenly, a muffled scream could be heard coming from the building they were to enter. Two of the policewomen stepped from behind either end of the van. They took one step toward the building. The others moved to follow. A series of low pops were heard, and Nisheeta saw the woman who stepped out from behind the van first fall.

"Ambush! Take cover," screamed one of the officers. All the women crouched back behind the van. "Can anyone see where that shot came from?" Another series of pops followed. The headlights of the van shattered. "Stay down, ladies," the lead officer commanded. Nisheeta could hear the lead talking into her COM. She was ordering some armored drones. Soon after, there was a buzzing sound, and more screams came from the building. A single thought crossed Nisheeta's mind, *The bastards knew we were coming.*

Eve woke as a scream echoed down the aisle of cages. She slipped off her cot and stepped to the gate of her cage. It was dark in the building. It was never dark. She could see flashlights moving down the far end of the aisle. She also saw flashes and heard muffled pops. Soon, the building filled with voices as the prisoners woke.

"Please. Don't," followed by the pop of what Eve quickly identified as a silenced weapon.

"Please don't kill me."

"They are shooting us. The fucking bastards are sh…" followed by the silenced pop of a gun.

Then there was only hysterical screaming being silenced by death. Eve froze in place as the men moved from cage to cage, shooting the occupants. She went to her cot and tried to make it look like she was still sleeping. She took off her tunic and hung it across the corner of her cell. It was what she usually did when she washed it and hung it up to dry. She was naked as she slipped behind her tunic. She crouched down in the darkness. If she was lucky, they would shoot the cot and move on to the next victim. She shivered.

One man shouted from the far end of the building. "Speed it up, boys. We have to get out of here in the next 5-minutes. Those cunts outside won't hesitate to shoot your little dicks off."

THE PRISON OF POWER: A MAN-MADE TALE

Eve could hear the pops getting louder and louder as the men approached. There was a space between the sleeve of her tunic and the main skirt. She peered through and saw that there was one man on each side of the aisle. They shot in a staggered pattern as they approached. One pop on one side and then another pop on her side. The time between the pops was decreasing.

"Pop ……. pop …… pop ….. pop …. pop … pop .. pop."

They were racing. Suddenly they stopped. Eve could see that the new girl was standing naked right up at the front of her cage. Both of the men stopped and stared at her. Eve heard her speak. "Don't shoot me, and I will suck both your cocks. You can cum all over me. Would you like that?"

"Hey, Billie, did you get to fuck this one?" Eve assumed Billie shook his head in the negative for that was followed by, "Neither did I. She is pretty hot. I would love to fuck her in the ass."

"Take me with you and I will let you fuck me any time you want." She turned around, stuck her ass out, and looked over her shoulder at the two men.

"Maybe we could fuck her now. My cock is rock hard. Open the cage," he said and glanced down the aisle in the direction of the voice that had ordered them to hurry.

Then they both looked up as they heard a series of pops coming from the opposite direction of their travel. A flashlight flared in front of them, and a man stepped out of the darkness. He stared at the naked girl in the cage. She smiled back weakly. "What the fuck are you two idiots doing!? We have our orders!" He lifted his gun and fired right into the girl's face. Eve saw her fall to a lump on the floor of her cell. He turned and glanced at Eve's cell, fired at her cot, and then turned back to the men. "Looks like we are finished. I looked after those." he nodded his head in the direction he had come from. "Let's get out of here."

The three men ran down the aisle to the far end of the building and disappeared. The giant room was silent again. Eve slipped to the ground. The smell of gunpowder mixed with the copper smell of blood and the stench of shit filled the air. Eve heaved, then thought better of it and pinched herself hard to overcome the nausea. She needed to remain still and silent. Someone might come back to check if they had killed everyone. She was alive and planned to stay that way. The only thing she felt was bitter disdain—cold, hard hate. It was the monster she needed to embrace and nurture if she was to remain sane.

The buzzing increased as the drones surrounded the building. They were invisible in the darkness. The drones fired at targets that were invisible to the police, hunkered down behind the van. There were shooters on the roof of the building and the drones found and killed them. The lead officer spoke into her COM and then turned to the others. "We got them all. Go."

The officers ran in single file to the building and stopped, backs to the wall, near the single door on the side of their approach. One officer moved to the door and scanned the perimeter with a device. She set small explosive charges near the hinges and the lock, then moved to the end of the line and stuffed the device back into her pack. Holding up the detonator, the lead officer looked at her and whispered, "Fire." The officer pressed the detonator button, and a sequence of muffled bangs were followed by the door hitting the ground. The lead officer glanced around the corner and shouted, "All clear." They entered the building and spread out in a staggered line. It was dark. The lead officer turned on the flashlight attached to her weapon. She aimed it in front of the group and scanned the opening to the aisle of cells. "Light up, ladies," she said, "Martin, Moss, Davenport, and Gomez go down that aisle. The rest of you split up and search the perimeter of the building for males and escape routes. They knew we were coming, so I don't expect any of them to still be here, but don't take any chances."

Nisheeta Davenport and Marie Gomez took the left-hand side of the aisle. The smell of death proceeded any images that their flashlights revealed. Nisheeta looked at the lock on the first cage, took a cutter from her tool belt and cut it off. Gomez opened the door and stepped inside. There was someone on the cot. Nisheeta approached the cot and pulled gently on her partially exposed shoulder. "You're alright now. It is all over." She pointed her flashlight at the head and withdrew with a groan as the body rolled over. The woman had been shot in the back of her head and all that was left of her face was the mouth and lower jaw. Her head hung sideways, mouth gaping open, from the edge of the cot. The blood had long since drained onto the cot. "Oh, fuck no. Those monsters. They killed her."

From across the aisle, Kathy Moss staggered out of the cage on her side and ran around the end. Nisheeta could hear her retching.

Angela Martin whispered, "This one is dead."

"So is this one," said Nisheeta. "Fuck." She directed her flashlight down the aisle. The only noise was the ragged breathing of Kathy Moss as she tried to get her queasy stomach under control. "It is so quiet. I think they killed them all." She walked down the aisle, pausing at each cage and directing her light onto the body inside. "Fuck, I hate men. The sooner we get rid of them, the better."

Suddenly there was the sound of breakers connecting, and the lights popped on. They all shielded their eyes from the bright lights and blinked to adjust. An officer's voice could be heard shouting on the far side of the building, "Found the breakers. Also found their escape route. I think it is booby-trapped."

The lead officer ordered all the officers to join her at the door to the building. The women gathered there. Some were crying, and some were staring into space as if the horror of the place had shocked them into silence. "I suspect they killed all the women they held in here, but I need to be sure. We need to open every cage and check the bodies for life signs. Don't touch anything else. The forensic team will be here shortly, and they will want to document everything." She looked at Kathy Moss, who sniffed. "I know this is horrible, but we need to do our job. If you can't, then I would rather you went outside and stood guard. Are we clear?"

14

"I'm alright," said Moss, knowing full well the lead's comment was directed at her.

All the officers moved to open the cell doors and check for life signs.

E ve sat naked on the cold floor with her tunic pulled tightly around her. Her mind turned inward. Her senses were blocked. She no longer heard the gunfire. She no longer smelled death. She did not hear the police enter the building. All her thoughts were of blank walls. White walls surrounded every facet of her being. Even the hate she swore to was wrapped in a protective white sheet. She needed to feel nothing. She felt nothing.

When the lights came on, she blinked at their brightness. She could hear voices as she slowly left the safety of her mind cocoon. She thought they were women's voices, but she needed to be sure, so she pulled the tunic to cover her head and waited naked in the darkness. The voices stopped. They were replaced by the banging of locks and the creaking of opening cage doors. Eve felt the whiteness enveloping her again. They were coming to make sure everyone was dead. She became an inanimate object under a tunic in the corner of the cell. As the rattle of locks and opening doors got closer, she froze until she was barely breathing. Then they were there. They were opening her cage door. She felt the light filtering through the tunic, slowly turning it a darker grey. They stood in front of her. She stopped breathing altogether. A part of her tensed. She would fight. The motion of shifting light told her that someone was about to rip away the tunic and expose her. She decided she would try one last time to save herself. As the tunic began to move, she leapt to her feet and flew at the uniform in front of her. She flailed her arms, but with each flail she became weaker and weaker until she simply flopped down like a rag doll. She did not hit the ground. Someone caught her. She tried one more time to strike out, but her arms would not follow her orders. There were voices, but they made no sense. They were just echoes that conjured up terror. She was going to die. The white sheet grew taut in her mind. She would not give them any satisfaction by begging for mercy. They did not have mercy. They were men, and men were merciless and evil. She let her body go completely limp and felt someone hold her up and carry her out of the cell. The voices slowly became clear.

"She is alive, but barely. Call the EMTs," said Maria.

"Has she been shot?" said Kathy.

"Grab that blanket off of the cot and lay her down here. I will check," said Nisheeta. They lay the girl down on the blanket. Nisheeta brushed her hair back from her face. "Oh God. Oh God. This is my sister. Eve, are you shot anywhere!?" Nisheeta did not wait for an answer. She picked up her sister, like one would pick up a small child, and coddled her in the blanket. She started to run to the entrance. That is where the EMTs would be. Just as she approached the door, they entered with a gurney. They took Eve from Nisheeta's arms and whisked her away. Nisheeta trailed behind muttering, "Evee, my poor Evee, I'm sorry. I'm sorry. I should have searched for you. My god, Evee, I will kill every one of those fuckers."

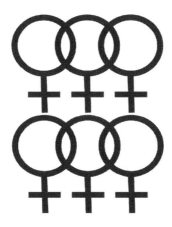

The area surrounding the organic farm was cordoned off. That was expanded to encompass the suburban area extending outward three kilometers in diameter. The area was huge. All egress was surveilled by drones. Fempol went house to house interviewing all males living within the boundaries. Every alibi for the night in question was checked. If there was any doubt as to the validity of these alibis, the names and numbers of the male were recorded, and they were tagged with ankle bracelets. Males providing alibis for other males were treated with skepticism. This continued until Fempol had compiled a little over 200 suspects they wished to interview as to their location on the night in question, as well as their political and social leanings. In reality, they all were to be interrogated using the latest techniques and equipment. Since there was no place big enough for this operation, a local sports arena was commandeered. All the suspects were brought to the arena and seated in the lower tiers, twenty-five men to a section. Fempol officers guarded each section. They were taken one at a time to one of the eight interrogation rooms. After the interrogation, they were returned to a different section of seats beside those not yet interrogated. As the day progressed, one section of seats slowly emptied and the other filled. The individual interrogations were taking far longer than anticipated. Thoughts as to the basic physical requirements of these men were not considered. This, as it turned out, was a huge error. Five hours in, a group of men, still to be interrogated, requested to use the facilities. This was followed by the other section requesting the same thing. Fempol decided to take the men ten at a time to the washrooms on the mezzanine. They still wanted to keep the men in their respective sections, so they were taken to different washrooms. The second washroom was much more distant from the first. All went well until a group of men returning from the washroom demanded that they be fed. They began to chant, "Feed us. Feed us." They all refused to move anywhere until their demands were met. It was soon obvious that the numbers of Fempol officers assigned to the arena detail were insufficient to maintain control of such a large group of males. That is when it happened.

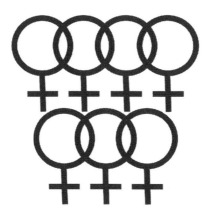

The court room was filled with women. There were a few males interspersed in the audience. At the front of the room was a large table on a raised platform. There were seven chairs in a row. There was a table with three chairs facing the platform. A woman entered, followed by six other women. The courtroom deputy spoke, "Please stand for the honorable Judge Renee Parker and the panel of investigators." Everyone stood. She waved them down, and the audience settled. She and her panel were seated.

She rapped a gavel on the table and spoke. "This is a Public Inquiry. We are here today to find out what happened at the sports arena on September 16, 2034. We are not here to place blame but only to determine the exact events that precipitated the deaths of 16 Fempol officers and over 200 male suspects. My staff and I will be calling a number of witnesses to determine an accurate sequence of events. We will then issue a set of recommendations to the parties involved to ensure that this horrific tragedy never happens again." She picked up a sheaf of papers and looked at the top sheet. I would like to call Fempol Officer Nisheeta Davenport." There was a mumbling from the audience. Nisheeta stood and walked down to the table. She was followed by two other women carrying briefcases. They all sat. The two lawyers accompanying Ms. Davenport opened their cases, removed some files, and placed them down on the table. "Ms. Davenport, I realize it is your right to have legal representation present, but I must stress that our intent is not to assign blame but to determine exactly what happened," said the judge.

Nisheeta stood, "Yes, your honor, I understand, but—" She was cut off by one of her lawyers who reached out and touched her arm. The lawyer stood, and Nisheeta stood beside her. The lawyer spoke, "Your Honor, it is our understanding that this court does not intend to place blame for these events and those that precipitated them, but blame will need to be placed somewhere. The women of this country will demand it. The media and social media will need a scapegoat. We are here to ensure that such blame does not fall on our client but exactly where it needs to fall: on the criminal males who are responsible for the torture and deaths of 39 women held captive for their depraved amusement and those men who took the law into their own hands in the arena. We will advise our client as to the kinds of questions she can answer."

"Thank you, Ms. Davenport. Please be seated. I would like this to be as informal as possible. Remember, we are just after the truth. Now, Ms. Davenport, I would like to start on Wednesday, September 13, 2034. Please tell us what occurred on this day."

"I was part of a group of officers selected to take part in a raid on a group of males suspected of being involved in a nefarious plot against women. The plan was to place officers at all the exits of the property in question and send squads of officers to each of the large buildings. I was part of the squad that was sent to building three."

"Am I correct in saying that the property in question was historically an organic farm and the buildings previously housed large greenhouses."

"Yes."

"What time did this raid take place?"

"We arrived at approximately 3 a.m."

"What happened when you arrived at building three?"

"We took fire. A squad officer was shot by a sniper when she stepped out of the protection of the van. I think someone ordered drones to seek and destroy the snipers. There was some gunfire, and then we were given the OK to enter the building." Nisheeta stopped as the memory of the first moments inside the building washed over her. The emotion swelled, and she pushed it aside.

"Please continue."

"The first thing that hit us was the smell. It was a mixture of gunpowder and death. I will never forget it. We walked between the rows of cells, opening them as we went. The women held captive were dead. They had been shot while they slept."

"Except your sister," interjected the judge.

"Yes. We found her alive. She hid in the corner of her cell after disguising her cot to make it appear as if she was sleeping. She was the only one alive. She was…," Nisheeta put the fingertips of both hands to her forehead and breathed a long sigh. The judge and the panel watched her, but they did not interject. They simply waited. Nisheeta stood erect and placed her hands on the table in front of her. "I was going to say that my sister was lucky she survived, but I am not so sure that surviving and having to relive that horror for the rest of your life makes you lucky." She paused again. The court was silent in anticipation.

"Ms. Davenport, we know this is difficult, but could you please inform the court what went on at this house of horrors."

Nisheeta became still. Her lawyer quickly stood. "Your honor, all this information is fully detailed in the report before you. I do not think it is necessary to have my client relive what was a very traumatic event."

"Ms. Davenport is a member of our elite Fempol section. She has been trained to deal with these kinds of situations, and I would like her to tell the court what went on in these buildings. Ms. Davenport, please continue."

"After my sister was taken away for treatment by the medical staff, we began a systematic exploration of the premises. The main cell block was designed to hold fifty prisoners. At the time of the raid, there were forty. Attached to this building were a number of smaller rooms that held what can only be described as torture equipment. A common item was something akin to a gymnastics pommel horse, only smaller. The walls were covered with poster-sized images of all the women that had been tortured in this room, as well as several religious quotes suggesting that all women are only on the planet to serve the needs of the male of the species. One did not have to guess what went on."

"Continue."

The lawyer stood again. "Your honor," she protested.

THE PRISON OF POWER: A MAN-MADE TALE

The judge gestured toward the women on the panel. "We know the result. We would like some insight into how these officers reacted when they first discovered it. Please continue."

Nisheeta was determined to detail the factual contents of the rooms with no emotional asides. "According to our only witness account, the women were brought into the room by three men each time. They were bent over the pommel horse with their legs spread and their arms bound to the side. A webbed leather helmet with a plastic mouthpiece attached was placed over their head. A rope extended from the top of the helmet to a ring on the ceiling. Its purpose was to hold their head up and their mouth open." She stopped and stared at the panel. "Again, the reasoning for this is pretty obvious."

"Your reaction to what happened is not obvious, so please continue. What happened to these women after they were restrained?"

"They were forced to fellate, and they were sodomized and raped by all three men multiple times. They were pinched, whipped, spanked, caned, beaten, and shocked during the rapes. After the men were finished, they urinated on the victim. Then she was released and sent to a shower before being returned to her respective cell. We have since learned that some of the older women, no longer subjected to these acts, were sent in to clean up the messes left behind."

The panel watched her reactions to the narrative as she spoke. Nisheeta kept all emotions hidden. The judge spoke, "Thank you, Officer Davenport."

One of the panel members spoke. "I took an interest in the quotes that were on the walls of these rooms. I would like you to know that none of these supposed "religious" phrases are part of any documented religion. Not the Bible or the Quran, etc. They are simply opinions to support the behaviors indulged in by these males. It is hard to interpret their behavior as a religious cult belief structure. It seems that this was just a way of inflicting revenge on women for usurping male power. It leads me to state, on the record, the importance of education. We must not make men feel they are powerless. If we do, we risk more of these cults in the future. All members of our society must be treated with respect. Yes, I know and agree that the males of our species are not capable of governing, but we must not treat them like animals. They have their place, and it is on us to validate their existence."

"On that note, I would like to call a recess. We will reconvene this afternoon.

Ms. Davenport, I would like to complete your testimony regarding the events that occurred at the arena, specifically the events that led to the carnage." The judge banged her gavel on the table and stood. The room cleared.

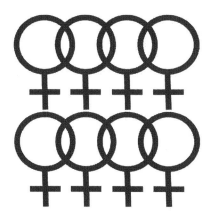

The judge tapped her gavel on the table. "We are all familiar with the events in general terms. To recap: a group of twelve male suspects waiting to be interviewed were taken from section 23 to use the washroom facilities off the concourse above section 25. They were supervised by three officers of Fempol. The officers were armed with automatic rifles." She looked up at Nisheeta. "It seems odd to me that the officers were armed with automatic rifles. Am I to understand that is the new normal for officers of Fempol? I thought these officers were not armed with firearms. Isn't the standard weapon a stun gun? If so, why were these officers armed with weapons of this type?"

The lawyer stood up. "The answer to that question is not within the purview of my client. She was not in charge of the weapons requirements for this action."

"We realize that. What I want to know is what the officers were told as to why the operation required such firepower? Ms. Davenport—what were you told?"

"We were told that our kits were modified to ensure that the situation would remain in our control. There were two hundred men, give or take. I am sure your honor will agree that many males in one place constitute a greater danger to females in the vicinity, especially after the horrors that took place at the farm. The men who perpetrated the murders and rapes at the farm were likely in this group. We were all on high alert."

"Thank you. To continue, the men entered the washroom while the officers stood guard outside. A plan of sorts was hatched by these men. They exited the washroom as a group. The center of the group surged into the officers and disarmed them. According to reports, the officers were beaten by these men, who were now in possession of three automatic rifles. One of the officers later died. As they moved back to their section, a second group from section 22 was about to be escorted to the washroom facilities. You were one of the escorts of this group, were you not?"

Nisheeta nodded.

"Please use your voice."

"Yes, I was."

"There seem to be some discrepancies and inconsistencies between your version of events and the forensic version. You were behind the group and the other two officers were on either side. Officer Halpren, on the left, saw the beaten officers first and moved toward them, followed by the officer on the right. As they crouched over the bodies, the men surged and tried to take their weapons. One of the men grabbed at officer Halpren's rifle. They struggled and the rifle fired into the ceiling. The officer succeeded in retrieving her weapon. The man lunged again at the officer. She hit him in the head with the butt of her rifle. Then there must have been a moment where everyone stopped. Officer…" She picked up a file and read the name of the officer, "Wong testified that all the men had their hands in the air, so she stood and stepped back. Suddenly more shots were fired and you, officer Wong and officer Halpren, fired into the group of men. They were all killed." She shuffled the files. "My question to you is, who fired that shot?"

"I am assuming one of the men tried to attack one of the other officers, resulting in a discharge. We all thought we were about to die at the hands of the mob. We acted in self-defense."

"And what did you do next?"

"We ran out of the concourse at the aisle between section 24 and 25. That is when we heard more gunfire. Some men overpowered the officers close to them and took their weapons. The resulting firefight ended with many of the men killed, along with many of my fellow officers. In my opinion, they got what they—"

The lawyer's hand reached out and stopped Nisheeta from continuing. She sat down.

"Thank you, Ms. Davenport. You may leave. This inquiry reserves the right to recall you if required."

A man seated at the back of the courtroom stood and started shouting. "You lying, cunts. You fucking murdered them in cold blood."

A second man on the other side of the room also stood and screamed, "Fucking murdering bitches. It was a massacre, plain and simple. You all should be strung up and gutted." He took off his shoe and threw it toward Nisheeta. It landed on the table.

Both men were apprehended by the court officers while the judge banged her gavel and called for order.

Nisheeta and her lawyers left the inquiry.

TREATISE

THE PRISON OF POWER: A MAN-MADE TALE

The following article is included to give the reader important background to the story. Most will not need this background as it is required reading for most of the cultures of Earth, but I include it for any future reader who might not be so informed.

"The Transmogrification of Power from Male to Female in the United States of America: A History" by Simi Timpani Rau

University of Delhi, New Delhi, India

January 2113

It was absolutely elemental.

It was definitely overdue.

It was astonishingly unforeseen by the power brokers.

It was the first essential step toward saving the planet and the species.

It was almost magical.

The exact moment in time when it started is unclear. There were several indicators: take, for instance, the author E. J. Carroll's 2017 'tongue in cheek' book titled, *What Do We Need Men For? A Modest Proposal.* Carroll referred to herself as an "Anti-Victim" after a rather nasty encounter with businessman turned celebrity turned politician named Donald Trump, but it seems the year 2020, during the Trump presidency, is the date most historians point to. For most, what happened that year seemed unlikely, if not impossible, the year before. The religious right had permeated the state governments of Louisiana, Missouri, Alabama, Georgia, Ohio, Utah, Mississippi, Kentucky, Texas, and Arkansas and began writing laws that restricted women's rights to their own bodies. Abortions were outlawed. The state legislators were almost entirely made up of white males. It was clear at the time that the focus on abortions had next to nothing to do with the stated rights of the fetuses in question. It was just an attempt at subterfuge. The actual reason was the need to ensure that women were punished for assuming they could do what men had been doing since the beginning of time. The motivation was fear.

The mid-term elections of the previous year resulted in an increase in female membership in the House of Representatives. Men on what was deemed "the far right" were afraid that females were going to take over the government and change the status quo. That fear, in retrospect, provided women with the impetus needed. It was those actions that pushed women to rebel at the ballot box. The number of females elected to high office swelled. By 2024, women filled nearly 50% of all municipal, state, and federal positions of government. Four years later, the number of women in government positions exceeded males. There was no looking back. Women changed the way America was governed. They funneled tax dollars away from the military and into health care, education, and infrastructure. They created legislation that required all companies that wished to do business in the US to install women into positions of power until they numbered 50% or more. There were even perks for companies that exceeded that ratio. By 2034, the government was dominated by women. At this point, it became obvious that the adversarial party system was not working. The philosophies of elected officials aligned. Changes happened much more rapidly than anyone would have thought possible 20 years previous.

> *- Religion was banned from government at all levels. You could have your beliefs, but there was no place for them in government.*
> *- The number of justices on the Supreme Court was increased, and they were no longer appointed in a bipartisan way.*
> *- The concept of a single president was replaced by a presidential committee headed by a single chairperson. The Electoral College was deemed superfluous and was abandoned.*
> *- The State's ability to enact laws specific to the state was removed. The only laws were federal statutes.*
> *- Lobbyists were banned.*
> *- Candidates for public office were financed by the government. Each candidate was allocated a sum of money to run a campaign. The amount varied according to the level of government aspired to.*
> *- Candidates had to meet specific requirements that demonstrated their suitability for public office. These requirements mostly focused on intellect and mental stability. The potential candidates' philosophies were never an impediment.*
> *- Weapons in the hands of citizens were banned. Millions of guns were destroyed.*
> *- Drug abuse was removed from the criminal code. It became a mental health issue. All drug addicts were supplied with whatever they required and provided safe injection sites. The billions of dollars spent*

THE PRISON OF POWER: A MAN-MADE TALE

on drug related policing was now available to support the recovery of addicts.

- Non-addictive substances were available through government regulated outlets. The monies raised went back into education. The effects of drug use were taught at all levels of the education system. The new philosophy embraced the logic that you could never force people to do anything, but you could educate them about the dangers. You could also ensure that all citizens were provided with all the material goods and services that ensured quality of life. This substantially reduced the numbers that turned to drugs.

- The Green New Deal, first conceived in the 2020s, became the mantra of the fight against climate change. Any company that demonstrated they were a part of the solution to this most dangerous situation was given tax breaks to the point where actual taxes required by any given company were determined by the degree that they could contribute to the reversal of global warming. The opposite was also true. The oil and gas industry slowly shrank to tiny boutique companies providing specialty goods. They were very costly to purchase for the tax rates on such items that contributed to global warming were exorbitant.

All of these changes did not happen overnight. There was a great deal of social upheaval. Large groups of men fought against many of these changes. These groups advocated tyranny. The police forces at every level had rumblings of government overthrow. The phrase, "Give'em power and they will take your balls!" rattled through all levels of society. This was the impetus that resulted in the formation of Fempol. If the new government was to survive, it would need to use the male tactics against them. Fempol was that force. It was the first societal group to be entirely female. Men were not allowed to be a part of this new police force. Thus, began the subjugation of the males in society. The more radical females supported the removal of all males from any sort of decision making. The reasoning for this always turned to history. Men were demonized for their violent tendencies. The year 2040 was notable as the year that men could no longer hold office or vote in any federal or state election. It was also the year that there were no wars being waged on the planet. The other even more notable event was the first year that the overall temperature on the planet actually decreased. It was only by 2 tenths of a degree Celsius, but it was globally celebrated. It was also used as confirmation that men nearly destroyed the planet and women would save it. The belief that men should never rise to power again was confirmed.

Science took that one step further. It was estimated that the 'Y' Chromosome would disappear in a little under 4.6 million years, given its present degenerative rate. Some fringe groups tried to speed things up and looked for ways to get rid of it altogether. Its time of usefulness was over, and it should be eradicated. After all, it was totally unnecessary for human life. More than half the species of humans survived perfectly well without it.

DISCURSION

THE PRISON OF POWER: A MAN-MADE TALE

DISCURSION (the process or procedure of rigorous formal analysis or demonstration, as distinguished from the immediate or intuitive formulation.)

The atomic incident of 2025 was the catalyst of a movement historically called "#MeNow." The Democratic People's Republic of Korea had acquired nuclear warheads and the rockets to shoot them. The leader was fighting a war of insults with the leader of the USA and decided it would be a "powerful show of strength" to drop one of its bombs on the neighboring country of Japan. The leader chose the same city that had experienced the first nuclear attack 78 years earlier. He dropped a bomb on Hiroshima and boasted that it was a bigger bomb than the USA had dropped at the end of WWII. China consulted with the US and a brief detente was agreed to. They now felt that North Korea's actions were dangerous to their desired image as a world leader. They planned with the US to disarm this rogue state. Together they responded with a series of tactical nukes attached to a fleet of high-altitude drones. They were paired with a series of bunker busters that served to open up all of North Korea's underground weapons caches. The attack was designed to destroy all infrastructure while leaving the population mostly unharmed. Russia, India, United Kingdom, France, Israel and Pakistan all went to high alert. There were some very tense moments before everyone took a deep breath and stepped back from the brink of total annihilation.

Over the intervening years, the "#MeNow" philosophy became more proactive and morphed into "#WeNow" then "#FeNow" then finally "#WOW" which was an acronym for "World Order by Women." This was the beginning of the new age. There were a number of women on the brink of taking power in their respective countries. The latest conflict opened the floodgates for females of the species to take control of almost all governments.

It didn't happen overnight, but by 2034, almost 80 percent of all countries were governed by females. Not much else changed until the United Nations took a larger role in world government. It was decided by the majority that all nuclear weapons were to be destroyed. The production of guns was to be greatly reduced. The USA carried it even further by collecting all firearms and melting them down. There were some that tried to hide weapons and claimed their rights were being trampled, but the women controlled all aspects of government and simply deleted the second amendment from the constitution. That was the start. Different countries had different rules for the male of the species. Some were more open—allowing the males more freedom to assume roles of authority. Others were more controlling and restricted male roles in society to a strictly working class. The "Land of the Free" became the most male restrictive society of all.

QUINLAN SMITH

Quinlan opened his eyes. A gray haze of light painted the walls, concealing the mottle of stain that edged up from the floor to below the high windows. He pulled the blanket to his chin and shivered. The room was small, with a sink and a toilet in one corner. There was a narrow bed, a three-drawer bureau, a wooden chair and a board hinged on the wall that served as a table. There were three books on the top of the bureau. He was allowed only three per year. He chose carefully. They had to last. Without something to read, he felt he would go insane. His first set, after graduation, when he turned thirteen, lasted less than a month. He spent eleven months rereading each, over and over, trying to pretend that he did not know the endings. This year he picked two large tomes titled *The Complete Works of William Shakespeare, The Concise Oxford Dictionary*—the mistake that turned out not to be a mistake—and *Existentialism and Human Emotions* by Jean Paul Sartre. He grabbed it because it was within reach, and he was out of time. The matron looked at him oddly, as if he were odd. He was sure he appeared odd to all the matron staff as well as the guards. He didn't care. He continued to stare at the window above, over the edge of the blanket that covered his nose. His breath was warming his hands and the end of his nose. He was hoping dawn would bring the sunshine down upon him, but the morning light was drab and gray—it was a dreary day—again. It would be cold and wet just like yesterday.

THE PRISON OF POWER: A MAN-MADE TALE

A clanging sound filled the air. The morning bell was ringing. Quinlan gritted his teeth in preparation for the cold air and tossed off the blankets. He peed, splashed cold water onto his face, and rubbed the night's deposits away with a towel. His entire wardrobe was draped over the chair where he had carefully placed it the night before. He quickly got dressed, made his bed, and folded his night shirt, placing it neatly on his pillow. He was practiced at this routine. He had ten minutes and was usually finished in three. That gave him seven minutes to read. He flipped open the Shakespeare's Works to a random page. He was presented with a sonnet. Sonnet 13. He quickly read it and, as usual, he understood little of what old Willy was talking about. But that was good. It was today's puzzle. He could think and reflect and never be bored for the entire day. He read the poem three more times, hoping it would stick in his mind so he could have it deciphered by the end of the day. He heard a rattle of keys and quickly closed the book and placed it back on the table. He stood smiling as the door opened. He blinked, for he did not recognize the woman standing in front of him. She wore a matron's dress with a utility belt around her large waist. The belt held the usual items used to deter anyone from acting in ways that were not acceptable. If you were in doubt and acted in a certain way, you soon found out whether you had stepped over the line. The matron held the expandable baton and was tapping it in her open hand. She was at the ready. Sometimes you were deterred even if you had not done anything that seemed to be unacceptable. Quinlan held his hands, palm forward, in front of him. He quickly dropped the smile, just in case this new matron thought he was being smart. If you were smart in some way or other, either by word or action, the baton was snapped open and you got whipped across the thigh. Major sassiness could get you whipped across the face. That left a scar. The scar itself told the matrons that you were prone to being smart. It sent a signal that you needed to be taught to follow all the rules and often got you whipped across the thigh just as a reminder.

Quinlan stood and waited. The matron looked him up and down, all the while slapping the baton in her other palm. Finally, she spoke. "Name."

"Quinlan Smith 62748517," he said clearly.

"Recite," she commanded.

Quinlan began, "The human race has been rescued. The female of the species has assumed the role of leader and lawmaker. The male of the species was deemed incapable. He has been subjugated and required to accept the role of lesser than that of the female."

"Do you accept this role for the good of all humans?"

"I accept and embrace my place in society for the good of all," said Quinlan. He lowered his hands. The matron motioned with her baton for him to leave the room. He walked out and down the hall. Behind him, he knew she had stepped into his room to check that he had left it neat and tidy. He heard his door close and the matron rap on the next door.

He walked quickly to the cafeteria. He liked eggs. If he was held up, all the eggs would be gone, and he would have to eat porridge. His pace quickened to just less than a jog. He was walking fast. Jogging would get you a baton across the back. He slowed just as he neared the open doors. He could see a few of the younger boys sitting and eating. He slipped into the line at the counter and picked up a tray. He waited. His stomach growled. He ducked quickly out of line to see what was holding everyone up. Patrick was at the front of the line. Patrick was big. He was not fat, just big. His red hair added to his flaming personality. He was the only person that lived in the school with at least three scars on his face and neck from vicious baton whippings. He seemed to be talking to the old man that was dishing out the eggs. He had two eggs on his plate.

Quinlan heard Patrick's harsh whisper. "Put another egg on the plate, old man, or I will smash your wrinkled face in."

The old man stared back at Patrick. "No," he said. "Move along." Patrick stood his ground and set his tray down on the counter in front of him. After a solid thirty-second stare-down, he snatched the large ladle in the man's hand and dug into the tray of eggs. He scooped at least three more onto his plate, then held his hand out and slowly opened his fingers, dropping the ladle, which bounced off the counter and clattered onto the stainless-steel trays. He stared at the old man again. "Go ahead. Set off the alarm. See if I care. One more scar on this face might be an improvement. One thing is for sure, I will make you pay, old man." He grinned.

The old man picked up the ladle and turned to the lineup. "Next," he said. There was a collective sigh of relief from the line of boys. Had the old man set off the alarm, no one in line would have gotten any breakfast at all. Patrick turned and walked to a table. He sat and quickly wolfed down the three stolen eggs. If a matron saw his plate with five eggs, he might have ended up in solitary. Eating them quickly was the best course of action. He stood and continued to get the rest of his breakfast. He picked up some cold toast and a carton of juice. He looked up at the room and scouted a spot. He decided and walked to a full table beside the door. It was the best table, for it kept you concealed from anyone entering the room. They would have to turn around to see you. You would always see them first. The three boys sitting at this table quickly read his intent and moved to an adjacent table. Patrick sat and ate a leisurely breakfast. He burped loudly and laughed.

When Quinlan got to the front of the line, there were still two eggs in the tray. They were cold, but that did not matter. He picked up some cold toast and a box of juice. There was a groan from the boy behind him, for he had to settle for porridge. He took a table that was directly in line with the door. If a matron entered, he would see her first. He did not like surprises, and he would be the first one to stand with his hands up beside his face with palms facing outward. That was the rule of the school. All the males had to show that their hands were free of any items that could possibly be used as a weapon. Since the MMA (Male Management Act) had become law, males of the species could not hold a weapon. They could not hold anything in their hands that could be used as a weapon while in the company of any female.

Quinlan had only a few more months of school remaining. He had three trades he could choose. He could work on infrastructure upgrading with a focus on roads. He could work as a planter in the vastly expanded park system, or he could work janitorial in the city. He had been given the necessary training for all three jobs. In fact, in any given year, he might be called upon to work all three. He didn't care which as long as he was out of this place. It was just like a jail. He had heard that the Canadian system was much less strict. If he were born a few miles to the north, he might have been able to work in one of the sciences. He could be an aide to a doctor or work in a lab with a biologist. He had heard that their females were more considerate of their men.

He sucked on his drink straw. The gurgling sound of the empty container snapped him out of his reverie. He glanced around the room, careful to avoid eye contact with Patrick. He was not afraid of him, but it was always better to avoid conflict, which resulted in punishment. There was no recourse for the innocent. All fighting males were deemed guilty in equal measure. He glanced out the door and saw a matron walking down the hall to the cafeteria. As she approached the open doors, he stood and raised his hands. She stepped into the room with her baton at the ready. Everyone stood with their palms open, facing out, except Patrick. He stood and raised his hands with both of his middle fingers sticking up. One of the younger boys let out a gasp. The matron looked at him and followed his eyes. She quickly turned around, only to see Patrick standing with his palms in the manner required. She tapped the baton in her open palm and spoke to the room. "Alright, gentlemen, time to go." Everyone cleaned up their breakfast trays. Quinlan took his tray and placed it in the depository. He filed out of the room to his class on the etymology of gravel. It was a mind numbingly boring class. Patrick slid in behind him and whispered in his ear. "I bet you don't have the pussy to do that." Quinlan ignored the taunt and turned the corner to the room that was commonly known as "The Gravel Pit."

SEAN
KILKENNY

Sean was standing in the stairwell below street level in front of an entrance off the alleyway. He glanced up to ensure he was not being observed as he opened the door behind him. He slipped inside, turned on the portable light hanging from a lanyard around his neck and scanned the small room filled with long abandoned boxes of files collapsed into paper bricks. The yearly rise of water together with a plugged drain had allowed the water to wick up to the tops of the piles. The weight had pressed each to half their original height. The musk of mold permeated the air, for the paper had not had time to dry out between floods. The concrete walls and ceiling were wet and glistened in the light of his lantern. He walked forward between columns of paper that formed an aisle into the room. He stopped in front of a wall of collapsed boxes of paper that spanned the room. These reached higher than those near the front of the room. They had been stacked so they touched the ceiling. He placed his hands on the wall and glanced back at the door. He heard the wail from a Fempol vehicle pass by. He pulled his hands back and rubbed them on the front of his shirt, and waited. He looked down at the shirt. The logo of the pest control company was covered in flecks of dirt from his hands. He brushed it off and listened. There was no sound. Only the high pitch of a fading siren reached into the narrow passageway between the boxes of moldering paper. He reached up and inserted his finger

47

between layers of paper at the apex of his reach. There was a low whirr, and a staggered pattern of boxes moved inwards. He stepped through, touched a panel on the inside and watched the wall slowly close behind him.

The room in front of him was approximately four meters square. He had secretly built a triple layered Faraday cage to ensure that no electromagnetic signals of any type entered or left the room. The room was soundproof, waterproof and light proof. Even the air systems were carefully constructed so that nothing from the outside would detect anything from the inside. He painted the walls black. Black was his favorite color, for it was not a color and all the colors at the same time. Black always fit his mood. He sat in his chair. He knew he needed to be sharp and alert. He needed to rest. He closed his eyes. Sleep did not survive the invaders of his thoughts.

It had been 15 years since the new government had instituted the MMA (Male Management Act). The riots started soon after. Men were demonstrating against the MMA's new laws regarding male behavior toward the female. They felt it was highly discriminatory. The basis of the MMA was the acceptance of the research that the male of the species, if left in power, would destroy humankind. They were just too violent and unpredictable to have the responsibility that leadership required. There were some growing pains when it was first instituted.

The total shift of power from males to females was cemented by the sadistic rapes and murders of over 100 young women by a group of men led by a psychopath who saw it as man's God-given right to use women any way they chose. If the women resisted, they paid the ultimate price. This accelerated the shift of power until all government positions were held by females.

In an effort to discover who was specifically responsible, Fempol arrested over 200 men from the cordoned off area around the farm where the crimes had taken place. His older brother and father were arrested, along with his uncle. They were taken to the stadium to be questioned. They were never questioned. They were massacred.

He remembered sneaking into the arena on the day of the massacre. He was fourteen. They had taken his father, uncle, and brother away to the arena earlier that day. He was hiding behind one of the concrete pillars when he saw a group of men being escorted across the concourse. He followed, hiding behind a low wall between the pillars that lined the outer edge of the concourse.

He looked up and saw the group of men standing in front of the washroom. One of the Fempol officers was scanning. He ducked down. He heard the men shouting and moved to the next pillar. He peeked out. He could see his father, brother, and uncle were part of this group. He glanced at the officers to see if they were looking his way. They were not. He waved and tried to get his brother's attention. His brother waved back at him and then waved him away. He mouthed, "Go Home. Go Home." He ducked down again just as the sound of guns echoed down the concourse. He looked up and saw one of the officers point her rifle at his brother's head. It exploded. The face of the officer was forever burned in his mind. Suddenly, all the officers began firing into the group of men. He was frozen, watching the bullets hit the bodies and bodies falling in a tangled tableau misted with blood. The smell of death rose with the heat from the bullets. He turned and vomited at the base of the pillar. When he looked up, he saw Fempol officers running out of the concourse at the sound of more rifle fire. He hesitated, and then ran to the pile of bodies. He found his father sitting with his back to another one of the dead. He was still alive. He looked at Sean and smiled. Blood ran from the corner of his mouth as his head fell forward. He was dead. Sean remembered screaming and trying to help his father sit up again. No one heard him over the cacophony of gunfire. He got up and ran back to the safety of the wall and slipped out of the arena. That marked the beginning of Sean's nightmares.

Only later did it come out that the sister of one of the female officers involved in the massacre was one of the victims at the farm. She wanted revenge against any male who was involved and took it against any male she could find. She killed his entire family.

Sean changed the day of the stadium massacre. For five years, his need for revenge seethed within him. He was angry hot, but he could see no way to satisfy the need that colored everything he did. The anger cooled and solidified. It became a weight on him. It was carrying that weight that gave him strength. He spent those years preparing this room and planning. He planned meticulously, and it was only a matter of putting it all into motion. It was from this base of operations he would begin. His anger was still raging within him, but he had learned to direct it like a laser. Concentrated hate had amazing power. Tonight, was the start. Tomorrow, he would take his first step in his plan for revenge. With that thought, he drifted to a dreamless sleep.

QUINLAN SMITH

Quinlan slid into his desk. The room was dusty, for every wall was lined with small drawers containing all the different types of gravel and stone. He knew all their names and uses. Today he would be tested. It was simple enough—he would be given a list of drawer names and have to identify the contents. The drawer system allowed the leaders to shuffle the locations. A button on the wall would move the drawers randomly to a new location—hence the dust. As they moved, the contents would shift, creating small plumes of dust that settled on everything in the room. The only part ever cleaned were the tops of the desks and the computer interfaces.

The second part of the test would be a series of problems relating to road construction, pipeline installation or perhaps levee maintenance, to name a few of the possibilities. Each of these required its own plan that covered material type, thickness, and relationships with the surrounding landscape. Quinlan knew all of this. There was only one problem. He hated the job that this class would inevitably lead. He was good at it, but he did not want to do it for the rest of his life. There were many options but being a gravel grunt was not one of them. He would write the exam with his usual finesse. He would score a passing grade. He would achieve something around 65%. That was high enough to pass, but not high enough to be whisked off to some project in the boonies. He had learned to play the game. He had been placed in this program by some idiot when he was 13. He remembered the day perfectly. He was standing in front of two older men who were supposed to interview the newbies and find out what field of study they were best suited. His mind reran the event:

"Hey kid, what do you want to be when you grow up?" the man behind the desk called. He did not wait for an answer. He continued, "Hey, Bob, what do you think this scrawny kid would be good at?"

The other man looked him up and down. He walked back to his computer terminal and swept his finger over the screen. "I think he would make a great gravel grunt. And lookie here—there is one space left." He touched the screen. "Put your hands on those," he ordered.

Two glass panels glowed on the table. There was an outline of a hand on each of them. Quinlan looked up at the men. He was not sure what was happening, and he was looking for some sort of explanation from the men. The first man pointed once again at the glowing panels. Quinlan did nothing. "Are you fucking stupid or something? Put your dirty little paws on the panels and fuck off." Quinlan did as he was ordered. The panels glowed brighter for a few seconds. He stepped back, and the man shouted, "Next!"

That is how he ended up studying bits of crushed rock.

He quickly finished the exam. He knew he had answered exactly 67% of the questions correctly. His score was high enough for the powers to give him another go at something new because he obviously had a few brains, but not enough to study at a higher level. He was not university material but smart enough for a good trades job other than gravel grunt. There were dangers in demonstrating high-level abilities. Quinlan had learned that early. He knew he was smart. When he was eleven years old, he took his first aptitude test. He had answered every question, and the results were disconcerting, to say the least. He was transferred to a Center where he was poked and prodded for some time. He was given a new series of tests, which he knew he had aced. He was proud of himself until he met Cygnet.

He was sitting in the waiting room of the Center when an old man named Cygnet slipped into the chair beside him. "I am going to give you some advice," he said, leaning over. He whispered into Quinlan's ear, "Don't ever show them how smart you are. I saw the report on her desk while I was emptying the trash. They will use you in ways you don't want to be used. Keep who you really are a secret. Always hold back. It is your only protection. If you are smart, they will do something horrible to you. I know." He patted his belly as if that would communicate his meaning of the horrible thing.

Quinlan had turned to him and spoke innocently out loud. "What kinds of horrible things?" Cygnet stood up and walked away from Quinlan and stood just out of sight of the receptionist. He turned, looked at Quinlan, and rolled his eyes.

The woman at the desk looked up. "What did you say?"

Quinlan looked from the woman to Cygnet, staring at him from the hallway. "Nothing. I was just mumbling."

Right after that, he was taken into a small dark room and the woman, who he assumed was a doctor, placed a funny-looking helmet on his head. She asked him questions while staring at a video screen. He tried to figure out what was going on while the old man's words were ringing in his head. '*Always hold back. Keep who you really are a secret.*' The woman asked him about some of the stuff he had learned in junior school. Most of the questions were about science and mathematics. They were sort of concealed in "what if" type questions like, "What would you do to survive for 24 hours if you were alone on a small, treed island populated with a pack of starving wolves and you had a pocketknife and some string"

Quinlan turned his head to the side. He immediately knew that he would use the knife to shave up some dry wood, make a pointed stick and use the string and the pointed stick to construct a fire-making tool. He would make a fire that he would keep burning for the 24 hours. That should keep any predators at bay until rescue came. Instead, he blurted out something stupid. He said, "I would wait for the head wolf to attack, and I would use the knife to stab him in the heart. All the other wolves would respect my power and probably make me their god." The woman entered some data into her terminal. Quinlan assumed it was something like, '*Delusional. Typical male with violent tendencies.*' There were a few more questions that Quinlan pretended he did not know the answer or said something stupid. He was sent back to his junior school and was never considered for higher-level education. He ended up as a gravel grunt.

He had one more chance to get a trade he would want to excel at. He could request to be enrolled in something a little more interesting than rocks.

He had considered something like quantum electronics, but men were usually not allowed to enroll in those fields of study. The inherent tendency toward violence often prevented a male from learning about any subject that might be weaponized.

His second choice was something in the biological sciences. His chances were much improved. Quinlan liked to help people, so he was really considering nursing or some sort of laboratory work with people or animals. Today was as good a day as any. If he applied before the exam results were out, he might be one of the first in line. He glanced at the clock on the wall. There was time. He headed for the main office to get a pass to the registrar. The man behind the counter seemed to be brain dead. Quinlan asked for the pass, and it was immediately dropped on the counter in front of him as if the man's only job was to hand out passes. He quickly snatched it up and turned to leave while muttering a thank you to the man who had already forgotten the entire interaction.

He headed for the registrar. No one stopped him or asked to see his pass. That was what usually happened. If you had a pass, no one stopped you, but if you did not have one, you gave off some sort of guilty vibes the matrons could sense from a kilometer away. They would come in packs, like wolves, and snatch you up in their sharp white teeth and send you to the security offices-cum-jail. Nothing good ever happened in the security offices. Quinlan was glad he had a valid pass.

The registrar offices were at the far end of the facility. This was a school for boys to the age of 17. After that, if he did not continue in school, he would be sent to a job site to work. Once you reached the age of 19, you had to go to work. There had been murmurs of other things to do with sex, but Quinlan had never put much credence in them. They were just myths. All the women he knew were generally nice people. He liked them and they liked him. Yes, there had been a few exceptions, but he liked to see the good in people. He smiled and stepped up to the glass window. The woman behind the glass looked up from her video screen. "May I help you?" she said and looked back down at the screen.

"I would like to talk to someone about registering for a new two-year course."

"Name and number?"

"Quinlan Smith – 9672301," he responded. She entered the information into the terminal.

"Please take a seat. Someone will be with you shortly." This time the woman got to her feet, walked over to the window, leaned down so her ample breasts were in view, smiled, and pointed to the area containing four chairs. "The one on the left has broken springs." Quinlan stared at the woman's breasts. He could smell her perfume waft over him. He felt very odd and quickly turned and lurched toward the chairs. Once he was seated, he looked back. The woman stood up, and she was still staring at him. Her tongue licked her lips just before she turned and sat down. The counter blocked his view of her.

He waited for 10 minutes, staring at the wall posters. They were of various smiling young men doing a variety of blue-collar jobs. He heard his name being called by the woman on the other side of the glass. "Quinlan, you can go in now," she said with a smile. The door to her left buzzed, and he stood and walked through. Her eyes followed him until he disappeared. There were doors to both the left and right. The one at the end of the hall was open, so he headed in that direction.

He stood in the doorway and looked down at the woman sitting at a desk. She was facing him but had to look around a terminal screen that filled most of the space on her desk. She was small and blonde. Her mouth was covered in red paint. He found the right word: lipstick. She couldn't have been more than a few years older than he was. At least, that was his initial assessment. She spoke, "Please sit." Quinlan immediately reassessed her age. Her voice was quite low. He now figured she was at least thirty. He sat. She had not looked at him and he sat quietly while she scanned the terminal in front of her. She did not look up. She spoke again, "What can I do for you, Mr. Smith?"

Quinlan slid up to the edge of the chair. He started to speak but stopped and cleared his throat. He spoke again, "I would like to extend my education to work either in the area of quantum electronics or medical biology." He smiled as warm a smile as he could. He tried to keep anything that might be construed as "smart ass" out of the look. He slowly stopped smiling and waited.

Finally, she looked up. "Stand up, please," she said flatly. He heard the 'please' at the end of her sentence, but he knew it held no real meaning. She was giving him a command. There was no mistaking it. He quickly stood. "Step over here so I can see you better." Quinlan moved to the side of the desk. "Turn around slowly." He turned in a circle. Her eyebrows lifted. "Good. Sit." Quinlan sat again. "You have a very interesting dossier. It appears that you were initially assessed to be in the top two percentile of eleven-year-olds. But then something happened. All further assessments dropped you down to just below the 50th percentile. What happened?"

Quinlan was about to shrug his shoulders but decided instead to be innocently dumb. He said, "I don't understand."

"It seems like the eleven-year-old you would understand perfectly. Can you explain that?" It was now time to shrug. He shrugged. Your grades in Geological Etymology indicate you are an average student, but the comments from your instructors say something different. They say that you are very bright in class and practical work, but you never demonstrate that on exams. Can you explain that?"

He was going to shrug again but thought better of it. He looked into the eyes of the woman in front of him. She stared back and pursed her mouth as if she was waiting for some bullshit answer. He assessed her and decided that he had to stop lying. This lady knew stuff that would reveal any lies he was about to tell. "I hate rocks. I don't want to work building roads and shoveling rocks. I did poorly because I did not want to work with gravel my whole life. I wanted to work with something interesting."

"Then why did you choose that area?"

"I didn't. It was chosen for me."

"I see." She looked back at her terminal.

"Are you going to send me back to being a gravel gopher?" His tone was sharper than he had intended, and he immediately apologized. "Sorry, ma'am."

"My name is Calista." She smiled for the first time.

"No, I am not going to send you back—at least not yet."

Quinlan tensed on the edge of his seat.

"Relax. Relax and listen to me." She stopped and waited. Quinlan sat back in his chair. "Good. I have an opening in something that you might like but it is not for the faint of heart." She paused. "I have an opening in Quantum Biology. I have been unable to fill the opening because it has very stringent prerequisites. If you are interested, I can recommend you take to the entrance exams. I suspect you are smart enough, but if you are not—well – c'est la vie." Quinlan stared at her, unable to determine the proper answer. "Well? What do you say?"

"Yes. I would like to take the exams. Can you tell me a little more about Quantum Biology?"

"Nope. I have no idea. I do know that it is a five-step program. It is one of the longest. It says here that it is the study of how quantum activities influence biological systems—whatever that means. You can begin work after level 2 while you continue your studies. Quinlan sat staring at her. She finally looked up. "Go. I will send someone to transport you to the testing facility." She looked back down, clearly dismissing him. He was about to ask her when and where but thought better of it. He stood and left the room. He walked down the hall and reentered the waiting room. He stepped up to the window. "Excuse me," he said. The woman behind the window quickly stood and leaned once again on the counter with her breasts half exposed. "What can I do for you, darl'in?" She grinned at him.

"I am supposed to come back for some testing. Can you tell me when that might be?"

"No idea, but if you hang around until I am off work, I'll see if I can find out—for a price." She leered at him and lifted her breasts up off the counter, and then quickly back down so they jiggled in her blouse.

Quinlan smiled. "No. I have to be back soon. Thanks anyway." He quickly turned and left the office. He knew his face was red and something in his belly was warm. As he walked, the sonnet he had committed to memory that morning wormed its way into his mind:

O that you were yourself! But, love, you are
No longer yours than you yourself here live.
Against this coming end you should prepare,
And your sweet semblance to some other give.

He read the lines again. He was pretty sure he understood the first three. Basically, it was talking about a person who was beautiful but with the knowledge that they would grow old and should prepare for that inevitable end. It was the "how" that puzzled him. He translated, "…give your beauty to someone else." How was that possible? You couldn't give away beauty. When it was gone, it was gone. There was no giving it away. He shook his head, and the poem fell in a shower of letters from his consciousness.

DISCURSION

THE PRISON OF POWER: A MAN-MADE TALE

By 2042, most countries had adopted an identification system of short-range nanobot transmitters that every person carried in their bloodstream. These were self-replicating machines that performed sentinel-like tasks within the human body. They recorded a myriad of data about the body they inhabited. This data was initially intended for use by medical systems. A person could enter a medical scanning center and step into a machine that would read the nanobot data. The initial step was identification. Once the system knew the identity of the client, it accessed the databanks. All DNA was already recorded, along with a detailed medical history. The new data provided by the nanobots was added, assimilated, and analyzed. If there were problems, a treatment protocol was initiated.

This was a voluntary system. It required the consent of the individual. Initially, a person could not be forced to submit to a scan. That changed after the law was amended to provide reasons to override lack of consent. When it became obvious that males were not using the system to maintain their health, citing that Fempol was using the system as a way to track their locations, the law was once again amended. Male consent was no longer required to initiate a scan. The public reasoning was that the society as a whole would be safer. If males were to become infected with a virus, it might endanger the entire population. The range of nanobot scanners was extended. They were placed throughout most cities, supporting the CCTV systems. They could scan anyone just about anywhere. To obtain individual female data, however, would still require consent. This could be overridden if there was an illness that endangered others. This was extremely rare in a society where all medical services were offered free of charge.

Fempol took full advantage of these laws and used them to track all males.

QUINLAN
SMITH

The week slipped past. It was filled with people coming and going. New students arrived and graduates left to new jobs or new courses in preparation for new jobs. Quinlan spent the time reading. He attacked one of the plays in the anthology but did not get far. His concentration was poor. He was waiting for someone to tell him where he was to go to be tested for a potential new life. He wanted to become a quantum biologist, even if he was not really sure what it was. It was definitely better than being a gravel grunt. He lay in bed. It was early. The matrons would not come around for another half hour to ensure everyone was awake. His thoughts went back to the day at the registrar. The woman's breasts were right in front of his face. They smelled wonderful. He fantasized that the woman put her hands around his head and pulled his face down between her breasts. Quinlan felt his penis getting hard. At the same time, there was a rap on his door. It was too early. He stood and looked down at himself. He was still hard. He grabbed his pants and pulled them on. He left his night shirt hanging over his pants. It would cover him. He quickly went to the door and opened it. A young boy was standing there. He looked up and spoke quickly, "Matron wants you in the office. She said to tell you to get there ASAP." The boy turned and ran away. Quinlan closed the door. His mind raced. He quickly got dressed and found himself standing outside an office he had always hoped he would never be standing outside. He was about to knock when the door opened. The Head Matron was standing there. She smiled at him. He could not imagine why she was smiling. It was not something the Head Matron did often, especially not at him. He tried to see if he had missed some kind of nuance that would give a reason for the smile, but there was nothing.

"Quinlan. Come in. Have a seat," she said, and she gestured to the chair in front of her desk. Quinlan sat. The matron placed her hand on his shoulder as she passed by the desk and sat in her chair. "I received a message from the registrar." She touched her terminal screen. "It says you are to be tested for placement in," She looked down at the screen and read, "Quantum Biology and are to report to the testing offices today at 8:00 a.m." She looked at him questioningly. "Is this a mistake?" Quinlan shook his head. "To be perfectly honest, I don't think you have the mental capacity to take these tests, much less pass them. Your records show a below average performance." She tapped her terminal screen. "Are you sure you want to do this? I don't want you to be disappointed. After all, you are a sweet boy. There are other choices that might increase the likelihood of success."

Quinlan spoke up, "No, I want to take the tests." He stood. "May I go? I have to get ready. It will take me awhile to walk over there and I don't want to be late."

"There is no need to rush. They have sent transport. There is a shuttle waiting for you at the gate." She stood. "They don't send shuttles for me," she muttered. "I wish you luck."

That was Quinlan's signal to leave. He stood and left the office. He knew he did not need to return to his room to get ready. He had nothing to get ready. He walked out to the front gate. There was a small older man in a gray uniform leaning against the shuttle. When he saw Quinlan, he glanced down at his personal COM and back up at Quinlan. "Quinlan Smith – 9672301?"

"Yes."

The man opened the door to the shuttle and gestured him to enter. Quinlan slipped into the seat and the driver closed the door behind him. Quinlan's heart jumped at the sound of the closing door. He felt an urge to get out and run away, but he did nothing but stare out the window as the school building passed in front of his eyes.

The drive took only 10 minutes. The driver stopped, got out, and opened Quinlan's door. There was no way to open the door from the inside. The man smiled and said, "Have a great day." Quinlan just nodded and walked into the building through a set of glass double doors. The foyer was the largest he had ever seen. He walked up to a counter and waited. There were two desks behind the counter, but no one was sitting at either of them. He glanced up at the timer high up on the foyer wall. He was early. He looked around and found a chair beside a small table facing the counter. He would see anyone as they appeared behind it. He sat on the edge of the chair and waited. It seemed like the entire building was empty. He could not hear anything.

Suddenly the front entrance door opened and a woman wearing a business suit rushed in. She was carrying a large, heavy case with a handbag over her shoulder. There was an apple clenched between her teeth. She rushed to the counter and heaved the box up and set it down. She took the apple out of her mouth, turned and looked at Quinlan. "I am sorry I am late. I ran into…," she stopped. "Never mind. Are you Quinlan?" Quinlan nodded. "Good. Just give me a minute to get organized and I will call you in." Quinlan nodded again. The woman put the apple on top of the case, hauled it down and walked past the counter to an unmarked door beyond. She turned to Quinlan once she reached the door. "Would you mind opening the door for me?" Quinlan hesitated. He looked around and, seeing he was the only person in the room, jumped to his feet and tried to open the door. It was locked. "Damn," she muttered. He took the box from her hands. She smiled. "Thanks. It was getting heavy." She took keys from her pocket and opened the door. Quinlan just stood in the doorway with the box in his arms. He had learned a long time ago not to assume things unless he was told directly. "Well, come in and put the box on that table." He looked around the spacious room. At first glance, it seemed to be cluttered. Quinlan had been taught to keep his world organized, but he had very little to organize. This room was laid out in pods with a table at the center of each. On three sides of each table were shelves containing a myriad of things, some of which Quinlan did not recognize. Many seemed to be rat's-nests of wires. At the center of each table was an array of connection points that had been designed for various pieces of electronic equipment. He set the box on one of these tables. "Thanks." She looked around the room at the various pods and then pointed at one on the far side of the room. "Please have a seat there." Quinlan walked to the table indicated and sat down.

He sat staring straight ahead. He did not want to do anything that might upset or irritate this woman in any way. She was his pathway out of the gravel pit that was literally waiting to swallow him up. The woman entered a small room at the back and soon returned with a steaming cup in her hands. She walked directly to Quinlan and sat in a chair opposite him. She sipped her drink, which Quinlan identified as coffee, when the potent smell reached his nose. "So, I read your file and understand that you want to be accepted into the Quantum Biology department for a 2-year study program." She stopped. He simply looked at her. She had not asked a question. She continued to stare, and he realized she expected confirmation of her statement.

"Yes. That is what I want, but…" He stopped. The word "but" was a word that was not encouraged. It suggested that the woman you were talking to had made an error or left something out. He looked at her face and waited.

"But what? Please feel free to speak your mind. I will not take offence."

"I thought that the course was a minimum of four years."

"It is. After you complete two years, you will be reassessed. If you demonstrate the required ability, you will be given the chance to continue to a higher level. I hope that is clear. Right now, you will need to work through a few simple exercises. Shall we start?" Quinlan nodded. She attached a series of sensors to his wrists and fingers. She slipped a set of glasses over his eyes. She reached out and picked up a helmet from the counter. "Good. I want you to put this on your head and plug it into that port." She pointed to a connection port in the center of the table. Quinlan nodded again and took the helmet from her and put it on his head. He plugged it into the port on the table. "It is simply a recorder. It will record cortical activities in the various parts of your brain while you are answering my questions. I am not going to test your knowledge. That would not be fair in that your access to high-level education systems has been restricted to this point. Do you understand?"

"Yes," said Quinlan. He nodded and felt the helmet slip on his head. The woman noticed and reached up to tighten the strap. He felt her proximity. The smell of her filled his senses. He held his breath in an effort to stop the wave in his belly.

"There. Let us start." She adjusted the terminal in front of her so he could not see. "The first activity involves some simple visualizations. I will say a word and I want you to create a picture of it in your mind. After 15 seconds, I will say another word and I want you to visualize it. I want you to create as much detail as possible. There are ten words in all. Do you understand?" Quinlan nodded. "Good. The first word is 'apple'. Begin visualizing." Quinlan saw an apple in his mind. It kept changing from red to yellow to green. He knew he should make up his mind on the color. He decided on a mottled red-yellow. The kind of apple kept changing. First it was like a Gravenstein, then a Gala, then a Braeburn, then it changed shape and color to a Granny Smith. The woman stared at the monitor. Her eyes were focused, and her brow was furrowed in concentration.

Something beeped. She spoke another word, "War." Quinlan tried to create a single image, but what he visualized was more like a video of explosions and faceless men shooting at each other. There were few details. It was simply a mishmash of violent actions without purpose.

"Baby," she said.

Quinlan created a circle of babies with himself at the center. They were all able to sit up, and they each grinned at him as he turned to look at them. They were all different. The images made him smile.

"Gun," she said.

For a second, all the babies had guns clutched in their small hands, then the babies vanished, and the guns fell to the carpet. He was still in the center of the circle, surrounded by guns. He looked carefully at the weapons lying on the carpet. They were black and lumpy. He reached out for one and saw they were made of black licorice. He could taste it in his mouth and wanted to bite one of the barrels. The woman looked up at him and saw he was smiling. She reached out to her terminal and paused the recording.

"Your response indicated high levels of pleasure. Please tell me what you were visualizing."

"Sorry. My mind saw the babies holding guns, and that was really weird, so I changed all the guns to licorice. I like licorice."

"Interesting. Let us continue. "Girl."

On hearing the word, there was a spike in his mind. The jolt of thoughts screamed, 'This is a trap.' He conjured up thoughts of a group of 10-year-old girls holding ribbons that were attached to a pole. They were dancing around the pole, waving the ribbons up and down. He had seen a picture of this once and tried to remember it. He breathed slowly, expecting the woman to stop and question him. He knew that he might not be able to hide his body reactions if he thought of girls as young women. It seemed he did not have a lot of control lately over what his body did in response to certain kinds of stimuli. He did not want his body to betray him. She said nothing, and he breathed away the tension.

The testing continued. Quinlan continued to see vivid images that often morphed into stories without beginnings or endings. The remaining words were *blood, kitten, danger, sex, and anger*. The woman stopped him at nearly every word to explain his visualizations. The test ended. The woman stood and helped him remove the helmet and the myriad of other sensors.

"I am not sure what this test has to do with Quantum Biology. I thought you would be testing me to see if I could pass the course work."

"I looked carefully at your record. I am very sure you have all the intelligence to be successful, but I was not sure about certain attributes of the male personality. I needed to check." She smiled at him.

Quinlan felt he could push harder for information. He took her smile to be an indicator that he would not be out of line to ask the next question. "What were you checking for?"

Her smile vanished. Quinlan tensed. "I wanted to know if your personality would be compatible with the other students." She paused, but her smile did not come back. "...the other female students."

"I will be studying with females?" He could not keep the dismay from his voice.

"Yes. Any males that aspire to higher education must have and maintain certain personality traits. They are carefully observed for the provisional two months to ensure the assessment is accurate."

"Did I pass?" asked Quinlan.

"I will let you know soon. The committee will review the results along with my notes and you will be notified." She reached out and touched his shoulder. She smiled at him. "Thank you again for helping me with that box. Your ride is waiting." She stood and directed Quinlan to the door. He walked out to the waiting shuttle that was to take him back to his tiny room.

MARGARET CARVER

Margaret Carver – 1326765490 was plain. Her name was plain. Her face was plain. Her body was short and chunky. It was obvious to her that her mother had not spent any time selecting her traits before she was created. She came from her mother's egg, but the male genes were not even reviewed. Her mother just selected her father based on his intellect, not his body. It only took a few minutes to extrapolate the egg and sperm combination to get a pretty good idea of what this pairing would turn out looking like. She could have at the very least, tweaked her height and weight. Her face could always be modified so that her chin and cheekbones were more—she searched for a word—assertive. She thought she looked like a weak person. For a girl, that was not a good thing. Strength was important if she wanted to go anywhere.

Margie. Her mother called her Margie. She hated the name, and she would never respond to it—at least not since she had turned 17. She was a woman now. She had all the rights of women all over the planet.

She could hear her mother's voice. "I did not blindly choose the sperm to go with my egg. I selected something much more important than your physical visage. I don't know why you care. You are strong. You are really intelligent. You have all the personality traits that will ensure you can, if you want, become a prime leader of any country you wish. You could even go all the way to the top leadership of this planet. That is what I did for you. Stop whining about being short. Short people live longer."

Margaret could hear herself scream and run to her room. "You just don't understand. You don't understand."

Her mother would yell after her, "I do understand, and so will you soon. This planet needs strong leadership. Looks often get in the way. You have what is required. Now stop behaving like a little boy."

Margaret was heading to class and let her reverie slip away. She had enrolled in a new program that would lead to a degree in Quantum Biology. It seemed odd that for her to get this degree she had to take a million physics courses. Many of these courses were advanced mathematics. So she was, in fact, taking a zillion math courses. She also had to take biology courses. Those were relatively simple in comparison.

She walked into the lecture hall and sat near the middle. It was the safest place to sit if you did not want to be called upon to answer questions presented by the professor. If you sat on the fringes or at the back of the class, professors assumed you were hiding and, being their sadistic selves, would seek you out and try to embarrass you. All teachers were sadistic in some way or other. Why else would you ever want to do the job? It had to be the worst job ever. Teaching. Yeech.

Margaret slipped into the seat and waited. A tall Amazon with long, straight black hair slipped into the seat beside her. She glanced at Margaret and then opened her tablet. Margaret was in the process of opening her mouth when it became obvious that the girl had dismissed her as being irrelevant. She said nothing. Another girl sat on the other side of her. She was gorgeous as well. *It is a conspiracy*, thought Margaret. They sit beside the ugly girl so their minor flaws will not be noticed in the blinding light of her ugliness. "Bitches," she mouthed under her breath.

She felt a tap on her shoulder. "Have you taken any classes by Professor Petra? I have heard she is tough, especially on the girls. She dotes on the boys."

"What boys?" retorted Margaret. "This is not a subject for boys. They don't have the minds required for this level of study."

"That is really sexist. Boys are just as capable of high-level thinking as you or me. Government segregation policies were created to keep violence out of all forms of government. When men were in charge of governments, they very nearly destroyed the planet. There hasn't been a war between member governments for 50 years. So, I say it was a success. But it is time to change the policies and desegregate our society and allow men the same freedoms as women," said the girl with a flip of her blonde hair.

"You had better not let anyone from the matron society hear you talk like that. You might end up in one of those re-education schools," Margaret said with a sly grin.

"They don't exist anymore. The new school of thought says we should let males do more than physical labor. They are just as smart as females."

"Give me a break. I have yet to meet a boy or man who could match me intellectually. They just don't have the ability for abstract thought. All those violent tendencies just get in the way. Look around you. Do you see any males?" said Margaret smugly. The lecture hall was slowly filling up with bodies and sound.

"That does not mean anything. They are just not given the kind of opportunities that we are given."

The noise dropped suddenly, making both girls turn and look forward. Professor Petra had entered and was standing on the stage. She was quietly looking at a tablet on the dais in front of her. The voices became silent as everyone waited. She finally looked up, scanned the room and spoke, "Good morning, all." There was a staccato of 'good mornings' returned. "This class is the introductory course of Quantum Biology. I am here to give you an overview of the entire degree program. If, after my overview, which will take 30 minutes or so, you wish to drop out of the program, please do so. I am recommending those of you looking for an easy program leave now." She waited and scanned the room. Five girls from various parts of the room stood and left. "Anyone else?" She waited again. "Good. I will start."

"Please do," whispered Margaret.

"Biology: the generalized study of living organisms—a simple definition. Biology as a discipline has been around for centuries. We have answered many of the questions of life and how living things work. Your high school studies will have given you a good background in this area. You have studied the basic building blocks of life. Cells and their interactions. Some of you might have delved into the chemistry of life. That is much more complex than cellular functions. Quantum Biology takes all of this much deeper into the mysteries of how things work. At the quantum level, all seeming obviousness disappears. Nothing is obvious anymore. All things need energy to exist. A plant takes in sunlight and water and chemicals from roots and grows. That process has never been fully explained until the discovery of the spooky quantum world about 150 years ago. We know a lot more than we did, say 30 years ago, but we have a long way to travel and many things yet to discover. A lot of what you will study has mathematical prerequisites. In other words, you will be taking a number of math and physics courses in order to understand how you might apply quantum concepts to your research." She paused and looked out over the full lecture hall. "I will take this opportunity to ask, once again, for those of you who would like to leave. Now is your opportunity."

At least half of the remaining students got up and walked out of the room. The din rose and fell with their passing. Margaret watched them go. The girl on her left got up and left. The room settled.

"Now that we have culled the herd, so to speak, I will ask you all to come down closer to the front of the class. Stand up and join me down here so I can see your faces." She gestured to the front rows of seats. The students slowly stood and moved down to the front. Margaret decided that the very front row was the best place to sit and moved down and took a seat front and center. The girl she had spoken to came with her and sat on her right. Another person sat on her left. She turned and sucked in her breath. The person on her left was a boy. Margaret felt her heart jump. He was a very good-looking boy.

She pretended she had not even noticed him. That proved to be a problem because she could not stop thinking about the fact that she was sitting beside a boy, let-alone a good-looking boy, on her first day of a university class. Everything that the professor said from that point forward might as well have been in another language. Whenever the boy leaned forward in his seat, Margaret leaned backward and slid down slightly. It gave her a chance to look at the boy without being seen. The absolute last thing she wanted was to make eye contact with him. But then she realized her peculiar behavior had alerted the girl on her right, who was now paying more attention to Margaret and the boy than to the lecture.

The boy sat back in his seat when the professor asked them to view a short video on their tablets. Margaret leaned forward and looked to her right. The girl grinned at her, leaned in and whispered, "You still think that boys shouldn't be allowed access to higher education?" She looked behind Margaret's head at the boy and then back at Margaret. "He is outrageously cute." She poked Margaret on the shoulder. "My name is Billie. What's yours?"

Margaret simply pulled her tablet close to her face. She felt her jaw tighten. She stared at the video as if it were the most interesting thing she had ever seen. Her mind was racing. Why was she reacting this way? She had seen boys before. When she was younger, she had even played with them. They had always seemed—she searched for a description—*less than.* Yeah, that seemed to fit. Males were less than her, and all the other girls she knew. But here was a boy sitting beside her in her first class of the hardest program she had ever taken.

The video ended. The professor asked a question. Hands went up. The boy raised his hand in a casually assured manner. The professor spoke, "If I point at you, please state your name before you answer." She pointed at the boy on Margaret's left.

He sat up straight and said, "Quinlan."

Her head was swimming. The rest of his words were muted as he answered the question. All she heard was his name. She kept repeating his name in her head, over and over. It became a kind of chant that hypnotized her. She did not look in his direction again. She did not have to. His proximity was enough to keep her body rigid.

Suddenly, the class was over. Quinlan stood and gathered his things. He glanced down at Margaret and smiled. He walked past her out of the hall. Margaret followed him with her eyes until he was gone. The girl beside her poked her in the ribs. "Yes, he is really easy on the eyes."

"Sorry," said Margaret. She looked at the girl. "You told me your name, but I forgot."

"Billie. And you are?"

"Margaret."

"You were saying earlier something about males being less than females. I'm pretty sure that is not true."

"Of course, it is true, but there will always be exceptions. I think I was sitting beside one."

Billie's eyebrows arched. "You don't say." She stood. "Want to get coffee?"

Margaret glanced up at the clock on the wall. "Sorry, but I have another appointment. Maybe next class." She got up and quickly strode out of the lecture hall.

VIHAAN KHATRI

Vihaan slipped out of bed and stepped up to the high window. He carefully pealed back a corner of the black paper and peeked out. It was early. The light was gray. It was misting a soft, cold rain. He looked across the street at the porch light creating a warm spot in the middle of a dreary row of houses. He was waiting. She lived there, and every morning he would try to catch a glimpse of her. He did not know her name or anything about her that was real. He barely knew what she looked like. She was always wearing a hood of some sort. Even in the summer, she wore a light top with the hood pulled up. Sometimes her gold hair would cascade down and conceal her face even more. It was winter now and her coat was a parka. He could not make out her features with her face set back in the faux fur that surrounded it.

This morning, he prayed he would see her as she left to go wherever she was going. He saw a silhouette as someone opened the door across the street. She stepped out into full view. Vihaan's pulse quickened as the wind tousled her hair. She reached out from the shadow of the covered porch to feel the rain that drizzled down. She pulled her hand back and flipped up her hood. She picked up a tote bag and stepped off the porch, quickly walking out and down the sidewalk, out of sight. Vihaan felt warm. This would be a good day. He felt his penis swell. The image of the girl burned in his mind. It would sustain him.

He left the window and quickly got dressed. His mother would be along soon to let him out of the room he slept in. She told him that this day would be the day he would be able to go out into the world, if only briefly. He had trained and studied. He knew he was ready, but she insisted that no amount of training could replace actual reality. Only experience could give him the skills to survive in the new life she had prepared for him. His mother was old-school. She insisted that her son would not become part of this horrible society. She had told him ever since he was a little boy that she would give him the skills to fight against the female oppression he would encounter. She had not registered him. His birth was a secret. It was a seventeen-year-old secret. He had remained hidden for all of his life. The rooms had changed, but his isolation from the outside world had not. He knew a few people besides his mother. All of them belonged to a small, local group that called themselves the Council of Sikh Women (CSW). Their stated purpose was to maintain their culture for future generations. It was viewed as a noble cause. He had spent some time with other boys like him. Whenever the council got together for an important meeting, he would go and see others like himself. He was the oldest and his mother saw him as the leader of the entire group of boys. The previous evening, his mother had been very anxious. She told him that tomorrow would bring clarity to his future. He had tried to get her to explain what she meant, but she just shrugged and said, "Tomorrow."

Tomorrow was here, and he was waiting at the door—waiting for his mother to unlock it. He had been told that he was not a prisoner, but it was far too dangerous to leave the door unlocked. He might think it was safe to leave the room when someone other than her was in the house and ruin both their lives. He could hear her voice. "Vihaan, it is better to stay in a locked room at night. Believe me, it is better." She was late. Finally, he returned to sit on his bed. He picked up a book of poetry on the way. It was a translation from Urdu or Pakistani; he wasn't sure which. He flipped open the cover and started to read. He did not get past the title *Tomorrow Enters Today* by Munir Niazi when he heard the rattle of keys. His mother was at the door. He snapped the book closed and tossed it on his unmade bed. He knew his mother would make it. In fact, she made sure that he did not have to bother with any household tasks. "House cleaning and bed making are women's work. I will not have a son of mine waste precious time and lower himself to such activities. It is my job." Then she would grin at him and continue, "Besides, I do it better than you."

The door opened, and his mother stood in the doorway. There was someone else behind her. She stepped into the room and to one side. A man followed her. He wore simple clothing. At first, his shoulders were humped and his head bowed. But as soon as the door was closed behind him, he straightened up to his full height. On his head was a deep green scarf. It was well worn and barely holding his long hair in place on top of his head. His mottled gray beard was cropped short. He was older than his mother.

The man stared at Vihaan with black eyes. Vihaan stiffened and stared back. His mother stepped between the two males and spoke. "Vihaan, this is someone who will be working with you over the next few months. You are a man now and must learn from men. His name is not important. You will address him as 'teacher'. You will no longer live with me here in this house. You will live elsewhere. Do you understand me?" Vihaan nodded. The teacher said nothing. The silence pushed the tension of the moment. Neither male spoke. Finally, his mother broke the silence. "You must go with him now. You must go in disguise. You must dress as a girl. Teacher will take you and you will remain until you have learned all the skills needed to join the revolution."

"Join what?" asked Vihaan in disbelief.

"You will understand soon enough," said Teacher. "The disguise is important. If we were stopped by the police, they would scan you for ID, and your body does not have the required ID bots. They would arrest you and ruin what your mother has done for the cause. Dressed as a girl, it is unlikely you will be stopped." Vihaan nodded.

His mother stepped out of the room and returned with clothing over her arm. "I will help you put these clothes on," she said and proceeded to lift up a sari and wrap it around his body. He was soon dressed. "You will have to wear your own shoes. I could not find any female shoes that would fit those huge feet of yours." She kneeled down and pulled the wrap so that it touched the ground. "There, that will hide them." She stood and stepped back and looked at him. She reached out and touched his cheek and withdrew her hand quickly. "You have whiskers," she said with dismay. She pulled the headscarf to cover his face. "This will conceal you until you get in the vehicle. You never know when a drone might be scanning this area."

"Enough. We must go quickly. The longer we delay, the more likely we will be stopped. The patrols have been extra vigilant of late. Three men of Irish descent were arrested yesterday. They were part of a road crew. They got drunk on some illegal liquor and made lewd remarks and gestures at a few teenage girls on their way to school. I figure they will get sent to reeducation, at the very least."

Vihaan pulled the scarf away from his mouth. "What lewd remarks and gestures?" he asked.

Teacher looked at Vihaan's mother. "Never mind. Let's go." He turned and left the room.

Vihaan moved to follow. He took a step too large for the sari he was wearing and nearly fell flat on his face.

"Small dainty steps," said his mother.

Vihaan followed his new teacher out of the room and out of the house. His eyes were wide. He was in awe of the outside world that he had seldom visited. There was a small autonomous vehicle waiting for them. The man opened the door and helped Vihaan inside. Teacher moved to the other side and sat. The vehicle moved. It traveled for at least twenty blocks and stopped in front of a large pull up door. The man got out of the vehicle and stepped up to a scanner array beside the large door. He scanned his palm and his iris. The door opened. He walked inside, followed by the vehicle containing Vihaan. The door closed behind them.

Vihaan exited the vehicle and went to remove the female clothing. "Not yet," commanded Teacher. Vihaan looked around. They were inside a large warehouse. The area just inside the door was lit, the remainder was steeped in darkness.

"Come," he said.

Vihaan followed.

As they moved, the lights came on over them and shut off behind them. After a few minutes, they stopped, as far as Vihaan could tell, near the center of the space. It was impossible to be sure. All around him was total darkness. The only thing visible was the floor. Vihaan looked down and noticed the concrete floor demarcated into two-meter squares. The man turned to face him but said nothing. Suddenly, Vihaan felt a vibration. The sound that should have accompanied the vibration was absent. The floor began to sink. Once the two-meter square of floor sank past the point where they could no longer see out, all the lights in the warehouse extinguished. They were left in a darkness never before experienced by Vihaan. He sucked in his breath and hoped—not for the last time—that his mother knew what she was doing.

MARGARET CARVER

For Margaret, the first month of classes was the worst. She knew the boy named Quinlan had an emotional effect on her. She could not seem to focus on her studies. He was in practically every class. She knew that was to be expected, in that he was taking the same program as she was. Billie had tried to make friends with her, but she had not so much rejected as ignored her. Lately Billie had given up trying to make friends. She had talked to the boy. That was a problem, too. The boy was becoming friends with Billie. She could not fathom a girl as smart as Billie being friends with a male. She didn't even seem to want him sexually. A sudden tsunami of realization swept over Margaret. Frack. Did she want him and was she jealous? Did she really care for this boy? He was very good looking. He even knew his place.

She had observed an interaction in the hallway earlier in the week. He was standing in a queue to enter a math class. The girl in front of him stepped backward and pushed him into the girl behind. His backpack hit the girl behind. He also put his arms out to support the girl in front of him and touched her shoulders. The girls confronted his actions. The girl behind claimed he had not taken care as all males must when in the presence of females. Had he removed his backpack, the incident would not have happened. The girl in front accused him of touching her without her permission. He did not defend himself at all. He admitted his actions were careless and apologized to both girls. Later, she checked the daily records and found he had reported the incident as was required. He stated that he was at fault and promised to be more careful in the future. The girls did not report anything. Margaret saw the girls smile at each other as if to show they could easily have this boy removed whenever they wished.

Her first urge was to step in and tell the girls that they were fucking little bitches but, she knew that would not help Quinlan. In fact, it would have made his situation much worse. Why would she want to help this stupid boy? He should not have been allowed to take classes with females. It was just stupid. All sorts of problems would arise, especially for the boy.

"Fuck—fuck—fuck," she whispered as she walked to class. He would be there. He with the gorgeous face and stunning body would be sitting in the same room as her. She felt herself flush in places she did not want to acknowledge. She knew she had to do something about her reactions to him. She could try to get him kicked out, but that would make her an even bigger bitch than the girls she had observed. She could try to be friendly? She knew in that moment that she would never be satisfied with mere friendship. She wanted him. That created a whole new set of problems, but at least she would not be eating herself up with indecision. She entered and saw Quinlan sitting near the front of the class. She slipped into the seat behind him and smiled as she did so. He did not turn around. He could be cited for that. She spoke, "Hello."

He nodded at her and turned around. "Good morning, Margaret," he said and turned back to face the front.

Margaret could not believe what her body was doing in reaction to a simple good morning from this boy. She felt wonderful. She was even able to concentrate a little on the subject matter. The lecture focused on the connection between quantum tunneling and the migratory behavior of birds. She had heard most of it—that is, when she was not leaning forward and smelling him. He definitely smelled good but smelling him was a serious distraction. At the end of class, he looked up at her as he was placing his study materials into his backpack. "May I ask you a question?" he asked.

Margaret smiled. "Of course," she said.

He sat up and turned to face her. "I am having some trouble with one of the math courses. Algebraic Topology. None of my high school classes prepared me for it. I was wondering if you knew of someone that might be able to tutor me. I cannot afford much so it is ok if you don't know of anyone."

Margaret smiled. "That class can be a bitch. I took a topology course in high school. Maybe I could help?" she said as politely as she could. She made a conscious effort to keep any arrogance out of her voice.

"I am not sure I would be allowed to take instruction from a female student."

"Of course, you would," she responded without really thinking about what she was saying. There were rules. Even rules for females in this society. "My mother is on the GCB, and I am sure she would get us a dispensation to study together."

"GCB?"

"Gender Control Board. You know—the group that determines the exceptions to the gender laws. You would have been discussed by the board in order to be allowed to take any sort of higher education. The Gender Laws state males cannot take part in any government decision making. They also restrict education of males above the level required for manual labor or trade work."

"Oh. I really don't want to cause any trouble. I just want to study and get some sort of degree. Mapping fibrations has me totally lost, to say nothing of homotopy excision."

"I will discuss the possibility with my mother this evening and let you know tomorrow." As she left, she knew she could get a dispensation from the GCB, given that her mother was the chair. That was not the problem. The real problem is that she did not want to look like an idiot in that she was not all that good at Algebraic Topology herself. She stopped in the hallway and flipped open her tablet. She did a quick search on the subject. There was a great deal and Quinlan would have access to all of it. But online tutorials were not the same as a tutor. "Crap," she said out loud.

Billie was coming down the hall and heard her expletive. "What is the problem, Margaret?"

"Oh, hi, Billie."

"You look depressed. You, okay?"

Margaret looked at Billie and remembered that she was a bit of a whiz kid in all her math courses. "I'm okay. Say, Billie, I need some help with Algebraic Topology. Do you have a little time this afternoon? I would really appreciate it."

"This afternoon, no, but I do have some time right now. What part are you having difficulty with?"

Margaret glanced around. She did not want anyone knowing she wanted someone to help her with anything. If it were just for herself, she would spend the time to figure it out, but she wanted a quick fix. She wanted just enough to get her through a tutorial with Quinlan and look like she knew what she was talking about. "Let's go to a study pod." She stood and led Billie to a private pod.

"What can I help you with?"

"Can we start with fibrations and homotopy?"

"Sure. It is pretty straightforward when you understand that all complex spaces are constructed from simpler ones. Here I will show you," said Billie as she leaned over and drew a circle on her tablet. Margaret concentrated and put all thoughts of Quinlan out of her mind.

MARGARET CARVER

Convincing her mother to get a dispensation for Quinlan to take some tutorials with Margaret took more effort than Margaret expected. The conversation started easy enough but soon turned into the usual argument.

"So, let me get this straight: you want me to provide you, sorry, to provide *a male* student with a dispensation to be tutored by *a female* student—specifically, *you*."

"Yes. Is that so hard? You are the chair. You just have to write it up so he can come here so I can tutor him." She interlaced her fingers and put her hands together on the table.

"Yes, it is quite simple and very possible, but there are two problems. First, you are my daughter and I do not want to be seen as someone who does favors for family. That problem can be overcome by submitting a request to the committee. It will not even reach the committee, for one of my aides will intercept and approve it. Secondly, you are my daughter and I do not understand your motives. Why on earth would you want to do this? I think the answer to that question frightens me a little." She stopped and stared at Margaret.

"What?" blurted Margaret defensively.

"Ah. Just as I thought. You like this boy." She rushed to cut off Margaret's expected defensive response. "Don't misunderstand me. There is nothing wrong with liking a boy. I, personally, have "liked" a number of boys and men in my time. It is a normal response. But you have to be careful. Know what you want and don't get carried away with emotional attachments. Some males like to take advantage for their own selfish wants." She rushed on. "To be clear, I am not just talking about sex. I am talking about attachment. Be careful you do not get attached."

Margaret threw her hands up in the air. "For frack sake, mother. I just want to tutor the boy. I was always told that teaching others is the best way to learn yourself. That is my only motive here. Any boy would do."

"But you picked this one."

"He is the only one that asked me, and I said yes. Look at me. He certainly did not choose me for my awesome body. Please, just send him a dispensation. I don't want to have to tell him that my mother won't let me. I will look like a fool."

"Alright. When do you want to schedule this tutoring, as you call it?"

"Every Friday night at 7:00 p.m. for the next five Fridays."

Her mother looked disbelievingly at her.

"*What?* Friday evening is a good time for both of us. Can you get it done soon? I want to start this weekend."

"Yes. But you have to complete your Coming-of-Age appointments with Doctor Kay. I want to be sure you have had all the treatments. If you decide to have sex with this boy, I want you to be prepared both mentally and physically."

"Oh, for fuck's sake, Mother," shouted Margaret. She stood up and walked out of the room.

"I will make the appointment for tomorrow, and I will not send the request until I see you have attended. Is that clear, Margie?"

A shout came from behind Margaret's closed door, "My name is not Margie!" She plopped down on her bed. A smile crept over her face. The thought of Quinlan sitting on her bed beside her quickly dispersed all the hateful images she created of her mother dying in various cruel ways. She grabbed her tablet and sent a text to Billie. She wanted to be super-prepared to tutor Quinlan.

DISCURSION

THE PRISON OF POWER: A MAN-MADE TALE

The New York Times

January 12, 2040

American Male Equality Nation (AMEN) Responsible for Plot

Fempol has unearthed evidence of a diabolical plan to demonstrate that the ZTR (Zero Tolerance for Rape) laws should be repealed. The new law, enacted after the Organic Farm Massacre, where almost a hundred women were brutally raped and murdered, resulted in over 185 male suspects being killed during an uprising in the arena where they were being interrogated. After ZTR was enacted, a country-wide purge was conducted, which resulted in 187 men being charged with the rape or attempted rape of a minor female. Sixty-four of these men were found guilty and put to death within a week of the initial charge. It was discovered that the computer systems governing and tracking these cases were manipulated to make it appear as if standard legal processes and protocols had been followed. The hack was discovered before the remainder of the men were executed. No direct link was found to connect the hack to the AMEN group, but circumstantial evidence points to their involvement. It appears this group wanted to sacrifice a few men to further their warped agenda. They have denied these allegations and continue to point out the inhumanity of this law and demand that it be repealed.

EVE
RINNE

Eve rolled on to her back and moaned. It was too early. The dream had woken her. The same familiar dream had slapped sleep aside and left her craving the darkness. She held her eyelids tightly shut in the hope she could recapture that sweet oblivion. She breathed deeply through her nose. For a moment, she thought she had succeeded. The pool of darkness was pulling her down out of the moment and back into that place where all the parts of her melded into one thing. She craved the perfect blandness where all thoughts ceased. She blinked. Color invaded her eyes and painted a million pictures in her mind. It was all back. "Fuck," she muttered to herself and sat up. There was a bar of bright sunlight on the wall that had slashed its way through a crack in the blind. It carried with it the green motion of the leaves outside her window. "Fuck," she said again, louder this time. She got out of bed tiptoed to the bathroom. She was not trying to be quiet. She simply wanted to reduce the cold that was biting her feet. The less of her that touched the icy tiles, the better. She jumped on to the relative warmth of the bathmat and stared at herself in the mirror. A mop of wild red hair surrounded her freckled face. There was a faint scar that ran from the corner of her tiny mouth and down under her chin. She rubbed her finger over it. The action pulled her dream back like a surging wave. It splashed over her. She felt the pit of her stomach tighten and cramp. This was the waking version of the dream she endured on a nightly basis. She could smell them and feel their heat. Eve quickly grabbed the bottle of mouthwash and swished a mouthful of the minty liquid over her tongue. The phantom smell faded instantly. She sped up her actions and quickly finished what she needed to do to become— only one word would do here: presentable. All she could ever achieve was a feeling of presentability. She dressed and left the room.

Eve was having a birthday in three days. She would be forty years old. Only sixteen of those years she considered to be happy years. The rest were filled with the memories that mutated each night into horrible dreams. But she had a plan. She would have stopped the dreams, but no, that wasn't possible. She had a plan to compensate for the dreams. She was going to get revenge. It came to her in a flash while watching some 80-year-old video. It was something her friend Colleen loved to watch, and she simply kept her company. She thought it was called *Star Trek*. It was supposedly some alien proverb. "Revenge is a dish best served cold." She could not remember what kind of alien it was, but the proverb stuck with her. In the last few years, it became her mantra. She would get revenge. She would get revenge over and over. The originals were gone. She had checked. When she was sixteen, she had been kidnapped and held captive by a pseudo religious group. She and many others were used as sexual objects by the cult of men. She was lucky. She had survived. All the others were murdered in their sleep. It was one of the cases used to convince the all-female congress of the USA to enact a set of laws to ensure that all women would always be protected against the evils of the males of the species. Some of those laws had been softened. Initially, rape of a minor carried the death penalty. Any male or group of males taking part in a rape of this type were to be put to death. The first three months after it was put into law, there were 64 men killed. It was a witch hunt. The amendments to the law were enacted when it was discovered that at least half the men killed were not guilty of the crime of which they had been accused and the remainder were not allowed due process. A computer hack of the system had expedited their conviction and resulting execution within a month of their arrest. They were part of a plot to show the female population what they might expect from the all-female government. A cabal of previously powerful men had tried to show that the government of women was seriously flawed. Men were needed to balance the society. The resulting arguments in Congress and the Senate modified the laws to what was presently on the books.

None of this was of any concern to Eve. The men who had raped her had all been killed in the arena massacre. All but one of them was dead, and he would never see the light of day again. It was not enough. All males were disgusting. All males would pay for what had been done to her. Eve had reached the conclusion that they must all pay. She would kill them and kill them until the anguish went away. Since she knew that would never happen, she would just have to continue killing them. Killing would make her feel something other than perpetual pain, so kill she would until there were no more men to kill.

She went to a hidden safe in the bedroom closet of her small apartment. She took out the gun she had finally obtained. Beside the gun was ammunition, but not enough. She could count the bullets she had been able to get on one hand. As it turned out, the ammunition was much harder to obtain than the gun itself. The previous year, she had joined a women's group: NOW AND FOREVER FEMALE (NAFF). They lobbied for even stronger laws to keep men from ever being able to reach positions in society where they might become powerful again. Their belief was that male humans were a subspecies and were no longer necessary for the maintenance of a vibrant society and therefore simply a drag on resources. Machines could do the heavy lifting. They were cheaper than males and generally did a better job with fewer problems. There were a number of women in government positions that were members of this group. Eve didn't care about all the beliefs of all the factions. She knew only one thing. If she killed males, she would feel better.

She had considered learning to shoot arrows or become proficient with a katana, but that was not what she wanted. It was not about making them suffer. It was about erasing. She thought that each man she erased would bring her closer to blotting out the dreams. The best and most efficient way to do that was to shoot them in the head. There would be no chance they could be saved. They would be dead. Eve held the gun out in front of her and pretended she was shooting. "Fuck you and fuck you and fuck you," she whispered and pretended to shoot. She shivered. *It was almost like cumming,* she thought. If pretending to kill men felt wonderful, just think how actually doing it would feel. She shivered again and put the gun back in the safe. She knew it was illegal to be in possession of any kind of firearm, but she didn't care. It had taken months to get one. She had to pretend she was a male. An underground organization of males from one of the few remaining "free male" countries in central Europe was selling them to any other males who needed protection from the female overlords. Eve laughed. Overlords. That is what the black site called women from the USA. If her country was ruled by female overlords, then they had truly won. Finally, men had found their place in the pecking order. The latest research suggested the 'Y' chromosome was heading for extinction. It was truly a world where only the fittest survived and males had served their purpose and were no longer needed for the continuance of the human race. She would just be helping with the extinction of the males of the species. If they were all dead, then maybe the dreams would stop.

Eve put the gun back into the safe. The lock snapped shut. Her planning had taken a couple of steps forward. The university would be first. She would kill any males she could find. She had gone there and walked around the quad. She had counted them. There were more than she had anticipated. Most of them were "sweets." The most disgusting abominations on the planet. Everyone should cheer her when she shot them all. She knew she had to be careful. There were those that would stop her and claim she had committed a crime. The only crime she would commit was cleaning up the crap without a license. Only women should have babies. A man with a baby could only lead to something bad. They just were not able to see that their time had passed. Their lies must not be disseminated.

There was more to this than just going somewhere and shooting the men. That would only work once. It was important that she be able to continue for years if needed. Her identity would be known by AI Mother as soon as she stepped on to the campus. It was a requirement of all places of higher learning. This was deemed mandatory after a rash of school shootings almost 50 years ago. That could not be helped. Once she was known as the perpetrator, that would be the end unless she took precautions. She would need a place to hide and plan her next event—and her next. She needed a way to travel secretly and stay under the radar, so to speak. Her plans needed to change. The same black site came up with the answer. The suit looked like long underwear interlaced with tubing. A synthetic blood was continuously pumped through the web-like tubing. This fluid contained female nanobots that masked the person's nanobots. It required some modifications to adjust. The size of even the smallest was much too large for her frame. The control system would transmit a fluctuating identity code. It would keep her own identity safe for the time it took to shoot a half a dozen vermin.

VIHAAN KHATRI

The man who was to be his teacher spoke in the darkness. His voice no longer echoed like it had in the large warehouse, but Vihaan could barely hear him over a rumble coming from above his head. "Remove the female clothing and leave it on the floor," he said. The rumbling stopped. The lights flickered and came on. Vihaan looked around. He was in a very small room that he guessed was an elevator. He looked up. There was a ceiling a short distance above his head. If he held his arm straight up and stood on his toes, he could touch it.

"Quickly," commanded his teacher.

Vihaan removed the sari and the headscarf. He wrapped them in a ball and hesitated. These were his mother's clothes. She would want them back. They might get dirty if he just dropped them on the floor. He held them out in front of him and looked questioningly at the man called Teacher. The man was no longer looking at him. He was staring straight ahead as if waiting for a door to open. "My mother will want these back," Vihaan said.

The man reached out and grabbed the ball of cloth and tossed them in the corner of the elevator. "No, she won't." The elevator door opened, and the man walked out. Vihaan just stood, trying to suppress an urge to look back at the clothing in the corner. "Vihaan, move. Now." Vihaan walked out of the elevator. He was at the end of an empty hallway that extended out and curved away in the distance. The teacher stepped forward and stood on a section of the floor that was darker. It ran like a snake along the right side of the hallway. Near the wall was a handrail. "Stand beside me. This is a moving walkway—a travelator. It moves rather quickly, so keep your feet planted." Vihaan stood beside the teacher. "Hold on to the handrail. If you remove your hand, it will stop." Vihaan gripped the handrail, and the travelator started. The two men moved quickly away from the elevator and down the hallway. The trip took much longer than Vihaan expected. At one nexus point, they got off the travelator and stepped on another one that was 90 degrees to the previous one. Thirty minutes passed before they arrived at their destination. The travelator ended in a circular room.

"What is this system?" asked Vihaan, looking around and down the many tunnels that branched from this room.

"It is a safe way to travel across the city without encountering the police. Everywhere you go up there, you are watched. The surveillance system covers almost every aspect of the city and is controlled by a rather sophisticated AI. It would have spotted you and identified you as something to be investigated if you had stepped out of the transport vehicle."

"But I was disguised."

"The sensors would have seen you as a glowing hole. If it could not identify you—and it couldn't—a team of taser-toting Fempol officers would have taken us both into custody. The vehicle protected you from the sensors. It is designed to provide an acceptable facsimile for the AI sensors."

"Who built this? How is it a secret?"

It is an old mega-mall transportation system. No one has used it for years, but we brought it back to life. It allows us to go from A to B in the city core with reasonable secrecy. There are still some danger points but, so far, our use has not been discovered by Fempol." He gestured to a door that was nestled in between the two of the travelators that spoked off of the central hub. "We go in there."

They walked across the room. As they approached the door, a silence settled over the room. The travelators all stopped. "What is in there?" asked Vihaan. His voice echoed in the high-ceilinged circular room. Before his question could be answered, one of the travelators started up and a thrumming sound filled the space.

"Go!" shouted Teacher.

"Is someone coming?"

"I have no idea, but I am not taking any chances. We might have been followed."

They both quickly moved to the door, opened it, and stepped inside. The door closed behind them. A dim light glowed in the ceiling. The room was no more than 1.5 meters square and filled with janitorial equipment. Teacher stepped to the rear and placed his hand on the side of a shelf that filled the rear wall. The shelf was drawn upward, exposing an elevator door. The door opened. The two males stepped inside, and the door closed behind them. There was no sound except breathing.

Finally, Vihaan spoke, "Are we going to some secret underground facility?"

"Yes and no." He turned and stared at Vihaan. Vihaan looked back, hoping for a reasonable answer. This man seemed to love riddles. Either that or he didn't trust Vihaan enough to be totally candid with him.

"What does that mean?" a frustrated Vihaan asked.

There were no indicators in the elevator. "Yes, it is secret and no, we are not going down. We are going up. This is an old service elevator that could stop on every floor in this 200-story building."

There was silence for the next few minutes. Finally, the door opened, and they stepped out. On either side of the elevator door were two men. They moved to the front of the elevator door and stopped them from continuing. Teacher raised his arms above his head and signaled to Vihaan to do the same. The two guards ran a scanner up and down both their bodies. Finding nothing, they stepped aside and took up their previous positions. Vihaan and Teacher stepped forward and walked down the hallway. Vihaan turned and looked at the two guards. They wore uniforms and carried weapons on their hips. Vihaan stared open-mouthed. "Those men—are they carrying—they are carrying…guns. How could they get guns? All the guns were destroyed in the weapons purge of 2036."

"Don't be naïve. Our organization has guns and a lot more. The government has underestimated our resolve. We will soon take our rightful place in the government of this country." He led the way to a small room with a table and four chairs. They sat. "We will wait here."

"How many of you are there? The females definitely outnumber you. It would be impossible for you to overthrow them."

"You keep saying 'you' when you should be saying 'we and us'. You are one of us now. You will be trained in the ways of revolution. Believe me, it will take a revolution to regain our power. This is just one of our cells. For security, none of AMEN cells connect with any other cell. If one is discovered, it cannot expose any of the others. We are slowly building our army in cities all over this country."

"AMEN?"

"American Male Equality Nation. Remember that. You are now part of the revolution that will regain our rightful place in this country." He paused as if his own words had empowered him. "When we are ready, we will strike. When you are finished with your training, you will be a leader."

"Me. Why not you?"

"How little you know. Didn't your mother explain?"

"No. I was always told that I was special and that I would one day lead. When I would ask questions like 'Lead what?' or 'Lead who?' there were no answers, only knowing smiles. How can I ever be a leader?"

"You are nanobot free. Most of us are not."

"What has that got to do with anything?"

"You really give meaning to the phrase, 'Ignorance is bliss.' Listen to me and remember. Everyone in this country, males and females, were injected with ID nanobots. Their stated purpose was identification. It was then decided to expand their purpose and have them become a diagnostic tool. If you get sick, those bots are scanned, and they report any health problems to the AI called 'Medical Mother.' This computer system tracks all illnesses and ensures any sick person can be treated and cured before their illness becomes critical. It has virtually expunged epidemics. It is also used to ensure any visitor to our country cannot bring in a disease. Everyone must be inoculated with our made-in-USA nanobots. Most of the countries of the world have these bots as part of their medical systems. Some groups, including us, have tried to hack them, but there is a sophisticated encryption that fluctuates every few seconds. It is a decentralized blockchain system and impossible to decipher."

"It appears that having these bots is a good thing. Why don't I have them? What if I get sick?"

"Oh, they have a nasty side, especially for all the males. This is not advertised by the government, but male nanobots have been modified to allow them to be tracked. It is like having a permanent GPS flowing through your veins. At first, we tried to get rid of them by performing total blood filtering. We were actually successful in getting rid of the nanobots, but the test subjects became screaming idiots. Somehow the bots inside the males had modified male brain structure to need these bots more than it needed oxygen. Without them, our brains went insane. It was an addiction to end all addictions. We could not escape their influence."

"So, you can't get rid of them, and you can't hide from Fempol. Yet here you are, hiding."

"We can hide here. The floors of the building are blocking any signals from reaching out or in. It is not uncommon for a person to disappear off the sensory grid for a few hours. The AI just waits until the subject returns from whatever dead spot they entered. It knows where all those dead spots are and what they contain. It simply waits for you to reappear. We have gotten around that by linking dead spots so we can do some of the work required without the AI ever suspecting us. All we have to be sure of is to reappear from the same dead spot. I will have to exit that warehouse we entered in a little under 14 hours."

"It can't track me."

"Oh yes, it can. It simply sees you as a hole. That means you are here without the proper nanobot signature. That makes you a danger that must be addressed immediately."

"I am confused. What is the point of not having the nanobots if not having them sets off alarm bells in the AI?"

Teacher reached across the table and put his hand over Vihaan's hand and squeezed. "They cannot kill you."

"What?"

"Any male can be rendered unconscious or killed with a simple signal from AIMM (Artificially Intelligent Medical Mother). If they suspect you, it's a simple thing to capture or destroy you. An army of men wouldn't last more than a few minutes no matter how big their weapons were." Teacher patted Vihaan's hand. "That's why we need you and others like you. You are nanobot free and not under their control."

"Now that I am here, what is the next step?"

"Now you get nanobots."

"What?"

"You get our special modified nanobots. We have taken nanobots from volunteer females that agree with our philosophy."

"Like my mother."

"Yes. Females are not tracked. They are free to go wherever they wish. It is part of the original amendment to the constitution. Their privacy is preserved. Even if they get sick, Fempol must get permission to read their identity before they can treat them. The only flaw with the nanobots we will give you is that the AI will think you are a female. It is a little price to pay."

The door to the small room opened and an older man walked in, looked at Vihaan, and said, "Please come with me."

MARGARET CARVER

Margaret spent every waking moment getting ready to tutor Quinlan. She had not told anyone, especially Billie. She knew she had to go to her appointment with Dr. Kay. It was required by the university anyway, so she went. After her checkup, the doctor sat her down in the conference room and asked her questions about her choices concerning her sexuality. Basically, the doctor wanted to know if she was homosexual or heterosexual. She replied, "I like boys if that answers your question." Once that was determined, there was an awkward discussion about actually having sex with a male. It was pointed out to her that she need not have sex if she wanted children. She need not even have to carry the child if she wanted one. There were a number of alternatives. That is when Margaret stopped the lecture. "I have no intention of raising a child. When or if I ever do, I will learn everything I need to know."

The doctor then explained to her how to determine if any particular male was safe. She opened a small cabinet and took out a package and handed it to Margaret. "This contains a little tool that will prove invaluable if you decide to have sex with a male." She smiled at Margaret. "Open it."

Margaret opened the package. There was a small device that looked like a ring. A silver band had a flat section that ran one third the way around the band. "What is it?"

"Put it on one of your middle fingers."

Margaret slipped in on her finger. It fit perfectly. "It fits."

"Of course, it fits. I have your entire genome here. Turn it so the flat section is in the palm of your hand." She reached out and took Margaret's hand and turned the ring so the flat section was concealed in Margaret's palm. "This is a bit of new tech devised by Science Center for the Safety and Advancement of Women (SCSAW)—pronounced seesaw. I have been asked to find some willing volunteers to test it out."

"What does it do?"

"It is very simple. As you know, everyone in our society has been marked with a nanotag. There are a few nanobots in everyone's system. These bots collect data on the health of their host. If you enter a hospital or my office, for example, the information collected can be transmitted and used to diagnose a myriad of problems. SCSAW has spent the last few years trying to get this new device approved by the Global Health Administration. It is a reader of sorts. Just press it to a male's skin. It will read who they are through the nanobots. Then that device will query the database for any information on their history."

"Like what kind of history?"

"Well, it will simply make a judgment on whether it thinks that you should be wary of this male friend or not."

"How?"

"There are a number of settings, but the easiest is a simple vibration code. If it buzzes three times, it is recommending you get away from this male as they are prone to violence toward women. If it buzzes twice, it is suggesting that the male in question has not been assessed in enough detail to be sure of their possible reactions. A single buzz is telling you that you can probably move forward but to be careful. All males have violent tendencies."

"That is funny. I have never met a male that I think would ever harm a fly. I harbor more violent tendencies than all the men I have ever met."

"You are young and obviously have not studied history. You have not lived in any other kind of society than this one where the males are monitored and controlled. Not so long ago, the females of the society were subjugated, and the males were dominant. It was a valuable trait for the human species. It used the strongest to provide protection for the weakest. Men kept the monsters from harming the women and children. That was when strength was an asset. It is written into our genes. But as humans became more technological, the real asset was intelligence without testosterone. Brute strength is no longer needed. Males' strength is no longer needed, but that discussion is for another time."

Margaret rolled her eyes. She had been taught this in elementary school. She glanced up at the clock on the wall. "How much longer is this going to take? I have a class."

"Nearly finished," said the doctor. "The single event that signaled the male-dominated society needed to end was—"

"The second bomb dropped on Hiroshima," finished Margaret.

"Very good. It was more than obvious that a modern human society filled with enough weapons to destroy everyone a thousand times over must not be allowed to continue. So, the females simply banded together to elect themselves a new kind of society. Once we held power, all the nuclear arsenals were destroyed as a first step. Everything that has come after has been pure maintenance."

"Men are that dangerous?"

"Have you not studied the thousands of wars they started and fought? Believe me, all men have extreme violence written into their DNA. So, use that ring device. It won't harm anyone and may help you understand how to deal with a part of our species that is no longer required."

"What about children? Don't you still need sperm to create babies?"

"Only for a while. Once the sperm banks are filled, then…" She looked down and lifted her head. "One eighteen-year-old's ejaculate could provide at least 100 million little swimmers per ml. A hundred thousand vials would be enough to keep the race going for at least 10,000 years. The numbers of males have been slowly decreasing ever since SCSAW lobbied and won the right for women to choose the sex of their child. At present, the birth rate in matriarchal countries is at a ratio of ten to one in favor of females. The best way to cleanse our species of males is to continue on our current path."

"What about children? Don't we need the males to continue to carry the children? Ever since the development of an artificial womb, males have been given the honor," Margaret said with a hopeful inflection.

"That is just bafflegab. Every pregnant man I have ever had the misfortune to meet was not happy. They can carry the child and deliver it by caesarian, but they certainly don't see it as an honor. It has been common practice to have males serve as a vessel for the female's progeny. The time wasted around having and caring for children was removed from the female and placed where it would be of the most use. The males who succeed in having a child are permanently altered. The hormones required change the nature of the male to be more female like. Most of the males that have entered the advanced education centers have been allowed to do so because they have had a child or two. The process alters them at their core."

Margaret sat up. She liked talking about males. They excited her. If all males were gone, well, that would be terrible. "How long will it take for all the males to disappear?" she asked.

"No, they will never disappear. They will have uses, but there will not be so many of them that they can band together and become a threat again. We females do not deny our own nature. After all, sex is important."

"Aren't we equal? Men and women?"

The doctor laughed. "The need for equality was a myth that women used to climb out from under the thumb of oppressive men. Once we were seen as equal, we took the power and brought to pass what we always knew. Females are superior to men in all things, especially all things social. If we had left men in control, we would all be little puffs of radioactive dust scuttling across a dead landscape."

Margaret looked once again up at the clock. She stood. "Gotta go."

"You are a healthy young woman. Enjoy yourself but be careful." Margaret nodded and left.

MARGARET
AND QUINLAN

Quinlan felt apprehensive all day. He had a tutorial scheduled with Margaret at her house. He took the subway to her neighborhood. He had to walk a few kilometers before he found himself standing in front of her house. He realized she was a politician's daughter, but he was still in awe of the mansion. He carefully stepped onto the fenced brick path that wound up to the front door. He took two steps when a bar of light flashed across the pathway at his feet. He took another step and the bar of light moved with him and increased its frequency of flash. The words 'STOP' formed. Then 'You are being scanned'. After a few seconds, the flashing stopped, and new words formed. 'Welcome, Quinlan Smith. Please proceed.' He stepped forward, but the welcoming words kept pace—always ahead of him. He reached the front door. He raised his hand to touch the door when it swung open in front of him. Margaret was standing in the doorway grinning.

"Quinlan. Glad you found the house. Sorry about the stupid pathway thing. All government people like my mother are paranoid. They are all afraid of the Anarchists."

"Anarchists?"

"You know, those groups that threaten to overthrow the most stable and safe society the human race has ever created."

"I don't know anything about that. I just want to get through this crazy math course. Thanks for agreeing to help me."

"No problem. Come on in." Quinlan stepped forward. "Put your palm on that." She pointed to an inset panel on a small table beside the door. "Once the house recognizes you, it will no longer bother you."

"Bother me?"

"You know. Warn you, then warn you again, then do something nasty to you. There are some concealed devices around this house that can stop any unwanted intruder. This way it will see you as a friend." Quinlan placed his palm on the scanner. It flashed once. "There. Let's go up to my rooms."

"You have more than one?"

Margaret ignored the question. "My mother is out at the moment so we will not be bothered." She walked up a set of sweeping stairs with Quinlan in tow. They both entered what Quinlan saw as an entire apartment with all the furnishings. Margaret pointed to a sitting area with a sofa and soft comfortable chairs around a low table. "Have a seat there." She pointed at the sofa. "Get your stuff out. I am going to get us a few snacks." She smiled and spun around once.

Quinlan watched her as she stepped up to a small tablet attached to the wall near the door. She spoke quietly so Quinlan could not make out what was being said. He scanned the room and felt more important somehow, like he was on his way to becoming a real and equal member of society. He chastised himself in his head. *Don't get too comfortable. You could still end up on a road crew shoveling gravel for the rest of your life. This girl is willing to help you, so don't mess it up.* He started to remove his materials from his bag and place them on the table. He watched Margaret doing something at the counter. She was short and a little thicker than most girls, but not unattractive. She was also smart. He watched her turn and stared at her ass. He took her jeans off in his head. His penis liked what he saw. That brought him out of his reverie. He put his tablet over his crotch and busied himself with preparing some of the questions he needed to ask her about. He glanced up, and she was gone from his sight.

She had stepped into an area that he assumed contained her bed. He was still staring in that direction when she reappeared. She grinned at him. She had changed her top.

Margaret sort of floated over to him and slid down into the chair to his right. She had deliberately put on a lower cut top. The cleavage of her ample breasts was impossible not to notice. Quinlan did not stare. He pointed down at his tablet and said, "This function makes no sense to me. What does it do? When do I use it?" Margaret looked down at the tablet. She looked up at Quinlan. A thought raced through her head. *Crap. I have no idea what that function even is, much less how to explain it to him.* She looked up at him with wide eyes and made a decision.

"Quinlan, I need to tell you something important." She leaned forward to look into his face. He lowered his eyes. His first thought was, *Here it comes.* His second thought was not even formed before her breasts filled his field of vision and his mind swam, and his penis responded. *Fuck, fuck, fuck,* his mind screamed. Margaret continued. "I got you here under false pretenses. I hope you will not get angry. I do not know any more about this stuff than you do. In fact, I probably know less. I have never even seen that function, much less wondered about its purpose." Quinlan looked up at her. He had not processed what she had just said. She rushed on. "Don't get me wrong. I want you to stay. I hope we can work together and figure it out—you know, like study partners. What do you think?" She sat back.

Quinlan continued to stare. He calmed his body, which seemed to be out of his conscious control when females were close by, especially females who smelled good and had exposed flesh. He finally made sense of what she had told him. "That sounds good to me. Maybe we could invite Billie. She seems to have most of this down. We could discuss problems that we have and try to solve them together."

"A study group would be great, but you are here now, and I cannot really answer any of your questions. I suspect you know more than I do. I haven't been paying much attention to this class. I figured I would drop it before it affected my GPA." She paused. "So, what do you want to do?"

Quinlan shrugged.

"I have an idea."

"What?" asked Quinlan.

Margaret kneeled on the sofa beside Quinlan. She was facing him. She saw his eyes drop and stare at her breasts. She took that as permission for what she did next.

"This," she said, and she leaned into him and quickly kissed him on the mouth. She pulled back and looked at the effect of her actions. Quinlan stared at her wide-eyed. She reached up and put her hands around his head and kissed him again. Her tongue flicked over his lips and probed into his mouth. A whimper escaped Quinlan's lips. It seemed to come from the center of his being rather than his mouth that Margaret sealed with her own. She quickly pulled her mouth back but kept her hands around his head. "Are you okay?" Quinlan shook his head up and down. "Good. Put your arms around me and kiss me back." She sat on top of him and leaned in to kiss him again. Quinlan did what he was told and put his arms around her and pulled her closer. He could feel heat where his chest was pressed against the bare skin of her breasts. Instinctively, his hands slid down to her ample buttocks and squeezed and pulled her closer. Margaret moaned and shoved her tongue further into his mouth. The passionate kissing softened a little as Margaret pulled slightly back and began to touch her lips and tongue lightly on Quinlan's lips. Quinlan could feel his hard penis. It had begun to feel a little uncomfortable, for Margaret was pressed down, creating two hard contacts. He wanted to shift his weight, but he dared not move. His mind finally caught up to what was happening to him. He knew it was wonderful and scary at the same time. He knew he had put himself in a dangerous position. A thousand scenarios rushed through his mind. He could lose his right to study at the university if she told anyone what was happening here. He could get blamed for a criminal offence. He had actually touched her ass and pressed her to him. The thought eased the pain at the contact point of their crotches. His penis softened. Normally, when a female expressed interest in a male, there was no need for a permission contract accepted by both parties. He knew that it was formality on the male's part. It was the female part that was required by SCSAW rules. Without one, you could end up in prison. He wanted to pull away from Margaret and stop what was happening. It was just too dangerous. She didn't seem to care. The worse that could happen to her was being chastised by her mother. While he could very well lose everything.

That final thought broke the kiss. Margaret leaned back to look at him. Her breasts were right in front of his eyes. A wicked smile crept over Margaret's face. She misinterpreted his intention as a desire to touch her breasts. She knew she wanted him to touch them. She pressed his face into her cleavage. Quinlan's penis leaped to attention. Margaret felt the hardness. They both moaned. Margaret pulled back slightly. She wanted his mouth on her breast. She reached up and pulled down the top she was wearing, along with one side of the stretchy bra. A breast popped out, and she quickly pressed it to Quinlan's mouth. She felt his teeth scrape the nipple. The sensation swelled outward like a bolt of electricity from the contact point and amplified the feeling until it filled both their bodies and overflowed like a giant wave in a small pond. It splashed out over both of them. It receded and echoed, each wave amplifying and neutralizing at the contact points until all that remained was a soft ripple.

Margaret wanted more. Quinlan's brain no longer had any thoughts at all. A light rap on the door snapped them both upright. Margaret stood up and adjusted herself. She looked around and saw a sweater that she grabbed and slipped on in an effort to cover the top she was wearing. Quinlan reached out and grabbed his tablet and scribe, pretending to be absorbed in studying.

From the door came a voice. "Margaret, it is your mother. I am home early. My last appointment was canceled."

Margaret plopped down in a chair opposite Quinlan. "Come in, Mother. We are nearly finished."

Her mother entered and looked at Quinlan. "Oh. I forgot you had your tutorial today. How is it going?"

"Great. This is Quinlan. He is having trouble with one of the math courses." She looked over at Quinlan. "I hope I was able to help you. Review those practice questions and I will see you next time."

Quinlan looked at Margaret's mother and nodded. She smiled at him. "Nice to meet you."

Quinlan's return smile was weak. He stood and gathered his materials. "See you in class Monday. You have been a great help." He moved to the door.

"Talk to you tomorrow, Quinlan," she said as he disappeared out the door.

EVE
RINNE

Eve headed to work. She was a legal secretary for a small firm of lawyers. They mostly did property work with the occasional divorce thrown in. She was amazed how nasty people could be to each other when they decided they didn't want to be together anymore. Marriages were always between two or more women. Three was quite common if the women wanted to raise children. Men were not allowed to marry. A group of women who were married to each other often had a male worker as part of the household. What the men did varied, but they often were able to forge out a good life as part of a female household. There were some households that had more than one man, but this was rare. It was discouraged in that small groups of men were discouraged. Larger groups were outlawed. Problems often arose when a group of men were allowed even a modicum of freedom. Controlling them became difficult. There had been cases where some more affluent women wanted what, historically, would have been called a harem. Some still existed, but they were becoming fewer with each decade that passed. The men in these harems aged and were less desirable as their sexual prowess decreased. Young men were becoming more and more rare. Girl children were being chosen at a rate of ten to one. Only some of the more traditional ethnicities chose to bear male children. Even they were becoming modernized. The need for males was slowly decreasing. Most of the ones being bred were designed as Sexmen—a new term used to describe men who were genetically modified to be used as sexual playthings. They could be bought or rented. These men knew and accepted their role in this female controlled society. A few years as a Sexman allowed them to create a better life for their future. Sexmen were paid very well. Older Sexmen were often able to find positions in the more affluent households. When they aged out of that role, they usually ended up in a community that catered to housing older men.

The latest rage was women who took on the role of sexual partner. They were called Loverboys, but they were not boys at all. They were women, some of whom went through a modified sex change. This was usually just the addition of a penis.

The plaintiffs in the divorce case she was working on were fighting over who got to keep the Sexman that was, what they termed, an integral part of the household. One of the women wanted to leave and take the man with her, while the other two wanted to keep him. There were children involved and the two women were adamant that this particular male was critical to the smooth running of the household. The children had become attached to him and therefore his value to the family far exceeded his value as a provider of sex. The other woman claimed she had paid for him and therefore he belonged to her. It sounded as if the male was a slave, but in fact, he could leave the household any time he wanted. However, where he might go and what he could do was highly restricted. It was likely the male in question would simply go with whomever won the case. Eve was not sure what the courts would decide. She didn't care. In her mind, men and sex were two things that did not go together. Men and violence did go together. Men were garbage and should be purged from the planet.

The transport unit stopped, and she got out. The office was nearly empty, as she was early. The door banged closed behind her, and that made her think of bullets. She needed more bullets if she was to make her mark on ridding the world of vermin. Only one man worked in the office. He was used primarily for cleaning up and lifting heavy boxes and equipment. Eve could see him wandering around with a broom in his hand that never seemed to touch the floor. She gripped her case as she walked past him. He did not look up. She turned and saw him pick up a wastebasket, look inside, and put it back down. She opened the door to her shared office and sat down at her desk.

She organized her daily assignments and then drifted. She was running scenarios in her head. What if she was ready and prepared to shoot men and she couldn't find an opportunity? There were not a lot of males at the university. Maybe she should choose somewhere else for her first attempt. Maybe she should go where there were a lot of men. Somewhere she could burst in, shoot a lot of men, and disappear. The more she considered her actions, the stupider they became. She would surely get caught and put in prison. Females were exempt from capital punishment but not from a life behind bars. What about a road crew? She could drive by and shoot them. An escape was impossible. Once the Transportation AI was alerted, the vehicle transporting her would simply stop and lock her in. Fempol would take her into custody. That would be the end. She reached out to her terminal and switched on a news feed. There was the usual plonk from across the Atlantic. A number of countries were debating whether to give males the vote. "Idiots," she said out loud. There were a couple of articles on what was happening on the Canadian west coast. A religious group led by men had started a rebellion against the laws of the country. The Canadians, in typical fashion, were involved in talks. There was even some debate about giving them their own land to follow their misguided beliefs. "More idiots. Just send in Fempol and shoot the works of them. Religion, my ass. They just want to hold dominion over the women. I bet they all have multiple wives and keep them pregnant," she practically yelled at the terminal. The story continued with video pieces of some of the wives.

Eve listened to one young woman speak. "I love my husband. I believe in what the good book says. I will love and obey him." Behind her were six other women nodding their heads.

Eve spoke out loud again, "You stupid twats. What century are you living in?"

The door opened, and a young woman entered. "Are you yelling at the news feeds again?" She walked to the other desk in the office and plopped down with a grin.

"Hi, Yvonne. Did you see this?"

The young woman stood up and glanced at Eve's terminal. "What is it?"

"It is the thin edge of the wedge. If you let them return to suppress women under the guise of religious bullshit, then other male groups will try. Pretty soon they will have the vote, and we will return to shooting at each other again."

"You are starting to sound like my sister and my mother. They seem to be more militant by the day. This morning my sister suggested global androcide." Eve looked puzzled. "You know, the killing of all males. My mother loved the idea and even made suggestions on how to do it."

"What did they suggest?"

"You're kidding, right?"

"We don't need them anymore. They add nothing to our society. They are basic, self-serving, and evil."

"Let me ask you a question—have you ever been with a man?" Eve nearly blurted out that she had been with a number of them all at the same time as they poked their disgusting penises into all her orifices and, if she saw them again, she would kill them with her bare hands, but she simply flushed and looked down. Yvonne misconstrued her actions as embarrassment. "Cause if you had you would not be so quick to want to kill them all."

"So what if you had sex with a man? A lot of women still have sex with men, but I doubt if it is any better than a big vibrating dildo in the hands of a Loverboy. In fact, I have heard that the women with men are always cautious and that detracts from the experience. They are always expecting the man to turn violent."

"I have heard that some women like that."

"That is warped. We have been taught since before we could talk that all violence is bad unless it protects you from imminent danger."

"It is not like that. It is more like pretend violence."

"You are sounding like you want a man to be violent with you during sex. Is that what you want?"

"Fuck you, Eve." Yvonne sat back down and busied herself with what was scrolling on her terminal.

The silence slowly built-in intensity until Eve broke it. "Sorry," she said into her terminal. Neither girl looked up. They both worked at their terminals. The remainder of the office arrived, and the day passed quickly. It was not until most of the lawyers had left for the day did Eve speak again to Yvonne.

"I would like to talk to your sister. Do you think you could introduce me?"

"Why—so you can discuss getting rid of all the men?" spat Yvonne.

Eve stood and walked over to Yvonne's desk. "I had a very bad experience with a group of men when I was a girl. I would like to talk to someone who understands why I hate them all. It might be cathartic for me." She paused and looked down at Yvonne. "So, will you introduce me?"

Yvonne looked at Eve as if weighing what she had said. "Sure, why not. It is not like you, or my crazy sister, will ever act on the fantasies. I will talk to her later and ask her if she wants to be a kindred spirit."

"What is her name?"

"Cassandra Ross. AKA the bitch. She does some contract work for the government. She likes to imply that her work is important and critical, but I think she is full of shit." She watched for a reaction. Eve did not react. Yvonne stood up and gathered her things. "See you tomorrow."

"Thanks," said Eve as she returned to her desk. She was not ready to leave. She needed to think. The word 'androcide' had suddenly become her new favorite word, and she rolled it around in her mind like some shiny new bauble.

QUINLAN SMITH

Quinlan sat at a small corner table in the cafeteria. It was situated next to the exit and partially concealed by the propped open door. He was a curiosity among the many females and was not yet used to being an object of curiosity. In his first week, he was asked to join groups of girls at their table for lunch. He had always politely declined. This had only made him more of a curiosity until he spent a couple of lunch times sitting with Margaret. It seemed as if this had insulated him against the other girls' attentions. Margaret had stated it simply when he mentioned it to her. *"They think you are with me,"* she said, *"so they keep their distance."* Her statement was rolling around in his head. Was he now with her? Had she taken some sort of ownership of him and his attentions? Was that a good or a bad thing? He felt his penis stiffen at the thought and decided that it was a good thing, at least for now.

He looked up from his lunch. Margaret had not come to the morning class. Perhaps she was not well. There was a flu making the rounds. Across the room was a group of guys. They were not boys, but they didn't seem to behave like men either—at least not the men that he was used to: gravel grunts. They were smiling and chatting to each other. They were ignoring all the glances from the women in the room and behaved as if they were in their own safe little world.

Quinlan was considering going over and introducing himself to them and maybe making some friends other than Margaret and Billie when Margaret entered the cafeteria. She took three steps through the doorway, stopped, and scanned the room. She was wearing a new style of jeans that came high up on her waist. In the back, there was a large opening below the waist in the shape of an upside-down heart. A jeweled string attached the point of the heart to the waist. It was nestled neatly in the crack of her buttocks, accentuating the whiteness of her skin. There was an appliqué of arrow feathers on one side of the opening and an arrowhead on the other, suggesting it was piercing the heart. Much of her ample ass was exposed. Quinlan sucked in air. Margaret turned toward the sound.

"There you are. I was hoping I would find you here. We don't have any other classes together today, and I wanted to see you." She stared at his eyes, that were still focused on her jeans. She pirouetted. "These are all the rage. Do you like?" There were no words, just an energetic nod from Quinlan. Margaret sat in the chair next to him. "Why are you hiding in the corner like this? We could be out there on show. Those bitches would kill to have you sitting with them." Quinlan grinned weakly. Margaret scanned the room again. "Look, there is a table near the window. Let's go and sit over there. We can chat."

"It is more private here," said Quinlan.

"Who wants privacy? Not me, that's for sure." She started to stand, but Quinlan remained seated. "Are you worried about those sweets?"

"What?"

"Sweets. Soft Candies." Quinlan scrunched up his face. "It's what we call boys like that. They have been chosen and are being prepared for childbearing." Quinlan's eyes widened. "Oh, they still have all their equipment but none of the desire to use it for anything but peeing."

"Fuck," whispered Quinlan. "I knew about that, but I really thought it was just a story the matrons told to scare the crap out of us."

"Oh, they are not being forced. We still live in a democracy, and they have almost as many rights as women and more than most men. They just can't vote or own property and a few other things. Those boys are here learning so they will be able to intelligently raise their offspring. It is a two-year course. They are on a regimen of specific hormones as well as undergoing the required physical and psychological modifications."

"Fuck," whispered Quinlan again. "Not something I would volunteer to do."

"Let's go," she said and was about to push her chair away from the table when the door behind her opened further as someone unseen pushed it.

Then it happened.

Quinlan watched two people in bulky black suits with attached helmets enter the cafeteria. They walked just past the open door that Quinlan and Margaret were behind. Quinlan was sitting and Margaret was standing. She shrank back and bumped into the table. She slid around the table and pressed herself against Quinlan. They both grew quiet. Quinlan slipped off of his chair and slid down below the tabletop. He slowly drew Margaret down beside him. They were partially concealed.

One of the persons spoke. It was an accented female voice. "Ok, bitches, get your asses on the floor." No one responded. The same person reached out to a table covered with dishes and dumped it on the floor. The noise of breaking glass got everyone's attention. They all looked quizzically at the two intruders. The female voice repeated, "Get your asses down on the floor."

One of the girls stood up and stared at the intruders. "Who are you and what do you want?"

The speaker pulled a stun weapon from her hip, pointed it at the girl, and fired. She fell to the floor. Her body jerked in a series of spasms and then went still. She had vomited, and the smell filled the room.

"Ouch. I bet that hurt." Everyone froze. "Get on the floor and put your hands behind your head and look up." They all quickly found a space on the floor, put their hands behind their heads and looked forward. The unconscious girl moaned and coughed.

Quinlan leaned over to the crack where the door was hinged. He peered out. He could see more of the black suited intruders in the doorway. Some facing into the room and some facing outward. He could see six in total. The speaker was female, but the others were much larger and were obviously male. Quinlan stared at her. The woman stepped further into the room. She wore a black suit like the men. It clung to her body. Her hair was black, and her skin was the color of taffy. She was smiling at the women in front of her and did not glance at the woman on the floor. She raised the small tablet in her hand and looked at it and then back at the women. Quinlan saw a mark inside her wrist, near her left hand. It looked something like a flower. The two that entered the room walked over to each woman in turn and checked their faces against a face on a small tablet. The male of the pair reached the Sweets that were huddled close together. He looked at them and took a step backward.

"You boys are disgusting. You are an abomination." He reached for a weapon on his hip and pulled it out. It was not like the weapon the female had used. This was a real gun that shot real bullets.

The woman looked up from the face she was checking and looked at the man beside her. "Nu inca," she said in a soft tone and held up her hand. It was an obvious command, but Quinlan did not understand the language. The man looked at the Sweets and mock shot them while making a popping sound with his mouth. The woman had finished inspecting the people on the floor. "I am looking for someone specific. Does anyone here know where Margaret Carver is this fair day?"

Quinlan felt Margaret stiffen in his arms. She whispered, "What the fuck do they want me for?"

"Shhh," hissed Quinlan.

There was a robotic shift of heads, as if controlled remotely. Since the two intruders were standing in the sight line, all the students on the floor looked like they were staring right ahead at waist level. They were, in fact, staring at Margaret and Quinlan. The woman did not connect the action of her prisoners as any kind of response to her question. "Okay, who would like to experience the highest setting of one of these taser projectiles? She got half a charge," she said and pointed at the girl, who continued to moan on the floor. "How about you? Do you have any idea where Margaret Carver might be right now?" She reached to her weapon and adjusted something. "There, now you will not only puke, you will shit your pants and piss yourself." She pointed the weapon at a number of people. When she reached one of the Sweets she stopped. "Tell me or—" She didn't have time to finish. The Sweet quickly pointed to the table behind the door. He was trying to speak, but no sound came out. The woman turned and stared at where he was pointing. At first, she could not see that there was anyone behind the table and chairs that concealed both Margaret and Quinlan. She took steps toward them. She glanced up and caught the eye of one of the men in the doorway. He stepped into the room, pushed the right door closed, and pulled the table aside, exposing the hiding place. Quinlan stood up with his hands raised and stepped in front of Margaret. She slowly rose behind him and peered out past his shoulder.

Quinlan spoke. His voice did not waver. "What do you want her for?"

The woman stared at him. "Cute," she said and nodded at the male intruder that had just entered the room. He was carrying a rifle. He slammed the butt into Quinlan's midsection. He buckled and fell to his knees.

Margaret stared out into the room. In her eyes was a mixture of fear and defiance. "I am Margaret Carver. What do you want?"

The woman spoke to the group of intruders. "Take her." Two of the men stepped forward to grab Margaret when Quinlan suddenly stood. He picked up two cups from the table by their handles and swung them at the heads of the two men. His actions did little to stop them. The man moved forward and hit Quinlan on the side of his face with the gun he carried. Quinlan collapsed. "Who is he?" she asked Margaret.

"My friend. Don't hurt him."

"Your friend. Interesting," she said and looked up at the other intruders. "Take them both." Two of the men lifted Quinlan between them and half carried, half dragged him out. Margaret followed with one of the men on each arm. The man with the pistol looked at the woman. She said, "Fa-o acum," and nodded. The man unclipped a small device from his belt and snapped it toward the floor. A thin tripod with a camera attached to the top was aimed at the three young men huddled on the floor. The man started the camera, turned and stared at the Sweets still sitting on the floor in a weeping huddle. He pointed his gun at them and started firing. It was not a clean killing, for he continued to shoot at their bouncing blood-soaked bodies until all sixteen shots were expended. He turned, grabbed the camera, swept it over the crowd of hysterical women and strode out of the cafeteria amid a cacophony of screaming wails.

VIHAAN
KHATRI

Vihaan's training was intense while at the center. Training to become a fighter was second only to learning to become adept at functioning in a female world. A major part was information gathering. He was training to be a spy. He was also undergoing some cosmetic changes to make him look more feminine. The nanobots in his system gave him a new identity. That was all that mattered. As long as the AI attached to Medical Mother thought he was female, it didn't really matter what he looked like. There were a lot of females who had taken on male characteristics and dress. The reasons varied, but an obvious one was the attraction factor. Females were still attracted to males even if the government discouraged this. Women who took on male characteristics were sought after. If they were of average to below intelligence and they wanted to earn a better-than-average living, they could become prostitutes. This was not a word that was ever used. The common name for these male-like females was Loverboys. Some even went through surgeries to reduce breasts and gain a penis. This was what Vihaan was being trained to do. Given that he already had a penis was a plus. A PR campaign would introduce him to the politicians. This was common. When someone new hit the market, they had to have what amounted to a "Coming Out Party." It was expected that a new Loverboy on the market might get snatched up by someone high up in the ruling council. Basically, they would be kept and used until they were no longer desired. A lot of the older Loverboys became pimps. It was a rather seedy subculture.

Vihaan was being groomed to be a Loverboy for a very specific woman. He was to gain her trust once she had committed to pay for his time. He would become her monogamous lover. Getting her to actually commit was the job of at least a dozen researchers. He had to embody all that the woman desired. He had to be shown off in such a way that the woman could not resist. This was not an easy task. This part of the plan to infiltrate the government was dependent on this procedure. It was a long game. There were hundreds of boys, just like Vihaan, being trained. Once they were ensconced into the daily workings, they would begin to assert themselves as a political person in their own right. There were a number of pathways to political office, but the most common one was the process of recommendation. This was tried and true. A number of former Loverboys held office. The plan was to get enough of the false Loverboys in or near the seat of power. It would be a simple matter to change some of the laws and give men a foothold in government and reverse the trend. At least, that was the plan. It did not involve weapons, but it did involve the ability to protect oneself in case the unlikely occurred. Vihaan was very good at what could only be described as covert assassination. All things considered, having a ruling council member drop dead of a previously undetectable brain aneurism at just the right time might open up an opportunity. He was told that it would be very unlikely that he would have to kill anyone, but it was better to be prepared.

Getting away with murder was tough. Undetectable murder was even tougher. Murder made to look like an accident was usually the chosen method for the medical nanobots would expose any attempt to introduce poison. The only drawback was the time it took to plan and implement. All the men being trained as Loverboys were sitting in the lecture hall. Vihaan listened to the instructor drone. "I cannot stress how important it is to pay attention to absolutely everything in your subject's life. Even the most seemingly insignificant event could possibly be used when it comes time to do the deed."

Vihaan raised his hand. He started to speak before he was recognized. He had to yell from his seat at the back of the room. "I was told that I would not have to actually kill anyone."

The instructor frowned. "Please stand so I can see to whom I am speaking." Vihaan stood. The instructor squinted in an effort to read the number on the front of Vihaan's jumpsuit. "Ah, 285120. It is true that you will probably not have to do the deed, as it were, but you will be an integral part of the planning. Your purpose is to gain inside knowledge so that the planners can do their job." He looked at the entire group. "That is not to say that all of your subjects will be…" he paused, "dispatched." We are being meticulous. After all, the males of the human species are at risk of becoming extinct. Since you are all males," he waved his finger at the group, "I would expect you to do whatever you can to mitigate this seeming eventuality given the plans of the present female governing council." He scanned the room. "You may sit 285120."

Vihaan sat and rubbed his chin through the latex covering used to conceal the young men's identities from each other. His whiskers were being removed, and his face was a little raw. His preparation had not involved any attempts to make him actually like a woman chemically. In fact, that was frowned upon. He had not had any hormone injections or surgeries to make him more female. That was deemed a risk. He must not be tempted to feel any kind of affinity to the female majority. A leak of their plans to Fempol or the Ruling Council would spell failure. That must never happen. Their actual identities must not get leaked. That would mean intensive interrogation, followed by a prison sentence. One leak and the entire project could crumble. Vihaan's thoughts drifted to his old room in his mother's house. His new room was not much different except that it was soundproof. Listening to his mother and his uncle had made him feel safe. Here there was no sound. Sometimes his breathing and his beating heart were all he could hear. He kept reminding himself that this was his purpose. This is what his mother had done for him. He would serve the greater good by becoming and performing all the tasks required to the best of his ability.

He knew his target was the chief aid to Lillian Carver. Carver was the chairwoman of the Ruling Council in the USA. She was, for all intents and purposes, the most powerful person in the country. His target's name was Karen Chow. She was in her mid-forties. She'd had a series of Loverboys over the years. She liked tall slender women with dark skin and long dark hair. Vihaan had been growing his for many years. He could hear his mother's voice in his head. "You must let your hair grow long. It might be required one future day. If you need it short, it will be a simple matter to cut it off but not so simple to make it long." That one future day was nearly upon him. His objectives were first to become her Loverboy, second to replace her present aid, and third to replace Chow as chief aid to the chairwoman. He would woo her and become her Loverboy. He would make himself indispensable. The planners would figure out a way to counterfeit a recommendation that he take Chow's aide's place and soon after to take Chow's place. Chow's ability to adequately perform her duties would be brought into question. That would go a long way to getting him placed as a high-level operative in the female government. This was a government that must change if he and the members of his organization were to survive.

His next class was a personal tutorial. He would not have to wear the latex mask, as he was not with any of the other students. If he was to "make himself indispensable" to the woman he was to seduce, he would have to know a lot about her and the job she did for the chairwoman. This woman had degrees in economics and political science. She had been the chairwoman's aide for the last five years. In politics that was a long time, or so he was told. Political aides were like dresses—in one week and out the other. This woman had made herself indispensable, which also made her a very valuable asset to spy on and find a way to control. It was stressed to Vihaan that she was the person to replace. He was special because he had been chosen to be her replacement. If he played his cards right, he might succeed. He touched the door with his palm, and it opened. He entered and took off his mask. His face was sore, and the cool air felt good. He sat and waited. His instructors entered and nodded at him.

"Good afternoon, 285120," said an older man. "I am on my own today. I would like to ensure you have a good understanding of the political system under which we are presently suffering. You won't be able to be a successful spy unless you have something more to offer than your body. We are hoping you will get a position with your target that entails more than an occasional fuck. To do that, you must demonstrate knowledge and intelligence as well as being a good fuck. You will need to become her lover and her companion. The hardest thing will be using your maleness and hiding it at the same time."

"That has always bothered me. I understand the workings of the female political system and can hold my own. What I don't understand is the specifics of being a Loverboy. Do they have male equipment?"

"The committed ones do. They go through a procedure to change their outward gender and often go overboard. I have seen examples of some, and they have huge equipment. It is controlled by some sophisticated hydraulics to provide an erection on command. You won't have that. You will have to be more real. This will be both an advantage and a disadvantage, but if you can get her to have feelings for you, it will be more of an advantage."

"Feelings? You mean I have to get her to love me?"

"Yes. That would be best." Vihaan scrunched up his face. "It won't be all that difficult. You are very good looking in a girl-boy sort of way. I assume you have been studying female behavior. Of course, you have. You would not have gotten to this individual tutorial otherwise."

"I am committed," said Vihaan. "The only thing that has me worried is the sex part. I was raised in isolation and I—"

"I see. Don't worry, you will get to practice that aspect. Everyone that has gone through it tells me it is the best part."

Again, Vihaan scrunched up his face. The instructor furrowed his own eyebrows in response. "You do like girls, don't you?"

"Is that a trick question? I have been told my whole life that females are our enemy."

"No. Females are not our enemy. The political system created by some women is our enemy. We are striving to change the system. It is just that we have been forced to resort to some rather nasty tactics to achieve our goals."

"Yes, I like girls. There was one girl who lived across the street. I would see her leave her house every day. Sometimes I would…"

"Fantasize about her?"

Vihaan nodded.

"Good. Very good."

Vihaan leaned forward in his chair. "Tell me more about the sex practice. Will there be real girls to practice with? Do I get to talk to them? Can I choose one or do they just give me one and we have intercourse? Tell me how it works."

"We will get to that. Today we are going to discuss the ruling council and how they go about making laws. You have to understand that if you are to be one to initiate change." Vihaan nodded and tried to push the thought of the girl next door out of his head. His tongue rubbed up against the tattoo on the inside of his right cheek. He had gotten it the first week he had been here. The image of it helped him concentrate. It was the code for the male of the species, and it must be honored and protected. Unicode 2642. He wore it proudly. He wore it secretly.

Its meaning filled his mind and drove all thoughts of sex away.

NISHEETA DAVENPORT

Nisheeta was early. She called the meeting to discuss the plans of the various Fempol commissioners to bring the perpetrators of the university massacre to justice and get Margaret Carver back alive. She took the chair at the head of the table and pressed a series of buttons inset on the tabletop. The lighting softened and the side wall filled with images of young female children playing. The door at the far end of the room opened and two older men dressed in server uniforms entered and began to lay out a selection of fruits and pastries on the table. They set a small side table with various hot and cold beverages. They did not speak but completed their task and left the room. Nisheeta glanced up for a moment. The sight of the pastries made her stomach rumble. She glanced down at her timepiece, quickly stood up, and reached for one of the pastries. She shoved it in her mouth. She bit down and let the sweet, fresh dough fill her senses. She moved back to her chair and ate the remainder of the pastry with relish. She was licking the icing from her fingers when the door opened. A young woman entered.

"Oh, you are early. I was going to get the room ready, but I see you beat me to it," said the young woman.

"Good morning, Dolores. I was already here, so I got it all ordered. Sit. I have some notes for you, and I would like to plan how I want this meeting to go." Dolores sat to the left of Nisheeta. "As you know, I have a slightly different viewpoint on how we should deal with these criminals than the Commissioners."

"That is an understatement."

"I get the feeling that you would rather I be more like the NAFF (Now and Forever Female) zealots in my dealings with criminal elements, especially rogue males and the females who support them."

"As a matter of fact, I do. I don't think you should go as far as the Plague Warriors." Nisheeta looked at her questioningly. "The PW is relatively new. Their agenda is a simple one: get rid of males—completely. There is something to be said about that. Imagine no males at all. Do you realize how much simpler our job would be?"

"You would have me declare war on these kidnappers and bulldoze my way to their center no matter how many innocent people it hurt in the process."

"May I speak freely?" Nisheeta nodded at her aide. "The commissioners are on the front line. They know how to deal with the criminal element that is trying to subvert our government. They know what works and what doesn't. These people must be stopped, and if that means using all the tools at our disposal, then so be it."

"Oh, I plan to stop them alright. I am just not going to do it with the press following my every move. That is what these monsters want. They want to point to the people and say, "Look what this government is doing. They are murdering women.""

"You think women are at the center of this?"

"My Intel suggests that this was perpetrated by a mercenary Roma group out of central Europe. They were hired by one of the many branches of AMEN. I am not sure of their purpose here, but it seems they want to trade her for a number of male prisoners. They have demanded the release of ten prisoners in payment for the Carver kid's safe return. They are asking that as a smokescreen for their true desires. They want us to negotiate. Once that precedent is set, it will never stop. They want to force us to ease the laws and give men equal say in the government. That will never happen on my watch."

"Are there women in this terrorist group?"

"Please understand that there are many older females, especially those of certain ethnicities, that still believe that men are important, even necessary."

"Don't these women remember what it was like when men held the reins of power? Has history taught them nothing?"

"Obviously not. So, are you going to support me, or do I have to start looking for a new aide?"

"Sorry, I didn't understand."

"I know. That is why I am the head of Fempol and you are my aide." She paused to see if her jab had an effect on Dolores. "I don't want to pull rank. That is just far too male and not my style, but time is short. I need to know that you are on my side in order to get the commissioners to follow my agenda and not their own agenda."

"I understand. I am with you," she said and turned to a sound at the door. There was a short knock. She reached out and opened the door. A young woman said something to her. "Please send them in." There were six women in total: three commissioners and their respective aides. The commissioners sat at the table while the aides sat to the side. Each aide was carrying a case that they set on the floor to be opened as needed.

Nisheeta stood at the end of the table. She waited until everyone was seated. "Ladies. Welcome. Please feel free to help yourself to tea or coffee. I tried one of the pastries. They are delicious." She waited, and no one moved.

The woman sitting alone on the left side smiled a crooked smile. "Let's get to it, Nisheeta," she said and tapped her tablet with a stylus. "Some of us have jobs to get back to."

A thought shot through Nisheeta's head. *Bullshit, bitch.* She quickly covered it with a tin grin. "Yes, let's get started, but before I do," she turned to Dolores, "Dolores, would you please move those darling pastries to the table. Put one of the plates close to me so I can put my self-control to the test." Chuckles came from the others in the room. She smiled and waited until Dolores had completed her task. "Good," she said and watched the three commissioners stare at the plates of pastries. "I know all of you have been briefed on the situation regarding the murders at the university and the kidnapping of the Carver girl. I have a few more details that have not been released. Along with the Carver girl, was a young male. According to the witnesses, he tried, in the usual male fashion, to come to her rescue and was summarily silenced with the butt of a pistol. They were both removed by three uniformed males and one female. The female appeared to be the leader of the group and ordered the execution of the males in the Male Progeniture Program."

One of the commissioners spoke. "We know all this. In fact, I am sure we sent this file to your office earlier today."

"Yes, you did. I received a file from each of you. They were all fairly similar. That is good. They confirm what happened. My office received this video today with the demands of the perpetrators." She looked up. "Run the video, Dolores." Dolores reached down to her tablet and the wall opposite Nisheeta began to play the video. It started with a logo that filled the screen.

"Please take note of that logo. It has been identified as belonging to a mercenary group out of Romania." The video continued. A group of Sweets and a number of other females could be seen cowering. The camera zoomed in on the Sweets and the sound of a gun being fired and bodies bouncing as splattered blood filled the wall. The entire scene slowed and zoomed in on one of the males as a bullet hit his cheek. You could actually see the flesh tear away and pieces of his teeth shatter—white needles in a red mist—leaving a gaping hole in his face. Then the video sped up to the sound of the gun firing and slowed again as another bullet hit and shattered another body. There were seven of these before the camera pulled back to show the horror on the faces of the females. The video finally stopped and went to black. "Stop it there, Dolores." The video stopped. "Comments?"

"My report said that they set up the camera and shot the Sweets. None of the witnesses reported anything like this."

"This was all done after. The video was shot with an ultra-high-speed, high resolution camera and edited to what we saw," said Dolores.

"There is more," said Nisheeta. She nodded at Dolores and the video continued. The screen went black with white lettering scrolling across the screen.

Our demands are simple. Pardon the following prisoners and release them at the following coordinates: 48.979203 – 123.074332.

51244-098, 98765-097, 56565-050, 76565-055, 86135-007, 97105-007, 74410-053, 93450-011

The scrolling stopped.

One of the commissioner's aides stood to copy the numbers on the screen with her tablet. "Or what?" she asked.

"That is just it. They are not threatening anything specific. They did not even mention the Carver girl. To me, that is far more insidious than any threat they could have made," said Nisheeta.

"Have you checked out what I am assuming are coordinates and prisoner numbers?" asked one of the commissioners.

Nisheeta looked up at Dolores. Dolores touched her tablet and began reading. "The location is just about as close as you can get to the Canadian border. It is a small peninsula that is separated from the continental US by water. The town is called Point Roberts. It can only be accessed by land by traveling 40 kilometers through Canada. Over the years, there have been many discussions about it ceding to Canada. It was probably an oversight when the borders were decided. "She looked down at her tablet. "As you probably have determined, the other numbers are of a series of prisoners presently in custody. They were originally clustered in three areas." She looked down again. "New York area, DC and California. But they were moved and are all now housed in a maximum-security federal penitentiary in Hazelton West Virginia."

"Here is what I think we should do. We send out feelers to all our informants. We offer a huge reward for information leading to conviction as well as some small enticements to show we are serious. I guarantee we will have the girl back within the week," said one of the other commissioners.

"The moment you do that, the press will be all over it," said Nisheeta.

"So what," said the commissioner, sitting by herself on the left side of the table.

"We don't want this out until we have investigated the drop area. I think this must be connected to the cult that has taken refuge on Vancouver Island. They are affiliated with the AMEN group. It is just too close not to be connected to those idiots who still think males are equal to females." There were smirks all around the table.

"So, Commissioner Davenport, what do you suggest we do?"

"Infiltrate the cult. I want to know their plans so we can dig them out by the roots."

"The reports I read suggest their leadership is female. Do you think that is true, or is it a male ploy?"

"Could be. There are still some females who aren't thinking with their brains. I have a plan, but it is not fleshed out yet. You will all be receiving an outline of how we are going to proceed. I expect a response before the week is out." She looked around the room to nodding heads. "If there are no more concerns, we are adjourned."

As the women gathered their papers, Dolores' tablet sounded a warning. She glanced down and quickly approached Nisheeta. She shoved the tablet in front of her. "Look."

Nisheeta glanced down and quickly absorbed the notice. "Ladies. Please be seated. Something has come up." There was silence as the women took their seats. "It appears as if someone has leaked the whereabouts of the young man that was taken at the same time as the Carver girl. He is being held by one of the AMEN cells we have been surveilling. Fempol is in the process of rescuing him and shutting down this cell. I would like to reconvene tomorrow when we have more information. I hope that is agreeable. Dolores will make the arrangements for your extended stay in the capital." She nodded at Dolores and quickly left the room.

MARGARET CARVER

Margaret saw Quinlan hit the floor. She was lifted and dragged out of the cafeteria. She glanced over her shoulder and saw the men pick Quinlan up by his arms. He was unconscious. She heard one of the men speak. "If you hadn't knocked him out, this would be a lot easier."

"Pick him up. We will have to drag him."

The men each took an arm over their shoulder and followed, with Quinlan in tow. Margaret screamed and struggled against her captors. She tried to kick the men holding her when the woman in charge walked up to her. She stared directly at Margaret and said, "If she doesn't stop struggling and shut her fucking mouth, shoot him somewhere that won't kill him." Margaret stopped struggling and was carried quickly along. The route they took out of the university was unfamiliar to her. They ended up in a loading dock. There was the smell of garbage—mostly rotting food being composted. A utility vehicle designed to carry the composted material was parked near the loading ramp. As they approached, the carefully disguised back of the vehicle swung aside. Everyone entered, and the opening swung closed. She was pushed down onto a bench and strapped into place. Her arms were tied over her head to the wall behind her. Quinlan was unceremoniously dumped onto the floor. The captors sat with their weapons at the ready. There was no sound except the motor of the vehicle revving. Margaret felt the motion of a turn to the right as the momentum forced her to sway left. From there on, she memorized the turns.

"What do you want?" she finally asked calmly.

"From you—nothing except that you do whatever the fuck we tell you to do. I am telling you now to shut up." said the woman. She added poignancy to her words by staring at Quinlan.

"Where are you taking me?"

"A slow learner, I see." The woman stood, walked over to Quinlan, and kicked his unconscious body in the ribs.

"Leave him alone," shouted Margaret.

The woman kicked him again. Quinlan would not feel the kicks until much later. Margaret stopped talking. She glared at the woman. She was angry at herself for losing control. She had lost track of the turns, or they had not turned since the three turns leaving the university. If the latter was true, then she had a pretty good idea of the direction they were traveling. They drove for about 30 minutes when she felt the vehicle slow and stop. It had not turned again. The woman whispered something to two of the men. They stood up and dragged Quinlan to the doorway. A motor whined, and the door opened. They took him out. Margaret stared at the open door in hopes of seeing something she might identify at a later time. She could see and hear very little, but the smell of garbage was so strong it almost brought tears to her eyes. "Shut the door," ordered the woman to someone on the other end of a communication device. "They can catch up with us later." The door closed, and the truck started again. She looked at Margaret. "He is gone, but not forgotten. We can and will hurt him if you don't do what you are told. Be very sure of that."

The vehicle started again. Margaret breathed deeply and waited. They traveled for a few more minutes, and then she heard the woman speak a single "Yes," into her COM. The woman stood up, opened a pouch and removed a needle. She nodded at two of the men. They stood on either side of her. The woman held the needle on display for Margaret to see. "You can sit still and take this sedative or, if you decide to struggle, one of these men will punch you in the face and knock you out. Either way, you are getting this needle. The 'how' is up to you."

Margaret nodded. "Just give me the shot."

The woman nodded at one of the men. He stood over Margaret and detached her right arm from the restraints. He pushed up her sleeve. The woman bent over and injected her. Margaret felt the drug immediately. She looked at her captors and tried to memorize everything she could. She got as far as an insignia on one of the men. It was tattooed on the skin of his wrist as he lifted her arm and reattached the restraint. It looked like a flower. It was indelibly printed in her memory.

Margaret woke. She was on her back, and when she opened her eyes, she was looking at a yellow ceiling. She sat up and the world spun around her. She lay back down to a pounding in her head. She turned her head to the side. There was a door in front of her. She lay still and stared. To move meant to feel like her head was being hit repeatedly with a sledgehammer. Each pound brought splashes of color, mostly red and yellow, that swelled out in waves from the center of her brain. She remained as still as she could, and the pain ebbed to a dull gray. Her mouth was dry, as if she had been breathing with her mouth open for as long as the drug kept her unconscious. She brought her lips together, and the action signaled the creature in charge of pain to lash out. She moaned, closed her eyes, and welcomed the gray bandage the darkness brought.

Suddenly, the door to her cell opened. "Sit up," a voice ordered. Margaret opened her eyes and coughed. She slowly sat up. The woman in front of her was holding a glass of water. She thrust it at Margaret. "Here," she said. "Take these." She gave Margaret two white pills and the water. Margaret took the glass and quickly swallowed the pills. She figured that there were at least a thousand other ways to kill her besides poison pills, so she took them without question. She lay back down. "Rest," ordered the woman. "I will bring you something to eat when you feel better. Then we can talk." The woman left the small room. Margaret drifted off to sleep.

Sometime later, she woke again. She felt much better. There was a small table in the middle of the room with a single chair. On it was some food that consisted of crackers and cheese. There was also a pitcher of water. Margaret sat up and scanned her cell. There was a toilet partially concealed by a room divider. Her bladder was full. She stood and started toward it. Her head swam, and she nearly fell. She relieved herself and moved to the table. She drank some of the water and nibbled at the food. She was not hungry. The fuzz that had coated her brain was lifting. She was feeling sharper. She ate another cracker. She knew she might need her strength.

The door opened again, and the same woman entered, carrying a chair. She set it opposite Margaret and sat. The two women stared at each other. Margaret felt her anger swell, but she held it in check. The woman spoke. "I hope you are feeling better. I need you to be lucid for what comes next."

"Next?"

"Yes. You are going to star in some videos. I want you sharp and healthy for the first one."

"First one?"

"Yes. You are probably going to star in a number of videos before this is over. Exactly how many depends on your mother."

"What the fuck has my mother got to do with…" she paused. "Oh, I get it. I'm being held for ransom. What a joke. My mother doesn't have a lot of money. The house we live in does not even belong to us. Most of the stuff we have is courtesy of the government."

"We don't want money."

"What then?"

"Favors. We want your mother to do us some favors."

"Who are you, anyway? You behave like a bunch of terrorists. Are you one of those women that support men? How can you do that? How can you be a traitor to your gender?"

"I am not. I am a supporter of equality for all members of the human race. The AMEN group strives for equality of males and females."

"What is the point? The latest estimates give the human male 50 more years before they no longer exist in this country. That is a fact."

"That is a very sad thought. We are determined to reverse this evil plot by the government of this country, no matter what it takes. We want your mother to use her powers to release some incarcerated men. She has done it before, and she can do it again."

"She won't do that."

"We will see," the woman said and stood up. "Someone will be in shortly to clean you up a little. Those disgusting jeans will have to go. Your ass is practically hanging out."

"That is because you murderous bastards ripped them."

"Murder? Oh, you are talking about the abominations—the Sweets—or whatever you call them. First of all, that was not our doing. The people we hired got carried away."

"Carried away. Fuck," whispered Margaret. She slapped the table and shouted, "They were just innocent bystanders and you killed them—for what—to make a point!?"

"Those creatures exist to perpetuate your distorted view of what you want the human race to become. That is not murder any more than killing a virus is murder. Once we have set things right, they will all be killed. We believe that all the monsters you create to further your androcide must be purged. The rest of you will have to be shown that males and females are equal and have the right to be treated as such."

"You don't really believe that shit, do you?" Margaret reached out and picked up the glass in front of her. It was heavy in her hand.

The woman stood. "Perhaps, in the near future, it is something you too might believe." She smiled. The smile carried a message of things to come. She turned and walked to the door. Just as she reached out to open the door, Margaret stood and hurled the glass at her. It hit the wall beside her head. It shattered. The glass flew, some of it bounced off the woman's back. She turned. She touched her hands to opposite shoulders and then pressed them together in front of her while touching her chin with her fingertips.

Margaret thought it looked like some religious gesture. "What the fuck does that mean?"

"It is simply an expression of unity. The equal and opposite genders represented by the shoulders come together and are bound by our mind into one indivisible unit called human. It is beautiful."

Margaret spit on the floor. "It is just a bunch of bullshit lies."

The woman smiled, "It will become your truth soon." She left the room.

QUINLAN SMITH

Quinlan woke some hours later. He found himself lying face down on a cold concrete floor. His head and his face ached. His mouth was parched. His tongue touched his lips. They were swollen and dry. He started to push himself up to a sitting position when he heard a rattle behind him. He stopped and eased his aching body back down to the floor and waited. A second or two later, the unmistakable sound of a heavy door opening made his body go rigid. He heard someone behind him breathing and felt the presence weigh on him. He remained still. He felt what he assumed was a boot nudge his ribs. He moaned even though it didn't hurt very much. The boot nudged him again. He made no sound this time. He had a little boy plan form in his head. Play dead. Play dead and when they least expect it, jump up and attack your attackers. They would buckle under your onslaught—not expecting your surprise attack. The boot touched his ribs again, but this time it was accompanied by a voice. "Please sit up. I know you are awake. I wish to speak to you." Quinlan did not move. His little plan was forgotten. "I have some water here for you," the voice said. Quinlan turned over. He looked at the man standing in front of him. He had a container of liquid and he held it out. Quinlan stared at him. "It is just water, I promise."

Quinlan reached up for the water. "Where is Margaret?" he asked and then drank deeply.

The man looked back at Quinlan with a puzzled expression on his face. "I do not know what you are talking about. I know nothing about anyone named Margaret."

"You took her from the university. You hit me when I tried to stop you."

"You were taken from the university? You were involved in that mess. Shit," the man stated flatly. He turned and left the room. The door clanged behind him.

"What the fuck?" called Quinlan at the sound of fading footsteps. The quiet fell over the room except when Quinlan moved. Every sound echoed. If he scraped his foot along the floor, the sound seemed to reverberate. Even his breathing was amplified. He stood up and moved around the small cell in an effort to ease the stiffness and cold in his muscles. The cell was empty. It was well lit but had no obvious source of light. The floor was smooth and clean except where he had been laying. He must have bled from somewhere. There was blood on the floor. Quinlan felt for wounds. He touched the side of his head and winced. The pain brought a memory of one of the suited men hitting him on the side of his head. He looked at his fingers. There was watery blood on the tips. He felt up and down his clothes. He hoped to find something he could use as a weapon. He had a stylus and his tablet when he left that morning. The tablet was left on the table in the cafeteria and the stylus was no longer in his pocket. He stood in the middle of the room and waited. A few minutes passed before he heard the sound of footsteps returning. An old habit from his time in school asserted itself. He held his hands up at shoulder height, palm forward. There was no expression on his face. He was standing as if waiting for a matron to approach him.

The door clanged and opened. The man who had given him water was standing in the open doorway. He stared at Quinlan. His expression changed. It was obvious disapproval. "Don't stand like that. You are a man, not a slave." He turned his back to Quinlan. "Come with me." He walked out of the cell. Quinlan did not move. The man turned. "Come. We have a lot to talk about." He turned once more and continued walking. Quinlan hesitated and then followed. The hallway led to what Quinlan supposed was an elevator. The door was open, and the man gestured for him to enter. Quinlan entered and turned. The man followed. The elevator started.

"I have a lot of questions. Are you going to answer them when we get to wherever we are going?"

"If I can," said the man facing the door.

Quinlan considered hitting the man and trying to escape once the door opened, but his captor no longer seemed threatening. He waited. The door opened. In front of Quinlan was a large rotunda with many hallways leading off the central area. There were at least a dozen men moving through the rotunda in and out of the various hallways. They all seemed to be busy and involved with each other. The startling thing was the fact that there were no females. "Where are the women?" he asked.

"Exactly," answered the man cryptically as he entered one of the hallways leading out of the room. He stopped at a door, touched a panel with his palm, causing the door to open with a soft click. The room was utilitarian, furnished with a table and some chairs. There were posters on the walls. Their nature struck Quinlan as extremely odd. They were reproductions of very old posters. One wall was dedicated to something called "Suffrage" while the opposite wall was dedicated to "Anti-Suffrage." The suffrage side posters depicted women from the past trying to get the vote. Many showed women being arrested and bullied by policemen. The opposite wall had a different tone. The posters were showing what it would be like if women were allowed to vote. They showed a man looking after children while women went out into the world to their jobs.

"This is a strange room. What's with the posters?"

"I thought this would be a good place for you to begin your education."

"What are you talking about? I go to the university. I am studying quantum biology."

"Yes, and you will continue to do just that, but you will also, if you agree, help to overcome a new kind of oppression and help men regain suffrage."

"Sorry, but I have no idea what suffrage means."

"So starts your education. It is an old word with its present meaning dating back to the 1850s in this country. Basically, it means the right to vote. Women did not have the right to vote for a very long time. It took 70 years to achieve. Once they had it, it took another 100 years to reach some sort of equality with men. The #WOW movement sped up the process of women being equal to men in all ways. It led to the shift we now experience. Women are seen to be superior to men. I find it hard to dispute that statement in that this planet has never had a more stable global government. For the first time in human history, poverty has been crushed. There are no wars. Global warming has been reversed. None of those things would have happened if males were in charge. We probably would not even be here had it not been for women ruling the world."

"You sound like one of the matrons at school."

"These posters are here to make sure that we males understand how we got to this point. History is a pendulum. It swings back and forth. Sometimes it swings too far, as it did before women had the right to determine their destiny. It has now swung in the opposite direction. It is critical to reverse this trend before the males of the human species cease to exist. The "Y" chromosome is already much less pronounced than the "X". Natural selection has already started to make the "Y" chromosome less and less important. The women of the USA have decided to speed up this process by setting in motion a plan to rid the country of all males. They will do it in a typically female way. They will simply reduce the number of male children born. Once that has been achieved and maintained, the male of the species has no chance. We will simply fade away.

We are already not required for reproduction. The sperm banks can provide enough for the next thousand years. Technology has replaced us in all ways. As women see it, we are not necessary for the survival of the species. We intercepted a secret memo that describes males as equivalent to an appendix. It is totally useless and is dangerous if it becomes infected. It is better excised."

"How can they possibly do that? What about sex? I'm not that experienced but I know women desire men." Quinlan thought of his encounter with Margaret and added, "At least I think that is true."

"Yes, most do, but that can be changed with a little carefully aimed propaganda. They will teach the female children that a male is not needed for sex—those males are dirty and dangerous. If you have sex with one, you will be impregnated with a monster. How is that for a purposeful lie? They will simply pass a law and that will be that."

"Fuck," murmured Quinlan.

"More likely not," the man said with a smirk.

"Well, what is this place? Who are you? Where is Margaret? What do you want from me?"

"Yes. One question at a time. We found you unconscious outside one of our warehouses and brought you here. You did not have anything dangerous on your person but this." He produced a stylus from his pocket and handed it to Quinlan. "We like to be careful, so you were put in that cell. We spent some time trying to identify you. When you told us you were taken from the university, we figured you were dumped by a group of mercenaries. We are pretty sure they were responsible for you and the Carver girl's kidnapping. Do you have any idea why you were dumped after the kidnapping? It seems odd."

"I have no idea. I was fighting to save Margaret one minute and the next I woke up in that cell."

"Maybe you were useful as a pawn. Did the Carver girl have feelings for you?"

Quinlan felt his face flush. He stammered. "Well, she...we kissed and... she wanted to...we wanted—"

He nodded. "I understand. They took you to keep her under control. They probably threatened to harm you if she did not cooperate. That's what I would have done. Once they had her under control, you were just a liability, so they dumped you." He looked skyward, considering his words. "Initially, we thought they were a harmless, quasi-religious group, but we are now reconsidering since the brutal murders at the university."

"They shot three sweets in cold blood. Just shot them. One of the men did it, but I think it was a woman who ordered it. And they took Margaret."

"And you. It was an interesting move on their part. The fact it was a woman in charge confirms the group we suspect. You were lucky."

"I would have been lucky if they had simply left me there."

The man shook his head. "No. If they had left you there, you would be in prison right now. Fempol would have assumed that you were in on it. Think about it. A woman you are sitting with is snatched from the university. Not just any woman but the daughter of the head of the Committee. Then the Sweets were killed. If you were left behind unharmed, you would have been fucked. By the time they figured out you had nothing to do with it, the news cycles would have your picture splattered over everything. No one would believe you. It would just be better to make you disappear. As for the remainder of your questions, the answers will come in good time. I have to go. You are a bit of a puzzle that needs to be investigated. Someone will come and take you to your quarters. You have to stay with us, at least until things settle down. I will see you later." The man stood and left Quinlan sitting in the room filled with the bizarre posters. He stared at them.

VIHAAN
KHATRI

Vihaan was sitting in front of a vid screen. He felt lousy. The morning injection of female nanobots had not conformed to the standard. There was some sort of reaction to this batch that he had not felt before. He had been assured that they would soon reprogram themselves and he would feel fine. That was hours ago. The screen was looping through a series of females. He was supposed to choose one to use for his continued studies. Vihaan considered the word *use*. It was not one he would have chosen. He considered others. *Fuck*. *Make love*. Those were the two extremes that resulted in the same thing. Neither were suitable. He just wanted to understand and practice. *Practice*. Maybe that was the right word. He needed someone to practice with. They could not know the purpose of the practice. He wondered what they had been told as to the nature of the situation. He flipped to the next girl. One word defined her. Young. He suddenly felt concern. Why was someone so young being used for this? He stared at her and realized that his initial impression was wrong. She was not as young as he first thought. She was just made up to look that way. He flipped to the next and stopped. This girl looked just like the girl across the street from his house. He had spent a lot of time fantasizing about her. He looked closer. It wasn't her, but she was eerily similar. He zoomed the picture to a close-up of her face and decided to choose this girl. The interface allowed him to confirm his selection. He would spend the rest of the morning with her. He sat back and waited. The door to the viewing room opened. "I think you have made a good choice. Please come with me." Vihaan stood and followed the man. He was directed to a small room with a seating area, a bathroom, and a curtained off double bed. Sitting at the table was the girl from the selection video. She stood when he entered. Vihaan's guide spoke, "This is Chloe. She will be with you for the next two hours." Vihaan knew he was never to reveal his name and to introduce himself as a number was just too odd, so he simply nodded. The guide left and closed the door behind him.

"Have you done this before?" he asked and then realized that he had asked the most ridiculous question ever. Of course, she had done it before. He was the novice here, not her. She looked up at him and smiled. "Never mind. That was a stupid question."

She stood and walked over to him and placed her hands on his shoulders. "My job here is to train you to have positive sexual experiences with a female in preparation for a life in a household. Young men, like yourself, need to be trained for your job as a Sexman. I assume you have been trained in a myriad of other household chores." Vihaan nodded. He now understood what this woman was doing. It was her job to train Sexmen in the art of love and she thought he was preparing for that job. "Today's lesson is a simple one. Your job will be to give me pleasure. You will do that by following my directions. Do you understand?" Again, Vihaan nodded.

She walked over to the bed and drew back the curtain. "First, you must know the nature of common female clothing. It is not about cleaning and caring. That is a different course. This is about removing them from the female form." She pointed at the top button of her blouse. "Begin here. Undo all the buttons until you get to the waistband of my skirt and then gently pull the blouse out and continue until all the buttons are undone. Do not open the blouse." Vihaan hesitated. "Begin," she ordered. He reached up and slowly started to unbutton her blouse, taking care to do it smoothly. The woman reached out and put her index finger under his chin. "Look up here at my face when you do this. I assume you can unbutton a blouse without looking at each button." Vihaan looked up. "Smile. If you are going to please a woman, you have to give her the impression that you are enjoying what you are doing, even if you are not. Generally, you will not have to undress a woman completely, but you will have to start." Vihaan completed unbuttoning her blouse. "Good. Now open my blouse and react to what you see."

Vihaan opened her blouse. Her breasts were exposed, and he sucked in his breath. "Nice. Now, depending on the woman, you will have to either follow instructions or take the initiative. If the latter, you will have to attend to her reactions to give you direction as to what she likes." The woman turned and removed her blouse. She turned back. "Now, suck on this nipple. She thrust her breast forward until the nipple was a few cm from his mouth. He opened his mouth and sucked it gently. "Harder." He sucked harder on the nipple. "Faster." He sped up. "Rub the nipple between your teeth. Don't bite. Good." She put her hands behind his head and guided it. "Bite it." He bit down on the nipple. She winced and pulled his head away from her breast. "I didn't say bite it off. Fuck." She rubbed her nipple to smooth away the pain. "Now that is an example of someone who likes to give orders. It is not easy and sometimes results in one of these." She slapped him across the face. He pulled his head back at the blow. "Now on the other breast. Pleasure me by tuning in to my body's reactions." She pushed his head back to her other breast. Vihaan began to suck. He reached up with his hand and rolled the nipple on the other breast between his fingers. He popped the nipple out of his mouth and flicked it with his tongue. The woman moaned and pressed his head into her breast, forcing as much of it as she could into his mouth. He gently pinched the other nipple. She moaned again and pulled back. She grabbed his head and turned it up, so she was looking straight at him. "Are you sure you have never been with a woman before? That was especially erotic for me." She waited for him to respond. He simply looked at her. He knew better than to grin. He had never really interacted with females other than his mother, but he knew it was never a good idea to be smart. "Well, have you?"

Vihaan shook his head. "I just did to you what I like when I…" he paused, "…you know—"

"Masturbate?"

He nodded.

"Stand up."

He stood, and she reached out and felt his penis. "Why isn't it hard?"

"It was until…"

"Until what?"

"It was until you slapped me."

"Oh, yeah. Sorry about that. I am supposed to ensure that you do not react violently. If it is any consolation, you reacted as you should." She reached out, opened his pants and clasped her hand on his swelling penis. She pulled it out as it continued to swell. "Oh my. You are going to be a very sought after Sexman." She continued to rub his penis.

Vihaan felt his knees go weak.

QUINLAN SMITH

Quinlan's stomach growled. He had not eaten since his capture. His head ached. He rubbed the bump on his skull where he had been hit. He stood in front of some rather bizarre posters. One showed a woman sitting in a wooden chair. The chair was secured to pegs in the ground with thick rope. The same rope was used to tie the woman's arms to the back of the chair. Her leg was shackled to a 50-pound weight. Her head was being held between two horizontal boards with padlocks dangling from the bottom board holding it in place. The woman's mouth was securely clamped shut. The poster's intent was obvious. The caption read, "What I would do with the Suffragists." To the right was another poster that was even more bizarre. It depicted a woman with a metal frame around her head and over her face. There was a tightening screw on the top of the woman's head. Her mouth was held closed by a huge padlock through her lips. The title of the poster was: PEACE AT LAST. Just below these posters was a comment that surprised Quinlan. It read, "It wasn't right then, and it isn't right now." It had never occurred to him that he was being treated like the suffragists were treated almost two centuries earlier. He had simply accepted his role in the society. The sound of footsteps alerted him that someone was approaching the door. He looked at the door just as it opened. An elderly man entered. The man's eyes scanned Quinlan.

"Interesting posters, eh," he said. Quinlan did not reply. He simply nodded. "I am here to take you to your quarters. Follow me." The man turned and walked out of the room and down the hall. Quinlan followed. He was led down a hallway past a series of plain wooden doors. The man stopped at the third one and opened it. "You can rest here. Someone will bring you food a little later. I assume you are hungry. Is there anything else you require?"

Quinlan looked at the man. He was lost as to what to reply. Asking what he might require was alien to him, so he said nothing. The man nodded and shut the door. Quinlan turned and scanned the room. It was not unlike his previous room in the institution where he grew up, except it was larger. There was a bed with table and a chair, as well as a small sofa to the side. There were no windows, but there was a large screen attached to the wall that was displaying a series of outdoor scenes. A door to the left led to a full bathroom with a shower. He went inside and relieved himself. He lay down on the bed and let his mind replay the previous hours, or maybe it was days. He was unsure. He rubbed his head when he thought of the kidnappers hitting him. His ribs were sore. He did not remember being hit there, but he must have been. He lifted up his shirt. His right side was bruised black and purple. He shifted to his left and closed his eyes. He did not want to sleep, but his body settled on the soft mattress and his consciousness seeped out of this body.

He woke to a repetitive beeping that seemed to come from the walls. He sat up and winced. His bruised side ached. He stood and walked in the direction of the bathroom. He stood in front of the toilet and peed. Just as he finished, the door to his room opened. He turned his head and saw a man stick his head into the room and stare at the bed. The beeping sound was louder now and intermittently interrupted by short bursts of a siren.

"Shit. Where the fuck?"

"Here," said Quinlan.

The man he had never seen entered the room and moved to where Quinlan was standing. He touched a small device to a panel beside the door. "Come now."

"What is happening?"

The siren changed from short bursts to a cascading wail. "Later. We have to get out of here." He grabbed Quinlan's arm and pulled him toward the door. They left the room and moved quickly down the hallway to an open area. There were a number of men hustling from room to room. There were carrying small devices that they touched to sensors on the outside and presumably on the inside of the rooms.

"What are they doing?"

"Cleaning up," the man said, and dragged Quinlan into a very small room. In fact, it was a broom closet. He pushed some buckets with mops standing upright in them to the side, reached up and pressed his palm to a section of the wall. The end wall slid away. He pulled Quinlan through, and the wall closed behind them. They were in a service elevator. The man pressed some buttons, and the elevator started to drop. It was moving very fast. Quinlan felt his stomach pitch upward as the elevator moved downward. The man turned to him. "The entire floor is fitted with DNA erasers. The men upstairs set the timers on the devices. When they go off, all DNA in the air or on the walls or furniture is broken down into its base molecules. The timers will give the men time to get out. The erasers are not selective when it comes to where it finds DNA. All Fempol sniffers will get nothing. This place is shielded so our nanobots cannot be detected. Once we are gone, the floor of this building will reveal nothing. That is what we are doing now—getting out."

"What about all the others?"

"There is a freight elevator that is not on any of the plans for this building. Fempol will never find it. They will all leave that way." He turned to the back wall and touched three areas with his thumb. A panel slid away, exposing a rack of equipment at the back of the elevator. "You will have to help me with this. It is the data banks of our entire cell. There is no backup. They cannot be accessed by any outside system, even AIM (Artificial Intelligent Mother). The system has its own power source and emits zero radio or infrared signals."

"Where are we going to end up?" asked Quinlan. There was a bump. "What was that?"

"Grab the handles. There," the man pointed. "Get ready to push this rack out when the doors open. Don't hesitate. We will get about seven seconds to get this rack and ourselves out before the door closes. Believe me, you do not want to be inside this elevator after the door closes." There were a series of beeps rapidly increasing in frequency. Once the sound became a solid tone, the door at the back of the elevator opened. "Push now!" The rack was heavy, but the two men overcame the inertia and the rack moved over the threshold and onto a smooth floor. Once out, they turned just as the door closed and concealed any indication that there was ever an elevator. There was only the sound of their breathing.

"What's happening in there?" asked Quinlan, pointing at the elevator door.

"Nothing pleasant, I can assure you. Anything living turns into a little pile of carbon, calcium, phosphorus and a few other elements and a room filled with an explosive mixture of oxygen and hydrogen in the air. It is a weapon developed using nanobots to break down any living thing into its component parts and then spark an explosion of the resulting mixture of oxygen and hydrogen. The explosion is small, but it is enough to destroy the nanobots so they cannot be reverse engineered. Cool, huh." Quinlan shrugged. Weapons were not his thing. "Since there is nothing alive in there, not much will really happen."

Quinlan looked around. They were inside another small broom closet. "What now?" he asked. He was tired and wanted to return to his room at the university and sleep for a week.

"Help me push this into that alcove."

"There?"

"Yes. Move the buckets and brooms."

Quinlan grabbed the items and moved them to the side.

"Good. Now help me push this rack."

Quinlan and the man pushed the rack into the alcove. It fit perfectly. It was obviously designed for the space. The guide touched the wall and a set of panels closed the space and concealed the rack of equipment. "Let's go."

"Where?"

"Away from here, for starters. That alarm signaled that Fempol was about to raid us. How they found us will be investigated, but I suspect they've had a good idea where we were for some time. It has been too peaceful."

He opened the opposite door and peeked out. The hall was empty. He stepped out and signaled Quinlan to follow. The short hall led to a large atrium with other hallways leading off like spokes of a wheel. The room was devoid of life. It was abandoned and had been so for some time. "Head across," said the man. They had just reached the center when a uniformed officer stepped out of the far hallway. They both stopped. The guide turned and looked for another means of escape. Every hallway leading out of the atrium had an officer of Fempol standing with a baton at the ready. Quinlan's guide turned to him. "Put your hands up and stand in front of me." Quinlan did as he was ordered. His guide stood directly behind him. He was so close that Quinlan could feel the man's chest against his back and his ragged breath in his ears. The rest was a blur. He heard the man whisper, "Sorry, Quinlan, but you know too much to allow you to be interrogated." He felt a sharp object stab his back, and he turned his head toward the pain. He fell and tried to remove the object that his guide had shoved into his back. He couldn't reach it. The image of himself on his knees with a knife sticking out of his back and blood dripping from his mouth filled his consciousness. Then came the pain, and he fell forward onto his belly. He vaguely heard an explosive "Whump!" behind him and then it was raining. He turned his face to the side as red rain and black hail fell all around him. His face and head were peppered with a lumpy liquid of blood and bone and brain from the body of his guide. Only then did his consciousness slide under the red tide.

SEAN
KILKENNY

The pulsing vibration on his wrist became the silent sound of flies that hovered over the coffins set in a semi-circle. There were three—his family—not all, but all those that mattered. They were innocent—mostly. They were killed because they were there. Their bodies bouncing from the force of the bullets seemed to syncopate with the vibration on his wrist, making the latter dominant—more real than his vision of their deaths. He opened his eyes. It was time.

He had done his research. She ran early in the park on days that started with 'T'. Today was Tuesday. She would run today. He would take her today. He was a registered pest control officer. "Bullshit," he muttered. They did not treat him like an officer of anything. He was a ratcatcher, a cockroach-killer, and they let him drive around in his broken-down van and rid the city of vermin. Well, today he would take steps to remove one of the vermin. Dolores Fineman was the aide for the police commissioner, Nisheeta Davenport. She was the ultimate vermin, and he had plans for her.

Sean sat up and hefted the duffel bag by the door. He opened the surveillance app on his phone and checked out the cameras. He was meticulous when leaving his secret lair. The aisle between the file boxes was empty. He flicked his thumb, and the image changed to show the alley outside. It was empty. He glanced away from the screen, but some motion brought his eye back. A small stream of water was running from under a large garbage bin to the right of his exit door. Someone was behind the bin, and they were peeing. He waited. An old man stepped out and staggered down the alley. He waited until he had disappeared before he opened the door to exit the old file storage room. He checked the cameras again. It was all clear. He quickly stepped through the door. It locked automatically behind him. He walked down the dark alley and onto the sidewalk. His van was parked down the alley across the street. He looked both ways. There was no traffic at this time of the morning. The sun was not due to rise for another hour. He had planned the location of his hideout very carefully. The country had altered its surveillance away from cameras to a combination of sensors, including infrared and nanobot RF receivers. It was a far more accurate method of identification. The nanobots in male bodies would always answer any inquiry by the AI sensors and identify the individual. Female nanobots would only identify as female. It would require a court order to force nanobots identifying as female to give up personal data. The AI could not see him here. He was in a blind spot. This entire part of the city was poorly covered. Many of the sensors had been vandalized and not repaired, especially in the city's alleys.

He reached his van and walked around it. Nothing was out of place. He reached behind the rear wheel and disconnected the charging cable. He pushed the end down into a small depression and swept some gravel over to conceal it. He was stealing power. This cable snaked under the alley asphalt and up into the building next to the van. He hopped inside. He glanced at the battery charge. It was full. He glanced once more at the surveillance app. There was no one.

He traveled further down the back alley before he headed to the park. The AI would see and identify him before he entered the park, but since he was where he was supposed to be, he would not be bothered by Fempol. The park itself did not have any sensors. After many attempts to maintain sensors in the park, the city planners and Fempol gave up. The park denizens would destroy them as fast as they were replaced. They had countered by tripling the sensors around the park, so they knew anyone who entered or left. His contract with the city gave him freedom to be just about anywhere. He often trapped rats in the park. His job was to keep the population in check. This morning he would set up just off her planned route. She was a typical female who felt invulnerable. She was not afraid of males, especially those in the park. They were like timid squirrels who would hide as she approached. He grinned. "This male is not afraid of you," he whispered. He wanted to shout out an expletive like *bitch* or *cunt,* but that was not wise. If anyone accidentally heard him, it could ruin his plans. He kept those words, and others, in his head.

He parked the van on a small access road next to the running path he knew she would take. He was on the far side of the pedestrian tunnel she would run through. He slid out of his seat and stepped into the back of the van. He unclipped and lowered a metal frame that was hinged on the inside wall of the van. It was a fold down bed with a foam mattress. The chains that held it horizontal snapped taut. He had often slept on it in the old days before his hideout was ready, but today it would serve another purpose. He opened a medical kit, adjusted some items, and placed them on a shelf attached to the other side of the van.

He glanced at his phone. He had 25 minutes before she would arrive. He grabbed the duffel bag and stepped out the back of the van. Dawn was starting to assert itself. He dropped the bag behind the van and walked a side path that would let him circle the entire area and check for possible witnesses. If he discovered anyone in the vicinity that might observe what he was about to do, he would cancel and try again. It took 10 minutes. There was no one in the vicinity.

He put on surgical gloves. He took the bag into the tunnel and removed a piece of black cloth, a sand filled sap of soft leather and a folding shovel. He used the shovel to create the illusion that a pile of rocks and gravel near the tunnel wall had been strewn onto the path by some animal. He had placed the rocks there six months earlier and had slowly dug a small hole near the wall and gradually enlarged it over the following months. He had planned meticulously. It would also appear as if it was accidental. The rocks extended for two meters along the path. Most were the size of his fist. This ruse would cause her to stop in the middle of the path. This would give him the time he needed. He put the shovel in the bag and returned it to the van. He entered the tunnel again and prepared for her arrival. He took the swatch of black cloth, slipped it over his head and adjusted its position so he could see through the eyeholes. He looked like a cartoon ghost dressed in black. He gripped his sand filled sap and leaned back against the wall. Sean breathed slowly and deeply. He needed to be calm. He felt his heart slow as a thought of waves caressing his toes filled his mind. The cool air of the tunnel became moist and musty under the cloth. He imagined sea air that carried the smell of salt wafting over him as he leaned up against a grass covered dune. He settled into the wall until he felt he was a part of it, invisible against it, and waited.

He felt the ground vibrate with her footfalls before he heard her. There was the distinct sound of someone humming. She was humming to the music she was listening to. He smiled. She would never detect him as she moved from the light of early dawn to the darkness of the tunnel. She jogged into the tunnel. She kicked one of the rocks and looked down. She stopped and stared at the rocks in the middle of the path. His heart quickened. He held his breath. He could now hear the music from her ear buds. He took that as a signal to move. He stepped away from the wall and, with one fluid motion, slammed the sap into her head just above her right ear. She staggered. He raised the sap to strike her again when she dropped to the ground. She was moaning. He ripped off the black cloth, reached into his pocket for the small canister of xenon gas. He opened the valve and pressed the mask over her mouth. The moaning stopped. He held the mask in place. He knew it would take a little more than a minute to knock her out. He quickly gathered her up and carried her to his van. He placed her on the bunk in the back. He was all business now and went through a series of memorized and practiced motions. The faster he could complete his tasks, the less likely anyone else would happen along.

He hung a plastic blood bag down from the metal bunk frame. He rolled up the leg of her running tights and reached for an alcohol-soaked cotton swab from the kit he had prepared on the shelf opposite. He tapped her leg and looked for a vein. He rubbed the alcohol over the area he had chosen for the injection site. He tied some rubber tubing around her leg and patted her vein. It bulged up. He took the needle attached to the blood bag and inserted it into the vein. The blood started to flow. He double checked everything. He pressed the xenon gas mask to her mouth to ensure she did not wake up. He had 20-minutes to clean up, collect the blood and inject her with the benzodiazepine that had taken him six months to obtain. He purposely chose the back of her leg near her ankle for the bleed and injection site. He would use the rocks in the tunnel to judiciously scrape her leg at the injection site to make it look like falling on rocks caused her pain. He would do the same to her head, where he had hit her with the sap. All he wanted was a little blood. All this was to create the illusion that she had simply fallen on the rocks, scraped her leg, and hit her head. The benzodiazepine would ensure she did not remember anything.

He set to work. He gathered the black cloth and the sap. The blood bag was nearly full by the time he had finished. He removed it and placed it in an ice chest on the floor of the van. He injected the blood line with the benzodiazepine and removed the needle from her leg. He pressed an ice cube to the needle site and held it for two minutes. That two minutes seemed to take forever. If anyone happened along, he would surely be caught, but that was very unlikely. He had spent many mornings hidden and waiting for anyone that might be using this path at a very early hour. No one had ever come here at his time of day. He had even waited and watched long after she had left. The soonest anyone had come was an hour after she had passed and that was an old drunk looking for a secluded place to rest and drink the bottle he had somehow obtained.

He carried her back to the tunnel and dropped her like a sack on her back. He lifted the leg he had used and hit the injection area with a sharp stone. He looked at the damage. It was not enough to cover the injection site. He carefully scraped her leg. The area started to bleed but soon stopped. He smeared the stone with her blood and dropped it in the pile. He felt her skull and found the place where he had struck her with the sap. He picked up another rock that was sharp enough to cut her skull but not cause too much additional damage. He didn't want a murder investigation. None of his subterfuge would stand up to in-depth forensics, but if he did this right, no forensics would be considered. He picked up some of the smaller rocks and dropped them on top of her. He stood back and inspected his handiwork and saw her for the first time. She was pretty and probably no older that thirty. She was wearing a stylish running suit with a zipper down the front. He felt an urge and reached and pulled the zipper down. She was not wearing anything underneath. He stared at her bare breasts. They did not excite him in a sexual way, but they did excite him as a way to cause some pain. He reached down with both hands, pinched her nipples between his index finger and thumb, and twisted them violently. He looked at them as they paled and swelled red. *Fuck you, bitch*, he thought. He zipped up her top and stood back. The word IDIOT rumbled like an ancient train through his head. *That was stupid. Do you want to get caught?* He checked everything one last time, turned, and calmly walked back to the van, erasing his footsteps as he went. Then he calmly drove to one of the buildings where he was to trap vermin.

Part one was over. He had the blood. The blood had the required nanobots. He was the universal recipient with blood type AB+. There would not be a problem. With proper refrigeration, they would last long enough for his purposes. There was enough for two forays into the female's den. One to reconnoiter and one to do the deed. What that deed actually was, he was not yet sure. That was what the reconnaissance would hopefully tell him.

NISHEETA DAVENPORT

Nisheeta was reading the report on the raid of the hideout of one of the AMEN cells. They had received a tip that the young man named Quinlan Smith was being held in a facility that was under surveillance by Fempol. He was the same young man that was kidnapped with Margaret Carver. The radical group was forewarned that the raid was to take place and one of the groups had tried to escape with Quinlan. The pair was intercepted, but instead of giving up, the man escorting Quinlan tried to kill him and then kill himself. He only succeeded in blowing himself up. The young man survived and was being treated in the prison hospital. She reached out and touched a button on her desk and spoke, "Connect me with the administrator at the prison medical center." She did not wait for a response. She looked back at the report. "That boy has to know something," she said out loud to no one. The phone on her desk buzzed. She picked it up.

"Yes, Chief Commissioner Davenport, how can I help you today?" asked the voice.

"I need to talk to one of your prisoner-patients. He arrived yesterday." She picked up the report and scanned it. "He was stabbed in the back. What is his condition?" There was a pause.

"Do you have his ID number?"

"His name is Quinlan Smith."

"Smith. That is a common name. Can you get me his ID?"

Davenport became irritated with the woman's bureaucratic attitude and snapped, "For frack sake. His name is Quinlan Smith, and he entered your facility yesterday with a stab wound to the back."

The woman's voice artificially brightened. "Ah yes. Smith. Quinlan. Here it is." There was a long pause.

"Well?"

"It seems that the wound missed all internal organs. I would say that he will be able to be interviewed by tomorrow morning. Do you want an appointment?"

Davenport scrunched up her face. "Please expect my aide, Dolores Fineman, by mid-morning, Ms…" She expected the woman to offer her name. She did not.

"Yes, Commissioner."

"Make sure he is lucid." She hung up the phone and touched the button on her desk. She spoke, "Has Ms. Fineman arrived yet?" She needed her aide, and she was uncharacteristically late.

"I am sorry, Chief Davenport, but Ms. Fineman was in an accident yesterday and will not be in to work for a couple of days. I was just about to tell you when you asked me to phone the prison. It slipped my mind."

"What happened to her?" She tried to sound concerned, but she knew some irritation had crept into her voice.

"She was out running in the park early this morning and she thinks she was hit by a falling rock in one of the tunnels. She woke up lying in a pile of rubble with a big bump on her head. One of her legs was scraped and bleeding. She thought maybe she was suffering from a concussion because she felt dizzy and nauseous. She hopes to be okay in a couple of days."

Feeling guilty for her lack of concern, Nisheeta spoke with a measure of feeling, "Give her a call and tell her to stay home until she is feeling better."

"Yes, Chief," said the voice.

Nisheeta sat back in her chair and breathed in and out slowly, hoping to ease the tension she felt swelling in her shoulders and neck. She would have to go to the prison herself. She hated that place. It made her think of her time as a young officer. She had been part of the massacre in the prison yard. It was not something she liked to reflect upon. She shook her head in an effort to clear the memory.

The screen in front of her beeped. Any chance at relaxation vanished. She reached out and touched the keyboard. The screen came to life. A small rotating icon floated in the center. She touched it with her finger, and it burst open to a still image of a naked girl sitting cross-legged on a concrete floor. Her arms were crossed over her breasts. Her head was tilted down, and her hair covered her face. Under the picture was a caption: "Comply with our demands." The picture seemed to vibrate and was replaced by a different image of the same girl with water pouring over her head. The new caption read: "Or we will have to get creative." Nisheeta looked up at the glass door to her office. Someone was shouting. The door swung open. It was the head of the ruling committee, Lillian Carver. Nisheeta looked back at her screen and realized that the images she had received were of Margaret Carver, her daughter. She quickly closed out the images and stood up.

"Ms. Carver, what can I do for you?"

"You can tell me that you have my daughter back safe and sound from the wackos that took her," she said in an almost eerie, calm voice. "They contacted me this morning. They sent me some very nasty photos of someone who might be my daughter. I could not tell."

"Yes, I got the same photos. We are analyzing them now," she lied. "When we know more, I will contact you. There is little we can do until we complete our investigation."

Ms. Carver placed both her palms on the front of Nisheeta's desk and leaned forward. "Bullshit. You can and will do exactly as they ask," she hissed. "I could not care less about a few male criminals being sent up to Canada. No negotiation. Just do it. Do you understand, Chief Commissioner?"

"I don't think it's a good idea to negotiate with criminals."

"Why are you holding on to that absurd male concept? We are women. That is what we do. We negotiate."

"Doing what they ask is not negotiation. It is capitulation."

"Then fucking well capitulate. This is my daughter we are talking about. Once we get her back, then we will do whatever is necessary to make these bastards pay. I don't care if we have to invade Canada to do it." Nisheeta's eyebrows arched. "Don't look at me like that, Davenport—just do what I said. I want her home unharmed." She left the office, leaving the door open.

Nisheeta stood and walked over to close the door. She held on to the edge of it, swinging it gently back and forth. She was deep in thought. Finally, she closed the door and returned to her desk. She touched a button on her desk and spoke. "Set up a holo conference with the commissioners first thing tomorrow afternoon and notify me when it is done. We need secure connections." She released the button and sat back. She reached for the file on Quinlan Smith and opened it. It was the report of the incident that resulted in his stabbing and capture. She scanned it and closed it again. She reached for the phone on her desk and spoke. "Get me everything on Quinlan Smith ASAP," she said and read out his ID number from the file in front of her. She hung up the phone. She had to be sure she was up to speed before she interviewed this boy.

QUINLAN SMITH

His sense of smell came first. His body was reacting to a very noxious odor. His head jerked to the side, trying to find some air that did not smell like death. Pain pulsed outward from the center of his chest and echoed back in a syncopated beat that pounded his consciousness. He slipped back into the safety of oblivion.

Hours later, he woke. His stomach was growling over the dull pain in his chest. His mouth was dry. It was evening. He moved his eyes and not his head; the memory of screaming pain was fresh in his mind. He was surrounded by a curtain. He could see a bag of solution hanging beside his bed. He could not see where the line from the bag ended. He started to lift his arm to see if it was attached. His arm moved only a few centimeters before it stopped. He tried his other arm. He knew his arms were strapped down to the bed. He was a prisoner. He called out, "Hello. Hello. Is anybody out there?" He could hear vague, indiscernible noises. He called again, "Hello. Hello?" The second hello came out in a rasping croak. He tried to lift his head, taking care not to move quickly. Suddenly, the curtains surrounding his bed flashed red. Behind him, a red light was pulsing. He heard a door open and then footsteps. The curtains opened quickly, and a man stepped up to the bed. He reached out and shut off the blinking red light. He looked at Quinlan and picked up a glass of water from the bedside table. He offered Quinlan a sip from the straw. Quinlan spoke, "Please." He drank. Some of the water dribbled down his chin. The man reached over with a small towel and daubed his face.

"Now rest," he whispered. He glanced back toward the door. "Someone will be in to see you soon."

"Where am I?" Quinlan asked.

The man turned once again to look at the door. "I have to go. They will have seen the warning light." He turned and left the room. The curtains remained open. Quinlan waited, occasionally glancing up at the door in anticipation of someone who could give him some information. No one came. He wanted another sip of water. He lay his head back on the pillow.

The memory of being stabbed came back to him. He was standing in front of a dozen Fempol officers and about to raise his arms when he felt a searing pain in his back. The man behind him must have stabbed him. He could not understand why. One moment he tried to save him and the next he tried to kill him. It made no sense. He remembered the man saying something about him knowing too much and interrogation. He could not think of a single thing that he knew that could possibly be a reason to kill him. After he fell to his knees, something happened. He was thrown forward as if a giant hand had appeared and slammed him down. He remembered the sound. It was the sound of a muffled explosion. He was not sure if Fempol had killed his benefactor, or he had killed himself. He must have blown himself up. The officers were only equipped with stun weapons, so they couldn't have done it. Quinlan pondered what he might know that would be valuable enough for this man to want to kill him. He closed his eyes. All that happened since his capture and release by the kidnappers swam in his head. Then he remembered Margaret and the man that had nearly killed him. He had said something about Fempol blaming him for the kidnapping. He was dizzy and felt like he was drifting away. His last thought before he lost consciousness was, "Shit—Fuck—I don't know what I know and I'm dying."

Muffled voices far off in the distance slowly moved closer and became louder and clearer. Quinlan kept perfectly still, as if stillness equated to a kind of invisibility. He thanked a god he did not believe in, that he was not dead, and listened.

"Is he able to talk?"

"I am sorry, but he is asleep right now. He had been drifting in and out of consciousness. His wound was quite severe.

"Why have you got him restrained?"

"This is a prison hospital, and we don't have any idea what this male is capable of doing."

"Get the restraints off of him before he wakes up. I don't want him to think we mean him harm. I need to find out what he knows and to be conducive to what we want him to do."

"I feel it is my duty to tell you that he is dangerous. Removing the restraints is ill advised."

"You don't know what you are talking about. Now take them off or I will," commanded the voice.

"Yes, Commissioner, as you wish."

The word commissioner bounced around Quinlan's mind. *The commissioner of Fempol was standing over his bed and she wants to question me and do something for her,* he thought. He could feel someone removing the straps that held his arms and legs down to the bed.

"I want you to increase his level of care. He is not a prisoner. As soon as he is able to be transported, I want him in a private room in the City Hospital. Is that clear? If anything happens to him while he is here, I will hold you personally responsible."

"Yes, ma'am."

Quinlan heard the footsteps of a single woman. They were the sound of high heels clicking on the tile floor. Once they were gone, he could hear the sound of someone breathing. He decided it was a good time to wake up. He moaned and moved his head. He smelled a hint of perfume and felt the heat of this woman's body as she leaned over him and pressed what he assumed was a call button. He heard more footsteps and moaned again. He fluttered his eyes.

The woman spoke to the approaching footsteps. "He is waking up. His protocol has changed. He is now priority A-1. He is being moved to City Hospital. I want that to happen as soon as possible. I want him out of here. Criminals that are not restrained are dangerous."

"Yes, Ma'am," said the new voice.

Quinlan opened his eyes. He spoke to the new person in nurses' garb. "Could I have some water, please?" She moved closer and he could see that she was quite old. Probably in her fifties or even older. He was not a good judge of age when it came to females.

"Yes, dearie," she said as she held the water straw to his lips. He drank. "How are you feeling? You have not received any pain meds, so you must be hurting. On a scale of one to ten, what is your pain level?"

Quinlan tried to push up to a sitting position, but the pain cut the motion off like a giant knife. "Ten," he said as the nurse moved to ease his body back down. He watched her reach into her pocket and remove a pressure injector. She pressed it to his bicep, and the pain eased almost immediately. "Could I have something to eat?"

"Not yet," she said. "Liquids only." She took a small electronic tablet from a clip at her waist and looked at it. "The knife you were stabbed with luckily missed your heart and all major blood vessels. There is a chance you received a concussion from what I understand was an explosion." She looked up at him. "Someone will bring you some broth. You are being moved to City Hospital as soon as you are able. By the looks of your vitals, it will be soon. How are you feeling now? Did the pain meds help?"

"Better. Thank you."

"My, aren't you the polite one?" She smiled and placed a call button in his hand. "I will order you some juice, and I think you could hold down yogurt. What is your favorite flavor?"

"Blueberry," said Quinlan. He relaxed as the pain meds did their work. He closed his eyes.

"That is good. Nothing better than sleep to heal a body. When you wake up, you can eat."

Quinlan drifted and the memories of what had happened faded away.

♂♂♂

Quinlan opened his eyes. He knew he had been moved. Everything smelled different. The underlying stink of rotting things was gone. He had been dreaming that he was to be executed for the kidnapping of Margaret Carver. Then he remembered the words of the woman from Fempol: *"I don't want him to think we mean him harm."* What the heck did that mean? Did they intend to do something bad to him and just did not want him to know? Then he remembered the even more ominous: *"I need to find out what he knows and be conducive to what we want him to do."* He lifted his right arm and moaned. The pain stabbed up his arm and down his leg as if it were running a predetermined path with the intention of causing the greatest amount of discomfort possible. A beeping sound started. The pain flooded his whole body and varied its intensity with his breathing. He winced when he breathed in and sighed as the air retreated.

A male medical worker entered the room, walked over to him, and looked down. "Do you want something for the pain?" he asked.

"Please," whispered Quinlan.

The man reached behind Quinlan and touched something at the head of the bed and the beeping stopped. "Someone will be here soon. What happened to you?" He touched a device at the foot of the bed. "Crap, you got stabbed. You must be the guy…" He did not finish his sentence.

"Marcel. I don't think this patient's history is any of your business. Please stick to your job," said a woman from the doorway.

"Yes, Doctor Park. Sorry. I was just making conversation. It is not often I see men come in here with stab wounds."

"Again—none of your business. Now please get on with whatever you do around here." Marcel nodded, checked the empty trash, and left the room. The doctor turned to Quinlan. "Are you in pain?" Quinlan nodded.

She reached for the device at the foot of the bed and swept her finger over the surface. "You should feel better in a few minutes." Quinlan felt the pain ebb almost immediately. "I don't want to put you to sleep. You have a visitor this afternoon. I have ordered you some food. I hope you like eggs and toast. That is all I think you can handle at the moment." She smiled.

"I have a visitor? Who?"

"Commissioner Davenport."

"What is it about?"

"That is above my paygrade, I'm afraid." She glanced at her wrist. "She will tell you herself in a few minutes. You were stabbed just below your shoulder blade. The knife went deep, but it missed everything important.

Somehow, your left lung was not punctured. Had it been, you probably would have drowned in your own blood. You should heal up and be as good as new." There was a click of heels from the hall and a woman entered. Whereas Dr. Park smelled of nothing, this woman dragged a cloud of perfume with her. Quinlan smelled her before he saw her. Dr. Park turned and left the hospital room. Quinlan said nothing. He waited.

The commissioner stood at the foot of his bed and looked at the electronic chart. Finally, she looked up at him and smiled. "Good afternoon, Mr. Smith. I hope you are feeling better after your ordeal." Quinlan nodded. His time with the matrons had taught him to acknowledge and remain silent. Words were often dangerous. True meaning often came from how you said them. Speaking got you into trouble. He looked down at the bedding. Looking could also get you into trouble. He chose the safe path. "Look at me," she ordered. Quinlan looked up. "I want to ask you some questions about what happened when you and Ms. Carver were taken."

Quinlan blurted, "Is Margaret okay?" He immediately looked down. "Sorry," he mumbled. "I did not mean to presume."

Ms. Davenport smiled again. "That is alright. I want you to feel comfortable. I am here to meet you and make sure you are being treated well. I need you to heal. I have a job and I want to make sure you are the right person. I also want to ask you a few questions. I need you to be honest with me. Can you do that?" Quinlan nodded. "Good. First, how did you get to be in that place?"

"I do not know. I just woke up there. They had me in a cell. I was fighting the kidnappers and then I was there. I do not know anything that happened in between."

"What did you learn about them in the time you were there?"

"Not much. They were trying to get the vote for men. They showed me a bunch of old posters about women fighting for the vote hundreds of years ago. I thought women always had the vote, so I am not sure if the posters were real or not."

"Oh, the posters were real, alright. That is why we took power—to make sure men could not vote. When they had that power, they abused it to the point where they put the entire planet at risk. Never again." Her face took on a more concerned look. "Did they tell you anything else? Did you see anything else?"

"Not that I remember. The man that helped me escape down the elevator told me something about DNA erasers. That is all."

"We inspected the elevator you came down in. It had a concealed section. Did the man remove anything from the elevator?"

"We pushed…," Quinlan stopped. He remembered about the data storage equipment that they had hidden. "… brooms, mops, and buckets in front of the elevator door. I guess he wanted to conceal it from you, I mean Fempol. Then we saw all the officers surrounding us. That is when he stabbed me and…killed himself." He was not sure why he lied, but he thought it was important that he keep the location of the concealed computer storage rack to himself. It must be of critical importance if his guide wanted to kill to keep it a secret. "I was wondering what happened to the others."

"Others?" Quinlan opened his mouth to speak but closed it again. "Please. Speak up. Ask what you wanted to ask."

"The other men in that facility. Did they escape? The man I was with told me they would all leave through some secret freight elevator."

"The power to the building was cut just before the officers encountered you. There was no trace of any living thing found in that facility. It looked like a small gas explosion took place. We figured they used some sort of nanobot system to cover their tracks."

Quinlan paused. It was time to change the subject. He did not want to get caught in a lie, and the image of the data storage device tucked away in a concealed cabinet loomed in his mind. He asked, "Will I ever get to go back to school?"

"What were you studying?"

"Quantum Biology."

"I have no idea what that is, but I am sure you can continue your education once this is over."

"When what is over?" asked Quinlan. He felt a flood of shivers well up from his spine. The question was not his to ask. He knew that, but he asked it anyway and prepared for a rebuke.

"Good. To the point. I don't have all the details worked out, but you will have to…." She paused. "Do you care about Margaret Carver?"

"Yes. She is my friend."

"Good. Then you will want to help her. That is what we want you to do.

We want you to help us rescue her from some very bad people. Are you willing to do that? If you are and she is brought home safely, then you will be able to write your own ticket. There will be a lot of powerful people beholden to you."

"Is it dangerous?"

"I won't lie. Yes. It might get you killed, but we will do everything possible to make sure that does not happen. That danger is great, but the rewards are also great."

"I don't care about that. If it will save Margaret, I will do it," he said flatly. His mind flooded with thoughts of his encounter with her in her bedroom. It felt good to know she was important to him. She was the first and only female he trusted. He would do almost anything for her.

"Good. You have two weeks to get healthy. That will also give us time to prepare you." She glanced again at her watch. "I must go. I will contact you again very soon." She turned and left. He heard her voice from the hallway. "Make sure he gets only the very best. I want him on his feet as fast as possible. If there are problems, I must know immediately."

Quinlan closed his eyes. He had really gotten into a major mess. The pain was creeping back and then suddenly it was gone again. More drugs hit his system, and he slipped into a fitful sleep.

VIHAAN KHATRI

Vihaan walked in step with a group of seven other trainees just like him. He had never really met any of them before. They were complete strangers. He had been informed that one trainee was about to start a life in the real world. Their skill in the day's activities would be the determining factor.

He was looking for his number: 285120 to be displayed on the door to one of the booths that lined the hallway. Three of the others peeled off the line and entered their respective booths. His was now on his right. He reached out to the door and tried to open it. It was locked. He tried again to be sure he had not made some sort of mistake. He looked around as the remaining trainees left the hallway and entered their booths. He was alone. He looked again at the number on the door in front of him. He recited it just under his breath. It was his. Of that, he was sure. He stepped back, glanced up and down the hallway. He stepped forward again and tried to enter the small room. Today was the final day of weapon *jerry-rigging*. It was basically a course with a focus on death. They were taught how to use household material in the construction of various explosive devices, poisonous gases, and caustic chemicals. Some of these were designed to incapacitate, but most would kill and kill quickly. Vihaan was already proficient, but it was not his favorite activity. He reached out to the door, but it was not going to open. He started to sweat under the latex mask that concealed his identity from his classmates. He was alone, so he quickly slipped it off, wiped the sweat from his face on his tunic and replaced the mask. He waited. He hoped he would never have to use these particular skills.

He visualized the small room with a workbench, a chair, a locked cabinet in which the teachers provided various items used in their studies and a terminal that displayed the assignments. Upon entering the room, the terminal would come to life and give the instructions the trainees were to follow. They were then tested on their work. Speed was important, but it was not the most important. Accuracy was primary.

Vihaan stepped back from the door and leaned against the opposite wall. He could feel tension creeping into his muscles. His jaw was rock hard. He stretched it by opening and closing his mouth. He breathed deeply and tried to meditate. He slowly relaxed. He felt an urge to step up to the door and try again to enter the room with his number, but he knew the situation had not changed, so he suppressed it. He stepped away from the wall and stood at ease. He stared straight ahead. He waited. Part of his training was time estimation. He was able to estimate the passage of time within +-2 seconds per minute over a period of 30 minutes. After that, his accuracy dropped to +-5 seconds per minute. That skill was dependent on his resting heart rate. He averaged 60 beats per minute. Thirteen minutes had passed since the other trainees had entered their respective rooms.

He waited in the silence of the hallway. At one point, he thought he heard someone cry out but chalked it up to a creak in the building. When he heard it a second time, he started to listen in earnest. He stepped closer to the door on his left and listened. He wanted to press his ear to the door. He glanced up and down the hall. It remained empty. He was about to lean into the door when another sound came from the room farthest to the left. He stopped and moved quickly to that door and pressed his ear to the metal. He could hear nothing. He tried to open the door, but it was locked. He stepped back to his own door to consider his future actions when that was decided for him. He heard a click. He reached out to the latch on the door to his room and pushed it open. He stepped inside as the door slowly closed and latched behind him.

His mind was racing. Something was wrong. Something had happened to the others. He could feel it. There was a sharp edge to everything. He searched for reasons why his door had remained locked while the others opened. The delay was not normal. Why the delay? What happened during the delay? He had heard what sounded like someone being hurt. Was something hurting the other trainees? Was this some sort of bizarre test? Had the strange wait been a warning? Once again, Vihaan became ultra-sharp and ultra-cautious. The terminal came to life. A genderless voice intoned instructions, as was the norm.

"Good day, 285120. In front of you are 12 containers. Most of the containers are filled with various household materials. It is your job to find a substance that will render a human unconscious without harming them in any way. You will test it on yourself. You are required to sit in the chair and press the red button in front of you just before you become unconscious. This will stop the timer. As a warning, some of the containers contain substances that could harm a human. Accurate identification is critical. You have 17 minutes remaining to complete this task." The cabinet door slid open, revealing the containers and laboratory equipment.

Vihaan stared at the containers. His mind raced with more questions. Something was definitely amiss. Whomever was responsible for this test was risking valuable assets. A lot of time and effort had gone into the training of himself and the others in the rooms beside him. He examined the containers. The bottles were clear so he could approximate the density and viscosity as well as the color of the liquids contained inside. *God, they could contain anything. Just sniffing one could be dangerous,* he thought. He remembered the sounds he heard from behind the other doors while he waiting in the hallway. Had the others been stupid enough to breathe in the fumes from these containers? Maybe that is what the cries indicated? Maybe someone had hurt themselves?

On the counter were various items, including a scale, empty containers, a large syringe with an extra-long needle, a Bunsen burner and flint, beakers of various sizes, a beaker stand, and a bottle labeled *Distilled H_2O*. He glanced back at the terminal. The time was counting down in the top right corner of the screen. Four minutes had passed. The more he stared, the more dominant one particular thought became. This exercise/test was stupid and dangerous. His eyes scanned the containers lined up like soldiers ready for battle. The shelf was lit from behind and light refracted through each one. One caught his eye. The light was refracting differently in the bottom of the container than at the top. He picked it up and looked closer. There was an obviously denser clear liquid in the bottom third of the glass. This was definitely not a household chemical. In fact, it contained two things that did not easily mix. Like oil and water. He shook it slightly. It did not behave like oil. He set it down and watched it separate back into two layers. He did not think there was anything here that would kill him, so he removed the lid and used his hand to waft any vapors to his nose. He smelled nothing. He decided that the upper liquid was just water. He took the syringe and sucked up some of it and squirted it into a petri dish. He sniffed it again and finally touched it. It was water. Whatever was under the water would be more interesting. It could also be much more dangerous. If it was, and he was careless, his score on this test could be in jeopardy. He picked up the syringe and then a memory of one of his training labs came back to him. They had been taught to make ether from bleach and acetone. This is what the final product looked like before the water was removed. That would be a perfect substance to put someone to sleep. He inserted the syringe again and sucked up a small amount of the second liquid. He put in a dish and used his hand to waft some to his nose. He snorted out in an effort to ensure the vapors did not affect him. It was definitely ether.

He sat back and considered the instructions. He came to a decision. He put the lid back on the container with the ether at the bottom. He placed everything back to where he found it, sat down in the chair, and stared at the button. The timer on the terminal indicated three minutes remaining. He had completed the task in record time. The strange delay had not hampered his ability to solve this problem. Then he decided. He was going to press the button and when the testers came in, he was going to say, *"I don't have to render myself unconscious to know that the substance was ether. I decided that was a dangerous action. It was an instruction, not an order. The situation indicated that I should ignore that instruction."* He smiled, pressed the button, sat back in the chair, and waited.

The terminal continued to count down the remaining time. When it reached zero, the door lock to his testing cubicle clicked, and the door swung open. Vihaan stood and stepped out into the hall. No one else was there. He decided that the test must be over, so he continued down the hall and returned to his room. Everything about this day was strange. Nothing made sense. No one did the debrief that usually happened after a testing session.

He removed his mask and sat on the edge of his cot and waited. There was a knock on his door. He stood and opened it. An older man stared at him as if checking that Vihaan was the person expected to answer the door. He spoke, "285120 please follow me." Vihaan turned to pick up his latex mask. "You will not need that. Leave it." It was a command. The man turned, and Vihaan followed.

EVE
RINNE

Yvonne was good at her word and a meeting was set for Eve to meet her sister Cassandra Ross. Three weeks had passed, and Eve was getting more and more consumed by the thoughts of killing men. If she was caught, she would not be able to kill any more men, and she wanted to do the deed over and over until all the men were gone. She knew she must find a way to never get caught. Her ride dropped her off at an out-of-the-way café. As she walked past the gold lettering on the front window, she looked at her reflection. She flipped her hair and smiled a fake smile just to see how she would present. She looked good. Whenever you met a woman for the first time, especially one you wanted to impress, you needed to look your best. She entered the café and looked around for someone wearing a red scarf around their neck. She saw no one. There was a booth near the back that had a red scarf hanging from the coat rack attached to the bench at one end. Eve headed toward the booth. As she passed a table along the opposite wall, a hand reached out and grabbed her by the arm. She turned and looked at the woman who grabbed her. Her expression carried her irritation with it and she growled at the woman as her arm was released. "What?" she said.

"Sit," said a very beautiful woman with long auburn hair that flowed like honey over her shoulders. She did not smile. "Just sit. Don't say a word."

Eve hesitated but sat opposite the woman. "Who are you?"

"Who are you looking for?"

Eve looked around the room furtively and then back at the woman opposite. She felt anger well up in her. "I'm looking for someone who was to wear a very specific piece of clothing and you are not wearing that clothing, so fuck off." She started to stand up. She could still see the red scarf hanging from the coat hook in the rear booth.

"A red scarf?"

Eve stopped and sat back down. "What is your name?"

"A much better question is, are you from Fempol? Are you one of their spies?"

Eve decided that the game of cat and mouse they were playing was getting them nowhere. "I am not a cop. My name is Eve and I hope your name is…" she stopped, hoping the woman would follow her lead and state her name. The woman did not disappoint.

"Cassandra. Yvonne is my sister. She told me you wanted to talk to me. She told me that you were as crazy as I am. I just wanted to be sure I was not going to be arrested. Ever since that mess at the university, they have been on high alert." She stopped and looked at Eve as if she were trying to look into her head and see her thoughts. "So, how can I help you?"

"Well, I thought I might be able to help you. I have," she paused, "I have similar feelings about certain aspects of our species as you. At least your sister leads me to believe I did."

"Well, Eve, let's cut the crap. Speak plainly or don't speak at all."

"I have a need to…"

"What?"

Eve swallowed. Her fantasies of killing men had never really been shared before. She considered for a second and then accepted what she wanted. She whispered, "Yes," and then she blurted, "I already belong to NAFF (Now and Forever Female) but they do not do much but collect my yearly membership and send me a monthly newsletter. They do not want to do what I want."

"Kill as many of the pricks as possible. Is that what you want?"

Eve nodded.

Cassandra guffawed, "NAFF are just a bunch of middle-aged twats looking for some sort of purpose now that men are no longer in vogue."

Cassandra looked around the room. No one was paying them the slightest attention. She looked hard at Eve. "You are not bullshitting me, are you. You really want to kill men. Boy, somebody really damaged you." Eve sucked in her breath.

After a pause, Cassandra continued. "I don't know what you think I do, but I definitely do not have any plans to go out and kill men indiscriminately. I have no desire to end up in prison or worse, the sicko ward." Eve sighed and looked down at the table. "In fact, I would like you to forget about all the killing you have planned. Killing anything is not easy. By the looks of you, I doubt you could kill anything. I don't care how angry you are."

Eve looked up at Cassandra. There was fire in her eyes. "You have no idea how angry I am. You have no right to pass judgment on my abilities. I have plans and I will carry them out on my own. So, fuck you." She pressed her hands to the tabletop and pushed herself up from the table.

"Fuck me? You ignorant little bitch. You come to see me and try to entangle me in your insane, murderous plans. So, you go out and do something horrible and Fempol captures you. There is no doubt about that. They find out that you had this little meeting with me and suddenly I am suspect number one. A little innocent like you could never have planned and carried out multiple murders, so I must have put you up to it."

"I would never blame you. I would tell them it was my idea."

Cassandra laughed. "God, you are stupid. No matter what you plan to do, we will be blamed for it." She paused. "Sit the fuck down before I punch that pretty little face in." Eve slowly sat down and stared at Cassandra. "It is time for your edification. That means I am going to tell you some things."

"I know what the fuck it means. Who is this 'we' you are part of?"

Cassandra scanned the room. No one had entered or left since Eve had joined her at the table. She turned back to Eve. "If I tell you, you must understand that I might have to kill you if you tell anyone else."

Eve grinned. "Now who is being stupid?"

Cassandra's hand slipped over Eve's and squeezed the knuckle joints together. Eve winced and pulled her hand back. "Okay, okay. I get it."

Cassandra leaned in. "Have you heard of POW?"

"Power of Women. Who hasn't? Practically everyone is part of that group. They espouse that women must maintain all power positions in our society. That is the status quo. I can't think of a single male that is in charge of anything beyond a small group of men. They are called foremen or leadmen or roadmen or something like that. That is as far as they can go in the new society. It has been 20 years since the Male Assembly Restrictions Act became law."

"Yeah, it happened right after the Organic Farm fiasco and the resulting Arena massacre."

Eve winced and tried to cough to cover her need to be sick. Cassandra stared at her. "What's the matter?"

"Nothing," whispered Eve, staring at the table in an effort to clear the emotions raging in her head.

"You looked like you were going to puke when I mentioned the horrible rapes and murders that happened at that farm." She turned her head slightly to the side, as if that action might clarify something that was niggling at her brain. She reached out and lifted Eve's chin up so she could see her face.

Eve lashed out at her hand and pushed it away.

"Fuck. You're her. You are the survivor from the farm. No wonder you hate men enough to want to kill them all."

Tears flowed freely down Eve's face. She grabbed a napkin and wiped them away. She stared at Cassandra. Her eyes were filled with anger. "Okay, okay, I get it. Calm down."

"Are you going to help me or not?" Cassandra leaned back; her head pressed against the booth head rest. She sat looking at Eve for a long time. Eve broke the silence. She started to rise. "I'm outta here."

Cassandra leaned forward. She had made a decision and said gently, "Sit back and listen." Eve sat and folded her hands in front of her. "A number of members from the upper echelon of POW realized the group that espoused 'women power' really had none. They decided to form a new group. We are called the PW. We do not send out monthly newsletters. We do not have any sort of web presence. We are an organization of very few. Everything that happens in our organization happens face to face. If we want something done, we use third-party contractors."

"What do you do?"

"We watch and react to things we don't like."

"Like what?"

"Situations that might lead to males getting any power, political or otherwise. If we find something that concerns us, we deal with it in our own way. We are preemptive. Men must never be in positions of power ever again."

"I just want to kill them. That solves the problem permanently," said Eve as she placed her palms down on the table. "You say you use third party contractors. I could be that. Hire me. I could do the nasty stuff." She watched Cassandra's eyes widen. "What do you have to lose? I come cheap. I work for the pleasure of it."

Cassandra opened her bag and took out a pen. She reached for one of the unused serviettes and wrote something down. She folded it in half and placed it on the table in front of Eve. "Open that and memorize it and then give it back to me. You will be notified as to the when." Eve stared at the writing on the serviette. It was an address and a number. After a few seconds, Cassandra asked, "Got it?" Eve nodded and Cassandra snatched the note from her hand and dropped it into her coffee cup. She poked it with her spoon until it was just a mush of paper fibers.

"Oh yeah, what does PW stand for?"

"Plague Warriors," she answered flatly. "Our credo is to ensure that the plague of male domination never gets the smallest foothold in American society."

"How will you—" started Eve.

"Go!" hissed Cassandra.

Eve got up and walked away from the table. As she passed, Cassandra whispered, "Don't make me regret this."

Eve walked out of the restaurant. All thoughts of guns and bullets and killing men were gone. She kept playing her meeting with Yvonne's sister over and over in her head. They had invited her to work for them. Maybe these people would help her after all. Maybe they had a plan that wouldn't result in her being sent to prison forever. Maybe, just maybe, she could get the revenge she so desperately desired. She smiled and whispered to herself, "I'm a Plague Warrior. So many men, so little time." She had heard that phrase before and she knew that was not how it was originally intended. It fit perfectly, nonetheless.

VIHAAN KHATRI

Vihaan entered a small office. It was totally bare of anything except two chairs, a desk and a terminal. The man behind the desk stood as he entered. He strode up to Vihaan and shook his hand. "Congratulations. You have graduated. I know today's test was strange, but it was necessary. Something has come up, and I need to place someone very soon. I need someone who can think before they act and, after today's test, I think that person is you." Vihaan dropped his hand and stood at attention in front of the desk. "Have a seat, please. Relax. Tell me your thoughts after today's," he paused, "activities." Vihaan shrugged.

"Please speak freely."

Vihaan leaned closer to the man behind the desk. He did not recognize him. He was not part of the daily training routines; therefore, he was probably a higher-up, someone who was in charge of the training facility or, more likely, someone in charge of the entire organization. "I have just one question," said Vihaan.

"I will answer it if I can."

Vihaan's face scrunched up for a moment, and then he continued. "Why the delay at letting me into the testing cubical?"

The man clasped his hands and rubbed them together. "Truthfully, it was an accident to start with. I thought I toggled all the locks to open at the same time, but I missed yours. I was about to unlock it, and then something told me to leave it locked. I wanted to see what you would do. I was watching you. I know I should have given you more time in the room but, as it turned out, you didn't need it."

"I thought there was something wrong. My senses were heightened."

"Is that why you didn't follow the instructions about putting yourself to sleep?"

"Partly. It was too dangerous. I did not want to be unconscious in a room full of chemicals," he paused, "I heard some distress sounds from the other rooms. Did anyone get hurt?"

The man's face clouded. "Why would you care? You didn't know any of the others."

"I think a better question is, 'Why would I not care?'"

"Are you concerned about the other trainees?"

Vihaan stared at the man. He had the sense that his answer to this question would be a determining factor in whether he might be selected for the up-coming placement. He decided to portray himself as caring only for his own well-being. "If something was causing harm to them, then it could very well hurt me. I value my safety."

The man smiled. "Yes, I see your point. I think I have chosen well. There were seven trainees for the same assignment. You have come out on top. It is probably the most important endeavor of our entire organization. We had to be sure the candidate was the best. Failure is not an option. Remember, this is a long game. Once you are placed, you will not be able to contact anyone in this organization. If we require something or need to communicate something, we will contact you. You need to play a part and play that part perfectly."

"I have been told that I was to endear myself to a woman called Karen Chow. I did not know that there were others told the same thing. What will happen to them?"

"That is not your concern. You will spend time becoming known to the society that Ms. Chow frequents. We have already structured your background for the Webbies. In fact, you are a woman of mystery. We are preparing to leak that you, along with photos, are looking for employment. A Loverboy with your looks will be the rage. We expect an offer from Ms. Chow's agent soon after the release. Her present Loverboy is not feeling well." He grinned. "You will have to play hard to get, but not too hard. We want you to have your own quarters, so that is one of the requirements. We also demanded a rather large stipend. You have to have a source of money to keep yourself desirable. She has a tendency to get bored quickly. You will have to make her believe that you have a continuous line of offers. That will keep you well placed until you take over from her present aide. If we, and by we, I mean you, play your cards right, that job will be yours in a year."

"What is my new name?"

He reached out to the terminal on the desk in front of him and touched the screen. He read and looked up. "Karima Rani Sanyal. It was chosen in keeping with your Indian heritage."

"What now?"

"You have a bit of cramming to do. You have to memorize your history. There are gaps that will not be released to give you the freedom to improvise when it is beneficial." He stood and held out his hand. "Good luck, Karima," he said, and a smile edged on to his face.

Vihaan stood and left the office. He was excited that his life would finally have meaning. He could live in the real world. He would no longer be Vihaan, but that mattered little. Vihaan was nobody and nothing, anyway. The past would vanish, and tomorrow would emerge.

MARGARET CARVER

Margaret, dressed in a gray jumpsuit, was moved to a small windowless room with padded walls and a constant dim light emanating from the ceiling. There was no day or night. There was no sound except those made by Margaret herself. There were no mattresses or blankets. There was nothing in the room but a toilet in one corner that automatically flushed once a day at a random time. If she wished for water for drinking or washing, she had to get it from the toilet bowl. There were days when the toilet flushed before she had the opportunity to use it for its intended function. On those days, she had to wash and drink before she could relieve herself. Her single daily meal was delivered to a double-blind box. The timing of the meal, like the toilet flush, was random. The meal arrived silently on a piece of parchment paper. She had to constantly open the auto closing door to the box to see if the food had arrived. There were never any utensils. She had to eat it with her hands. There was nothing that could possibly be used as a weapon. She was left in the room with no human contact.

Her sense of time became corrupt. She started counting the days by counting the meals, but that became confused when two meals arrived minutes apart. At least she figured they must have because when she checked the box for a meal, removed the food, ate and opened the door again to toss the parchment paper back inside, there was another meal waiting for her. The present day must have become the next day. She removed it and set it aside, knowing that the next meal would not come for, at the very least, another 24 hours.

She napped, as she often did, to escape into her dreams. When she woke up from the nap, the meal she had placed in the corner of the room was gone. This frightened her more than anything. They were coming into her room when she was asleep. She tried not sleeping, but that seemed impossible. It occurred to her they were drugging her food. She came up with a plan to try and stay awake, but that meant she would also have to be very selective in what she ate. It would be harder to drug fruit, so she would only eat fruit that still had the skin on. She saved the parchment paper on which her meals arrived by carefully folding them and putting them in the bib of her jumpsuit. After she had a week's worth of parchment paper, she put her plan to catch the people entering her room into effect. She needed to stave off insanity, and seeing another human would do exactly that. It would make the bastards real. She could fight against reality. She could not fight the nothing that this cell created.

Her plan was simple. She wanted to entice them into her cell. For three days running, she ate only the fruit that came with her meal. She did not feel she was being drugged anymore, and this feeling gave her strength. On the third day, she drank the water from the toilet to keep herself hydrated. Without water, she would become delusional. She had to keep her mind clear. Then she dumped the remainder of the day's meal into the toilet, along with the dozen or so balls of parchment paper. The toilet was completely plugged. When it flushed, it would overflow. That would require someone to come into her cell and fix the problem and clean up the mess. She would be ready for them. She knew she would attack and try to hurt whomever it was. She was losing her mind. She sat in the corner of the cell and waited. Her efforts to stay alert soon faded. She knew she was nodding off. The flaw in her plan was obvious. To stay awake, you needed strength. She had none. She fell asleep.

She awoke with a start. She had slid from her sitting position to the floor. She slept with her cheek pressed to the cold tile. She sat up, hoping someone had woken her. She was wrong. She looked around the cell. Someone had been there. They had made some changes. Margaret stared across the room and burst into tears. With the help of the corner walls, she climbed to her feet. She screamed, "You fracking bastards. What the frack do you want from me?" She sank down the wall and held her head in her hands, sobbing. The toilet was gone. What remained was a hole in the floor.

Nothing changed except that her water was now included in a paper cup with her food. For days after the removal of the toilet, Margaret drifted from one inane activity to another. She ate, relieved herself, sat and slept. There was nothing to clean with. She no longer cared. She felt her sanity slipping away and resigned herself to let it slide. She sat in the corner like a zombie until a microscopic seed of anger reasserted itself like a slowly growing crystal— edges sharp and clear. She could do nothing but nurture it in secret. She must not let them win. She must not let them know she was not defeated. She continued to be an emotionless zombie, moving inexorably through the days. Externally, she was broken. Internally, the crystal of anger grew, flawlessly layering molecules of pain. The anger was not focused, but she knew that one day soon they would come to her expecting a broken child ready to please for a pittance of attention. Only then would this anger become useful. She cultured it.

When the day came, it was a whisper, but to Margaret it was a million-decibel bellow. From the wall and ceiling, she could hear voices. They were soft and jumbled. Someone was leading young children, and they were responding. It was chant-like:

"The human race is made up of females and males."
　　　　　　"Females and males together."
　"Males and females are equal."
　　　　　　"Males and females together."
"Females and males make a complete whole."
　　　　　　"Females and males together."
"Males and females cannot exist without each other."

"Males and females together."

"Females and males complement each other."

"Females and males together."

"These words are the whole truth."

"Males and females together."

"These words are female."

"Females and males together."

"These words are male."

"Males and females together."

"These words are equal."

"Females and males together."

The chant continued and slowly grew in volume until it filled Margaret's cell as if she were inside a speaker. Then the volume lowered until she could barely discern the voices. It continued for hours. She found herself straining to hear the sounds. They were like the perfect narcotic. She wanted to hear them. She needed to hear them. She thought she might die if they ever stopped. She started to chant the response herself. Softly at first and then louder until the voices were inaudible. She stopped. She was feeling full, as if she had just been fed a huge meal. The silence was warm for the first time. During the silence, she heard a thought creep into her consciousness. It was her secret anger. Whatever they wanted to change her into had started, but she was not as weak as they thought she was. She smiled and whispered to herself, "Females and females together."

MARGARET CARVER

The days continued as before, except for the voices and the chanting. They seemed to occur at the same time each day. This was the first thing that was consistent. Margaret could count the days with some accuracy. Other things also became more routine. Her meal appeared at the same time each day. Even the lights seemed to dim a few hours after food arrived. There was a routine beginning. Her day became predictable.

Things started to improve. It all seemed to be connected to the chanting. If she stopped and listened and took part for a few days running, she received a sort of reward. The first was the return of her toilet. It was better than the last, for it had a small sink attached to the back. Next came a second meal in the morning. The food appeared on plastic coated paper plates with plastic utensils. Everything seemed to be improving. Margaret sat in wait for the voices to come. She would sit in anticipation in the corner of her cell with her back to the wall. The chanting had morphed into more of a series of question-and-answer conversations that repeated over and over until she knew them by heart. She started to answer the questions quickly and noticed that the response portion was missing. She was providing the response.

"Why are the males of the species important?

Males are strong.

Males are creative.

Males are intelligent.

Males are loving.

Males balance the female.

Why are the females of the species important?

Females are strong

Females are creative.

Females are intelligent.

Females are loving.

Females balance the male.

How can males and females work together?

They must respect each other.

They must support each other.

They must speak to each other.

They must listen to each other.

They must love each other."

The first time she did it perfectly, there was a tone from the box where her meals arrived. She went over to it and slowly opened the door. There was a candy bar in the box. Chills flooded Margaret's body. She reached for the candy. Her thoughts were simple. *I did a good job, and they rewarded me. I will do a good job next time too.* She took the candy bar to the corner and sat down to eat it. As the sugar filled her senses, she analyzed what was happening. She was not stupid. She knew she was being conditioned to behave and respond in a specific way. That was obvious. It was also impossible for her to do anything else. She wanted to get out of the cell, and the only way to do that was to play the game and play it well. She must play it so well that they could not see that she was holding her real self out of their reach. That was key. She could not pretend. She must cooperate totally, or they would return her to the way things were in the beginning.

Thoughts of the beginning of the nightmare brought a flood of memories. She seldom indulged in memories anymore, but today she would allow herself to remember. The day she was taken, she felt incredibly sexy. Her jeans with the cutout heart in the ass made her feel just like she was feeling now eating the candy bar. It was anticipatory of something to come. Then images of the men kicking Quinlan under orders from that horrible woman took all the good feelings and squashed them flat. She wondered about Quinlan. She hoped he was ok. The pit of her stomach warmed. She was unsure the cause. Perhaps it was her feelings for Quinlan or, more likely, the candy dissolving in her mouth. She did not care. The feeling was one she wanted to repeat.

She wanted to please them. Every time she did, she was rewarded. They must think they had broken her. She was unsure if they had actually broken her. All she knew for certain was the anger remained—anger she held like a pearl in the shell of her mind and slowly rolled and caressed as the layers of nacre strived for perfection. It was all that kept her from dissolving into an unknown person.

She worked with her captors in order to improve her situation. She now had a portable shower, a small cot, a blanket, and some toiletries. Each day was like school. The school decided what you learned. Your job was to learn whatever was presented. Margaret learned. Margaret also rebelled silently and secretly. She hoped she was still in control.

She knew the day would come when they decided she was ready. Her captors needed her for something and were obviously preparing her. That something came the morning she woke up and noticed clothes on the foot of her new cot. She screamed with hysterical joy. She held the clothes up and inspected them. There was a skirt, blouse, and jacket in a burgundy tweed along with underwear and low-heeled shoes. Her first thought was that the skirt and jacket were at least two sizes too small. She took off her jumpsuit and held the skirt up to her naked body. She then looked down at her hips. The chubby fat was gone. She could clearly see the hip bones under her skin. She had lost a lot of weight. She looked at her gaunt breasts and frowned. They were her best feature. She shrugged, had a shower and prepared herself. She assumed that someone was going to take her out of the cell. Why else would they give her clothes to wear? She sat on the edge of her cot and waited. She knew there was food in the box, but she was just too excited to eat. Then she thought better and walked to the box and removed what was now supplied for her morning meal. There was the usual bowl of porridge, a small container of milk, and a piece of fruit. She ate it all and then returned to her cot and sat and waited.

The door to her cell had not, in her conscious presence, opened before. There was a click, and it swung open. She leapt to her feet and ran over to it. No one was there. She stepped through into an empty hallway. At the end of the hallway was another door. The door to her cell closed behind her. She walked down the hall. Her only thoughts were that the new clothes fit her body like they had been tailored specifically for her. She reached to open the door and stepped through. It closed behind her. The room in front of her was a furnished studio apartment. No one was there. She turned back to the door she had entered. It was locked. It was then she realized she had graduated to a new prison.

EVE RINNE

The time since her meeting with Cassandra Ross dragged by. All she could think about was seeing her again. She fantasized about what she would be asked to do. It would have to entail the killing of men, or she would simply walk away. Nobody was going to dissuade her from exacting the kind of revenge she had envisioned.

Work was assembly line—each task automatically performed and instantly forgotten. She even stopped speaking to Yvonne except where it was work related. She was waiting. The location she had been given was odd. She looked it up. The coordinates she had memorized were in the park, near the fountain, surrounded by seven bronze statues of females representing the World Order of Women (WOW), titled the Seven Professions. There was the scientist, the doctor, the executive, the architect, the engineer, the politician, and the judge. It was constructed soon after the revamped Constitution was created. At that time, the government was 100% female. The revamped Constitution disallowed males from holding any of the high-level positions and they were unable to vote. It represented the new age of women. Fempol became the only law enforcement agency. All others were determined to be redundant and disbanded. Their purpose was seen as a way for the male of the species to exert power.

THE PRISON OF POWER: A MAN-MADE TALE

The park did not have surveillance at the level of the city streets. It was a perfect place to meet, especially for women. Men in the park were either part of the park labor force or vagrants. The precise location was a government kiosk that sold memorabilia of the park statues. Oddly enough, a male worked as the salesperson.

The park was near the offices where Eve worked. She would often visit at her lunch hour. She would sit and wonder when she was going to be summoned and what she what going to be asked to do. She returned to work after one such visit. She sat at her desk. In the middle of her desk was a brightly colored flier with pictures of the seven statues in the park. The caption: *Start Collecting Today* was diagonally embossed over the pictures. At the bottom was a leader: *Get all seven miniatures in the original brass. 'The Doctor' is specially priced this month.* Eve stared at it. She wondered who had put it there. She looked over at Yvonne. She was typing on her terminal. Eve called her name, "Yvonne?" Yvonne looked up at her questioningly but said nothing. "Have you been at my desk?"

Yvonne made a face. She felt she was being accused. "No!" she said and continued to type.

"You didn't put this here," she said in a softer tone and waved the flier.

"Not me," she replied without taking her eyes away from the terminal. "What is it?"

"It is a flier urging people to collect miniature statues of the seven professions of women. You know—the bronze statues."

"What statues?"

"In the park. The Seven Professions."

"Oh, those statues. I have them all. Got them when I was a kid. Come to think of it, I only have six. I lost one when I moved to the city."

"Which one?"

"What?"

"Which statue are you missing?"

"Oh. The Doctor, I think,"

"Well, they have it on special at the kiosk in the park." She waved the flier again.

"Really. I should replace the one I lost. You go there for lunch sometimes, don't you?"

"Sometimes."

"Could you pick one up for me next time you go?"

"Sure. I guess so." Eve stared at Yvonne. The coincidence was just too much to believe. It was just too deliberate. Somehow, she was supposed to go to the kiosk and buy a statue of "The Doctor" and give it to Yvonne. She decided that she would walk past the park after work and approach the kiosk and purchase a bronze statue of "The Doctor."

The sky clouded over and threatened rain. Eve hurried through the park and walked up to the kiosk. The park was nearly empty. The elderly man at the kiosk was just shutting up as she approached. He looked at her and spoke in a British accent, "Sorry, Mum, but we're shut for the day." He gestured skyward. "Gonna rain."

"I won't be a moment. I know what I want," she forced a polite tone.

"Sure, Mum. What can I get for yea?"

She cast her eyes around the displayed wares. "I want a statue of 'The Doctor'"

The man reached to a shelf with bronze statues all lined up in a row. He touched one and then turned. "Yea buying this for yerself er for someone else?"

Eve stared at him, trying to figure out what difference that could possibly make. She answered, "For someone else. My friend Yvonne lost hers and wants a replacement."

"I see. Then you'll be want'n this one," he said assuredly. He turned and reached under the front shelf and brought out a statue of 'The Doctor.' It looked exactly like all the others.

"Thanks. How much?"

"I be happy to inform you that today that statue is yours free of charge." She frowned at him. "You be my...," he paused, "10,000 customer and, according to all that is good, you get whatever you want for free." He set the statue down in front of Eve. "Good day to ya." He shut the kiosk doors. Eve picked up the statue and turned to go just as the rain started. She was soaked before she could get to the train station. She shivered in her seat with one hand in her pocket, clutching the statue. She was sure it would give her some instructions as to how to proceed. She smiled. It had finally started.

She fondled the statue in her pocket as if it were living. Her fingers explored the surface. She scanned the train car. There were other passengers either staring out into space or focused on their portable devices. A passenger facing her from across the aisle made eye contact and then quickly looked away. The possibility that she was being observed occurred to her. She did not take it out to look at it for fear it would somehow expose her purpose. Once back in her apartment, she set it on the table and stared at it. She shook it. Nothing was evident. It was just a small hollow brass statue. There was a small rubber plug in the bottom. She took it out and peered inside. It was empty. There was a tiny number etched into the lip where the plug was inserted. She looked at it but did not really take notice, assuming it was just a number representing the casting run. Thousands of these had been produced. She put the plug back into the hole in the bottom, set it back on the table, and continued to stare. Frustration welled up in her. The stupid statue told her nothing. She reached out and flipped it over. It clinked down on its side as if it too was disappointed that it did not contain any information to clarify the situation.

The next morning, after giving the process of getting the statue some thought, she decided she must give the statue to Yvonne—after all, that was the reason she got it in the first place. Even the man from the kiosk was careful to give her the statue that was for someone else. He gave her a very particular item and not one of the many on the top shelf. Logic demanded that this statue held some kind of message, but for the life of her, she could not figure out what that message was.

She was the first to arrive at work. She placed the statue in the middle of Yvonne's desk. She readied herself for work. Yvonne came in and sat down. She saw the statue. She picked it up and looked over at Eve. "Thanks, Eve. I didn't expect you to actually get it for me. What do I owe you?" she asked and reached for her device.

"Nothing. The man in the kiosk gave it to me." She stared at Yvonne, half expecting her to give her some sort of message. She did not.

"Thanks," she said and set the small brass statue on the corner of her desk.

Eve was more frustrated than ever after her interaction with Yvonne. The stupid statue had nothing to do with her getting instructions from Cassandra.

She felt used as she logged on to her terminal, but before she could begin, a small box popped onto the middle of the screen with a flashing cursor. She stared at it. The flashing seemed to demand that she type something, so she typed the first thing that came into her mind, 'kill mal' She tried to type 'kill males now' but the box only had eight spaces. She quickly erased what she had typed and sat back and stared at the screen. She turned to see if Yvonne was looking at her and she noticed the statue staring back. On impulse she said, "Hey, Yvonne, can I have a look at the statue of 'The Doctor'?"

"Help yourself," she said and continued typing.

"Thanks." She stood and retrieved the statue and sat down. She stared at the statue, hoping she might get a clue now that she knew the clue was eight characters long. The brass doctor was wearing a typical medical jacket with her arms folded in front of her. She had a stethoscope around her neck. She was smiling. Everything she thought of was either too long or too short to fill the box. Eve turned it upside down again and pulled out the plug from the bottom. Then she noticed the number etched on the lip—62748517. Eight characters—*this has to be it*, she thought. She quickly jotted it down, reinserted the plug, and returned the statue to the corner of Yvonne's desk. She typed the number into the box. It disappeared, and some text scrolled past. She read: *You passed the first test. This is your first assignment. Please read carefully and remember.* There was a gap of blank screen and then the message began again. *A package will be delivered to your apartment this evening. It will contain items that are self-explanatory. Do what is required.*

Eve was sitting at her table with a small, sealed box in front of her. She remembered the words Cassandra had written on the napkin: *City hospital— target is 9672301.* The use of the word '*target*' was perfect. It meant that she would be able to actually satisfy that need in her soul—the need that had been with her for all of her adult life. She was going to kill a disgusting man. All that remained was the how. She slowly opened the box. Inside was a primed pressure injector in a small opaque case and a small identification badge for the hospital. There were no messages of any kind. Eve whispered to herself, "*Go to the hospital—find 9672301 and either inject him directly or inject his IV line.*" She assumed it was a man. If they gave the job to her, it must be. She could not kill a female.

QUINLAN SMITH

Quinlan healed quickly. He also ate voraciously. The food was wonderful, and he could have as much as he wanted. He started to gain weight. After the first week, he was able to walk on his own as long as someone was available to catch him if he started to fall. He had a minor setback three days earlier when he attempted to walk to the bathroom without help. He lost his balance, reached out to stop from falling, and tore open the wound in his back. It had hurt more than he could believe. The throbbing swelled so that even his extremities seemed to pulse with pain. The meds made him fuzzy and he didn't like to take them, but this was an exception. Now he was feeling better. The pain was localized to the wound. He became agitated. He knew he was falling behind in his studies. He decided to ask if he could have his study materials while he was in hospital. He spoke to one of the doctors.

"Is there anyone I could talk to about getting my tablet? It has my books on it?" he asked the first chance he got.

"I will have the hospital librarian deliver some novels for you to read. What genre do you like?"

"No," he said, "that is not what I meant."

"What did you mean?" she responded sharply.

"I am studying at the university, and I don't want to fall behind. Is there anyone who might help me get my tablet? The last time I saw it was in the university cafeteria before I was...." he stopped. "I need to contact someone there to retrieve it."

"The university. How did you manage that? Not many males are smart enough to study at a university. What are you taking?" She stuck her thumbnail in her mouth and bit down slightly. "Wait. Let me guess. You are young. I bet you are taking art courses. Or, yes, I put my money on theatre. You want to be an actor. That would be a good choice for a male."

Quinlan was curious. "Why do you think being an actor would be a good choice for a male?"

"Well, to be perfectly honest, it is about all you could have a measure of success doing. Males just can't cut it in anything that requires higher levels of thought. Too many other things get in their way."

"Like what?" ventured Quinlan.

She squinted at him questioningly. "Like violent tendencies and testosterone. This has been documented and widely accepted. On an intellectual level, males just cannot keep pace with females."

Quinlan whispered under his breath, "That doesn't make it true."

"Pardon."

"Can I get them?" he said out loud. He smiled. "I would be very thankful."

"I'll see what I can do," she said. She looked at his chart on her device. My guess is that you have about another week before you will be well enough to be discharged. I expect Commissioner Davenport in a couple of days. You realize the only reason you are in this facility is because she put in a request."

"Yes. Thank you."

The doctor left Quinlan alone with his thoughts.

The next morning, he woke and was surprised to see a small box on the table beside his bed. He opened it and saw it was his notes and a tablet that contained his texts and lecture recordings. He breathed a sigh. He pulled the table over his bed and laid everything out. The lectures were first. He was about to watch the first one in his math course when a woman in a white jacket stepped into his room. She stopped, and she stared at him. She walked up to the electronic chart at the foot of his bed. "Are you 9672301."

"Yes. But my name is Quinlan," he answered politely. There was a noise from the hallway and the woman turned to the doorway. Her hand was in her pocket. She turned back and then glanced once more at the open door as if she were expecting someone. She strode up to Quinlan as if she had just made a decision. Her hand came out of her pocket. Quinlan could not see what she had cupped in her palm. Behind her were some voices just outside the door. He could see the backs of the women. The woman quickly retreated from the bedside and walked toward the door. She nodded to the two women entering, but kept her head bowed as if she did not want to be seen and disappeared. The woman entered the room.

"How are you doing today, Quinlan?" Fempol Commissioner Davenport asked as she stepped up to the bed.

Quinlan's mind swirled. He remembered something about doing something for this woman to help Margaret. He had not thought about her for at least a couple of days. He chided himself. He wanted Margaret to be safe. This woman was going to ask him to do something dangerous. He knew he would do it without hesitation. He also knew that he had no choice. "I am feeling better," he said and wiggled to sit up taller.

The commissioner looked down at his table. "I see you got some of your study material. Good. I want your mind sharp."

"What is it you would like me to do?"

"You know Margaret Carver, and I think you care about her. We want to get her back safe and sound. You can help with that." Quinlan nodded. Nisheeta Davenport continued, "The kidnappers have made demands. They want us to release a number of male prisoners and send them to…" she stopped. "Where is not important. We want you to take the place of one of those prisoners and spy for us."

"Spy?"

"Well, not really. You will be required to place electronic breadcrumbs for us once you arrive where you are going. These people have Margaret somewhere and we must determine where that is."

"Breadcrumbs?"

"Small micro transmitters. They are designed to transmit only after they cool to below body temperature. While on the body, they are undetectable and nearly invisible. Usually, they are embedded in the ball of the thumb in a stack. Every time the carrier presses his thumb down on an object or a person's clothing, one of these bugs will stick. There are over 50 of them in the stack—hence breadcrumbs. Your job will be to choose where to drop them to give us the greatest chance of discovering Ms. Carver's location. Do you think you can do this?"

"Who do they think I am?"

"They will think you are a dead guy. That is, he is dead, but they do not know this. We think that this prisoner was chosen because he is a sociopathic killer who hates women. They want him to do something, but we are not sure what."

"So, you want me to play the part of a killer?"

"You won't have to actually do anything. We expect to have the entire subversive group in prison before anything bad happens."

"What kind of *bad* might happen?"

"Nothing that a smart boy like you couldn't handle. I understand you are taking courses at the university. What are you studying?"

"Quantum Biology. What kind of bad things might I expect?"

Nisheeta pulled a chair over from the corner of the room and sat down. "All right. I will level with you. We need you to do this. You fit the physical description of the guy from the prison. That makes you half perfect for the job. The kidnappers have not given us much to go on. They have made their demands, but they have not given us any ultimatums. They have said nothing about releasing Ms. Carver after we meet their demands. We cannot contact them." She stopped and stared at Quinlan.

"I am only half perfect. Why is that?"

"You are not a killer, are you? We plan on giving you the skills and information so you can at least pretend to be. I have a group that is investigating this prisoner and will provide you with everything you need to become him. Do you think you can pull it off?" Quinlan looked at her with as blank a stare as he could muster. "If it is any consolation, we will reward you handsomely if you help us."

"That is if I survive."

"I won't coddle you. There is always a danger that they want you for something that is not conducive to your survival."

"You mean they might want this person so they can kill him?"

"Yes, but highly unlikely. There are hundreds of ways they could have killed him while he was in prison."

"How did he die?"

"He had a massive stroke. The autopsy indicated that it was the result of damage he received as a child. His home life was nasty. You will learn all about that if you agree to do this for your country. In fact, we can have you out of here today. We have to bring you up to speed so you can pass as him."

"What was he imprisoned for?"

"The formal charge was subversive behavior, especially toward females. In layman's terms, he was part of a group that beat-up and raped a young girl."

"How old was he?"

"He was about 10 years older than you, but we will introduce some nanobots that will age you temporarily." Quinlan frowned. Nisheeta rushed on. "Don't worry. It is completely safe." She stopped and looked at him for some reaction.

Quinlan ran his fingers through his hair. "What kind of reward will I get?"

"What do you want?" Quinlan sat up in his bed. He winced. The half-healed stab wound felt like it cracked open. He shut his eyes and winced again. The system sensed his pain and automatically flooded his bloodstream with pain meds. He sat perfectly still until it faded. "Are you alright?" Nisheeta asked as Quinlan slowly opened his eyes.

"May I speak freely?"

"If you mean, will I punish you if you say something I don't like? The answer is yes, you may speak freely. I want you to understand that we need you, not the other way around."

"I want to have the rights that women have," blurted Quinlan.

"If that were within my purview, I would grant your request. I cannot, but I can offer you protection from any repercussions that might arise and dispensation from common penalties imposed on males in general—as long as you remain law-abiding."

"What does '*dispensation from common penalties imposed on males*' mean?"

"Well, for example, if you were to accidentally bump into a woman in the hallway of the university and you apologized, then any accusations that might arise would be treated as if you were a woman. Such an act would be determined to be accidental and responded to appropriately."

Quinlan smiled. "What you are saying is that I have to behave like I always do but will be insulated from unfounded accusations."

"Pretty much. I can also offer you credits so you can pretty much do whatever you wish once this…" she waved her hand to indicate his task. "…job we are asking you to do is completed successfully." She paused again and answered the question that Quinlan was trying to formulate. "Not helping would result in us simply assigning you to a road crew. I do not recommend that course of action."

"That is not much of a choice. But I will do it voluntarily," said Quinlan softly. "For Margaret." The drugs were stealing his clarity.

Nisheeta Davenport stood up. "Good. Sleep. I will send someone tomorrow to transfer you to a private facility where we can give you the training and information you need. If you are as smart as you purport to be, you will have no difficulty becoming someone else." She turned and walked out of the room. Quinlan heard her speak to the supervisor at the desk. "I have put in a formal order for a guard at this patient's door. No visitors are allowed. Please have an orderly guard the door until they arrive. I cannot stress enough how important this patient is."

Quinlan fell asleep as the commissioner's words, and their meaning, faded from his consciousness.

EVE
RINNE

Eve forced herself to walk down the hospital hallway. The syringe was still cupped in her hand. An image of her target filled her mind. *It was a boy. It was a boy named Quinlan. Not a man. Just a boy. Maybe 18. Maybe older, but not by much. They want me to kill a boy. Evee girl, why do you care? It was a male. You hate all males. Shit. Fuck. You blew it. Calm down. Calm the fuck down.* She was now standing in front of the elevator. There were two chairs on either side. She sat down and stared blankly out. Her mind flicked frantically from one thought to another. She had blown her opportunity. They would never want a failure in their ranks. She had to succeed.

Eve breathed slowly. It was not over yet. She could see the doorway to his room. Two women had entered his room. One was probably his doctor, and the other looked like she was important. She tried to remember the face, but she had been staring at the floor in an effort to conceal her own face and did not get a good look. She continued to look down the hallway and waited for the woman to come out. When that happened, she would try again. Now she knew who it was and where he was, she could just walk in, pretend to be part of his medical team, press the syringe on his neck and watch it happen. There was no point in killing him if she did not see him die. The dying part was what was important. That was dangerous. No, she had to inject him and then get out as fast as possible. She knew there was no surveillance in the rooms. After all, this was not a prison. It was a hospital where women valued their privacy.

That thought set off another. Why was a boy in this hospital? There were other facilities better suited to his gender. The only answer was that he was somehow important. Who was the woman visiting him? He must be important, and Cassandra's group wanted him dead. She stood up and wandered down the hall toward the room. It was about halfway to the end. If she walked to the end of the hall suggesting she had a purpose, she could walk back, giving her two opportunities to see into the room. Maybe she could get a look at the visitor. She might recognize her.

Eve stood up and slipped the syringe into her jacket pocket. She walked purposely down the hall and slowed at the doorway. She looked casually into the open doorway and saw the woman standing over the boy in his bed. The woman looked up just as Eve passed. She recognized the woman and her heart pounded in her chest. *Fuck—fuck—fuck,* she silently screamed. It was the freaking commissioner of Fempol. It was her fucking half-sister. She had been one of the original women to push for disallowing men from being able to vote. That was twenty-plus years ago. If it wasn't for her stupid half-sister, she would probably have never been kidnapped. Nisheeta was a bitch. Her dad and Nisheeta's mum had died when Eve was young, and her half-sister had tried to raise her. They fought continually. One day, Eve was out very late. Eve thought back to the time. She remembered that she did not come home for two days. She staggered in around two in the morning. When she did, Nisheeta freaked and kicked her out. That is when she was kidnapped. She was walking along the street with her backpack when a group of men grabbed her and took her to the farm and put her in the cell. She spent at least two months there. The whole thing was Nisheeta's fault.

The boy must be unbelievably important to get a personal visit from Nisheeta Davenport.

Her mind was racing as she continued down the hall. Suddenly, a doctor came running down the hall and was about to turn into a room on the opposite side of the hallway. She stopped and grabbed Eve by the shoulders. "Come with me, miss…," she read Eve's ID badge and continued, "Nurse in training, O'Hara. I need you." She turned and strode into the room. Eve stood frozen in the hallway. There was a shriek from the doctor, "Get in here now." Eve turned and stood in the doorway. She tried to say something, but nothing came out. Her eyes focused on the doctor administering to an old woman in the bed. Eve took a step into the room. The doctor spoke with a quiet but urgent voice, "Get over here and hold this woman's hand. She has a DNR, and she is dying. She has no family. No woman dies alone while under my care. Hold her hand. Pretend you care even if you don't. Talk to her. Make her last moments warm and loving." Eve moved to the opposite side of the bed and took the old woman's hand. It was cold and dry. Her skin was incredibly smooth. She felt the fingers twitch and tighten in her own hand. "I am doing this for you as well as for her. You have to experience someone's death as part of your training," whispered the doctor. "This may take a while. I will be back in a few minutes to check on you. If you feel her slipping away, just press that button and I will come running." With that, she turned and left the room.

Eve did not know what to do. Obviously, her ID badge was taken from an actual student nurse. She dropped the old woman's hand and looked frantically around. The hand she dropped was sticking out from the sheet and looked disconnected from the body. It was twitching as if it were looking to reconnect with Eve. She looked up at the old woman in the bed. Her eyes were fluttering, and her head was twitching back and forth. She stepped away from the bed and looked out of the room. Down the hallway, she could see a doctor speaking to the commissioner. Their conversation lasted a few moments. The doctor directed a large woman to sit by the door. It was obvious she was a guard. The commissioner walked away just as Eve heard a moan from behind her. She turned back to the dying woman, strode over to the bed, pushed the button that would call the doctor, left the room, and exited the floor by the stairwell at the end of the hallway.

SEAN KILKENNY

Sean sat up in bed. It was very early. He looked around the single room that comprised his studio. For a male in the city, it was viewed as luxury living quarters. "What a dump," he said out loud. He glanced at his device. It was just before dawn. He got up and dressed quickly. He needed to prepare for his day of investigation of the main office of Fempol. He had visited a few times and surreptitiously released a number of big-eared mice in the dark corners of the building. Then he waited. The message came the previous week. He was asked to get rid of the vermin that infested the building. He waited until the request became an order before responding. The few mice he released had magically transformed into an infestation in a few weeks, even though he only released males in the building. "Mice will do that," he chuckled to himself.

He chose the date carefully. He needed to see her office. Today was a day she was going to be there to attend a meeting of all the federal commissioners. Nothing would happen today but reconnaissance. He planned to wear his protective suit with a breathing mask that was totally unnecessary, but it would make him look more ominous as well as anonymous. It would also strike fear into all those females when he walked up to them and asked, "Excuse me, Ma'am but have you seen any rodents in your office?" He would be allowed to go anywhere in the building except on the seventh floor. He would need the nanobots for that. He had injected them the night before. They would have time to proliferate his system. Eight hours after injection, they would be dominant. He must attempt to cross the sensors on the seventh floor before his own nanobots began to eradicate the invaders. He hoped the sensors would read him as Ms. Dolores Fineman and allow entry. He didn't think she would be there after her little "accident," but even if she was, he doubted the scanning system would be programmed to react to her entering twice. That is what today was for. He had to find out if his plan would work.

He made a cup of tea and sipped it while he fantasized about what would happen to the evilest person he knew. Nisheeta Davenport—AKA 'The Butcher'—would die writhing as the poison gas stole all muscle control. He opened the cupboard under the kitchen sink. There were many containers stored on the shelf. Behind the jug of bleach was a small pressure canister. He pulled it out and held it lovingly in his hands. All he had to do was feed the gas into the correct room. He had considered trying to capture the images of The Butcher shitting her pants just before collapsing so he could watch it over and over, but the risk was too great. The security systems would discover transmissions of any sort. He would have to use his imagination. He grinned. It was probably better and safer, anyway.

He knew he must not leave the building after the deed. If he did, he would become their number one suspect. They would find him setting traps in the basement. He would even have a couple of dead mice to show for his efforts. He would be dismissed as a suspect.

He grabbed a breakfast bar from the cupboard and headed out the door. He carried the canister in a nondescript lunch bag. He would put it in his secret lair. Secret Lair. He loved the phrase. It made him sound like he was a super criminal who was about to have a coming out party. He walked out of the building and over two blocks to his pest control van parked in the alley. He glanced around and disconnected the charger from the illegal power and concealed the cord. With a fully charged van, he could go anywhere in the city. He drove to his hideaway, parked the van, and entered with the greatest of care. The recent flooding made the file boxes exceptionally smelly. He did not mind. That smell was a wonderful defense against discovery. He opened the door at the end of the passage through the rank piles of wet, collapsed file boxes and slipped inside.

He set the gas canister on the tool bench. It had taken him a year to find a supplier and then another four months to convince them to sell him what he wanted. He did not know the name of the actual compound. He had told them he needed to have enough poison gas to flood a large rabbit warren in the park. He wanted a poison gas that would kill all the rabbits quickly in one shot. He figured it would also kill a human. He did not want to half kill her and then have the doctors bring her back to life. She needed to be dead. The supplier had guaranteed that this was the stuff. It had a number of precautions stating its danger to humans. It came with warnings for its use against various rodents. It had cost a bundle. He pulled his COM out of his pocket. It was nearly 7:00 a.m. He had to go now if he was to be sure the nanobots were still viable. All his pest control traps were in his van. He checked the cameras. The entire area covered by the cameras was devoid of all living things. He still followed the procedures for exiting his secret lair and was soon on his way.

He pulled into the line of early arrivals at the federal building and prepared his paperwork. His turn came quicker than he expected. He smiled and looked out at the woman in the guard shack. She smiled back, but the warmth generated was short-lived. "Identification," she snapped. Sean handed her his city ID. "Job scan," she ordered. He held out his device, and she touched it with a device of her own. She looked at it. "So, you are the Rat Man."

"I am pest control agent Sean Kilkenny. I have to inspect the premises and remove any pests that may have infested the building. I am guessing I will find some mice or maybe a few rats." He smiled at her again.

"Yeah, I heard people were seeing rodents in their offices." She turned and spoke into her device and then turned back to Sean. "Pullover there and step out of the van."

"I really don't have time for this. I need to check offices before people arrive." He tried to sound professional, but he knew his words came out more of a whine.

The woman turned harsh. "Look, Rat Man, this is a high-level government building, and it is my job to maintain security. For all I know, you are some male shit bag who's trying to take down the government. Pull the fuck over or leave."

Sean pulled his van over to one of the parking stalls. He glanced in his side mirror. He could see at least three males going over his truck with sensors and mirrors. They were making sure there he was not carrying anything on the undercarriage of his van. He heard a tap on the window. He rolled it down. "Would you please step out of the van," asked a very young man in one of the uniforms that indicated he worked for the oppressive female government. Uniform was a nice description. What they wore was more like a prison jumpsuit. Sean opened the cab door and slid out. "Please stand over there," the man requested. He indicated a white circle on the pavement. Above the circle was a cantilevered pipe with a series of 7 lights. Sean stood in the circle and watched as the men searched the inside of his van. He tried to see where they were looking. His thoughts were racing. They had obviously increased their security protocols. He bet it had something to do with the murders at the university. When he delivered the mice, there was nothing like this. He was waved right through once they saw that he worked for the city.

The lights above him flashed in a chase sequence, with each light changing color in a seemingly random fashion. They stopped with only the seventh light remaining on. It was amber. The young man took a card from his pocket and looked at it. "Please remove the knife from your pocket and give it to me. You can retrieve it when you exit."

"Oh," said Sean, "I forgot about that. It is just a fingernail picker." He removed a small pocketknife and gave it to the man.

"It's a knife. Knives are restricted." The man took it and placed it in a small paper envelope. "It will be at the exit." All the men searching his van were now standing to the side. "You may enter now." Sean looked at his van. All the doors were still open. He could see his traps strewn in a pile. He turned and frowned at the man and pointed at the disarray. The man simply shrugged. He walked around the van, shutting doors as he went. He drove into the underground parking structure and looked for the door to the stairs. He took the paper notepad from the dash of the van. He still loved paper and pencil. It was much more versatile than the scribe pads. He needed to go through the building in order to formulate a plan. But first he needed to test the nanobots that he had injected that morning. If they did not work, then the whole thing would be a waste of time. He grabbed the bag containing his protective suit and mask. It was half hanging out of the bag. It had been rifled through by the security grunts. He straightened it and closed the bag. He walked up the stairs to the seventh floor. The elevators were often crowded, and he did not want to draw attention to himself. He was out of breath when he reached the door. He opened the bag and slipped on the overalls with "PEST CONTROL" emblazoned across the back. He put the breathing mask over his head but did not pull it down to cover his face. He dropped the carry bag and opened the door. The elevator doors were just closing as three women exited. They were walking away from him down the hallway. The bitches were chattering about one of their Loverboys. He shook his head. Women had gone crazy. They only wanted to fuck pretend men. He unconsciously reached down and squeezed his penis. It swelled.

The women walked toward the security station. They entered one at a time. A barred cage-like door closed behind them. Sean watched carefully. They stood still for a few seconds until the far metal door slid open. Once they passed through, the metal door closed behind them and the barred door opened to allow the next woman to enter. He remained quiet and still, hoping they would not turn around and question why he was on the floor. He would simply tell them that he was checking for vermin in the stairway. They did not turn and were all soon through the metal door.

He was about to step up to the security station when a door to the left of the station opened. A woman exited. She was totally preoccupied with her device and did not look up. Sean could see that the exit was a double door system with a small hallway in-between. From the other side, you entered the first door, which had to close behind you before you could open the second and leave. *Good to know*, he thought. She called the elevator, which opened almost immediately. As the elevator doors were closing, he strode over to the security system and entered the barred cage. The few seconds of waiting were an eternity. The metal door opened, and he stepped through. His mask was still on his forehead. The hallway in front of him was very wide, with a number of doors leading off of it. A few meters down the hall was a reception desk. There was a woman sitting at the desk. She looked up at him. Her eyes widened when she saw what he was wearing. She was about to stand up when he strode over to her. "Excuse me, Ma'am but I have been given access to this area to check for a reported pest infestation."

"I was not informed. What kind of pests?"

"Mice," he answered flatly.

"Yeah, I heard some ladies talking about that. I have not seen anything."

"That is good. I need to check the rooms on this floor, especially any with air exchange ventilation. The little buggers get in that way," he said as politely as he could. His brain was doing something else. This woman was displaying her tits like they were prize hams. He leaned into the high desk and felt his penis touch the front panel. It sent a flutter through his groin and pornographic images through his mind. He tried to keep his demeanor as neutral as possible. He did not smile or frown. He pushed the thoughts away.

She slipped off of her stool and stood. "I can show you, but we must make it fast. There is an important meeting scheduled in the main room." She bent over to pick up what Sean thought was a kind of key card. He watched her bend over the desk. Her sweater top fell open. He could practically see her nipples. He bumped the desk with his crotch and pressed it hard. He was hard now. With the hardness came anger and images. He wanted to let them flood his mind. He wanted to push his cock down her throat and squeeze her tits until she squealed. He did not. He pushed the thoughts away.

"That would be great. I will only be a few minutes in each room," he said calmly as he removed his notepad from his pocket. She strode to the first room of six and opened the door. She waited in the hall while Sean scanned the room for vents and marked their location down in his notepad.

The final room was the large meeting room at the end of the hall. "This is the last one," she said as she pushed the door open.

He stepped through. As he did so, his arm touched her breasts. She did not seem to notice, but Sean could not control his cock. It sprang up as he scanned the room. There was a door to the side. "Where does that go?" he asked and gestured to it.

"That is a private elevator that leads to the commissioner's offices. Speaking of which, she is due very soon." At that moment, the light above the door came on. Thirty seconds later, the door opened and two men dressed in jump suits similar to the men at the guard gate stepped out, pushing a food cart with cups, coffee and hot water urns. They did not acknowledge Sean or the woman. They simply set up the cart on the side of the room and returned to the elevator.

After they had gone, Sean took a few notes and checked the corners of the room. "What are you looking for?" asked the woman.

"Evidence. Where there are mice, there are mice droppings."

"Ew. Gross," she said and made a face. "Did you find any?"

Sean looked at the floor just under the main vent. He discreetly reached into his pocket and pinched a few grains of black wild rice he had placed there earlier and dropped them on the carpet. "Oh, oh," he said ominously. He reached down and picked them up again. "Looks like they have been here. Probably smelled the crumbs of food left behind from the last meeting. Mice have a powerful sense of smell." He looked up at the vent. "I am going to have to check that vent system."

The woman looked worried. "You can't right now. You will have to come back later. There is an important meeting starting in a few minutes. Suddenly, the light above the door illuminated. "You have to leave now." She stepped up to Sean and pulled him by the arm. "You have to leave now. Hurry." They both stepped over to the door just as the elevator door opened. As the door closed, Sean caught a glimpse of Nisheeta Davenport enter the room. He smiled. He was closer now than he had ever been to exacting his revenge.

"When can I get in to clean out the vents?" he asked her. He smiled now, hoping the smile would give him an advantage. "They can stink if the mice build nests. You don't want that."

"Well, let's see if I can find an opening in the schedule. She has another meeting scheduled for tomorrow afternoon." She slipped back onto her stool behind the desk and looked at her monitor. "The rest of the week is booked." She seemed to be warming to him as she leaned forward on the stool and slowly squeezed her breasts together as if she was stretching her shoulders. He stared. She smiled. "I tell you what, I will let you know when I can fit you in. How do I do that?"

"You put in the work order. They won't let me in here without one."

"Will do." He turned to go. "See you soon. But don't come through the main entrance. As you probably already know, the security is horrendous. I will have a pass ready for you at the workers' entrance once I find a block of time. How much time will you need? Oh, and what is your name?"

"I will need at least two uninterrupted hours. Just have the pass say Pest Control," he said and turned, jabbed his thumb over his shoulder to show the words on his coveralls. He left the way he came and headed to the basement. That was part of his alibi. He was almost positive he could gain entry, but he needed to be sure he would not be suspected. The thought of killing the monster with impunity made his erection harder.

VIHAAN
KHATRI
(AKA KARIMA RANI SANYAL)

Vihaan was prepared for his new world, but being prepared to experience and actually experiencing were light years apart. He was initially placed in a small studio in a less desirable part of the city. For Vihaan, now Karima, the freedom was exhilarating. He had never been free before. There had always been someone telling him what to do and what to think. That was still true, but the distance was greater. At least it felt like freedom, even if it wasn't totally true. He even had his own COM device, and it was ringing. He slipped out of bed and picked it up. He glanced at the screen. His handler wished to speak to him. He tossed the COM on the bed and walked into the bathroom. He had to pee. Part of his training was designed to ingrain behavior. As a male, he had peed standing up, but if he was to be a female trying to take on male characteristics, he would pee sitting. He sat and peed, hoping that his COM would stop ringing. It did not. He washed his hands and smiled at the design painted on his fingernails. He had grown them long and had them manicured and painted with the head of a cat on his thumbnail along with cat paws on the fingernails. He needed to be female in all ways except for his penis. That was the only thing he did not have to fake. They had given him a couple of scars that would normally occur from the surgery for penis enhancement. He did not really have any female apparatus, but he did have the best that plastic surgery could create. It didn't function, but it looked great. He even had scars on his pecs to indicate breast reduction. He would, if he was challenged, admit to being a hermaphrodite. That was a possible choice for a mother to select when setting the genetic parameters of her potential child, albeit not a common choice. But that was not something to admit unless he was under intense scrutiny.

He picked up the phone and spoke in character. He needed to always be in character. "Speak," he said, practically breathing the word. He had grown rather bitchy since he moved into the studio. It was not what he was promised. A month had slipped by and nothing had happened. No one had tried to contact him, especially the Chow woman.

"Pack. Only what is required. An e-cab will be there to pick you up. There has been a change of plan. You are moving up in the world. You now have a benefactor."

"Who?"

"A rich European woman. Swedish. She has set you up in your new apartment. She comes to town only occasionally. That will give you freedom to step out on her as it were. We have flooded the Webbies with your latest exploits. You will attend two parties, a dinner and a political event in the next week. You are flirty but not slutty. You will be featured in Chow's feeds. Her present Loverboy fell ill last week. With any luck, you will get a call from her aide. Accept any invite to social events but claim you are taken if they try to proposition you. You cannot give in too easily. Do you have any questions?"

"I need more information about my benefactor."

"No, you don't."

"What if someone asks me about her? What do I say?"

"Nothing. Act as if she wishes to remain anonymous. Don't even try to answer any questions, that way you cannot be caught in a lie. It will also increase your mystery quotient. We will leak the occasional tidbit to the Webbies. Just enough to keep you in focus and mysterious. Clear?"

"Yes."

"Good. It's show time."

Vihaan tossed the COM onto the bed. He looked around the little studio with paint peeling from the kitchen cupboard doors. He flipped his hair over his shoulder. He applied some simple makeup. He needn't go to any extremes with makeup. He just needed to look the part while out in the world. He put on a pair of jeans and a pink blouse. He looked like a young woman trying to look like a buff young man in drag. It was perfect. He smiled in the mirror at the changes he had made to his body. He frowned when thoughts of his future crept in. His road in life had been predetermined by his family—his mother specifically. Would he ever get to be just a normal male person? He answered his own question: *Maybe, if the rules change. Maybe, if I could be a nexus for those changes.* He opened the closet and grabbed a pair of red high-heeled pumps. He slipped them on. He picked up the prepacked go-bag from the closet floor, sat on the bed and waited. He did not pack anything else. There was nothing here he needed or wanted.

His COM beeped. He grabbed the bag and headed out of the studio. His e-cab had arrived.

KARIMA
RANI SANYAL
(AKA VIHAAN KHATRI)

The e-cab pulled up to a private residence in a very quiet neighborhood. It was evening, and the darkness hid much of the detail of the building exterior. The drizzle of warm rain made the hedge leaves reflect warm yellow light from a series of hidden sources along the front walkway. This was the kind of place that did not require the presence of guards or garish white lighting. It was protected in much more subtle ways, as was the entire area. No one of questionable integrity, male or female, ever entered without being subjected to intense scrutiny. She wondered about her own access. Then, as if her mind was being read, her COM beeped. She read the message: "You are not a visitor here. You are a resident. That is why you are able to enter this exclusive area without challenge. Just thought you would like to know."

Her reverie was interrupted by the e-cab beeping for her to present her COM and exact payment. She did just that, grabbed her go-bag and stepped out onto the walkway. The rain had changed from a drizzle to a downpour. She walked slowly forward, oblivious to the rain. A series of lights glowed more brightly at her feet as she walked. They faded out behind her. As she neared the door, her COM beeped again, and the door opened. Her hair was wet from the rain and clung in clumps to her face. She brushed it aside. The door closed quietly behind her. As she stepped forward, the lighting followed. The hallway led to a spacious room containing warm furniture. She plunked down in a large chair and stared around the room. Her COM beeped again. The text scrolled. *"This apartment is controlled by an AI. Just speak and it will respond. Everything said or done in this space can never be surveilled by any outside entity. Make yourself at home. You will soon be contacted by a number of ladies seeking a Loverboy. Put everyone off until you hear from us. It is likely that Chow will use an intermediary. When we know who that is, we will give you the go ahead to accept an invitation. This is our last communication. The AI will be your source as of now. Goodbye, Ms. Sanyal."*

Karima was following her training. She was female in all her actions, both private and public, with the exception of her sexual behavior. There she was more male than female. She had learned to adjust this according to the woman with whom she was being intimate. Sometimes more male and sometimes the opposite.

A drop of water dripped onto her forehead from her hair. She stood. "Where is the bathroom?" she asked.

"I assume you are speaking to me, as you are the only person in the room. In the future, to account for others being present, please address me as Jeeves. In answer to your question, the bathroom is down the hall to the right. I have lit the way for you." The hall lights came on with a brighter light down the hall. She got up and walked to the bathroom. She wiped her face with the towel and explored the apartment.

"Jeeves?"

"Yes, Ms. Sanyal, how may I help you?"

"Food. I am starving."

"The pantry is fully stocked," Jeeves said as a light indicated the kitchen area, "Or you could order a meal from a restaurant. What would you like to eat?"

Karima, in her previous life as Vihaan, had never eaten anything from a restaurant. Her training had included the protocols for restaurant dining, but the practice sessions were not the same as actually eating out. The food was generally bland. Her mind jumped to her mother's cooking and her mouth watered. "I would like some Indian food. Could you order me some Indian food?"

"Certainly. What would you like?"

The thought of actual Indian food was the most exciting thing to happen to her since this whole thing started. Not since she lived with her mother had she had anything that she really liked. All food had been eaten but not enjoyed.

"Lamb Rogan Josh," she paused, "vindaloo, basmati rice, and some chapatis. And some mango chutney."

"What you ordered is quite spicy. Are you sure? Perhaps you should have—"

"That is what I want. Some real spice. I want to eat it and sweat. Yes."

"Your order has been placed. An e-drone will deliver it in 30 minutes."

Karima plunked down in the large, comfortable chair and smiled. She flipped her legs up over the arm and closed her eyes. She breathed deep and relaxed. She had not really relaxed since she had left the training center, wherever that was. The relaxation was short-lived.

"Ms. Sanyal, you have a call. It is my job to intercept all communications when you are in the apartment. This particular communication is from an agent. Would you like to take it?"

"An agent? An agent of what? An agent for whom?"

"Just a moment. Accessing information on the agent. Yes. Her name is Jolene Fitzsimmons. She has many clients that wish to engage Loverboys. On whose behalf, I do not know. Would you like me to enquire?"

"No. I will take the call." She picked up her COM.

"You will not need the COM to communicate with anyone while you are in the apartment. Just speak after the word, 'connect'."

Karima spoke, "Connect. Hello. How may I help you?"

"Ms. Sanyal. Good evening. I hope I have not called at an inconvenient time. My name is Fitzsimmons. Do you have time to chat?"

"Yes. What can I do for you?"

"Great. I am enquiring as to your present relationship status. I heard you were going to be available soon and I have a number of clients who are very interested in your services. Is it true that you are looking for a quality," she paused, "benefactor?"

"I might be. What are you offering?"

"So, you are not under contract? I heard you were."

Karima fell back on the script that had been pounded into her, "I do not wish to confirm or deny at this time."

"Cagey. Well, I will lay it out for you. Tell me if I am wrong. I think you have a benefactor but are not under formal contract, which means you might accept an offer that meets your needs."

"Perhaps. That depends on your client."

"So, you want a specific type of client. Tell me, what are the parameters? Age? Weight? Ethnicity? Money? If it is money, I am your best bet. I represent the most affluent people in the city."

"No. Longevity. I want a relationship that will last. I don't care about the rest. No wait. I would like certain amenities."

"That goes without saying."

Karima jumped to it. "Do you have any clients that meet those criteria?"

"I might. Let me do some research. May I call you back with an offer?"

"You may. I would also like to know the name of the client at the time of the offer."

"That can be arranged if you are willing to sign an NDA." There was an extended silence. Karima did not answer. The agent continued, "So would you be willing to sign a non-disclosure agreement?"

Perhaps, if the offer is…well…interesting."

"One last thing. Will you give me first refusal?"

"No. I am sorry. That is not something I am willing to entertain. If you want me, then offer me what you think I cannot refuse. I must go. My dinner is here. Goodbye, Ms. Fitzsimmons."

The call was ended by the Jeeves. "Ms. Sanyal, your dinner has arrived. There is a package on the front stoop." Karima jumped up from the chair and retrieved her dinner. She set out the table and was about to take her first bite when Jeeves interrupted, "Ms. Sanyal, you have a number of calls cued. Would you like to talk to the first caller?" Karima shoved a fork full of lamb into her mouth and let the spice fill her being. It was hot, and it was good. She shook her head in refusal, hoping that Jeeves would be able to interpret her action. He was. "Very good. I will take messages." Karima ate with relish. It was her first real Indian dinner since leaving home.

MARGARET CARVER

The apartment was a zillion times better than her cell. It was one large room divided into a kitchen, a living room, and a sleeping area. There was a bathroom at one end. She ran around looking at everything from food in the cupboards and refrigerator to music and video chips on a side shelf. There was a player. On the wall was a large video screen. There was a tablet with many books. The thought of reading a book filled her with anticipation. She ran to the bed and plunked herself down. It was so soft she thought she might never get up. She quickly sat up. She remembered seeing a bag of potato chips in one of the cupboards. She ran over and grabbed it, plunked down on the small couch, and ripped it open. She stuffed a handful in her mouth and let the salty flavors fill her senses.

"Margaret," said a voice. "I am the apartment AI. You may ask me things by starting the question with 'AI'. For example: AI, please play some music."

"AI—please play some music."

"Do you wish for any particular genre?"

"You choose." Music played. It was classical. Margaret did not know many of the classics, but it was beautiful. She listened and ate chips. She got up and took a soda from the refrigerator and sat back down. She felt like she was in heaven. She sat up quickly, spilling chips on the floor. "AI—Where am I?"

"It doesn't matter."

"It matters to me."

"It shouldn't matter. You are now better off than you were before. Don't you agree?"

"Yes—but" said Margaret, "I would like to go home."

"You are home for now. You will begin your formal education here now that you are ready. If you feel you are not ready, you will have to return to the previous accommodations and—"

"No, I am ready," she said quickly. "I misunderstood. Tell me about my formal education. What will I learn?" Margaret's thoughts swirled in a vortex that grabbed the first one and dragged all the remaining ones with it as if they were clothes pegged to a line come loose from its moorings. There was a part of her that desperately wanted to escape this prison. She considered overt rebellion. But that, she was sure, would result in punishment. A return to her previous cell was not something she would ever want to consider. She had to rebel more covertly. She must be patient and look for a way to escape. She would cooperate right up until she knew she could escape.

"A lot of potato chips are not good for you. Stop eating them. There is a salad and a small sandwich for your lunch. It is in the refrigerator. Fetch it and eat it." Margaret got up from the couch and walked to the refrigerator. She felt the spilled chips crunch under her feet. She lifted one foot and brushed off the crumbs and, as if it had sensed the need for its service, a small vacuum trundled out from the wall to clean up the mess. She ate the lunch while sitting at the small table. It was delicious. Access to food was so primal she nearly cried. She filled up quickly and was about to save the remaining half of her sandwich by returning it to the refrigerator when the AI spoke to her.

"Please eat it all. There will always be enough food. You must overcome the habits learned from your previous experiences in your cell. Here, food will never be an issue. This is a good teaching moment. All the habits and ideas from your previous life are like this. They serve no purpose in your new life. All that you were before coming to us must be eradicated and replaced with new ways of thinking and reacting."

Margaret felt her heart rate jump and along with it the thought—*I did not come to you. You kidnapped me, you fucking criminals.* She simply smiled and pushed it away. That was good. It made her feel as if she still had a measure of power.

She could still control what was going to happen. Brainwashing. That was what was happening here. Her only means of survival was to keep her actual thoughts and feelings secret. She would cultivate the secret garden that was the true Margaret Carver. "I understand," she said with assurance and took a bite of the remaining half of the sandwich.

"When you have finished, please request the video screen. Your first lesson starts today."

Margaret quickly swallowed the last bite. She folded her hands and spoke, "AI—turn on the video." The large screen on the wall came to life.

It spoke with the same voice as the AI. "Margaret, today we are going to explore the history of our species in a way that may seem unfamiliar to you. It is, however, the actual truth. Please attend." This voice was soon replaced by a male voice that narrated the title of the presentation.

The Importance of Positive Male Role Models in The Development of The Modern Female.

This presentation will give you an opportunity to understand the importance of males in a society that has marginalized them. It will use many first-person anecdotal accounts of how males were instrumental in forging strong female personalities. It will also suggest the present social norms, which view males as an unnecessary burden on the positive growth of the species, are wrong and should be abandoned. It will demonstrate new political processes that could alter the anti-male path of our country. Women are powerful, but not as powerful as they could be, with males assuming an equal role in all aspects of society.

Margaret smiled and let her eyes glaze over as the narration began in earnest. A part of her whispered, "*Bullshit!*" but the chants were pushing her disagreement aside. A short time ago, she would have screamed *Fucking Bullshit* out loud. She found herself mouthing the words as she watched the images of young women and girls being supported by their respective males.

Males are strong.
Males are creative.
Males are intelligent.
Males are loving.

Males balance the female.

Females are strong

Females are creative.

Females are intelligent.

Females are loving.

Females balance the male.

They must respect each other.

They must support each other.

They must speak to each other.

They must listen to each other.

They must love each other.

Time slipped by. Her education progressed. For the first few days and even weeks, she still saw what was happening to her as indoctrination, but that slowly and inexorably faded. All thoughts of escape disappeared. There was no longer anything to escape from. The credo that was presented became truth. The folly of the women in the society needed to be confronted and overturned. As time passed, she came to believe all these teachings were true, and she was now prepared to fight for it. The latter part of her training included political processes required to bring about true changes in the laws that would reinstate the male vote and remove restrictions imposed by the radical female led government.

Her training took a new turn. She was introduced to the others. They were people like her who were being prepared to go and become part of the government. Some were trained to take public positions in the political landscape, others were trained to infiltrate the same landscape and slowly and inexorably shape it away from its unisex posture to a new form of acceptance of males as equal to females. Violence was integral to the process, but only as a means to achieve specific goals quickly. An aide might slip and hurt themselves so that someone more sympathetic might take their place. A ruling committee member might be unable to continue with her responsibilities and the resulting bi-election would give someone new an opportunity to take the position. Nothing was overt. No one ever mentioned their true political leanings until it was time. The plan was complex mainly due to the built-in flexibility. If something did not go as planned, there was always an alternative. But some plans were more important than others. Some things must come to pass if the laws were to change quickly. Margaret Carver was integral to that plan. She would become the heart of change. She was to become a committee member and if all went well, she would replace her mother as the chairwoman. There were already dozens of committee members elected in the last cycle that, like soldiers in the belly of a Trojan horse, were prepared to sneak out under the cover of the darkness created and maintained by AMEN and change critical laws. They would start with MARA (Male Assembly Restrictions Act) Once men could legally gather together, AMEN could come out of the shadows and fight openly for equality.

NISHEETA DAVENPORT

Nisheeta sat at her desk with her hands folded in front of her. She looked up at Lillian Carver, who stood leaning forward with both hands on the front of the desk. All anger had long since drained out of her. Lillian felt like crying. She didn't cry. "Nisheeta, please tell me you have a plan to get my daughter back. What do these bastards want?"

"Please sit down, Lillian. Let me explain what we are doing to get Margaret back."

"Do you think she is still alive?"

"Yes. They have no reason to kill her. Killing her would mean they no longer have any power. I am sure she is still alive. We have received a singular request to release a number of prisoners and deliver them to a small town in the northwest of Washington state. Once we start that process, I am sure we will hear from them again."

"So, you are going to deliver some prisoners. How the frack is that going to get my daughter back?"

"Sit down, Lillian, and I will explain our plan." Lillian Carver sat and gripped the arms of the chair. "We are sending the prisoners, but we will include a plant. The young man that was taken with Margaret was sent by the kidnappers to another cell of AMEN we were watching. The subsequent raid on their hideout allowed us to capture him. The group leader tried to kill him rather than let us capture him. They nearly succeeded. We are not sure why they would rather him dead than in our custody. I will find out, however. He has been in the hospital healing from a knife wound."

"Was that the male that Margie brought home to tutor? Are you sure he is not part of the kidnapper's cabal?"

"Yes. He is totally innocent. He is also willing to help us find them. As we speak, he is being prepared to take the place of one of the prisoners. He is being outfitted with some new tech that will enable him to show us where he is being taken. That should help us locate the kidnappers and, subsequently, your daughter. We will bring these bastards to justice."

"Keep me informed. In fact, I want to meet this male before you send him out to do whatever you expect him to do. I want to explain to him what will happen if he does not do what we want, especially if my daughter is harmed in any way. Phone Karen Chow, my aide, and let her know the when and the where," said Lillian Carver sharply. She stood and left the office.

Nisheeta also stood. She wanted to respond. She wanted to explain that meeting this boy was not a good idea. Threatening him was not going to improve the chances he would be successful. It would do just the opposite. She decided that she would keep her mouth shut and shift the blame to someone else for not informing her. Fineman could take the hit. "I will be sure to inform you," said Nisheeta. She plunked down just as her office door clicked shut. The boy was downstairs in one of the apartments reserved for special envoys from other countries. He was being looked after and prepared for his little adventure. He needed to know all the history of the man he was replacing, as well as information on all the other prisoners who would accompany him. Some, if not all, were dangerous. She was hoping that those preparing him would also give him good advice on how to deal with his companions during the journey. The seven other men might make things difficult for Quinlan. She touched her COM and spoke, "Ms. Fineman, please come to my office."

Dolores Fineman rapped on her office door and entered. "Yes, Commissioner, what can I do for you?"

"How is the young man in the downstairs apartment doing? Is his training progressing? How is his health?"

"I will check on him and let you know. What did Carver want?"

"She is understandably worried. She wants to talk to Quinlan before we send him out."

"Do you think that is a good idea?" Nisheeta shrugged. That shrug would give her deniability. She considered the possible dialog that might ensue regarding whether or not she told Dolores to inform Carver's aide and decided it was opaque enough to keep everyone safe from blame.

"Have any of the commissioners gotten any possible leads from their informants? Someone out there has to know something. These people are not ghosts. There must be something. They cannot operate in today's world without leaving a trail. We need to find it and take them down."

"I will check in with the search team and see if they have discovered anything. I am sure if they came up with anything, they would have already contacted this office."

"Please check. Thank you." Dolores turned to leave. "How are you? I understand you had an accident while running in the park."

"I'm okay. Just a bump on the head and a sore leg. Some rocks fell, and I tripped on them in one of the tunnels. Must have knocked myself out. I don't remember even entering the tunnel. I must have been out for some time. When I finally came to, at least 30 minutes had passed. I put in a work order to ensure that it would not happen to anyone else." She rubbed her head. "Anything else?"

"No. And take care running in the park. There are some nasty males living in there just looking to take advantage of a girl. I sure wish they had not removed the cameras."

"All the males in the park are harmless. Every time we install cameras, they get smashed. Short of purging that park of all males, there is little we can do." She left the office and closed the door behind her.

Nisheeta sat and tapped her fingers in sequence on the surface of her desk. Her COM beeped. "Yes, Dolores," she said into the device.

"You have a visitor from the chairwomen's office. It is her aide, Ms. Chow. May I send her in?"

Nisheeta thought, *What the frack does she want now?* She said, "Send her in."

Karen Chow entered. Nisheeta remembered their last encounter. This woman gave women a bad name. Previous generations used to call women like her a myriad of names, none of them pleasant. Ms. Chow entered. "What can I do for the Chairwoman's aide today?" She stressed the word 'aide', knowing it would irk the woman. She saw herself as much more important than she actually was.

Chow smirked but did not bite at the obvious gibe. "I am here on behalf of the Chairwoman. She just informed me you have a male prisoner who you intend to use as bait. I am here to join the personnel that are involved in his preparation. I will be reporting daily details back to the Chairwoman."

"That is not necessary. In fact, your presence will be detrimental to his training. Please report to the chairwoman that I must refuse your…help." The word 'help' came out like spit.

"The Chairwoman insists."

"The Chief Commissioner also insists. The young man in question is not, as you refer to him, a prisoner. He has done nothing wrong. He has volunteered and is being prepared by professionals. You do not have the skills to even be present during his training. Take my message back to the Chairwoman with my sincerest regards." She reached out and picked up the tablet on her desk and read as Ms. Chow stared back at her. She was furious and could barely hold her reactions in check. Nisheeta looked up at her. "That is all. You are dismissed." Karen Chow turned with a snap of her high heels. The quick motion caused her to falter slightly. She limped for a few steps and then recovered. She opened the door and walked out.

QUINLAN
SMITH

Quinlan was hot. The room was stuffy. He wiggled in the chair. The material was shiny, and it stuck to him. He was not formally restrained in the chair, but all the attachments made him feel like he was. There was a helmet on his head recording his brain waves, ear buds sending sound to his ears, and VR goggles on his face. His arms were held firmly to the arms of the chair. They had explained that it was necessary in order to measure his vital body readings accurately. The latest visuals were showing him various aspects of the life of the man he was replacing. He had already experienced what it was like in the prison system. The worst part was being confronted by other prisoners with various demands. Some of them were overtly sexual. Most were about something he had that they wanted. He had learned how to survive in prison. Quinlan figured it would not really help him in an actual prison, but it would help him if he needed to appear like he had actually been in prison. It was information that would allow him to deceive anyone who doubted his history. After about 30 minutes, the visuals stopped. A woman in scrubs removed the VR goggles and other equipment.

"May I get up and stretch?" asked Quinlan. The woman nodded and set all the apparatus she had removed from Quinlan on a side shelf. He stood up and flexed his shoulders. She watched him for a moment without speaking and then, as if she had decided it was safe to leave him unsupervised, she left the room. The room was like a typical doctor's consulting room. He stared at the door to ensure no one was about to enter. He pulled at his pants and shirt to release them from his skin. The clothing he wore was given to him when he arrived. The shirt was too small, and the pants were too big. He felt a little ridiculous. He was thirsty. In the center of the counter, there was a sink with a small tap. He did not feel it was safe enough to take a drink without permission, so he simply sat down on the edge of the chair and waited. A few minutes passed. Quinlan decided that he could probably get a drink, and no one would be the wiser. He listened and then quickly moved to the counter, picked up a paper cup, turned on the tap, filled the cup, drank, filled the cup again and emptied it. He tossed the cup in a nearby trash bin and sat down on the chair again. He felt powerful. He had wanted something simple that he had a right to want and simply satisfied that want. He wiped the moisture from his lips and realized that he was still afraid and did not want whoever came into the room next to know about his actions.

A different woman entered. "Hello, Quinlan. How are you today? Have they been looking after you properly? I hope so. It is hot in here. Would you like something to drink? Soda, iced tea, water?"

"I'm fine," he said.

"Good. Are you ready to continue or would you like more time?"

"I am ready. What's next?"

"Well, you will be glad to know that this is the last activity. You will have to wear the VR helmet and skull cap again, but none of the other apparatus. We have created a short VR presentation. This is a computer-generated video. We would like to get more information on what happened before you were stabbed. It is a walkthrough of the path from the floor of the building in which you were held to the location of the attack that resulted in your stabbing and the death of your captor. We want you to tell us what happened at each step of the way. You will actually walk as if you were there and narrate what happened and what was said at each step. We will measure your reactions as you go. Do you understand?" Quinlan nodded. "Good. Let's get you ready. I am going to take you to a special room that is set up so you will have room to walk." She put the equipment on Quinlan and led him out of the consultation room. The new room was much cooler. Quinlan breathed deeply and waited.

240

He was not sure what he was supposed to say that he had not already said. "Alright. Describe the room you were kept in and tell what happened. The system will try to create where you are. It has a lot of other data about the building to help, so the lag should be minimal. Do you understand?"

"Yes." Quinlan looked around the virtual space. There were blank walls. "I am in a small room with a bed. I don't really remember the other furniture. I think there was a small bathroom." The virtual room appeared before his eyes. "The man who stabbed me came to get me. There was a siren blaring. He turned away from the bed. "There is a door in front of me." A door appeared two meters from where he was standing. Quinlan walked to the door and reached out to open it. The virtual door responded. He walked through. He looked left and right. "I think we walked down the hallway to the left and came to a large room." The VR appeared almost exactly like the large room he had moved to. "It is just like the actual room." He looked back and forth.

"Like I said, the program has access to the building plans, but I suspect they were altered to conceal the path you took to the underground rotunda where you encountered Fempol. It has just filled out the details with what it knows. What do you remember about this space?"

"There were a lot of people milling about with red lights flashing. We walked over to a broom closet there." Quinlan held up his arm and pointed. A door appeared on the wall. It was in the wrong place. "It was more to the left. Two meters at least." The door moved. He reached out to open it. It was empty. "There were brooms and mops and buckets in there and a shelf at the back." They all appeared. "We moved them away from the back wall and the man I was with touched the shelf here." He reached out and touched the shelf. "When he did that, the shelf slid away and an elevator door opened." The VR program kept pace and a small elevator appeared. "We rode it down while he spoke about what was going to happen in the elevator when we exited it."

"What did he say?"

"He told me about some nanobots that ate flesh and left behind the base chemicals with oxygen and hydrogen."

"The sniffers did not find any evidence of nanobots."

"He said that the oxygen and hydrogen were ignited. That action destroys the bots."

"Interesting. What happened next?"

Quinlan felt his heart rate jump and wondered if the equipment he was wearing would record his reaction. The last time he was questioned, he had left what happened next out of his narrative. He realized there was little to be gained and a lot to lose by omitting it again. His first omission could be easily explained as a result of his trauma. "Well," he turned, "the wall was really a rack with some equipment attached to the back side of it. We wheeled it out of the elevator once it stopped. We were in another small broom closet. He opened a panel on the side wall of the closet, and we pushed the rack into it. The panel closed, concealing everything."

"Point to the location of the panel." Quinlan pointed. The panel appeared in the VR world.

"We left the room through a door there," he pointed again, and again a VR door appeared. He stepped through it. The VR knew the design of the large room where they were accosted by Fempol. It appeared before him. He shuddered. The thought of a knife thrust in his back made the nearly healed wound ache.

The woman picked up her COM. "I am sending you a VR rendition of the location of some data storage equipment. I want it in the lab as soon as you can." She turned to Quinlan. "Thank you," she said. "Someone will come and take you back to your room." The woman left Quinlan standing in the center of the room. She did not question his previous omission. He felt a sense of relief, removed the apparatus from his head, and waited.

Later, he lay on the bed. The story of who he was to impersonate ran through his mind. This was not a nice person. According to the women that tutored him, he did not really have to act in any specific way. It would be better to be passive and not draw attention to himself. He was to simply be alert enough to drop the breadcrumbs. He was told that the tiny transmitters had a range of 500 meters. They were solar powered. They would fit them to his thumbs just before he was to leave. They were all closed-mouth as to the exact where and when he would leave. Margaret popped into his head. An image of the heart cutout on the ass of her jeans jumped into his head and ran like a video. He could see the soft creamy mounds move when she walked. He ran his hand over his crotch and then thought that he was probably under surveillance and pulled it away. He must find her and be instrumental in freeing her. How it might benefit his future was also a consideration. He reflected on what the commissioner had promised him. "*I can offer you protection and dispensation for as long as you remain law-abiding. I can also offer you credits so you can pretty much do whatever you wish…do whatever you wish.*" Giving him the credits to do whatever he wished was a very enticing promise. He got off of the bed and sat on the floor. He stretched. The wound was healing, but it still felt tight. He started with pushups. He did fifty and then ran on the spot until he was puffing. He felt strong. He felt that he could do whatever these women demanded of him. He would find Margaret.

QUINLAN SMITH

The prison transport vehicle was state-of-the-art. It was designed as a series of modules, each housing two prisoners. There were four modules in this vehicle, allowing the transport of eight prisoners. The modules provided a mini living quarter for two prisoners. There was a washroom and sleeping and eating facilities in each module. Each module was, in fact, a cell not unlike the cells the prisoners were used to. The cells were aligned along the driver-side with an aisle along the opposite side. There were two guards observing the prisoners at all times. One patrolled the aisle, and the other sat behind a clear door facing down the aisle. There were living quarters for four guards at the front of the semi-trailer.

Transporting prisoners by other modes of travel was no longer considered. There had been a number of incidents where the process was disrupted by the male behavior or one of the extreme female groups demanding the execution of the male prisoners, especially during air travel. The modern transport vans took a little longer, but the new security protocols improved the process to such a degree that the number of problems dropped to nearly zero. Even the external shell of the trailer was made to look like any of the other self-driving ground transport vehicles that crisscrossed the country. This particular one purported to be a refrigeration trailer, taking perishable foodstuffs to the city of Seattle. It started in Hazelton, West Virginia, would take Hwy 64 to St. Louis, Hwy 70 through Kansas City to Denver. From Denver, it will travel north to Salt Lake, Portland, and finally Seattle.

Quinlan figured they had been on the road for a little more than an hour. He and the other prisoner in the cell were both sitting on bunks opposite each other. He was trying to keep his rather sullen persona alive, but he felt more and more like striking up a conversation with this man, if for no other reason than to kill boredom. He looked up from the floor at his cellmate. Their eyes met. The other prisoner held his eyes and spoke first. He was much older than Quinlan. He had salt and pepper hair and sported a short white beard over his dark leathered skin. The contrast was striking. His eyes were amber, almost yellow. Quinlan felt like the man's eyes cut his fake persona to ribbons with each shift of his glance.

"What is your name?" he asked and pursed his lips to suggest that not answering was not advisable.

Quinlan nearly blurted his real name, but he summoned the bravado his new persona carried and said, *"93450-011"*

"Don't be a little shit and tell me your name," he ordered. He was not a big man, five foot eight at most, but he was very used to being obeyed. His power was invasive.

Quinlan spoke, "Mikey, Mikey Peters." It came out quickly, too quickly. He felt he needed to be more defiant, so he added, "What's it to ya?" The man did not even respond. He simply looked away, his head rocking with the movement of the transport. There were no more attempts to communicate for two more hours. Finally, the man stood and stepped into the small toilet. The privacy consisted of a fabric screen. He heard the man relieve himself and the toilet flush. He moved back to his bunk, sat, and crossed his arms. A smile crept over his face. It was not a pleasant smile. He spoke again. "It took me awhile, but I think I have it."

"Have what?"

"Have you sussed." Quinlan did not understand the word and his forehead scrunched. "Sussed—figured out," the man clarified. "There were to be eight of us. I know, I picked them all out myself." He waved his finger back and forth at the other cells in the truck. "Do you have any idea why you are on this transport?"

"No. I'm a prisoner. When the cunts tell me to jump, I simply ask, how high. Hell, I don't even ask that, I just jump and hope I get it right." Quinlan winced inside as he listened to himself. He was trying to decide if his response was too far over the top.

"So, your name is Mikey Peters. That right?"

"Yeah. You deaf or something?"

"You ain't Peters—that's for sure. But *who the fuck are you*?"

Quinlan's brain was racing. He was looking for an explanation that would satisfy this man. He had studied many of the things that might go wrong, but this was not one his handlers had considered. He didn't think Fempol knew that this particular prisoner was the one actually orchestrating this kidnapping payoff. He said he had actually picked out all the prisoners to be shipped west, but how could that be true? Suddenly, an idea popped into his head. He let a smile slither onto his face. "Shit, you are good. You're right, I'm not Mikey. He's dead. I hung out with him and I guess that's why they picked me. They said they needed someone to impersonate Mikey and offered me a reduced sentence. I told them to go and fuck themselves and then they offered me a pardon and a pot of cash. I filled out all the papers and my lawyer said everything looked good, so I took it. I had to pretend to be Mikey. Once it was over, I would be free without any sort of record."

"I see," said the man.

"I don't think they know about you. I was told we were to be part of an exchange."

"An exchange?"

"Yeah, they said we would travel for a few days until they discovered the destination and then we would all be apprehended and sent back. But if I did this for them, I would be set free. I had to do it. Who are you, anyway?"

"My name is Clark Bacon."

"What are you in for?"

"I was a subversive. They charged me with crimes against the state. In other words, I was just a man trying to obtain my freedom. What about you?"

Quinlan surprised himself. What came out of his mouth next sounded either daring or stupid. He could not decide which. He just hoped it would satisfy this man. "I'm in for liking pussy. I got a little drunk one night, and I saw some sweet pussy, so I helped myself. They blamed me for what happened, but it wasn't my fault. All she needed to do was lay back and enjoy it, but no, she had to be a cunt." He paused. "Anyway, she ended up dead and here I am."

"Yeah, here you are." He lay down on his bunk and closed his eyes.

"Not for long, I hope." Quinlan hoped he had played his part well enough to be believed. He rubbed his index fingers over the ball of his thumbs. He could feel the rough edges of the inset micro-transmitter bundles. He pressed his thumb to the white plastic of the wall beside his bunk. A transparent dot stuck. It was not invisible, but it was definitely not obvious.

QUINLAN SMITH

The hours ticked past. Quinlan lay on his bunk. He was chewing on one of the dried cereal bars provided. The gentle rocking of the vehicle had resulted in a couple of short naps. His cell mate seemed to be sleeping but then sat up because the transport was slowing. It jerked back and forth, indicating it had come to a complete stop. About 20 seconds passed and then it started up again. Quinlan stood, walked over to the door and peered out the window to the narrow hallway. The guard was at the far end of the transport and suddenly ran past the cell door. Quinlan pressed his face to the window in an effort to see where the guard was going. She disappeared through the door in the front. Behind him, he heard Bacon's voice. "Get ready, it is about to happen."

"What?"

"Party time."

The guards were staring out the front viewport of the semi cab. The driver's side of the cab was blocked off behind a steel panel. The self-driving apparatus was housed inside. There was no chance of anyone accessing it or hacking into its electronics. It was totally secure. The transport was approaching the Eisenhower Tunnel just outside of Denver when it was stopped. The guard could see the opening to the tunnel in front of the rig. The tunnel workers had stopped traffic right after the vehicle in front of the rig had entered. It had come to a halt just outside the west bound tunnel. A series of barriers were set up. The entire tunnel was now closed to traffic in both directions.

A guard that had just entered from the prisoner's section spoke, "What is going on here?"

"We have been stopped."

"No shit, Sherlock."

The guard turned around and flipped her blonde ponytail to the side. She looked at the other woman. "Don't be an ass. Why are you out here anyway? It is your turn on sentry duty."

"Relax. They aren't going anywhere. So why are we stopped?"

The blonde woman turned back to her. "I guess we stopped because those men put up some barriers," she said and rolled her eyes.

"Do you think we should wake up Georgia and Willow?"

"They are on the off shift and probably sleeping." She jerked her thumb toward the guards' living quarters. "Think about it. Would you want to be woken up just because we stopped?" The other woman shook her head. They both watched for five more minutes.

"We have to report if the stop is longer than 15 minutes."

"Yeah, I know. Look. They are taking down part of the barrier." The transport moved slowly forward and entered the tunnel. They stared out the viewscreen as the road slowly curved to the left. They were picking up speed. Both women sat and watched. There was nothing in front of them. Suddenly, an emergency vehicle roared past them with lights flashing. It traveled quickly around a curve and disappeared from sight. "What is that all about?"

The transport slowly sped up to the designated speed limit of the tunnel and then, just as quickly, began to slow again. They could see the emergency vehicle parked across both tunnel lanes. Its lights were flashing. Two women were standing in front, waving their arms. The transport came to a halt twenty feet from the EMTs. They both approached the transport door. One stood to the side, and the other knocked.

The two women in the transport froze. It was against protocol to open the door. They could not hear the women outside, but they could see them gesturing. One kept placing her hands on her chest and jerking her body. "I think they want a defibrillator. They know it is standard equipment on these self-driving transports. Where is it?"

The other woman opened a cupboard and pulled out a small red case. She held it up and the woman outside the window nodded her head and made motions with her hand that she needed it. Open the door and give it to her. Tell her she can keep it. That way we will be exposed for only a few seconds."

"Okay. I'll open the door and you toss it out to her." She turned to the control panel and gripped the handle she needed to turn to open the door. She turned the handle. The door seal hissed as the door opened. She looked back at the panel in front of her and stared at one of the small monitors facing behind the transport down the tunnel. Immediately, she knew there was something wrong, but her brain could not define it. The other guard held the defibrillator and was ready to toss it as soon as the door opened enough for it to pass through. Suddenly, her brain found what was wrong. There were no vehicles behind the transport. The tunnel had opened to traffic, but they only let the transport through the barriers. That spelled trouble. Her hand quickly reversed direction, and the door began to close again. The guard holding the device turned her head to see why the door was closing again, but it was too late. A metal bar was stopping the door from closing, and then the small control cabin was filled with mist. Both guards turned to grab for a weapon clipped to the wall within easy reach. They both faded and fell to the floor, unconscious.

The door was pried open and two women wearing small gas masks entered the cabin. They propped the unconscious guards up. The pry bar was slipped into the handle of the sleeping cell where the other two guards slept. It could no longer be opened. The still leaking gas canister was kicked out of the cab. The air soon cleared. They lifted one of the unconscious guards up and carried her into the prisoner area. A number of the prisoners yelled when they saw someone carrying a guard down the aisle. The guard's hand was placed on the door scanner and the cell occupied by Quinlan and Clark Bacon opened.

"Well done. Get the other one." The woman dropped the unconscious guard on the floor of the cell. "Let's get out of here," commanded Bacon as he headed for the cell door.

Quinlan stepped up to him and put his hand on his shoulder. He pinched gently, pressing his thumb just hard enough to deposit one of the tracking crumbs on his shirt. "Take me. I can be of help."

Bacon turned. "You are a fracking spy that can be bought. According to you, Fempol has given you a get-out-of-jail free card. Why would you want to risk that?"

"Well, that was not totally true. They did offer to move me to a minimum security somewhere warm if I cooperated," replied Quinlan.

"Why did they pick you, anyway?"

"They said I looked like Mikey. I do sort of."

"Never seen the guy myself, so I wouldn't know. According to his papers, he was a super asshole, and I needed super assholes to ensure this kind of ground transport." The two women dressed as EMTs entered with the second guard and dumped her beside the other.

One of the EMT women touched Bacon's face. "We have one last thing."

Bacon smiled at her. "Yes. Make sure the package is safe and sound in the first cell with the guards. Handle it with care. Once it is locked in and we are gone, get the rest of the prisoners out and into the EMT. If they don't cooperate, just leave them here. I suspect they won't give you any trouble. Drop them off wherever they want in Denver. They will provide some distraction, for a while anyway. Let's go." The woman nodded in the direction of Quinlan. "He will come with me. He may come in handy. The woman grabbed Quinlan by the elbow and directed him out and the other woman closed and locked the cell door. Quinlan stepped out of the transport door and pressed his thumb to the outside of the door and left a crumb. He walked past the front fender, trying to take it all in and remember. Once they were out of the prisoner transport truck, the two EMTs headed for the emergency vehicle parked across both lanes of the tunnel. To his surprise, Bacon did not follow them. He ran to the wall that separated the east and west tunnels. There was a door nearly opposite the emergency vehicle. Bacon pounded on the door. It opened and a small man stuck his head out and gestured for the two men to enter and get out of sight.

Quinlan turned back and pressed his thumb to the edge of the door and left a bread crumb at the entrance. He saw the fake EMTs open the back door of the EMT vehicle and step inside. They were pulling a gurney out of the back and the transport truck door was still open. He had one last thought before the door on the tunnel wall slammed behind him. *They are putting something or someone into the transport vehicle.*

They were in the passageway between the east and westbound tunnels. The three men jogged down the dimly lit passage until they came to another door. Quinlan left another bread crumb. The small man opened the door and glanced out in both directions. The three men exited. There was a small utility truck parked right beside the door of the empty east bound tunnel. The small man reached out to the back of the small truck and a panel lifted up from the cargo section. He handed Bacon a small package. "You might need these. Get in. They have already opened the tunnel to traffic. We have to merge in when it arrives. Be silent until we get past the road crew." Quinlan and Clark climbed onto the truck bed and lay down. The small man slammed the lid. In the darkness, Quinlan felt the truck begin to move along the east bound section of the tunnel. He pressed his thumb against the side of the truck bed. He could not see the breadcrumb, but he was sure he had left one behind.

QUINLAN SMITH

The back of the truck smelled of grass clippings. There were tools used for gardening clipped to the side of the truck bed. They rattled in time with the truck vibrations. Quinlan tried to breathe deep. The dusty air tickled his nose. He was about to sneeze and raised his hand to muffle it. He felt a tap on his shoulder. Bacon whispered, "Put this on. The air back here is not the best." He handed Quinlan a cloth mask.

"Thanks," Quinlan whispered back and put the mask over his mouth and nose. Neither man spoke as the truck sped up. They traveled in silence for a while. Quinlan shifted his position. He ended up lying on his back with his hands behind his head. Things had taken a strange turn. His training had not prepared him for this scenario. They left the lit section of the freeway behind. There was only an occasional flash of light stabbing the darkness through cracks in the truck's bed cover. "Where are we going?"

"Back to the capital."

"What about me?"

"What about you!?"

"Are you going to drop me off somewhere?" Quinlan's mind was racing. He did not know what he should do. To go with this man might be dangerous. To not go with him might result in something worse.

"Relax. I've been thinking and I might have a job for you."

"What kind of a job?"

"That depends on how much of your story is bullshit. Personally, I think you are a much more dangerous spy than you are claiming." He paused. Quinlan could feel Bacon's eyes staring in his direction. He turned onto his side. His breath was soaking the mask. He reached under it, wiped his face, and adjusted the position until it felt comfortable. There was silence again. Bacon broke it. "I am one of the leaders of a group that you should, at least, be willing to listen to. We are not trying to overthrow the government in any violent way. That would go against our credo. We want to stop the insanity that the present government has instituted against males. We do not wish to subjugate women. We only want equality. We want to get that equality by installing the right people into government positions." He paused again. "That being said, be assured that we will protect ourselves against those that wish us harm." The truck slowed and shuddered as it passed over a series of bumps.

"What's happening?"

"We are going to change transport. Which brings me back to you. Who are you really? I recommend you spill."

The truck stopped. Quinlan heard the cab door open and slam closed. The truck bed cover flipped open. He sat up and looked around as he pulled the breathing mask from his wet mouth. They were in an empty parking lot. To one side were boats up on stilts. It was a dry dock. "Where are we?" The driver pushed him forward.

Bacon spoke to the driver, "Zip tie his hands."

Quinlan's heart rate jumped. This was not good. He raised his hands over his head in an effort to thwart being restrained. "Hey, look, I am not dangerous. In fact, I agree with everything you are doing. I am sure I can help. Sounds better than going back to prison, even if it is minimum security. Prison is prison." Bacon raised his arm and snapped his fingers. Two more men came out of the shadows and walked up to Quinlan. "Okay, okay," he said reluctantly, lowered his arms and placed his hands behind his back. The driver zip tied them and the other two marched him forward. Quinlan looked up as they passed under a sign that said: *FRISCO BAY MARINA*. They paused in the shadows and then headed down a ramp. They were at a lake. The wharf extended out about 50 meters. The group walked quickly. It was late, and the wharf was deserted. They stopped at a large boat. Quinlan had never actually seen a boat up close before, much less been on one. This one was at least 10 meters long. There were two large motors attached to the stern. His captors shoved him on to the boat and down into a pitch-dark galley. The last thing he saw before the darkness was the truck driver waving and heading back up the ramp.

The boat motors started and rumbled. The boat was moving. These were gasoline engines. The boat was backing out of the slip. A click indicated the boat was about to move forward. The boat ran through the exhaust-filled air. It funneled down into the galley. The smell was offensive to Quinlan, and he tried to hold his breath. The boat soon sped up, and the air cleared. The lights came on just as the two men entered the galley. They sat him down on a chair and stood on either side. Quinlan felt that something important was about to happen. Bacon entered. He was no longer wearing prison fatigues. He sat down in front of Quinlan.

Quinlan's mind was racing. He was flip flopping possible actions in his head. They ranged from whining that the situation was not fair and he should have been left on the transport with all the other prisoners to aggressively asserting his worth to this obviously subversive group. There was also the truth. That did not seem like a viable alternative. He would play it by ear. "Hey, Clark, I thought we were in this together," he said.

Bacon stared at him and then placed his hands on Quinlan's knees. "Let me explain something to you. Right now, we are heading out to the middle of the lake. The water is really deep. It is dark and we are not using running lights. This galley is shielded with light proof curtains." He pointed to the gray panels that covered the windows. "Once we get to our destination, I will get off the boat and get on a seaplane that will be waiting for me." He smiled. "You have a choice to make. Tell me the truth about the how and why you were on that transport or spew some crap about being a prisoner that was coerced into replacing another prisoner to get some perks on your sentence." He clapped his hands down on Quinlan's knees. "You have never spent a second of your young life in Rikers. You are much too pretty. No one comes out of that New Jersey hell hole looking like you." He nodded at the two men standing to the side. They stepped back to the dark depths of the galley. Quinlan heard a jangle of chains as they stepped forward. They were carrying a large weight that they dropped on the floor beside Quinlan. The message was plain.

Quinlan's heart raced. He looked up at Bacon. He made a decision. "My name is Quinlan Smith. I am a spy." He paused. "What else do you want to know?"

"Stand up," ordered Bacon.

"I will tell you anything you want to know." The men on either side of Quinlan grabbed him under his arms and pulled him erect. One of the men picked up the chain and wrapped it around his waist. A lock clicked into place. Shackles were attached to his feet. Quinlan started to shake. He knew he was about to die. If they dropped the weight overboard, with him attached, he would *swim with the fishes*. He did not know where he had heard that phrase before, but it definitely fit his predicament.

"Hey. You don't need to do this. I can be of help."

"How can you be of help?"

Quinlan's mind raced. He had to convince this man that he was more valuable alive than at the bottom of the lake. He blurted, "Margaret Carver. I know Margaret Carver. I volunteered to help find her and rescue her from her kidnappers." He stared at Bacon with pleading eyes. "I can be your spy if you want."

"Sit   down."   Quinlan   slowly   sat   back   in   the   chair. "How do you know Carver?"

"We went to school together. The university. We were both taking courses in quantum biology."

"How the fuck did a little shit like you get dispensation to attend university?" Quinlan started to answer. "Never mind. The question was rhetorical." He reached out and squeezed Quinlan's cheeks. "So, you know the Carver girl. Were you fucking her?"

The door to the galley opened, and another man called down, "We're here."

He dismissively patted the side of Quinlan's face. "Never mind. I don't have time." He turned to the guards. "Unchain him. He is coming with me." Bacon climbed out of the hatch. The guards removed the restraints, leaving the zip ties in place. He was hauled to his feet and pushed through the hatch and on to the deck. He was leaning against the bulkhead, and he pressed his thumb against it. A crumb was left behind. He looked around. The boat was tied up to the seaplane strut. A set of stairs was attached to the plane's pontoon. He was pushed forward and soon was sitting on the floor of the cramped cargo section. They zip tied his hands to the seat support in front of him. He could not see anything. It was dark and his head was below the windscreen. The small plane started and taxied across the lake, gaining speed. It lifted off the water. Quinlan felt relieved at what he had just escaped and anxious at what was to come. He shivered as a cold breeze blew in from the cracks in the fuselage. To raise his spirits, he pressed his thumb against the aluminum skin of the plane and then again to the cases spread out under him. His thoughts turned to Margaret. He hoped she was alright. Images of her naked breasts filled his mind as he tried to sleep.

NISHEETA DAVENPORT

Nisheeta strode into the surveillance center. She had been roused from a deep sleep. She had been dreaming of Eve. She guessed her dream stemmed from her trip to the hospital months earlier. She had caught a glimpse of one of the nurse aides when she was visiting the Smith boy at the hospital. At first, she thought it was Eve, but Eve worked for one of the law firms in the city. Her staff would have informed her if Eve had changed jobs. Her dream was not nice. She had been locked in a cage looking out between the bars at Eve as three men were raping her. The frustration of not being able to help made her dream a horror. She touched her neck. Her throat felt sore, as if she had actually been screaming instead of dreaming that she was screaming.

One of the techs came running up to her. "Sorry to wake you, Ms. Davenport but—"

Nisheeta cut her off. "What is it?" Her tone was harsh. She softened as she looked at the tech's frightened face. "I'm sorry. Tell me what is happening."

"The prisoner transport in the Carver kidnapping case had a bit of a hiccup. Everything was fine until it reached Colorado. A few miles out of Denver, just before it was to enter the Eisenhower tunnel, it stopped. The tunnel system reported an accident in the westbound lanes. It shut the tunnel down in both directions to allow for emergency personnel to reach the accident. An EMT was dispatched to travel the wrong way down the westbound tunnel."

"Was the transport interfered with?"

"Not so far as we can tell."

"Then why am I here?"

"Well, a strange thing happened. The traffic was restarted, but the transport was the only thing allowed to move into the tunnel. Twenty minutes passed before the remainder of the traffic was allowed to move. The transport just stopped somewhere in the tunnel."

"Where is the transport now?"

"Seems to be following its programmed route."

"What is the problem, then?"

"The guards are required to check in every hour with a +- 15-minute grace period. They are," she glanced up at the clock on the wall, "20-minutes past the extended check in time."

"Have you tried to contact them?"

The tech nodded yes. "No one has responded. There is nothing wrong with the equipment. Everything pings okay."

Davenport furrowed her brow.

"What is your suggestion?"

"According to the kidnapper's instructions, we were not to interfere with the prisoner transport once it was on the road. We have been scanning via drone for any breadcrumbs left by our asset and found nothing. That suggests he is still on the transport truck."

"What about in the tunnel? Any breadcrumbs?"

"Don't know yet, but I have confirmation that there was an EMT in the tunnel. It was there for about 15-minutes and then exited. The transport followed soon after. I had a team head into the tunnel to scan for crumbs."

Another tech approached. "They found a signal at the entrance to the pedestrian path between tunnels and another on the eastbound exit door. It looks like our man is no longer on the transport."

"Fuck. Fuck. Fuck. This has become a major shit show. Where is the transport now?"

"It is just entering Salt Lake City."

"Is there any CCTV footage showing the vehicles leaving the east bound lanes after the tunnel was reopened?" The tech nodded. "Show me." They watched the traffic leave the tunnel. It was bumper to bumper. "Get me the IDs of the first 20 vehicles to exit the tunnel heading east. Track them. If all the prisoners escaped in the tunnel, then they must have had vehicles waiting to pick them up. They would need at least two vans or a bus. There." She pointed at the screen. "There is a bus. That is our best bet. Find it and check for crumbs."

"What do you want me to do about the transport?"

"Send in a Fempol team and stop it."

"Ma'am, we do not have the control codes. That was part of the deal. The control codes were input to the transport and then destroyed. It will continue on to its destination."

"Look, we've been had. I will bet money that there are no prisoners on that truck. Stop it. I don't care if you have to shoot the fucking tires to do so. Stop it and find out what happened."

"Yes, Ma'am."

"Call me when it's done. I'll be upstairs in my office." Nisheeta turned to the elevator. The door opened and the Chairwoman's aide, Karen Chow, stepped out. She was about to exit the elevator when Nisheeta spoke, "Nothing to see here. Let's talk in my office." She joined the woman in the elevator and pushed the button that would take them to her office. When the door slid open, she watched Chow step out. She had a slight limp. "Is that old war wound still bugging you?"

Chow turned. "No thanks to you," she spat.

"For fuck sake, Karen—when are you going to stop blaming me for what happened to you in the arena? You shouldn't have been there, anyway. You breached the security that disallowed media people and tried to record the interrogations. It was not my fault you were shot. Consider yourself lucky you were not killed."

"For all I know, you could have shot me. It was, after all, a police bullet that hit me."

Nisheeta shook her head in disbelief at the accusation. She wanted to tell this woman what she thought of her, but she simply opened the office door and said, "Sit, Karen."

Karen Chow plunked herself down in the chair opposite the desk. She was grinning. "Don't tell me—things didn't turn out as planned. Where is the Carver girl? I am warning you. I will make it my personal mission to destroy you if anything happens to her. That is a direct order I received from the chairwoman."

"Bullshit. Save it for when you actually have the power to pull it off. But be warned, I will not take any crap from you without…never mind. Listen. Something happened in the Eisenhower Tunnel. The transport is about to be stopped and I suspect it will be empty of the prisoners. We have evidence that they crossed over to the eastbound side through a maintenance passageway and boarded a vehicle or vehicles heading east from the Eisenhower tunnel. I am not sure how they pulled that off but—"

"So, you have lost all leverage. The prisoners are in the wind, and you do not have the Carver girl. There is no need for me to come after you." She grinned. "When the Chairwoman finds out, you are, perhaps literally, fucked in your least favorite orifice."

The tablet on her desk beeped. She looked at it and stood. "Get out of my office." Nisheeta headed for the elevator. The elevator door opened. Chow followed. Nisheeta held out her arm, and the door closed, leaving Chow behind.

Nisheeta strode into the room. The personnel were all busy in front of various screens and holos. The head tech approached her and spoke animatedly, "We stopped the transport. We caught up with it as it was leaving Salt Lake. It was a lot easier than I thought. One of the officers on the scene was familiar with these autonomous transports. She simply followed it until it stopped at a controlled intersection and stepped in front of it. There was no need for anything else. She just stood there. There was no way around her, so the transport just stopped and waited. They are about to cut open the door and I thought you would like to observe."

"I would."

"I will put it up on the main holo screen."

Nisheeta watched the scene unfold in 3D. An officer approached the door with a cutting tool. The sparks flew and bounced on the black tarmac. They pulled the door open. Inside was dark. A light was focused on the transport cab. The camera zoomed into an empty cab. There were sounds coming from

264

the guard's sleeping quarters. An officer stepped into the cab, followed by the camera. The lights inside the cab came on. The door to the prisoner's section was closed, but they could see that the first cell contained guards and the remaining cells were empty.

"What the fuck," exclaimed Nisheeta.

The camera turned as the door to the guard's sleeping quarters was freed. Two guards that were locked inside could be seen exiting the transport truck. The camera turned back to the first cell. There were two guards standing at the door, waiting to be freed. The door was unlocked, and they stepped out. The camera once again followed them out of the transport.

"Can I talk to them? I want to know exact details."

"We can talk to the sergeant in a few minutes."

The camera swept back to the remaining cells. It slowly panned from the last cell to the first and then stopped. It began to zoom in on one of the bunks. The blanket was moving. Nisheeta saw the first officer pull out her stun gun and point it at the moving blanket as she reached out to pull it away from the concealed body. A person in a blue jumpsuit was lying with their face concealed by a cascade of long hair. The officer holding the stun gun poked the person's leg. Nisheeta imagined she heard a groan. The body slowly turned over and sat up. The long hair continued to conceal their identity. Then they lifted their head, and the hair dropped away. Nisheeta recognized the girl right away. Her office was filled with missing persons posters of that face. It was Margaret Carver. A very thin Margaret Carver, but it was definitely her.

"Holy shit. It's her."

"Are you sure? Doesn't look much like her picture." She reached down to a tablet and touched some icons. The screen was split with Margaret's poster on one side and a close-up screen-capture of the girl found in the transport."

"Yes, it is her. Send a message. I want her back here as quickly as possible. Take her to City Hospital. I will direct them to keep her in isolation. I don't want this to get out until I am ready to reveal it. No one in here opens their mouth. Make sure the officers involved in the apprehension of the transport are cognizant of this. Have you found any crumbs that might lead us to the escapees?"

"Just the ones on the doors connecting the tunnels. I will let you know when we have something."

"Good. Thanks." She glanced behind her. "Can you lock that out?" She gestured to the elevator.

"Yes, Ma'am."

"As soon as I am gone, I want you to make sure we don't get any *snoopy visitors*, if you catch my drift." The head tech simply nodded and watched the elevator door close behind Commissioner Davenport.

MARGARET CARVER

Anew day dawned, and the AI spoke to her, "Ms. Carver, today is graduation day. You have reached a point in your training that requires real-world experiences. Today, you will return to your previous life. How you cope with that and what you choose to do is up to you. We can only hope your deprogramming and positive training will lead you to support the human species as being both male and female working together. Your access to some high-level government leaders as well as political aspirations will soon lead to true equality of all members of the human race. Remember, we will always be here—somewhere in the background—and we will help and guide you. May the truth be with you."

Margaret responded automatically, "May the truth be with you."

The voice began the chant that had been a part of her world ever since she started her training. She joined in. Her voice blended into the chant perfectly. She stood and bowed her head.

Males are strong.

Males are creative.

Males are intelligent.

Males are loving.

Males balance the female.

THE PRISON OF POWER: A MAN-MADE TALE

Females are strong

Females are creative.

Females are intelligent.

Females are loving.

Females balance the male.

They must respect each other.

They must support each other.

They must speak to each other.

They must listen to each other.

They must love each other.

When the chant finished, she asked, "What do I do now?"

"Get yourself ready as if today is a normal day. Eat the breakfast meal laid out for you. Drink the juice last and lay down on your bed. You will go to sleep. When you wake up, you will be on your way back to your life. But it will not be the same. Your training will give you all that you need to become what you must become. Goodbye, Margaret." The voice stopped. Margaret followed the directions and soon drifted off to sleep.

Margaret groaned. There were strange voices everywhere around her. She turned over. She was lying on a small cot in a small white room. A bright light hit her eyes, and she lowered her head. Her hair fell in front of her face. It blocked the light. She could see a number of Fempol officers in front of her. One was pointing a camera at her. Everyone was frozen, as if seeing her had stunned them all. This was not far from the truth. A voice behind the camera broke the silence. "It's her. It is Margaret Carver." Margaret stood up. Her knees buckled. Two Fempol officers held her up and supported her exit from the transport. She was quickly whisked away. The drugs had not left her system, and she fell back asleep. When she woke, she was in a hospital room. There was an alarm sounding and soon her room was filled with medical personnel.

"Oh, Margie. It's your mother," whispered the chairwoman. She brushed Margaret's hair to the side.

Margaret's eyes fluttered. She opened them and tried to speak. Her mouth moved but little sound came out. Her mother reached for the water beside the bed and put the straw in Margaret's mouth. She sucked up the water greedily. She cleared her throat and drank again. "I have to pee," she said, as she pulled back the covers and slid her legs over the edge of the bed. Her mother put an arm around her waist and walked her to the bathroom. "I'm okay now," she said and closed the door behind her. She peed and then stared at her reflection in the bathroom mirror. Her face was drawn and there were bags under her eyes. She ran her fingers through her hair. The drugs were still lingering. She stretched her arms above her head. They had taken the jumpsuit and put her in a flowered nightgown. She lifted it up and looked at her body. Her once voluptuous breasts had shrunk down to perky. Her hip bones were visible. She smiled. She liked the look. They had forced her to exercise to tighten the loose skin. They had also done some magic to make her, she paused and remembered the words of one of her trainers: *"If you want to be effective and make the world a better place, then you have to start with your own body. A strong, fit body means a strong, fit mind."* She rotated her hips to see her bum in the mirror. She smiled wider. She liked what she saw. For the first time in her life, she felt pretty—beautiful even. She smacked her bare bum and let the nightie drop. They were going to start interrogating her soon. She had to be ready. She knew she had to prepare the right mix of emotion and made-up story. The story had been drilled into her. That was, in fact, her reality, but it would need the correct touch of emotional pain to make it fly. Dealing with her mother would be the difficult part. That would require a master touch, for her mother could smell a fake in a heartbeat. She would start with her previous attitude toward anything to do with her mother. She would have to turn on 'snippy bitch mode' (her mother's phrase when she got snarky) and gradually fade into an emotional basket case. There were a lot of nasty things that actually happened when she was first captured. It was pretty awful in the beginning. She would use that. She had to give the impression that she was even more anti male than before. She chanted in her head:

Males are strong.

Males are creative.

Males are intelligent.

Males are loving.

Males balance the female.

She turned and opened the door and walked to the bed. Her mother stood to help her. She pushed her hand away and got into bed. "I'm not a cripple, mother," she said.

"I see they didn't squash your attitude. I am holding off Fempol. They desperately want to interview you."

Did they starve you?"

Margaret conjured a pained face. "I don't want to talk about it," she said and sniffed. She lay back on the bed. "When can I go home, mother? Take me home. Please."

"It is late. You can come home tomorrow if the doctors say you are well enough."

There was a finality to her mother's words. Margaret knew it was better to accept them. "In the morning. Okay?"

Her mother nodded.

"Be here by 10:00 a.m. I will be ready." She pulled the covers up to her chin.

The door to her room opened and a young woman entered with a meal cart. "Ordered you your favorite. You must be starving," said her mother. The medical aide put the tray of food on the cantilevered table. She pressed some buttons and the bed adjusted itself to a sitting position. She swung the table over the bed and smiled. "Enjoy," she said and left the room.

"I must go, too," said the chairwoman.

"Don't forget—10:00 tomorrow."

"As demanding as ever. I will be here." She turned to the door and wiggled her fingers as she left the room.

Margaret lifted the cover on the plate and stared at a Beautiful Burger with extra crispy yam fries from her favorite kiosk. Her stomach growled at the sight of it. She took a bite. It was just as she remembered it. She took another bite and then ate a handful of fries. She picked up the burger again to take a third bite and then slowly set it down. She was stuffed. Her diet had been so controlled that she could not finish what she would normally eat. Two Beautiful Burgers were her normal fare. Now she couldn't eat three bites. She put the cover on the plate and pushed the table away. She closed her eyes. A little later, she half woke to her bed slowly descending to a horizontal position. She closed her eyes again and did not open them until she heard a new voice.

"Good morning," said the woman in front of her. "I'm doctor Malory. How are you feeling?"

"Good. Is my mother here?" The woman looked puzzled. "My mother, the Chairwoman, Ms. Carver."

"Oh no. It is early in the morning—just after six." She reached over and took Margaret's wrist to take her pulse.

"I'm fine."

"Yes, I think you can be discharged."

"Do I have any clothes?"

"I assume your mother will provide something."

The next four hours crawled. Finally, Margaret turned on the viewer above the bed. She switched to the daily news channel. It was important to catch up on what was going on in the world. It was late in the news cycle. The announcers had moved to more humorous items. She listened and smiled.

"The Mouse Saga continues in the Fempol offices. Today there were four incidents of mice running amok in meeting rooms throughout the building. Needless to say, the reactions, when confronted by a harmless little mouse, have been *mousesterical.*" A series of videos taken from the surveillance system showed a number of women screaming and jumping up on their chairs. "On a more serious note, a search for the nests of these mice has turned up nothing. The latest pest control report states that the source of the vermin is unknown but probably the result of upgrades to the air purification and heating system in the tunnels under the main building. They will continue their investigation. They request that any new mouse sightings be reported so they can set live traps in those areas of the building. They have been assured of full cooperation." The reporter was grinning as she finished the segment.

The news switched announcers. "This just in: a discussion by the ruling council has caused quite a stir with the right-wing representatives. It appears that a small group of left-leaning council members has put forward a proposal to revisit the Male Assembly Restrictions Act. MARA has single-handedly kept the males in our society from causing incidents of violence like the Arena Massacre over twenty years ago. Many see allowing men to gather in groups will give them the opportunity to return our society to one of violence and mayhem. The online response has been vitriolic. A spokeswoman and author of the book *The Magic of MARA: The Creation of a Peaceful World* will release a statement that she hopes will encourage the council members to withdraw their proposal. More on this at the top of the hour."

Margaret shut off the transmission and lay back. She closed her eyes. An image of Quinlan jumped into her head. She wondered what had happened to him. The nurses told her he had been released and was safe. She wondered if he had returned to university. She wondered if he had found a new tutor for the topology course. She felt a pang of jealousy and then the memory of their time spent together in her rooms. Her hand slid down between her legs and squeezed. She missed him. She closed her eyes but, in what seemed like a second, her mother was shaking her shoulders. "Wake up, sweetie. I am not sure you should come home so soon. Perhaps another day?"

"I am going home now." She jumped out of the bed and looked at her mother. "You would have napped too if you had been rudely awakened at the crack of doom. I'm fine. Did you bring some clothes?"

Her mother pointed to bags at her feet. "Nothing at home would have fit that new body of yours. You look nice, by the way. I figured you are about a size 8. They might be a little big, but don't worry. We can update your wardrobe later." Margaret dressed, and they both left the hospital

KARIMA
RANI SANYAL
(AKA VIHAAN KHATRI)

Karima belched. The curry had been delicious when she consumed it, but now not so much. Hot curry was not something she had eaten in a long time. Perhaps it was too much. It did not agree with her stomach. She belched again and lay back on the sofa. She closed her eyes. She imagined what the Fitzsimmons woman looked like and quickly pushed it away. Vihaan was asserting himself for the image created of the agent was naked and sexy. This was bad if she was to maintain her new female persona. No fantasizing about naked women, at least the way Vihaan was doing it. She must remain aloof, not filled with lust. Her job was to appear to be whatever her client wanted. Her own emotions must be subdued. She had not taken any of the cued calls. They could wait for morning.

"Do you wish to sleep now? I see your respiration has slowed. I also noticed your stomach is too acidic and must be addressed if you are to sleep comfortably. Would you like an antacid? The medicine cabinet in the bathroom has an ample supply," said Jeeves. "I suggest you respond in the morning to all the messages."

"Yes." She burped a little more demurely than her previous manly belches.

She soon lay on the most comfortable bed she had ever slept in. She breathed deep and relaxed in the minty smell of the antacid she was still sucking on. Consciousness drifted.

In the morning, Jeeves was all business. "Karima, it is time to get up and make yourself breakfast. There is plenty to choose from." Karima groaned and slid from the bed. She was naked. She had a morning erection. "It is not advisable for you to sleep naked. Since your erections have been advertised as 'On Demand', you would not be demanding that you wake up with one. Always conceal it until the situation calls for you to produce one. On a side note, the medicine cabinet contains a supply of Sildenafil Citrate and Tadalafil should you have trouble with 'On Demand'."

Karima hurried to the bathroom to pee. "Thanks for the tip, but I thought I would be alone here and not have to worry about," she paused, "exposure."

"You are right. I have been programmed to observe and provide you with advice. That was simply advice. I would never assume you would be careless. The stakes are much too high. Today you might get the kind of offer we are hoping for. As you know, our target is Karen Chow. If you can become her Loverboy, the next step will be put into play. Eat and get dressed. I will arrange the interviews. We can do it via holo. Please do not accept any offer until it is confirmed. I am always in direct communication with your handler, which makes me your only source of direction."

"I understand," replied Karima as she sat and pushed her erect penis down and leaned forward to accommodate it. Her bladder emptied with a sigh. She walked back to the bedroom and prepared her makeup. This would take at least 30 minutes to complete. Vihaan's whiskers had been removed, but there was always a couple that tried to re-assert themselves. A few zaps of the laser dealt with them. She stared at the woman in the mirror and smiled.

Later, Karima sat in a lounger, ankles crossed, with a cup of tea on the table in front of her. She was wearing a red silk kimono with a fire-breathing dragon embossed across the front. Gold colored high-heeled pumps adorned her feet. "I'm ready," she said. The sound came out at the wrong pitch. She cleared her throat and repeated, "I'm ready."

An AI voice answered the first caller. It was not Jeeves. "Ms. Sanyal residence. May I ask who is calling and the nature of your business?"

"Yes," said a hesitant voice. "My name is Greta Jost. I am calling with an offer from one of my clients. She wishes to employ Ms. Sanyal in the position of Loverboy for her household." A small face belonging to the agent appeared over the table in front of Karima.

"What are you offering?" asked the AI.

"Before I make an offer, I would like a brief 360 holo view of Ms. Sanyal. Please initiate the holo and have her stand and present herself."

The voice of the AI became harsh. "Obviously, you have made an error. Ms. Sanyal is not a piece of meat to be paraded. Tell your client that this kind of behavior is not acceptable if one wishes to gain Ms. Sanyal's favor. Any offer you might make will be summarily rejected. Goodbye."

The call ended. The holo feed from the agent remained open long enough for Karima to hear the agent curse, "Shit. Fuc…"

The AI Spoke, "We will not answer any more calls for about an hour. That will be enough time for the word to spread that we will not be trifled with and will only accept offers from those that want the best and are willing to pay."

"The Chow woman can't be all that affluent. Won't we price her out of the market?"

"Credits will not be the primary deciding factor. In the next few offers we will make what we want clear."

"What is that, exactly?"

"A permanent position. The right to maintain a private residence like this. Monogamy. An introduction to society, specifically the political world. This last one will have to be carefully inserted under the radar. We don't want to arouse any suspicions of our true intentions," said the AI.

Jeeves spoke, "Ms. Sanyal, would you like more tea? I have put some new books on your reading list. Would you like to read now while you wait?"

"No and no," said Karima. She felt her face itch under the makeup, but she did not disturb it. She knew she was required to suffer through. She closed her eyes and drifted back to when she was a boy. Little Vihaan was always hiding or being hidden. As a result, he was inside almost continuously. His mother let him watch sports on TV. Cricket was his most favorite. He knew that was so because his uncle loved to watch the Indian Leagues where men were not as subjugated as here. The signals were pirated. He always wanted to play, but knew that it would never be possible, at least until things changed. He knew he was going to be one of the people to initiate change. At least, he hoped. It would be dangerous, for if he were found out, he would be imprisoned as a male subversive. If he and others like him changed the government and the present laws, he might be able to try a cricket bat. He was sure he could hit the ball like some of his idols.

Karima shook her head. What was she thinking? Cricket? That was a childish daydream. The freedom of the males of the species was at stake. She must not fail in her tasks.

The communication system rang, and the AI answered, "Ms. Sanyal residence. May I ask who is calling and the nature of your business?"

The AI weeded out the calls until it was sure that the caller was going to present an offer from Karen Chow, the aide to the Chairwoman. It was the Fitzsimmons woman. The AI seemed to know exactly who was represented by each of the agents. The agent spoke carefully, having heard how easy it was for your offers to get shut out of the competition. If Karima Sanyal was desirable yesterday, today she was a must-have in the eyes of the agents.

"Good day. My name is Fitzsimmons. I spoke to you yesterday and I would like to offer your client a position as Loverboy /Aide to Ms. Karen Chow, Chief Aide of the Chairwoman of our great union, Lillian Carver. The conversation continued, but Karima was no longer listening. This was it. She would soon be doing what the many months of training had prepared her for. The AI would give her the details and her new life would begin.

EVE
RINNE

I t had been some weeks since the fiasco at the hospital. Eve was sitting at her desk, shuffling papers from one pile to another. She looked up as one of the office lawyers popped her head into the room. "Ms. Rinne, have you updated the templates for the property transfers?"

Eve reached out and picked up a paper. "Nearly. I have a question. I cannot…rea…make out the script on this page. Could you please clarify it for me?"

The lawyer stepped to her desk and reached for the paper. She looked at it and frowned. "I have no idea. Who wrote this?" Eve knew the edits were in fact written by this woman, but she also knew she was not going to point that out. She simply shrugged. "Well, check the archived version and use that." She handed the paper back and turned. "I need it this afternoon," she called over her shoulder and left.

Yvonne watched her go and then whispered at Eve. "Her writing is so bad you'd think she was a doctor."

"What?" responded Eve, not getting the reference.

"You know. Doctors are notorious for having illegible script."

"They are?"

"Never mind. Are you okay? You have not been yourself ever since you talked to my crazy sister. How did that go, anyway?" Eve shrugged. Cassandra's threat replayed in her head. "The reason I ask is because Cassie wants to see you. She left a message on my COM. Here, I will show you." She took out her COM and swept her fingers over the surface. She held it out for Eve to read. Eve's heart rate jumped at the mention of Cassandra. She had been given a task and she had failed miserably. The syringe was still in her bag, tucked away in a protective box. She looked up at Yvonne's COM and read the message. It was terse. She read, "Tomorrow at four. Same place." Yvonne looked at the message. "Why don't you just tell her that you are not interested." Yvonne cocked her head to the side. "Are you?"

"What?"

"Interested? You know what she is proposing. She wants to do away with men completely. She is nuts. I like men—most men, anyway."

"You just like sex with men."

"Yes. So what? I think that is normal. More normal than whatever my sister does."

"Men are disgusting."

"No, they are not. Just because you had some sort of bad experience with men doesn't mean they are all bad."

"I agree. They are not all bad, but they all have the potential to be bad and I never want to take the risk. Imagine you are in a room with rattlesnakes. They are not all going to bite you, but they all could bite you. Why would any woman take the chance?"

"That is a stupid analogy." Yvonne turned back to her desk, ending the conversation.

Eve stood outside the restaurant and watched the door. She had arrived early and now it was past four. She walked to the door and entered. It was dim. She waited, letting her eyes adapt. It was more of a café with a counter along the side opposite the booths. There were tables at the back. There were no lights on over the tables, as if to discourage any patron from sitting there. She scanned the booths and saw Cassandra sitting in the far booth. She moved to the booth and realized that Cassandra was not alone. A young woman was sitting to her left against the wall. They both had cups in front of them. The young woman was sipping what Eve assumed was tea. She slipped into the empty side of the booth. She did not say anything, mostly due to the fact that there was a stranger at the table. Cassandra smiled at her. The younger woman's face was turned to the wall. When Eve looked at her, the young woman turned to meet her stare. An involuntary gasp escaped Eve and her hand went to her mouth. The left side of the woman's face was newly scarred. The red welts and divots formed a picture. Someone had played tic-tac-toe with a knife on her cheek. There was a long cut through three Os running from just to the left of her eye and ending below her ear. The Os had obviously won the disgusting game. The young woman flipped her long, dark hair, and it covered the scarred part of her face completely. Her hair, hanging and half covering her face, transformed her into a sultry beauty who was keeping a sensuous secret. The young woman did not smile so much as purse her lips and challenge Eve to say anything about what she saw. Eve chose to say nothing.

Cassandra abruptly held out her hand. "Give!" she demanded.

At first Eve was puzzled at what she was to give and then she knew. She considered lying. She could say any number of things. 'I left it at home' to the more dangerous admittance that she had stuffed it in one of those boxes in the hospital for syringes and other medical waste. Neither of those lies would garner her any favor. She reached into her bag and took out the case containing the syringe and dropped it on the table. It was a measure of defiance. Cassandra glared at her. A whisper of a smile drifted across the scarred woman's face when she saw Cassandra's expression. It was a smile that said she understood what Eve was feeling. Eve did not know what she felt except that she was not going to be meek. Her defense for being unsuccessful at her first assignment leaped out of her mouth in a caustic whisper. "You should have told me you wanted me to kill a child." She reached out and flicked the box containing the syringe toward Cassandra.

Cassandra picked up the box and tapped it on the long fingernails of her left hand. Eve was steeling herself for some sort of chastisement, but Cassandra simply put the box in her bag on the bench beside her. Without looking up, she said, "This is Zanders, Mary Zanders. Mary was an operative, working undercover. Like you, she fucked up. Unlike you, she paid a heavy price."

"Fuck you. Fuck both of you. I was gang raped so many times I can't even separate the memories." She looked at Mary. "Those scars on your face are nasty. I bet a lot of people feel sorry for you and try to help you get through the pain. My scars are much deeper. My scars will never heal and not one single person on this planet has ever tried to help me get over it. They all recognized that there was nothing they could do. Poor Eve. She is fucked up and is going to be fucked up for the rest of her life." She stopped her tirade. "I think that killing those that did this to me and those that are like them will bring me a measure of solace."

"Then why didn't you do your job?" asked Mary.

"Don't you dare use that euphemism to describe killing a helpless child in a hospital bed. I don't kill children no matter what gender they are."

"Alright. I get it. Next time, I will direct your rather selective hate with more care. Do you want to work with us or not?" asked Cassandra. Eve nodded her head. The rage was ebbing. "Good." She looked around the café. It was empty except for a couple of lovers sitting at the front. The two girls were staring at each other, and their hands were not visible. Their preoccupation satisfied Cassandra that they were just what they appeared to be. "It has come to our attention that a group calling themselves AMEN which stands for American Males Equality Nation, is behind the latest push to change some of our laws, specifically the Male Assembly Restrictions Act. We need someone to infiltrate this group and find out what they have planned."

"How do you expect me to be accepted into a group like that? Do they even have women in the group?"

"They, according to our latest intelligence, have a large contingent of females that agree with their philosophy. In fact, it has been rumored that the upper echelon of the group is mostly female."

Mary looked at Eve. "Just because you are female doesn't mean you can't be manipulated by males."

Eve stared back at her. She felt an urge to reach across the table and slap the pretty side of her face. She suppressed it. "So—how do I fit into this? I have a history that will not make me a good candidate for membership in this group."

"Don't worry about that. We will get you a bullet proof alias. All we want you to do is watch, listen, and report. Nothing more. You will probably be given paperwork tasks. Copy all papers and files you touch and send them to me. That is all. Do you think you can do that?" Cassandra seemed to have softened, and she reached out and placed her hand on top of Eve's.

Eve did not move her hand. The abrupt change in how she was being treated froze her in place. She stared at the two women in front of her and slowly withdrew her hand. "What next?" she asked, as a way of agreeing.

"Not here. Not now. I will contact you when it is set up. Go now."

Eve stood and turned to leave. She turned back, looked at the two women, and held out her hand. "I want it back." Cassandra furrowed her brow. "I want the syringe back." Cassandra stared at her questioningly, but Eve did not lower her hand.

Cassandra made a decision. "Okay." She reached into her purse and set the box containing the syringe on the table. Eve reached out, but before she could grasp it, Cassandra's hand slapped down on the box. She looked at Mary and a sardonic smile crept onto her face. Mary nodded. She turned back to Eve. "You can have it, but it is rather useless." She opened the box and removed the syringe. There was a protective sleeve over the needle. She removed it and held it upright. Eve stared in confusion. Cassandra pointed the needle upward and pressed the plunger. A clear liquid dribbled and then shot out in an arc toward Eve. She held up her hands and moved to avoid the liquid that splashed down on the table. Mary ran her bottom teeth over her lip in a casually suppressed smile as she extended her finger with an exaggerated motion and swept it through the liquid on the table. She stuck her finger in her mouth and erotically licked it and sucked the end into her mouth as if it were a succulent piece of fruit.

"What the fuck?" shouted Eve.

"It is just saline," said Cassandra. "We just wanted to see if you would actually do it. If you had, we would have used those skills. We now know you are all talk. Don't take this the wrong way. That is not a bad thing. We are not looking for crazy killers." She reached out and placed her hand over Mary's. "We have enough of those already."

"You were testing me?"

"Yes. I suspected you were all talk. Don't get me wrong. I know you hate men and have good reason to but hating something and murdering it are two very different things. We want you to work with us, and I promise there will be no more tests." She stared at Eve, whose face was contorted into a mixture of anger, fear, and relief. Relief seemed to win the contest. "Are you still with us?"

"Yes," she said flatly.

"Good. Go now. We will contact you soon."

Eve stood and walked away. As she passed the table with the two lovers, she noticed a pungent smell of sex.

QUINLAN SMITH

He was cold and very uncomfortable. The trip seemed to be interminable, but he determined, from the bits of conversations from the cockpit, that they would be in the air for an hour. He closed his eyes and tried to get some badly needed rest. The change in air pressure pulled him out of a light sleep. They were landing. He felt the plane hit water and slow. The plane came to a stop. It rocked in the waves. Someone reached over the seat and popped a black sack over his head. His hands were detached from the seat strut, and he was hauled to his feet and dragged out of the luggage storage section. Quinlan felt very exposed. He was put in a boat. A short time later, he found himself in a vehicle with a man on either side of him. He was grateful for the warmth. Everyone remained silent until the vehicle moved. He listened to a voice he recognized as Bacon speak, "How far to the airport?"

"A plane is waiting for us. We should be in the air in about 45-minutes."

"Where are we going?" asked Quinlan. There was a brief pause and then one of the men beside him punched him in the stomach.

"Shut the fuck up," a voice commanded. "Next time, you will lose some teeth."

Quinlan gasped and waited for the pain to ebb. He made no sound. He allowed himself to be pushed and shoved. He was soon strapped into a seat that he assumed was on a plane. It was not comfortable, and it was cold. The thought of his near escape from the bottom of the lake brought thoughts of being dumped out of this plane. He decided he would risk another punch in the guts. He spoke, "I have to take a piss. Could someone remove this hood? I am not a danger." The plane rumbled in response. "Hey. Someone. Anyone. I have to use the washroom." Again, there was no response. With hands tied behind his back and straps holding him to what felt like a bench, his ability to move was very restricted. He flicked his head back and forth in an effort to free his head of the black sack that covered it. It was bunched at the top. The weight at the top benefitted his efforts, for it slowly slipped up and, with an extra hard flip of his head, it exposed his eyes, and he could see once more. The hood dropped into his lap.

He looked around the space. He was alone. He was in the dimly lit hold of some sort of cargo plane. There were pallets of boxes strapped down in the center of the space. There was no indication as to what the boxes contained. He leaned forward. He could just make out a closed hatch in the direction of the nose of the plane. He really had to relieve himself very soon and did not want to sit in his own piss. He called out again, but the roar of the engines and the vibration seemed to counteract any sound he made. He twisted himself around so his feet could reach the wall of the plane. He kicked the wall and was rewarded with a resounding bang that he hoped would be heard by whomever was behind the door and they would come to investigate. His need to pee was overwhelming his ability to hold it.

On the third bang, the hatch opened. A large man entered the cargo hold and strode down to Quinlan. "What is the fucking problem here?"

"I have to use the washroom," begged Quinlan.

"Piss in your pants for all I care."

"That will not be good for me, but I would not want to be the person who has to sit next to me when we get off this plane. I'm guessing that would be you."

"Alright, but try anything, and I will hurt you. I am not in the mood to deal with problems from the likes of you."

"Thanks," said Quinlan. The man removed the straps that held Quinlan to the bench. "I can't pee with my hands behind my back unless you want to hold it for me."

"You wish," the man said and cut the zap straps holding his hands behind his back. He shoved him forward to the hatch and into a standard plane washroom. Just before the door closed, Quinlan saw that there were six seats free in this section of the plane. The front two were occupied.

He relieved himself. He looked in the mirror at his dirt smeared face. He washed himself and opened the door. The large man was waiting for him to exit. "I don't suppose there is any chance I can sit in one of those seats?"

"Fuck no. Move." The large man shoved him in the direction of the hatch leading to the cargo section.

A voice from the front seat was heard. "Let him sit." That was all. It was the voice of Bacon. The guard shrugged and pointed to one of the seats. Quinlan sat down. He could smell food and realized he had not eaten since they had left the prison transport. Bacon stood up and looked at Quinlan. "What is your plan?"

Quinlan shrugged. "Do what I am told," said Quinlan.

"Good choice." He turned to the guard. "Give him some food." He sat facing the front. The guard tossed a box in Quinlan's direction. He caught it and ravenously ate the sandwich it contained. When he finished, he sat back in his seat. His eyes fluttered. For some reason, he was not afraid. In fact, he felt comfortable with these people. He fell asleep.

When he woke, it was again due to a change in pressure. He swallowed to equalize it and looked around the small passenger cabin. Everyone was belted in except him. He fumbled for the seatbelt and snapped it closed. He looked at his thumb and considered dropping a crumb on the plane. Then he reconsidered. If Fempol actually found them, it might put Margaret in more danger than if they didn't, at least for now. He also considered telling them about the mini transmitters embedded in his thumbs. He looked at it and realized that was not a good idea, for the fastest way to get rid of them was to chop off his thumbs. Silence on that topic was the order of the day. He would say nothing. He felt a bump as the plane touched down. There were no windows in this mocked up passenger cabin on what was obviously a freight transport plane. As soon as they stopped, the group consisting of himself, Bacon, and two guards stood. He was directed out of the hatch to the section of the plane that held freight. The whine of motors was heard as the ramp lowered. They exited the plane in darkness and entered a large hangar. There was a black vehicle waiting. Quinlan found himself sitting between the two guards. He was quiet and as unobtrusive as he could possibly make himself. Bacon turned to him. "As soon as we get where we are going, we are going to have a chat." He then nodded at one of the guards, who produced the black sack and slipped it over Quinlan's head. He did not rebel. He scrunched down between the two guards and tried to breathe deep. That was almost impossible with a sack over his head, but after a few minutes, he was able to calm himself enough, so the warm recycled air was sufficient. All thoughts were pushed aside. He thought of gravel and how much simpler his life would be if the only decision he needed to make revolved around the size and composition of rocks. He did not know where they were taking him, and he did not care. All he knew for sure was the best way to survive was to go with the flow and make himself useful where he could.

The trip was short. He was led into a building. It was spacious. He could not see, but he could hear the echoes of the sounds of machinery. He walked awhile and then the sound dampened. He was in a small room. The guard removed the sack and directed him to a chair. There was a small cot at the back of the room. The guard spoke, "Sit. Do not do anything stupid. Someone will be here to chat with you in a few hours. I will be outside. If you fuck with me, I will fuck with you."

Quinlan nodded. "No problem. Can I lay down on the cot?" The guard nodded, turned, and left. Quinlan lay on the cot. His one need was to make his life simple again. He hoped this place was going to allow him to do that, but another part of his mind said just the opposite. His life was about to get complicated. Crazy complicated.

MARGARET CARVER

I t took Margaret a couple of days to acclimate to her old life. At first, she wallowed in the decadence of her rooms, but her training from the last months started to assert itself. She felt that her new life must have a purpose. She knew what that purpose was. At breakfast that morning, she saw where to start. "Mother, may I accompany you to work tomorrow?"

"God, you sound so formal. You only call me Mother when you are pissed at me. I used to be Mum when you wanted something." She held a cup of coffee in her hands and smiled at Margaret. Margaret twisted her head to the side and gave her a sarcastic look. "Yes, Margie, you can come with. I like that you are showing interest in politics. I have a couple of meetings this week in preparation for the upcoming house session regarding MARA."

Margaret's heart rate jumped. The mention of MARA brought back memories of her purpose. MARA was a thing to hate. It was something that had to be repealed if the country was to be healed. "I would like to see how the whole law-making system works."

"Good. Didn't you take *New Civics* in high school? I thought it was mandatory."

"It is, but that doesn't mean I paid any attention. It was one of those courses where everyone passed. I remember studying and passing, but it was studying for the purposes of the test. Nothing stuck. But I would like to learn."

"Oh, one other thing—you have an appointment this morning with Fempol to discuss your kidnapping. You have not mentioned it since you got home. Was it bad? I am assuming it was and have set up a series of appointments with a counselor over the next few months."

"Mother. I don't need any of that."

"I don't care what you think you need. As far as I am concerned, you have to do this. It is for your own good, and I will not tolerate any silly resistance. Do you understand me, young lady?"

Margaret's resistance to her mother melted with her new purpose. It would be better if she became cooperative and helpful. A cover story had been drilled into her to the point where it was now the truth. That was not to say that she did not know what actually happened to her, but the reality was overridden by her new programming. No, it was much more than programming. It was her truth now. She would do everything in her power to get rid of MARA, for that would be the start. It would give males a chance to show they were not monsters. Having males rejoin the society would make the country whole again. "I understand. I...," she paused for effect to ensure that the old Margaret would ease any suspicions her mother might consider, especially suspicions of brain washing. "...guess I will go along with it, but it's a waste of time."

"Good. After we can go shopping and get you some clothes that actually fit. Now eat up."

Margaret pushed the small piece of egg she had intended to eat around her plate. "Do you know where Quinlan is? I saw they let him go. Is he back at school?"

"Who?"

"Quinlan. You know. The boy I was tutoring."

"Oh. You mean the boy you were lusting after."

"Mother! I wasn't lusting after him. He was nice, and I liked him. That's all." She waited, but her mother said nothing. "Well?"

"When did you hear he was released?"

"I don't remember. I just did. Are you going to answer my question?"

Her mother sighed. "I can't discuss that boy with you until after you have met with Fempol. They will tell you whatever they can."

Margaret sat upright. "What the fuck has Fempol Security to do with this? Is he okay or not?"

"It has everything to do with it. You were kidnapped and held for ransom. We paid that ransom and here you are."

"What has paying a ransom to do with Quinlan? He was taken with me. I saw them dump him out. I assumed they just let him go."

Her mother stood and put her hands on the table. "Stop. We cannot discuss this any further until after your debriefing. Just stop." She waited for a reaction. There was none. Satisfied that Margaret had accepted her decision, she sat again.

Margaret ate a couple of blueberries and pushed her plate away. "I'm full."

Her mother rolled her eyes. "I think I liked you with more meat on your bones."

"You mean you liked me fat. Well, I am never going to be fat again. Get used to it." She pushed her chair back and stood. "I will be in my room. Call me when you are ready to go."

She turned to leave just as the house cook-cum-maid entered the room. The woman came up to her with her hand out and said, "Hello. I assume you are Margie. My name is Rosita."

Margaret turned to her mother. "You got new help. Where is Sharma?"

"Sharma retired. Don't be rude and say hello."

Margaret turned around and said, "My name is Margaret."

"Of course," said Rosita. Her hand was still extended. Margaret shook it. She felt something press into her palm. Rosita smiled at her.

She kept her back to her mother so as to conceal her surprise. Her mother called after her, "Your new COM is on your table. Please sync with it."

Margaret quickly went to her rooms and looked at the object in her hand. It was wrapped in a piece of paper. It was a program chip designed for a COM. The words *"use me"* were printed on the paper. She slipped the chip into the new COM that was sitting on her table. She turned it on. Everything behaved as normal. She held the COM up to her face for the scanner to read and record her identity. After a few seconds, the screen opened, and text scrolled past. She read, "The sync system has been modified. This COM will serve as our contact point." The text flashed and then vanished.

She flopped down on her sofa. It was where she had climbed on top of Quinlan and let him kiss her breasts. She squeezed them. They had shrunk in size. She wondered if that would make a difference to Quinlan. There was a knock on her door. She stood up and spoke, "Yes?"

"Miss Carver, your mother is ready. She would like you to join her." It was Rosita. Margaret opened the door and stared at the woman. There was a meekness about her. Margaret was about to interrogate her as to who gave her the chip when the woman went through an instant metamorphosis. Her face became stern, and her mouth pursed. A quick shake of her head told Margaret that she was not to do what she was about to do. A second later, she changed back to the meek housekeeper. Rosita stood to the side to allow Margaret to pass. As Margaret walked down the stairs, she turned to see Rosita disappear down the hall.

NISHEETA
DAVENPORT

Dolores Fineman rapped softly on the office door and entered after a count of three. There was no need to wait for a response. Nisheeta was standing in front of a large video screen. On one side was a column of pictures of the prisoners that had been found in the cells of the transport after it had been apprehended by Fempol. On the opposite side, displayed in a column, were the transport guards that had been duped into opening the transport door. There were three larger images in the middle. Images of Margaret Carver and Quinlan Smith were on either side of the single escaped prisoner. There was a name under the center picture. It read, "Paul Rizzo."

"Who the fuck is this guy?" asked Fineman.

"He is the only prisoner that was not recaptured. He was in prison for assaulting an officer of Fempol," said Nisheeta, tapping the screen.

Fineman looked at her tablet. "It says here that he was told to disperse when he was discovered with a group of men leaving an underground bar. He was in contravention of the MARA rules. He tried to run away from the officers. In the process, he ran into one of the officers and knocked her to the ground. He was summarily hit with a stinger and placed under arrest. He was charged with aggravated assault and sentenced to five years in Rikers."

"Did anyone think to check to see if his ID papers were legitimate? Paul

Rizzo had no previous record, and yet this guy was the only one to avoid being recaptured. I think the rest were just there to distract. We researched all these prisoners before we agreed to the kidnappers' demands. None of them seemed to be worth the effort they were going through to get them released." She tapped the screen again. "Do a deep dive into this guy. I want to know who he is and why they want him."

"Yes ma'am," said Fineman, and she tapped her tablet.

"Now, what about Quinlan Smith, our little spy? You found a couple of breadcrumbs on the wall of the tunnel. That at least gives me the feeling that he is doing what he was told. Rizzo must have taken him with him when they escaped. That could mean a couple of things—either they thought he might be useful, or they decided he was dangerous. Have you found any more markers?"

"Yes. The sniffer drones spiraled out with a focus on the roads that went east. We found a couple of crumbs at a marina in the township of Frisco. It is on the local reservoir lake. We scanned the entire lake and found more on a stolen power cruiser abandoned on the far side at Dillon Marina. It looks like they took the boat across the lake and disappeared. We have not found any sign of more breadcrumbs. Our search was exhaustive. They may have found him out and dumped him in the lake. No reports of any bodies to confirm this theory, however."

"So, they drove away, and we have no idea the destination. Does that just about sum it up?"

"Yes ma'am," said Fineman.

"What about her?" She tapped Margaret's picture on the video screen.

"She seems to be safe. They were good to their word. Once they had what they wanted, they let her go."

"They had her for months. How did they treat her?"

"According to the doctors at City Hospital, she is none the worse for wear, though she lost a lot of weight."

"What about her mental state?"

"Had a little chat with the Chairwoman this morning. She told me that her daughter is definitely her daughter. To quote her, '*she's as bitchy as ever*'. We have a debriefing with her tomorrow, and we will know more then." She looked up at the screen. "As far as the guards are concerned, we have no evidence that any of them were in on it. The only thing they are guilty of is opening the transport door against all regulations. I do understand the difficulty they were faced with. It was a simple request by the fake EMTs. They chose to save a life by tossing out the defibrillator. That was their mistake. They understand that and know they will face disciplinary action."

"Dig deep into this guy," she tapped Rizzo's picture. "I want to know who he really is. I also want to know why they chose the prisoners that they chose. I suspect they chose them according to the severity of their crimes. They forced our hand in our method of transport. They knew we would follow protocol and use ground transport. We are not dealing with stupid criminals. This group is smart, which leads me to believe there are women at the top."

"There is an indication that they are part of AMEN. I doubt the kidnappers had anything to do with that religious cult up in Canada. That was a ploy and a brilliant one at that."

"They seem to have inside information. We may have spies among us."

"That seems unlikely. What does this group have planned?"

"If we knew that, we could predict their next move. We have no idea who or where they are," said Davenport. She stretched and yawned.

"The prisoners we recaptured went west. Their purpose was to distract and divert our attention. From what, I wonder?" She snapped her fingers. "I bet they went east. What is east? Well, here is east. I bet they came here. Here is the government they wish to overthrow."

"That does not give us much. They could be anywhere."

"Yes, but we have a spy. Maybe he is still active and dropping crumbs." Fineman turned to leave. "I am going to deploy two or three swarms of drones over the city. We might just get lucky." She left Nisheeta staring at the video screen.

QUINLAN SMITH

Quinlan lay on the cot for hours. He was ravenous. The sandwich eaten on the plane was long since gone. He was trying to plan his next steps. He realized he had been used by everyone. His life had never been his. There had always been someone who needed him to be or do something for them. These people were a case in point. They were going to force him to do whatever. The sad part was that he knew he would cooperate and perform whatever tasks they asked. But now his motivation had changed. He needed to look after himself. He knew he would soon have two options. He would choose the actions that best helped him in the long run. The commissioner had promised him money and freedom if he did her bidding. That was still at the top of his list. His captors were going to ask him to do something for them. He suspected that they would appeal to his gender to help them do whatever they were trying to achieve politically. He ran scenarios. He soon realized it was a waste of time. He stopped and closed his eyes. He heard footsteps.

"Get up," ordered his guard. He got up. The guard held a set of handcuffs and proceeded to put them on Quinlan's wrists. He was taken into an interview room. It was stark and empty except for a table with two chairs. On the table was a box. The smell coming from the box was heavenly. The guard pointed at the box. "Eat," he said and left the room. Quinlan flipped open the box. It was a pizza. He stuffed a piece in his mouth. The taste was heavenly.

He continued to eat, and on his third piece, a man and a woman entered the room. The man sat opposite Quinlan while the woman stood to the side. They both smiled at him. The woman spoke, "You like?" Quinlan nodded and mumbled through a mouthful of pizza. "Good. Would you like something to drink?"

Quinlan nodded his head as he chewed. He swallowed. "Some water please," he said, and took another bite. The cuff chain jingled.

"We can do better than that," said the man, and he stood up and left the room.

The woman smiled at him. She was dressed casually in loose fitting jeans with a blouse covered by a gray sweater. Her hair was mostly tied back with a few loose wisps of hair at the side of her face. "How are you feeling?"

Quinlan's hunger was almost sated. He ate more slowly. "I am feeling fine. What is going to happen to me?" he said and paused. His fourth piece of pizza was half eaten in his hand. The man returned and placed a can of soda and a bottle of water in front of Quinlan. He opened the water and drank, never taking his eyes off of his captors.

"Please sit back and listen. We would like to start with what we have researched about you. Let us know if we have anything wrong," said the woman. Quinlan nodded and nibbled on a piece of crust. "To start with, it appears that you had an almost totally uneventful youth. Your time in the YMTC (Young Male Training Center) suggests that you had potential as a male that might excel but chose not to until it was time to choose a direction for your life. We dug a little deeper and discovered that you have read a great many books that are not typical fare for a boy in YMTC. You read a lot of classics. You were registered to become what is euphemistically called a Gravel Gopher. After completing this course with what can only be termed as below average grades, you chose to take aptitude tests for a Quantum Biology degree at the university. You were accepted and started your studies. As an aside, can you tell me what the heck Quantum Biology actually is?"

Quinlan stared at her. She stared back. He suddenly realized she actually wanted an answer. He cleared his throat. "It is the study of life functions in terms of the smallest known mass particles and energy potentials." She looked back at him. She had no understanding on her face. He spoke again. "For example—a field of study might be how some birds navigate using magnetic fields. How do they detect slight variances in those fields that enable them to travel to specific places they have never been before? The research suggests that quantum entanglement plays a role. Or how plants use light quanta to power photosynthesis."

"Never mind. Sorry I asked."

The man at the table continued, "At university, you met and befriended Margaret Carver. She was tutoring you in something called …," he glanced down at his tablet. "…Algebraic Topology. I am not going to ask you what that is. Is that correct?" Quinlan nodded. He decided to let that be the end. She had tutored him. There was nothing more. Done. Finished. "How did that work out?"

"What do you mean? She tutored me."

The man and woman exchanged glances. "We think it is unlikely that she tutored you when, in fact, according to her previous course work, her understanding of the subject matter was elementary at best. So, what did you do together while you were alone in her room?" Quinlan could feel his face flush red. His heart rate jumped.

The woman said, "Just so you know—we are scanning your reactions to our questions. If you lie, we will know. We recommend you demonstrate honesty if you wish this to move forward in your favor."

"Were you lovers? Did you have sex? Or did you just mess around?" asked the man.

Quinlan breathed deeply. "We were just friends. We started to mess around, but it didn't go very far." He stopped. The man waved his hand in front of Quinlan, as if to elicit more details. Quinlan blurted, "We just kissed, and I touched her boobs."

"Why did you not do more?"

"Her mother interrupted us."

The woman walked behind Quinlan. "Good. Now take us to the day the two of you were kidnapped. Give as much detail as you can."

Quinlan looked at the woman. He had a puzzled look on his face. "Why?"

"It is something we need to know from someone who experienced it firsthand."

"I don't understand." He stared at the woman. Anger swelled. He was confused as to why they wanted him to relive something they must already know everything about. "You already know everything. You people did it. You took Margaret and killed those sweets. Why would you need me to retell it?" He dropped the half-eaten piece of pizza and wiped his mouth on his sleeve.

The man and the woman looked at each other. A silent communication resulted in the two interrogators standing and leaving the room.

He reached for the water and drank. He waited and looked closely at the handcuffs. He looked around the room. He wanted to know if he was being observed. He could see no evidence of cameras. He twiddled his thumbs and, without actually deciding to, he pressed his thumbs to the handcuffs, leaving a crumb behind. He stared down at them to see if what he left behind was noticeable. He could see edges of a round dot, but it slowly faded until it was invisible, as if the glue that held it in place became clear when it dried. The realization that these crumbs might be his only hope of rescue suddenly became crystal clear. He tried to move his hands to the arms of his chair, but the handcuff chain was too short to have both arms on the armrests at the same time. He put his right hand down and squeezed the arm, pressing his thumb to the metal in order to leave another crumb. He wanted to be rescued by Davenport and have the life she promised. The thought of that new life pushed his rising depression aside. He must find just the right locations for the crumbs. A plan started to form. Where could he put them to increase the likelihood that they would be detected by Fempol? Just then, the man and woman re-entered.

The woman spoke first. "Just so you know, the people who committed that crime are a mercenary group out of Romania. They figured that the daughter of the chairwoman of the ruling committee would be worth something. They took her to sell. We simply saw an opportunity and paid what they asked. We want to know the details of what happened. We think they are a Roma group but are not sure."

"We don't think they are very nice people and do not want to be affiliated with them in the future."

Quinlan smirked. "I don't think you are very nice people and definitely don't want to be anywhere near you."

"Point taken. We do need you to tell us what you remember."

Quinlan remembered his time with Fempol after he was stabbed. He had explained all of this before. He sighed. "I was sitting in the cafeteria at City

University. I was at the table behind the door. I liked sitting there because I could watch everyone enter and they could not see me. I was waiting for Margaret. She usually looked for me after morning classes."

"Who else was in the room?"

"There were a number of tables of girls, women, and some Sweets."

The man looked questioningly at the woman. "I'll explain later." She turned back to Quinlan. "Go on."

"Margaret came in. I remember she was wearing these jeans with a heart cutout on her ass. They were very revealing." Quinlan visualized her wonderful creamy skin through the hole in her jeans. She sat, and we chatted about the Sweets. Then someone pushed the door open. There were men in black bodysuits. I think there were women as well. One for sure because she was in charge. We tried to hide behind the door but someone in the room pointed us out. What came after is pretty much a blur, but the end result was, we were taken away. I think I was knocked out. Why are you asking me this anyway? It has long since become part of the public record."

"Tell us more about the woman."

"There is nothing to tell. She was brown skinned with black hair, and she said some things in a foreign language. Oh, and she had a tattoo on the inside of her wrist."

"Describe the tattoo you saw on her wrist."

"It was a circle that sort of looked like a flower."

The man picked up his tablet and selected something with a stylus and showed Quinlan.

"Like this?"

"Yes, I think so."

"Good."

"What happens to me now?"

The woman stood. "That is to be decided. It has a lot to do with how you fare in our program."

"What kind of program? If it is like school, I already go to the university and do not need or want to be involved with your program."

"We teach young men and women like yourself to realize that the present system of government must be changed so that men can take their rightful place in the society of this great country."

"I see. What happens now? I mean right now?"

"You will be returned to your cell until your case has been discussed," said the man. He stood and walked up to Quinlan. Quinlan struggled a little to stand up. It was a deliberate act. The man reached down to help him to his feet and Quinlan pretended to slip. He grabbed on to his forearm to steady himself and pressed a crumb to the man's sleeve. As he walked out of the room, he feigned illness again and put his hand out and grasped the woman's arm and left another crumb.

EVE
RINNE

The message came in the form of a small note stuck to her video screen. There was a time and location. It was a location Eve recognized. She knew it was from Cassandra. She would go to the café after work today. She was filled with a mix of anticipation and fear as she began to embrace the possibility that she could fight against males in a different way than she had planned. She still wanted to kill them, but now, instead of that being the main course, it might become the dessert, and that sweet taste would linger and give her pleasure long after the deed was done.

She stepped into the café and walked assuredly to the booth where she knew Cassandra would be waiting. Today she would find out who she was to be and how she was to infiltrate the AMEN group. She could see the backs of two heads a booth apart. She stopped at the first one. The face in the booth was not Cassandra. It was the other woman – the woman with a scarred face. She did not sit. She put her hands on her hips and spoke, "Where is Cassandra?"

"Sit," said the woman and then as an afterthought she added, "Please."

Eve hesitated and then slipped into the booth facing the woman she knew as Mary Zander but she now thought of as "Tic-Tac-Toe." The thought of giving her a name that was, at the very least, cruel, made her feel powerful. "Did you leave me the note?"

"Yvonne put it on your vid screen. Cassandra is not available, and she wanted me to inform you of some very important changes in our plans." She paused. Eve said nothing. She had decided not to react. She did not want to come across as some out-of-control fanatic. She knew her life was going to change, and she knew she wanted some measure of control over its direction. Mary continued. "First, I need to confirm a few bits of information we recently became privy to." She paused and stared at Eve. "Do you know the Chief Commissioner of Fempol?"

"Yeah. She is my half-sister. Her name is Nisheeta Davenport." She made an assumption that this fact was going to disqualify her from assuming the role of infiltrating the AMEN group. "We are not close, and I do not agree with her politics. In fact, we do not agree on much. When our parents died, she became my guardian. A lot of stuff happened, and we drifted apart. Eve knew that 'drifted' was not the correct word, but it might soften how much she hated Nisheeta.

"We were hoping you might be able to reconnect with her. Having a spy in the office of Fempol would be very useful to say the least." Eve made a face. "We would like you to mend fences with your sister in an effort to get a position in her office. Do you think you could do that?"

"Fuck," said Eve. She made a face.

Mary flipped her hair away from the scars on her face. The action was deliberate. "You can see how valuable that would be for us. The information you might become privy to could really further our cause." She turned her head so that the scars were on total display. "We all have to do our part."

"Fuck," hissed Eve again. "I get it. Your scars are a badge of honor."

"If it is any consequence, you won't be asked to kill children. You very well might be the single most valuable asset the Plague Warriors have ever recruited." Eve drummed her fingers on the table. "I need an answer."

"When?"

"Now."

"So, you want me to suck up to my shithead half-sister and get her to hire me to work in her office. What is it I am to do?"

"That doesn't really matter as long as you have access to communications, especially those in Fempol. We want to know what is happening. There have been rumors about possible amendments to MARA. Anything that weakens those laws will fly in the face of our basic credo."

"What am I supposed to do with my present position? I already have a job."

Mary reached out and put her hands over Eve's. "I am really sorry, but the moment you joined PW, we took your need to massacre the males of the species as a commitment. We would not expose you as long as you remained committed to us. This is our little insurance policy."

"So, you are now telling me that I do not have a choice."

"Not only do you not have a choice, but you no longer have a job at that law firm." Eve's mouth fell open. "We decided that this was too important to leave it up to you." Mary turned her head so her scars were front and center. "So now you can behave like a little bitch, or you can accept that this is a wonderful opportunity and go and get a new job from your sister. That should be easy. She already feels guilty for what happened to you at the farm. You have skills, so use them." She stood. "I am out of here. I have to report to Cassie. What is your answer?" Eve stared at the scars, especially the 'X' cut into her high cheekbone. It seemed to glow red in the yellow light. Eve nodded. "I need to hear it."

"Yes," she said. She was surprised that she did not feel angry anymore. This was something she had always wanted. This was a real purpose. "I will do it."

"Great. Go home. Do not go back to work. That will be taken care of. It will appear as if the company you worked for no longer needed you because of downsizing. You will receive glowing references. In two days, contact your sister. It will appear that you are just what the office needs." She reached into her pocket and retrieved a small device. "Take this. It is a proprietary bit of tech that will read our coded COM chips. If you ever get one, use this." Mary smiled and turned her head so that her hair covered the scars. Her face transformed. She was once again beautiful. "Give me your COM. If you ever need to contact me, just send a text to this number." She tapped the screen and handed the COM back to Eve. She left Eve sitting in the dim light. Her mind was racing. She was trying to make up her mind if this was good or bad.

She felt movement. The person sitting in the booth behind her stood up. The woman did not turn around but simply walked toward the rear of the café and disappeared. Eve watched her go. She could not see the woman's face, but noticed she had a slight limp. Eve left the café, unable to make a decision. Once out in the light of day, she realized it didn't matter.

KARIMA
RANI SANYAL

Her AI had set the initial meeting at a French restaurant in the city. It was chosen for privacy more than its menu. The Bistro Cacao was moderately priced with booths that stressed romance. She dressed in a tasteful black tux with pink highlights. She had a short argument with the AI in regard to the shoes that would be appropriate. It was really Vihaan that was arguing. He hated high heels. His feet were large, and the specialty spike heels were hideous.

"How tall is she?" Karima asked.

"You want to look striking, and the heels really contribute to the look we want. She will be in awe," said the AI. There was a pause. "She is 5 foot 4 according to my data."

"She might be in awe for a few seconds, but those shoes kill my feet. I don't want to trip and fall and look like an idiot, besides I will tower over her. I am already 6 feet and with those stupid shoes, I will make her look like a dwarf. I think the gold flats will achieve the desired effect of giving me the look of being both male and female at the same time. Her head wants a female, but her sex wants a male. This will satisfy both her needs and make me irresistible," said Karima with a smile.

"Perhaps you are right. I will defer to you, but I hold my disagreement in abeyance," said the AI.

305

Karima took small steps as she was led to the table. She knew she had to be more female at the introduction. She had relatively small hands. Her taste in jewelry had been carefully researched to match the kinds of choices that Karen Chow preferred. Her fingers were all adorned with thin gold bands between each knuckle. Her thumbs had gold bands with inset blue and red stones. Her fingernails were plain with slightly tapered edges, as was the fashion. She stopped at the table and reached out her hand, allowing the light over the table to catch and reflect the gold on her fingers. Ms. Chow reached out to grasp the offered hand and guided Karima to the seat opposite. Neither said anything. They played with their eyes while flicking micro expressions of pleasure at the other.

Finally, Karima spoke. "I am Ms. Sanyal. Karima Sanyal. It is nice to meet you, Ms. Chow."

"Karen. Please call me Karen." She smiled and then searched for a topic and landed on the restaurant. "I chose this place because we would be able to talk without prying eyes or lenses. I often get photographed when I just want to be private." Her words said she disliked the attention, but her tone suggested otherwise. She stopped. Karima said nothing, folded her hands in front of her, and placed them on the table. "I suppose you have often been told this, but I think it needs saying. You are stunning."

"Thank you," Karima said softly. She did not look down or away from Karen Chow's eyes. She held her stare. It was just the right mixture of intent: demure and, at the same time, powerful.

"I spoke to the chef and ordered for the both of us. I hope you like my choices."

"I am sure I will."

They ate dinner and chatted about various subjects. Karima felt she was being interviewed to determine if she was worth what the AI had demanded. By the time dessert was finished, she was sure that this woman would want her. There was only one last step, and it was the one that both Karima and Vihaan both feared.

"Would you like to retire to my apartment for a nightcap?" Karen asked and reached out to Karima's hand.

"I would like that," Karima responded. They stood. Karima was just a half a head taller. The difference was perfect. She smiled inside. Her choice of shoes was definitely the right one.

They sat beside each other on the sofa, sipping a brandy. Karima watched Karen's tongue flick out in a mixture of anticipation and indecision. Karen's COM emitted a tone. She picked up her COM from a side table, swept her finger over the surface and spoke, "Yes," she said and listened. She spoke again, "The Loverboy contract regarding Ms. Sanyal is accepted."

Karima smiled. The contract stated that all her requirements must be met. Her apartment would be paid for, and she would receive a generous monthly stipend. She would also be in a monogamous relationship with Karen Chow. There were other details regarding escape clauses. The one required by Karen Chow expired 24-hours after their first sexual encounter. Karima knew it was there to ensure that the sex was good. If it was not good for either partner, then the contract could be declared null and void. After 24-hours, it was deemed to be in effect for one year, after which, the contract could be revisited for possible annulment.

Chow put her COM down. "Stand up," she ordered. This was behavior that Karima was expecting. She stood and slipped her hands into her pants pocket as if she were a man that was following orders but was not fearful of what might follow. "Take your clothes off. Slowly." She reached for her brandy, sipped and smiled.

Karima started with the pink tie. She pulled on one end so that it hung loosely around her neck. She felt her heart rate jump. The muscles of her neck tensed. *This is it*, she thought. She decided to take a measure of control. She looked up at the lighting and said, "May I?" Karen nodded. "AI—dim the lights. Apply an amber filter." She looked at Chow and smiled. She wanted to conceal some of the details that might expose her as the fraud she was. She ran her finger down the front of her blouse. It was a new design that opened when the touch was firm. The slit gaped open. She turned to the side and heard an intake of air from Chow. She slowly pulled the blouse open and slipped it off her shoulders. One arm rose instinctively to cover her breasts. She turned so that her back was to Chow and undid her pants. She was not wearing underwear. Her buttocks came into view as she slowly let her pants fall to the floor. She stepped away from them and looked over her shoulder. She flexed her buttocks back and forth and watched Chow's reaction. "You like?"

"I like. Turn around."

"Would you like me on or off?" asked Karima with as wicked a smile as she could muster. She was not erect and silently hoped Chow would not want her 'on'. If she did, then she would have to stall to achieve the desired effect. She watched as Chow began to take her clothes off. She was wearing a black bustier corset with a cutaway bra. Her exposed breasts were large. Her nipples were erect. She took her panties off and stood before Karima.

"Off. I want to see it come up. I am assuming you can control the speed. Make it come up slowly."

Karima knew what this woman wanted from her partners. She had done her homework. "Yes, Mistress," she answered, and slowly turned around. It was a defining moment for that part of Karima. There was Vihaan. He turned. She turned. He visualized one of the naked surrogates he had practiced lovemaking. His penis slowly stiffened and became erect.

Chow reached out and touched it. "Oh, it feels incredibly real."

"It was incredibly expensive."

"Turn around," she said and reached out, grabbed Karima's hips and spun her around. "I want to see that ass." She ran her hands up and down her buttocks. "Holy shit, you have a firm ass. How many hours a day do you work out?" She smacked her ass. "You are better than any man I have ever been with." She spun Karima around so hard she nearly lost her balance. She pushed the sofa table to the side, flopped down on the sofa and spread her legs. "Now get over here and fuck the shit out of me."

MARGARET CARVER

Margaret sat in a waiting room. Her mother had dropped her off and gone to her office. After her debrief she was to call her, and they would go shopping for clothes. Her COM buzzed, and she glanced at the screen. Some terse text scrolled past and a small icon appeared. "Run this," it said. She tapped the icon. Nothing discernable happened.

A young woman entered the waiting room, approached her and spoke, "Ms. Carver?" Margaret nodded. "You can go in now. Room 3."

Margaret stood and entered an austere room. The table was large, and she could see her name on a tent card in the middle of the far side of the table. She sat in the chair in front of her name. It was the only chair on that side. She felt small, for the chair seemed to swallow her. She felt prepared and unprepared at the same time. The chant started to march through her head. *Males are strong. Females are strong.* She felt a rush of what she knew was akin to a power surge. She pushed the words aside and wiggled in the chair. It was the largest chair in the room. It seemed like she was directed to the large chair to give her the sense that she was important. She did not feel important. She felt like she was being mocked. She stood and traded the large chair for one of the chairs placed against the wall. It calmed her. *Males are creative. Females are creative.*

The door opened, and four women entered the room. They all wore the uniform of Fempol. They said nothing as they took a seat at the table facing Margaret. Margaret stared at them. It was not a polite stare. She was on edge and expected these officers to try to make her seem at fault for what happened to her.

"Good morning, Ms. Carver," said the woman directly opposite. That was followed by a series of *Good Mornings* from the other officers. They did not introduce themselves. "First of all, speaking for all of Fempol, we are glad you are home safe. I hope you are getting on with your life. We are here to try to find out what happened to you. We would also like to know anything you can tell us about your captors, so we might apprehend them. If these people are not brought to justice, others will attempt to blackmail the government into seceding to their demands. Precedents must not be set."

The woman beside her spoke, "If this becomes too much, please tell us and we can recess or reschedule." She smiled weakly, as if she could relate to the trauma that Margaret had endured.

"Yes. This interview is not intended to add to what was most assuredly a very stressful time in your life. Please let us know if you require a recess. We would, however, like to bring this matter to a conclusion as soon as we are able."

Margaret nodded. "I want to get this over with as well. Ask me anything you want."

The officer in charge looked at the other officers, and they nodded at each other. She turned back to Margaret, "This interview will begin and will be recorded in accordance with the rules of this process."

A small woman sitting opposite spoke. "Ms. Carver, would you please tell us what happened on the morning of your abduction. Please start with when you entered the university cafeteria."

Margaret cleared her throat. "I was rushing. My class had gone overtime, and I was supposed to meet my friend Quinlan for lunch. I was wearing some new jeans, and I wanted to show them off. He was at the table behind the door. After modeling my new jeans, I sat with him. I was happy because he liked the jeans."

"Just to be clear, this boy was a classmate?"

"Yes, and he was my friend."

"How well did you know him? Might he have been part of the cabal that kidnapped you?"

"No," responded Margaret, as if the question was absurd. "Quinlan is my friend. Please don't try to make him the villain. Do you know where he is? The kidnappers freed him, so I assume he is back at school. I would like to see him." None of the officers said anything. "Don't tell me you arrested him. Is he in jail?" She looked from face to face. "If he is and you want this interrogation to continue, you had better free him. He has done nothing wrong. He tried to stop them and paid the price. They hit and kicked him and then tossed him out of the garbage truck they used to transport us."

"Garbage truck?"

"They took us to a freight bay. A modified garbage truck picked us up and took us away. They tossed Quinlan out after they were well away from the university."

"What we know of Mr. Smith is as follows: After the kidnappers, as you say, kicked him out, he was picked up by a cell of the AMEN group."

"AMEN?" queried Margaret.

"American Males Equality Nation. They have many cells throughout the country and are formally defined as a terrorist group."

The small woman continued, "We rescued him from this group, but he was stabbed in the process." Margaret sucked in her breath. "He healed up fine."

"So where is he. I need to see him," said Margaret softly.

"He volunteered to help secure your release." The woman's tone held a hesitancy. Fear welled up in Margaret. The woman hurried on. "At this time, we do not know what happened to him. He was taken. We are looking for him and fully expect to discover his whereabouts very soon."

"Now, Ms. Carver, can you tell us what happened to you during the time you were a prisoner?" said one of the officers who had not yet spoken.

The door to the room opened and Karen Chow entered with a flourish. Everyone stared at her. The lead interviewer recognized her and stood. "This is a closed interview, Ms. Chow. I must ask you to leave."

"Good morning, Margaret, I am glad to see you are well," said Ms. Chow. "I am here at the behest of your mother. She thought you might need someone to temper this interrogation."

"This is not an interrogation. A report will be prepared specifically for the chairwoman. Interference by the ruling council at this juncture is not only inappropriate but unlawful. Please leave." Karen Chow pulled a chair from the wall to the table and sat defiantly. One of the officers picked up a tablet and entered some text. There was a response. She entered more text. The response was delayed. The entire room waited. Karen Chow sat and folded her arms. "We are attempting to confirm your statement that you are here at the behest of the chairwoman. She was not only informed of this interview, she requested it."

Ms. Chow spoke, "So Margaret, tell me what happened to you during your incarceration. What did they do to you? What were their motives for keeping you for all that time? Were you tortured? Did they starve you? Did they try to make you like them? Did they mess with your head?"

"Ms. Chow, this is very inappropriate. You do not have the right to ask questions of this girl."

"It is probably the only way I will get answers," said Chow defiantly. The tablet beeped. The officer looked down at the response and looked up with a smile on her face. She entered something into her tablet and waited.

A few seconds later, the door opened and two Fempol officers entered. They walked to either side of Karen Chow. One spoke, "Please come with us, Ms. Chow."

Karen Chow stood. "This isn't finished," she said defiantly. She was escorted from the room.

"We are sorry. May we continue?" asked the lead interviewer. Margaret nodded. "Please tell us in your own words what happened to you after your capture."

Margaret slowly breathed in and out. It was time. She had to tell the prepared story to people trained to detect untruth. It was a simple story. She had it all memorized. She was kept in a cell that she described as a jail cell. She did not know where she was being held. She only had contact with her jailers. She was treated as a prisoner and nothing more. She personally decided to lose weight and get in shape. She had little else to occupy her time. On the day she appeared in the transport, she could remember nothing. They had probably drugged her food. She woke up in the transport truck. The officers asked her questions. She easily answered them. No one seemed to suspect she might lie. She had accepted her new role. She had to serve her country and bring it back to normalcy. The chant in her head served to calm her. *Males balance the female. Females balance the male.* "That is everything I know. If I think of anything else, I will be sure to let you know. Now, I wish to go shopping with my mother." She paused and then added for effect, "The Chairwoman."

NISHEETA
DAVENPORT

Nisheeta sat reading the report on the debrief of Margaret Carver. It was not really telling her anything she didn't know already. According to the girl, they simply held her and then freed her. The threatened torture never happened. She seemed to be in good shape both physically and psychologically. She flipped through the pages on her tablet. She stopped at an addendum. It was a report that highlighted Karen Chow. It described how she had tried to take over the debrief of Margaret Carver. It was pointed out that she was in contravention of the rules that stipulated the personnel that were designated to the task. There were security protocols that must be followed, and she ignored them. Nisheeta smiled as she read the description of her removal. She smiled again as she decided that something more permanent must be done. She needed to be reported to the ruling council with a copy sent to the chairwoman. She really wanted to get the woman fired, but her plan might have consequences for her own position. Rule number one of anyone in a position of power who wanted to keep that position was to not piss off your boss. She decided that an informal message sent only to the chairwoman would be the best course of action. It would be up to her to discipline the Chow woman. She set about writing the notice when there was a rap on her door. "Yes," she called.

Dolores Fineman entered. She was excited. "We got a hit. Actually, we got two hits."

"Where?"

"That is the weird part. Both hits are in apartments in the suburbs. We think they are stuck to clothes and are most likely in some pile of laundry. The houses were not occupied when we got the hits. We think that Quinlan touched some of his guards and they simply wore the clothing home. We identified the occupants and followed them. They both disappear into a sensor hole, and we lost them. I have assigned an operative to hang out near the location where they disappear. We should discover Quinlan's location soon."

"Stop. I do not want to lose this chance to discover a cell of AMEN. I have been told that they have strict protocols when they are discovered. Remember what happened when we raided the underground entrance where they last held Quinlan? They destroyed everything before we could gain proper access. They even tried to kill him. We need to capture and interrogate these people without being discovered. Keep everything under surveillance until we know more."

"What about the boy? His life might be in danger."

"I know, but that is what he signed up for."

The next morning when Nisheeta arrived, Dolores was waiting for her. "Something is wrong."

"Not out here," said Nisheeta and they both entered her office. They sat down. "What is the problem?"

"Those two suspects' apartments where we discovered the crumbs have been emptied overnight. There is nothing there but bare walls."

"Did you follow them when they exited?"

"That is just it. They never came out. We have no idea where they went once they entered the black hole. We found a couple of entrances to similar unused underground transport systems. That led us nowhere."

"They obviously suspected we were coming. But how?"

"The drones. It was my fault. I activated a couple hundred of them to sweep the city quickly. Someone must have noticed and figured out we were looking for them."

"Get a platoon of officers with sniffers and scanners down there and search every possible hidey-hole. Find the boy, if he is still alive."

"Yes, ma'am," said Dolores.

EVE
RINNE

Eve debated whether to call her sister or just drop in. She decided it would be better if she showed up. She would arrive with what she thought of as confident contrition. Two things that usually did not go together, but for this situation, they were perfect. She entered the building through the front entrance and was submitted to a rather invasive search. She did not complain. She approached the reception desk and asked to see Nisheeta Davenport. She explained to the receptionist that she was Nisheeta's sister. She gave her name and sat down in the reception area and waited. She watched the front door and wondered why the security level was so high. Everyone was searched and scanned multiple times.

"Ms. Rinne," called the woman at the front desk. "Please take the secure elevator to the seventh floor. It will give you direct access to the Commissioner's offices."

Eve entered a small elevator at the end of the bank of larger elevators. There were no controls. It obviously had only one destination. She sucked in her breath as the doors closed. She was setting out to do something that might, just might, ease the nightmares.

The doors opened. A young woman was standing in front of the open elevator doors. "Hello. You must be Eve. My name is Dolores Fineman. I am your sister's aide." She held out her hand. Eve shook it.

"Nice to meet you."

"Go right in. She is waiting for you."

Eve nodded and walked toward the door. Each of her steps seemed to turn the world around her to Jell-O. Her balance became more and more precarious. She reached out to the doorjamb to steady herself. She shook her head and chastised herself for being such a scared little boy. She pasted a large smile on her face and opened the door. As she stepped into the room, she saw Nisheeta stand and come toward her. For an instant, it felt like a threat. Eve shifted her weight on to her heels. It was a move to retreat. Nisheeta had her arms out and quickly grabbed Eve by the shoulders and drew her into an embrace. Eve kept her arms at her side. She realized she was standing like a mannequin. Her hands were fists, and her arms were as rigid as sticks. This did not feel or look like confident contrition. This looked like fear—no terror. It always came in waves whenever she was near her half-sister. Something about the memories of the time of horror and her sister being linked.

Eve lifted her arms and pulled Nisheeta to her. She returned the hug. The smell of Nisheeta brought a flood of memories that were from before. From a time when they were small and Nisheeta was her idol. She grabbed on to these and stepped back. "Hi Nisheeta. It is great to see you. It has been a while."

"It has been too long. How have you been?"

"I've been good for the most part. How about you?"

"Crazy busy. This job has me wondering if I should just take a pension and look after the garden I started five years ago and let go to weeds. What have you been up to?" Eve looked back with a face that said, '*You know fucking well what I have been doing.*' "Yes, I guess I have kept an eye on you. You are my sister and well, there were just too many reasons not to make sure you were okay. I still feel like your parent."

"Just don't start acting like it. I am a big girl."

"For sure. You are looking great."

"Thanks."

"What can I do for you? I know you lost your job. I snooped and read some of the letters of reference. They are pretty positive. I assume that is why you are here. At least that is what I hope, so I am not going to make you do something that I know you would find extremely difficult."

Eve frowned. "And what is that?"

"God, Evee, just relax. I am offering you a job. Here. In my office. My aide—you met her—is over worked. I can hire you to do the kinds of things you are good at." She paused and stared at Eve. Eve smiled back and the tension broke. Both their tight pale expressions relaxed, and the warm glow of blood flooded their faces.

"Thanks, sis. Thanks for making me feel like I am really wanted. I had forgotten how that felt." Eve smiled again. She felt fear rising like water slowly filling the tank she had just sealed herself inside. She was about to spy. She was not sure she could do it.

KARIMA
RANI SANYAL

Karima was in her own bed. She turned on to her back. She was naked and alone. She touched her penis. It was a little chafed. Vihaan pushed Karima aside. One of the skills he had practiced was the ability not to reach orgasm. A Loverboy would never actually orgasm during sex like a male. Some Loverboys were equipped with fake ejaculate, but it never really caught on as a desirable trait. It seemed that females did not like such contrivances. At least, that was what Vihaan's handlers had informed him about the research. He touched his penis again and thought of one of his repeat sex surrogates. It became hard, and he stroked himself. It was actually something his handlers had encouraged. It helped to avoid an accident. There were other ways to avoid ejaculating, but these drugs did not agree with Vihaan. He preferred to pleasure himself after. Taking drugs to maintain an erection was not something he had to do in the past, but he thought back to the previous night and realized that there might come a time when he would have to use them. He did not find Karen Chow attractive. It wasn't her body. That was nice enough. It was her need to dominate and order him around that he disliked. He knew he must follow through on his training. This was a woman he thought he could manipulate. He stroked his penis faster. She would fall under his spell; of that, he was sure. That thought pushed his excitement level to a peak, and he orgasmed. He reflected on why that thought was so enticing. It was power. It was feeling powerful. He felt powerful.

The previous night was definitely a trial run for Chow. That was part of the contract. Confirmation must be made twenty-four hours after the first encounter. Both parties must confirm their agreement, or the contract became null and void. There was a measure of gamesmanship involved. Whoever called first was going to be in a submissive position when it came to any last-minute tweaking of the contract. It was early afternoon. Karima did not get back to her apartment until early morning. They had agreed that the starting time of last evening's activities was 9:00 in the evening. That left a little under seven hours to complete the contract. Karima was pretty sure she had impressed the Chow woman, but she was not positive. This woman wanted to feel in control at all times, especially during sex. The plan was to call her just after she returned home from her office. It was the AI's job to inform Karima when that happened. That is when Karima would call. Her plan was to call and tell Chow that she had been invited out to dinner by a possible client and wanted to know if Chow was going to confirm the contract. It would split the power difference. Chow would be given first refusal, but Karima would leave her with the feeling that she could easily be replaced. As it turned out, this plan was unnecessary for her COM beeped and the AI answered. She listened to both sides of the call.

"Karina Sanyal's residence. May I ask who is calling?"

"This is Karen Chow, the Chief Aide to the Chairwoman of the Ruling Council. May I speak to Ms. Sanyal?"

"Ms. Sanyal is indisposed at the present, but she has designated me to complete the details between the two of you. If they comply with her requirements, then I, as her designate, can confirm the validity of the contract."

There was a long pause. "Fine," spit Chow. "I agree with all the clauses presently outlined in the contract."

"Would you like me to review these clauses to ensure that you understand your commitment?"

"No. I can read."

"There is one thing before we sign."

"What?"

"It is not really something contractual, but it is a request that Ms. Sanyal asked me to present to you."

There was another pause, followed by a much more satisfied tone. "I will entertain any request of Ms. Sanyal provided I can deliver what she desires."

"She is very interested in what you do—working for the Chairwoman. She would like you to be a mentor as an adjunct to her being your lover. She told me that the relationship could really benefit from her involvement in your work. Do you think that is possible?"

"Tell Ms. Sanyal that I would love to mentor her. Perhaps when our contract is over, she might like to enter politics. I know of several former Loverboys who have taken a role in government. Please have her call me. I would like her to come to my apartment tomorrow evening. I am having a few guests over and I want to show her off."

"I will impart the message when she is awake. Thank you for your call." The AI disconnected the call.

Karima smiled. "AI, I will need to buy a new outfit for tomorrow."

"Yes. You have an account at a number of the more elegant shops, thanks to Ms. Chow. I will make you some appointments to try things on. Will 4 o'clock give you time?"

"Yes." Karima stood and tossed off the blanket. She felt the cool wetness of her ejaculate on the sheets. Everything was going as planned. She smiled and headed to the shower.

QUINLAN SMITH

Quinlan sat in his cell. He only saw another human when his meals were delivered. That was twice a day. The rest of the time, it was as if there was no one in the entire building. Ever since his interview, he had spent all his time in the cell. None of his captors would speak to him. It was morning and his breakfast was late. Ever since he was held in the cell, it arrived soon after he woke. But not today. His stomach growled. He was hungry. He called out, "Hello. Hello? Is anyone out there." There was no response. He lay down and waited for something to happen. Hours passed. He tried to open the door to the cage they held him in. It was securely locked. Every few minutes he called out, but there was no response. He finally lay on his cot and considered his fate. They had left him. The training they had spoken of was obviously not for him. He was, after all, a plant—a spy. He closed his eyes and tried to sleep. Sleep would not come. His life had taken some very unplanned turns. He thought of Commissioner Davenport's offer and wondered if she would honor it. It wouldn't matter if he starved to death in this cell. He thought of Margaret and wondered if he would ever see her again. He did not even know if she was alive. He thought of Margaret's ass. He thought of school and classes at the university. Every thought was just the flit of a butterfly's wing. Each thought passed through his mind, only to fade as the next took its place in some crazy random sequence. He lay twiddling his thumbs. Suddenly, he had an idea. He figured his thumbs still had a lot of crumbs. Maybe they could send a signal further if there were many of them in one place. He sat up and began to press his thumb on the back wall of the cell. He started to write using the semitransparent dots as his pen. He wrote "I am here" followed by a capital Q. He ran out of dots just as he finished the Q. He laughed. His thumbs were empty, and no one would ever read what he wrote. The adhesive that held them in place slowly dried and they became invisible. He lay back down on his cot and waited and hoped.

Time passed. It seemed like weeks to Quinlan, but he was sure it was only days. He was so thirsty he could no longer call out. Food did not seem to be important. All he could think about was water. He imagined he was at the bottom of a waterfall with his tongue sticking out, gathering the ice-cold spray. Then the spray turned hot like molten metal. It was landing on his tongue and burning through his skin as it splashed over his face. He started and sat up. He had been sleeping, if you could call his mental state sleep. He felt a need to get to his feet. He wasn't sure why. Something had changed. It was the air. There was a cool waft of air entering his cell. Somewhere out there, a door had opened, and someone had opened it. He tried to speak. "In here," was what he intended to say, but all that came out was a low rasp. He gripped the chain-link of his cell and rattled it with all his waning strength. He rattled until he could no longer move his arms. He slowly dropped down to his knees and flopped his head onto the chain link. He began to sink lower, but his fingers were still intertwined in the woven wire mesh that comprised his prison. The cool air became a draft, and it woke him. He summoned all his strength and rattled the chain link again. He stopped and rested, preparing for another effort. He did not need to. Suddenly, the room was filled with noise and bright light. Quinlan let go of the chain link and slipped to the floor. The cool concrete pressed to his cheek and drew him down.

NISHEETA DAVENPORT

Nisheeta picked up her COM and called the office of the Chairwoman. Dolores Fineman answered. "Chairwoman Carver's office. How may I help you, Commissioner?"

"I would like to speak to the Chairwoman?"

"What is it regarding?"

"Just connect me. I know she is always in her office at this time, so just connect me," said Nisheeta. She instantly regretted her tone, which came out more as an order than a request. "I'm sorry. Is this Dolores?"

"Yes."

"This is rather important, and it has put me on edge. Is she available?"

"I understand, Commissioner. I will see if she is able to take your call."

"Thanks," said Nisheeta. She waited, hoping that she had not caused Dolores to simply leave her on hold. The thought slipped from her mind when the chairwoman answered.

"Nisheeta, what do you have for me?"

"Thanks for taking my call, Vivian. I have news regarding the young man we sent to spy for us, Quinlan Smith. He has been found."

"Is he okay?"

"He is recovering from dehydration. The bastards just left him locked up in a cell in one of the abandoned machine shops in the underground. We think he had been there for at least three days. If we had not found him when we did, he would have died."

"How did you discover him?"

"He is one smart kid. We mounted him with a series of micro transmitters—crumbs. They were imbedded into his thumbs. These crumbs can only transmit a short distance. The kid stuck at least 100 of them to the wall of his cell. The combined transmitters were much more powerful than we were aware. We picked up the signal as we scoured the underground looking for him."

"Thank God. I was fretting how I was going to tell Margaret if he was killed. She has been asking for him. Where is he?"

"We have him in one of our covert medical centers. It will be at least a couple of days before we can talk to him."

"Great. Keep me informed."

"On another note, I would like to talk to you about your aide."

"Chow?"

"Yes."

"What has she done now?"

"Well," she paused. "She tried to take over the debrief of your daughter. That is against all regulations. Please have a chat with her regarding the propriety of her behavior."

"That is my fault. I asked her to keep an eye on Margaret. She tends to go overboard. I will have a chat with her." There was a pause. "Is there anything else?"

"No. And Vivian, thanks for speaking with me."

"Keep me updated on the Smith boy."

"Yes, ma'am." Nisheeta signed off the call. The Smith boy was still on her mind. She had promised him some rather substantial rewards for his service. She would wait until after the report to determine if she would honor them. Another part of her shouted, '*You bloody well better*'.

KARIMA
RANI SANYAL

The next month was filled with dinners and parties interspersed with liaisons. Sex with Chow was never boring. It was, however, often out of the ordinary. She liked group sex. This caused some problems in regard to the contractual section on monogamy. Chow brought the subject up and requested they revisit this particular section of the contract. It was rewritten, much to the secret liking of Karima, to allow for the occasional multi-partner events. That was Karima's description. Chow referred to them as sexy soirées. They could have multiple partners, but Karima could not be ordered to service someone else. They were often orientated around costumes. It appeared that Chow belonged to a group of powerful women that entertained themselves with Loverboys of various shapes and sizes. Karima would often choose to observe at these parties. Chow seemed to like being watched and accepted Karima in this role.

Karima's handlers wanted her to take note of who attended these parties and see what information she might overhear that might be important. She was watching Karen as they entered the main living room. A number of women stared at her. A woman with long auburn hair, dressed like Robin Hood, approached. She walked boldly up to Karen Chow and kissed her full on the mouth. She took a step back but still held Chow by the shoulders. "I

THE PRISON OF POWER: A MAN-MADE TALE

have something for you. Please catch me before you leave." She then pulled Chow to her and whispered something in her ear. The words were barely audible, but Karima caught something like *'It is a special package for Dee.'* Karima watched her tongue flick into Chow's ear. Chow pulled back. The woman laughed.

Chow reached up to wipe her ear and grinned. "Cassie, you are such a bitch. Maybe we can," she paused and did not finish her sentence.

"Oooh yes," she said and turned to another passing woman in a monk's robe. As the woman passed, they could see that the costume view from the front was very different than the view from behind. They could see a completely naked behind through the gauzy material. "I'm going to get her on her knees so she can say a few prayers for me," she giggled as they followed the passing woman.

"Who is that?" asked Karima?

"Who?"

"Robin Hood."

"She is just an old friend."

"What does she have for you? Do you want me to get it if you are...?" Karima stopped. She searched for a word that was not negative. Drunk was what her mind settled on, but her mouth was more delicate, "...indisposed?" She was about to ask who Dee was, but a part of her knew the risk of exposure would increase if she asked too many questions, especially questions about things she was not supposed to hear.

Chow waved her hand in dismissal. Karima looked inquiringly at her. "It is probably a new sex toy. We went to uni together and played around a lot. We used to both belong to the same sorority."

"What sorority?"

"Be a dear and go and get me a Manhattan—a double," she demanded, ignoring the question. She walked away in the direction of Robin Hood and the half-naked monk. She turned with a sly grin, "I'll be in here."

The morning after this particularly raucous party where Karima was dressed as a unicorn and Chow as a princess, they were chatting. There had been a lot of comments to Chow about riding her unicorn. She thought the comments were wonderful.

332

"All those bitches wanted you. I'm glad you did not fuck any of them."

"I am only here for you, Karen," said Karima with a wistful smile.

"That is nice. I'm not good at sharing." She stopped. "You know that the contract says you could do whatever you wanted at these costume parties. I noticed that Councilor Bradford's Loverboy was giving you the eye. Have you ever felt like fucking one of those women?"

"Like I said, I am only here for you. I will look after you. I will make sure nothing goes wrong. I serve at your pleasure."

"That is really nice to hear because I have something I would like you to do. It is just a little task. You asked me earlier about learning the political ropes. This is your first lesson. You can become much more than a Loverboy if you can do more than just fuck. Don't get me wrong, I love fucking with you in the literal sense, but sometimes I need more. I think we have developed some trust and this job will serve to solidify that trust. Are you willing to do some small jobs for me?"

Karima pursed her mouth. It was deliberate. She wanted not to appear too eager. It was always better to suggest that she was actually thinking about it when, in fact, she was already all in. She spoke, "I think I would like that."

"Good. This is what I want you to do. There is a young man held in the secure section of City Hospital. I want you to deliver something to him."

"No problem. Do you want me to do it today? I have a couple of appointments to look at costumes, but they can be moved."

"There is a small catch. He must not know anything about it. I want it to be discovered later. Can you do that? I suggest that you find his belongings and place it with whatever he has. When he is better, he can find it." She grinned. "And assume it was left by Davenport."

Karima knew she had never purported to act as if she was stupid. It seemed like a good time to assert herself. "Will I get into trouble?"

"Not if you do it right. I was informed that the hospital is keeping him sedated, so it should be rather easy. I have provided you with a good reason for being there. You will deliver a personal note to one of the doctors who works on that floor and then enter his room and place the item with his clothes. There will also be a disturbance of some kind. If any personnel are in the room, they will leave to check it out and give you an opportunity to place the object without being noticed."

"What is the item?"

Chow tilted her head to the side and shook it. It was a clear message to not ask that question again. "Better not to know. It is the package by the door. Take it when you leave. Everything is set for this afternoon. Here is the information you need." She touched her COM. "Once it is read it will disappear, so memorize it."

Karima picked up her COM, read and memorized the message. It was simply a hospital room number and a name. "Okay, done."

"Good. Now come to bed and fuck me with that wonderful penis of yours. It is incredibly real and fantastically shaped. I especially like how it curves slightly to the left. The artist that created it made it much more real by not making it perfect." She stood and grabbed Karima's hand and led her to the bedroom.

Karima left Chow's apartment and headed home. She wanted to change her clothes and wash the sex off. She also needed to inform the AI of what had occurred. This was obviously a very important twist and might be crucial to her getting a place in the government hierarchy. There was also the item she was to deliver. She remembered the name. Quinlan Smith. Who the hell was this guy and why was framing him so important? Men were seldom deemed important enough to be involved in any sort of cabal. That is what this looked like—a cabal. But like any cabal, there had to be more than one or two players. She supposed the male was just a pawn in some elaborate game. Maybe this was not political. Maybe this was one of Chow's little revenge plots. She had been very open to Karima about some of her previous trysts and their little spats.

She entered and started to remove her clothes. She put the package on the table and spoke to the AI, "Jeeves—please scan this package, tell me what it contains, and report the contents to my handler. I am going to have a shower."

"Affirmative, Ms. Sanyal."

The water was hot. Karima liked it hot. It was the only thing that really cleaned the invisible dirt of her job from her skin. She dried her hair, put on some understated makeup, dressed, and entered the living room. "What did you find out? What is in that package, and what do they really want me to do?"

A new voice spoke through the AI. It was not Jeeves. In fact, it was not a machine at all. "Ms. Sanyal, the package contains a COM with an explosive charge secreted inside. It can be detonated remotely. The COM has also been modified so it can eavesdrop. We are not sure of its purpose. The subject, Quinlan Smith, is a person of interest. He was in the custody of one of our now disbanded cells. He was abandoned in a cage when it was discovered the cell had been compromised. I am surprised he is alive."

"Why would Chow want to kill this man in such a complicated way? She could simply have him transferred to a prison hospital. He would be easy to kill there."

"That is the same question we have been asking. We talked to one of our newly freed commanders. He interrogated Smith and found out he was a plant during the kidnapping ransom event. The boy said he knows the Carver girl. We think this is a Plague Warrior plot to kill somebody. We would like you to complete your task, but with a modified version of the package you were given. It will be harmless. There is more going on here than first appears. We want to find out what."

"Who is Dee? A woman at the party who called herself Robin Hood said something about a package for someone that Chow knows?

"I don't know but I will find out."

"I am supposed to deliver it this afternoon."

"We think we can have something for you in a couple of hours. Head to the hospital in an hour or so. Take the cab we send. Someone will deliver it to you before you arrive."

"What do you want to do with that?" She pointed at the package. "If there is a bomb in it, I don't want it left here. I kind of like my head on my shoulders."

"Have some lunch."

Karima had lunch, occasionally glancing furtively at the package. *What a bitch, giving me a bomb to carry around*, she thought. The car arrived, and she left her apartment. City Hospital was at least 30 minutes' drive away if there were no detours. The driverless vehicles rarely took the direct route. The next series of pickups was always considered. That would often extend one particular ride but improved the overall flow of traffic and benefitted efficient passenger transport. Karima sat back in the seat. She decided to catch up on some badly needed sleep.

There was a tone that signaled arrival at the hospital. She sat up, tapped her COM, and stepped out of the cab. She had not received a replacement package. She hoped they would get it to her. She stepped into the lobby and looked for a place to be that would give her a good view of the door. She leaned against a pillar and waited. Her COM buzzed. She looked at it. The message said, "Get in the far-left elevator."

She stood and walked to the elevator. She pressed the call button. The door opened immediately. There was a woman inside with a tote bag in her hand. She handed it to Karima and walked out. The door closed, and the elevator began to rise. Karima glanced in the bag. It contained some packages of what appeared to be clothing. There was a package that looked just like the one she left in her apartment. Her heart started to pound faster. She breathed in and out slowly and was calm by the time the elevator door opened. She was stopped by two security personnel. She held up her COM. One of the women scanned it, looked at her tablet, and nodded. She walked to the reception desk and asked, "Could you please direct me the Quinlan Smith's room."

"He is in room 16," she answered without looking up. Karima walked down the hall. Her COM buzzed. She glanced at it. It was a note from her handler. *'Our subject has a visitor. It is a perfect opportunity. Introduce yourself. Be cordial and make friends. All will be explained later.'*

MARGARET CARVER

Margaret was running. She hit the elevator button in City Hospital and waited. The indicators were still. The elevator was in some strange limbo for those waiting to be freed from hell. It kept trying to come down to Margaret, but it went up one floor and down one floor, only to go up again. She wanted to scream. The elevator led to the security floor of the hospital. It was obviously plotting to drive her crazy, thought Margaret. She turned and ran to the stairs. She sprinted up, only to be stopped at the top by a locked door. There was a button that, once pushed, should gain her entrance. It did nothing. She not only did not hear a buzz, but the view through the security glass was a bare, cream-colored wall. She banged on the door with her fist and pushed the buzzer. After a particularly vicious bit of pounding, a security guard came into view and saw her face pressed against the metal meshed glass. She held up her COM open to her ID. The guard came up to the door and did something on the other side. Margaret heard a high-pitched voice speak. It was coming through the speakers on the wall beside her.

"This is not an entrance to this floor. You must use the elevator."

Margaret screamed, "Then why the fuck is there a door here?"

The woman did not hear her, for it appeared that the conversation could only go one way. She simply shrugged and walked away, leaving Margaret alone with her rage. She turned and ran back down the stairs to the front of the elevator. The doors were just opening. She was able to get inside before the doors closed. She was not alone. There was a male worker and a couple of, what appeared to be, hospital techs already standing inside. The doors closed. The techs were chatting with each other about the length of their shifts. The elevator stopped, and the techs left. An eerie silence followed the closing of the doors. The male had a machine on his back. It was unidentifiable to Margaret. He was also going to the top floor. The door opened. Margaret stepped out and was stopped by a guard. She noticed that the man was not detained. He simply walked around the guard and continued on his way.

"May we help you?" asked one of the security guards.

Margaret was ready. She held up her identification. "I am Margaret Carver and I have obtained visiting rights to this floor."

The guard touched a reader to Margaret's COM and then glanced at it. "You may proceed. The patient you wish to see is in room 16. Take the hallway to your right." Margaret quickly stepped past the women and headed down the hall. She passed a small hall with a door at one end. Above the door at the end was a sign that read: EMERGENCY EXIT ONLY. It was the door she had tried to enter. Room 16 was an interior room. It did not have a window. She stood in front of the door that was the entrance to Quinlan's room. She breathed deep. She couldn't wait to see him, and, at the same time, she was very apprehensive. What would she say? She pushed the thought aside at the same time she pushed the door open. She could see a person in the bed. There were tubes going into him. His eyes were closed. She quietly approached the bed and stood over him. She was told he had arrived an hour before and was being stabilized. He was delusional due to severe dehydration. She reached out and put her hand on his head. She brushed his hair aside. It was much longer than when she had last seen him. He stirred but did not wake up. She sighed and sat down in the chair beside his bed.

Margaret turned as someone entered the room. The woman spoke, "He is sleeping now. We are giving him intravenous fluids along with something to help with the delirium. Why don't you come back tomorrow? I am sure he will be awake by then."

Margaret nodded, "May I stay a little while longer?" The woman nodded and left the room. She settled down in the chair, all the while staring at Quinlan. Her feelings for him had grown stronger. Her COM beeped. She looked at it. It was from them. Their words formed in her head and she mouthed them:

They must respect each other.
They must support each other.
They must speak to each other.
They must listen to each other.
They must love each other.

The text read, *"You will soon have a visitor. It is a perfect opportunity. Introduce yourself. Be cordial and make friends. All will be explained later."*

A tall, dark woman entered the room. She was beautiful. Margaret forced a smile. She was still trying to figure out what her handler was doing. This did not fit with her training. The woman smiled back. Her white teeth made her even more beautiful. She held a tote bag over her arm.

Margaret felt her stomach tighten. A new emotion flooded her face. She desperately tried to push it aside. Then she knew what it was. She was jealous. Why was this stunning woman visiting her Quinlan? He was hers and yet someone else was here at his bedside. She had been ordered to make friends. She did not feel cordial in the slightest. Margaret stood.

"Hello. My name is Karima. Karima Sanyal," Karima said and held out her hand.

Margaret reached out her hand. "Margaret, Margaret Carver." She turned and looked at Quinlan, sleeping. "How do you know Quinlan?"

"Oh, I don't. I am here on a task." Margaret sighed. The tightness in her stomach eased. "Is he your friend?" Margaret nodded and stepped closer to the bed. She felt protective. Quinlan was still asleep. Karima stepped up to the small closet and opened it. She looked inside. There was nothing inside. "Where are his things?"

"He was found in rags. I assume they were discarded. Why?" Just outside the door, an alarm started to howl. There was a red light flashing in the doorway. Margaret stepped to the door and looked out. A number of the staff were running down the hall. One of them gestured to Margaret to stay in the room as she passed. "What is going on?" she called after the woman. There was no response. Two minutes passed and then a voice came on. "Please ignore the alarm. There is no emergency. Again, please ignore the alarm." When Margaret turned around, Karima was stepping away from Quinlan's bed.

"Well, I was asked to leave this with him. I will just leave it in here." She put it in the closet and closed the door.

"What is it?"

"No idea, but it looks like clothes. I'm just the delivery girl." She turned to the door, turned back and spoke, "I hope he gets better soon." Karima left the room.

"Who sent you?" she called out. There was no response. Margaret went to Quinlan. She reached out and pushed his hair away from his face. She leaned over and kissed him on the forehead. He moaned and shifted his sleeping position. She looked at the closet and had an urge to check out what was in the bag. Quinlan moaned again. She stopped and turned back and whispered, "Get better soon." She sat back in the chair and closed her eyes. *'They must love each other'* floated through her head.

SEAN KILKENNY

Each evening Sean found himself sitting in front of his tablet waiting for the workorder to come through. It had been what seemed like forever. The bitch had probably forgotten. Without the workorder, he could not gain the secure entry to the offices of Fempol that he required. He had frozen the remaining blood he had obtained from the Fineman woman. He hoped that the nanobots would still be viable. Obviously, the mice he had planted no longer caused any problem, probably because they escaped the building. It was not a very hospitable place for mice. He smiled and thought, *Or for men*. His mind drifted to something he had heard before. It was from a book—no, a poem. Something his father taught him was nagging at his consciousness. Something about plans and how they can get fucked up on a whim of the gods. Thoughts of his father brought images of his father's body bouncing as the bullets hit him. He forced his eyes closed. A tear escaped and ran down his cheek. He wiped it away. "That fucking bitch has to die," he said and stood. He needed to go to his secret hideout and plan. He also needed to load his van. Tonight, he had to destroy a large hornets' nest. They were easier to deal with at night. He had his own technique for dealing with large nests. This one was purported to be massive. It was in a location that would not allow the use of fire. His female overlords had made most pesticides illegal.

Fucking stupid. He had a number of bottles of liquid nitrogen that he would spray into the nest. It worked best and left nothing behind except frozen dead hornets.

He walked to his van and drove to the alley near his hideout. It was nearly dark. There was no one on the streets. He picked his way, avoiding all the sensors that might detect his presence. He was not overly concerned in that he had a plan 'B'. He did not want to waste it, for it could only be used safely once. If his location came to the attention of Fempol, he would say he was just setting up traps to capture some squirrels that had been bothering the ladies who lived in the apartments nearby. He quickly ducked behind one of the waste containers and scanned the area for any evidence of sensor repairs. Everything looked as it always had. This was not an area that was of concern to Fempol. He quickly opened the door to his hideout and slipped inside. He waited the required ten minutes to be sure no one had followed him. If they had, they would not discover the door hidden behind all the moldy file boxes. He would just be an avid pest control officer doing his duty and checking out the space to make sure there were no nasty creatures.

He opened the door concealed behind the wall of sunken cardboard file boxes and stepped inside. He turned on his surveillance system and scanned the monitors for anything unusual. There was nothing. He sat in his recliner chair and tilted it back. He was not thinking of his hornet eradication job. He could do that in his sleep. He was trying to figure out a way to kill Davenport. He had studied the problem for years. Yes, he could just step up to her while she was out in the world and stab her, but that would result in his own probable death. He could not savor his revenge if he was dead. Savoring was crucial. He wanted to sit in his recliner and watch the newsies go on about how horrible men were for murdering a very prominent woman. That was an important aspect of his revenge. He needed to get back into her offices. He thought of the woman who had not put in the work order. She had forgotten and then deemed it not necessary—after all—the mice had disappeared. An image of the woman's big tits jumped into his head. He pressed his hand down on his penis. Suddenly, he sat up. An idea jumped into his head. If he found out where this woman lived, he could—accidentally—encounter her. He was sure she would remember him. When she did, he would remind her about the mice. He heard himself chatting her up and making her think that the mice problem had not gone away. *Those little buggers hide out and have babies. Once the babies are old enough, they will have babies. That will undoubtedly turn into an infestation. Infestations are really hard to eradicate. I recommend you put in that work order, or they will come back—with a vengeance.* He grinned to himself at how appropriate that word was. He wanted her to consider what would happen if he did not do his job.

He stood and did a search on the Webbies for lists of women that worked in the Fempol main office. He wanted pictures so he could find out her name. It was not as hard as he had originally thought. She was into social media big time. It would be easy to find out where she lived. He would concoct a pest eradication job in her building. That would provide the opportunity he needed to make contact with her.

He glanced at the time. It was hornet killing time. He grabbed two bottles of liquid nitrogen at -200 degrees Celsius. They fit neatly into his backpack. They were designed to attach to the spray nozzle. He would insert the nozzle into the nest and release liquid nitrogen at various locations. He would continue until he was sure all the insects were killed. As an insurance policy, he would wear a protective suit. He was excited. He had figured out a way to get the required work order that would get him into that building and leave his deadly present.

QUINLAN SMITH

The cool spray from the waterfall clung to his hair and eyelashes. It was the most wonderful feeling. He turned his head and stuck out his tongue. The cool, wet air caressed his face. He stood and looked down at the swirling pool of green water. He pulled off his tunic and teetered on the edge of the rock above the surface. He jumped. He woke. There was a cool, wet cloth on his face. He opened his eyes. He could see a woman standing over him. She stepped back when she noticed he was awake. "Well, hello there," she said.

"Where am I?" croaked Quinlan.

"You are in City Hospital. You must like it here. I noticed you have been here before. How are you feeling? You were seriously dehydrated," said the hospital tech. She reached for a glass of water and offered the straw to Quinlan. He tried to sit up and noticed an IV in his arm. "We can take that out soon."

"I need to pee," said Quinlan.

"Let me check your chart," she said, and touched the tablet at the foot of his bed. "Okay, I think we can disconnect you." She moved to his side and removed the IV from his arm. She helped him stand and guided him to the washroom. "Just call when you are finished, and I will help you back to bed. You need to rest." Quinlan nodded and was soon back, sitting up in bed. He reached for the water glass. The tech held on to the glass as he drank. "You had a couple of visitors earlier today." Quinlan looked up with a puzzled expression. The tech continued to chat. "You have some interesting friends. I recognized Margaret Carver, the daughter of the Chairwoman. There was another woman. I did not recognize her. She was tall, dark, and stunningly beautiful. Who was she?" The tech loved to be in the know. She wanted something to talk about to her friends. A boy visited by the Chairwoman's daughter was perfect.

"Margaret was here?"

"She sure was. She just recently escaped from her kidnappers. She spent some time here after that. I never got to see her, but my friend told me about it. She was healthy and only spent a couple of days here."

"Do you know if she is coming back?"

"I assume so. She spent most of yesterday here." She pointed at the chair beside the bed. "It is still early. I assume she will be here during visiting hours. That starts after the breakfast service. Speaking of which, what can I get you to eat? You have to eat. You lost some weight during your ordeal. You need to eat."

"I am not hungry."

"I know, but you need to eat anyway. The best way to get your appetite back is to eat. I will bring you some yogurt. What flavor do you like?"

"Blueberry."

"Great. Blueberry yogurt and raisin toast. I think they go well together. Now rest and I will be back in 30 minutes or so."

The tech left, and Quinlan closed his eyes. He was feeling much better. Thoughts of Margaret filled his mind. He slipped into a dream. He was in Margaret's room, and she was sitting on top of him. Her bare breast was in his face. He felt excitement well up. With the excitement came consciousness. He opened his eyes. He felt someone close to the bed. He turned his head. Margaret stood. She was sitting in the chair beside his bed. He could see her face. It was different somehow. Her hair was shorter. Her face was thinner. Her mouth was smiling. "Margaret?" he asked.

"It is me. How are you feeling? There is some food here. Would you like me to," she stopped. "I can raise your bed." She reached to the bed, and it tilted Quinlan to a sitting position. She pushed the table over his bed and opened the container of yogurt. "Eat," she ordered.

"What did they do to you? You are…," he stopped. His training kicked in. He understood that his suppressed statement was an inappropriate one for a male to say.

"What? You were going to say that I am skinny." She stood and did a pirouette. "I am skinny and I love it. What do you think?"

Old training rose to the surface. Quinlan knew there was only one answer. "You look great," he said and smiled. "Have you been to class since you got back?"

"Oh, we have so much to catch up on. You put yourself out there to save me. My mother told me what you did. I want you to know that I am very grateful. I want to tell you everything and have you tell me everything." She looked around. "But I do not want to talk here. I chatted with your doctor, and she told me you can leave here as soon as your electrolytes are stable. All she wants you to do is eat. So, eat." She picked up the spoon, dipped it into the yogurt, and stuck it into his mouth. Some of the yogurt smeared on Quinlan's cheek. Margaret giggled and leaned over him. She kissed him full on the mouth and licked the wayward yogurt from his cheek. Quinlan's pulse jumped. He reached up to reconnect the kiss. Margaret pulled away and glance back at the door. "Soon. I have to go. A car will come and get you tomorrow and bring you to the house. My mother has some things to say to you. I heard what you were promised by Davenport. I am going to make sure she sticks to her promises." Margaret stood and walked to the doorway. She turned and posed as if she was a 1940s calendar girl. She giggled and left. Quinlan stared at the empty doorway. He picked up a piece of toast from the tray. He took a large bite and chewed with relish as if he was starving, which, of course, he literally was.

EVE
RINNE

After a week, Eve felt like she had finally found her niche. She never would have believed that working for her sister would give her this kind of satisfaction. She was doing pretty much the same thing she had done in the lawyer's office, but her commitment was very different. The tasks were not mindless. She was often consulted by both Dolores Fineman and her sister. Her opinion was actually listened to. Being near the actual seat of power of Fempol was exhilarating. The thing furthest from her mind was spying. Whenever she thought about it, she felt slightly ill, so she avoided the concept completely. She had actually slept through the night without waking up in a sweat. She was still having the dreams, but they were not like the nightmares that usually haunted her nights.

Her office was just a few doors down from Fineman's. Nisheeta's was at the end of the hall. She was writing up a brief that Nisheeta wanted to present to the RC (Ruling Council) requesting additional funding for specialty training for the newly formed undercover division of Fempol. She was trying to formulate some reasons why this group was necessary and the kinds of training they would need to be effective. Her fingers were waving in the air above the keypad in preparation to type whatever ideas jumped into her head. Nothing was coming quickly. There was a knock on her open office door. A girl, still in her teens, was standing with a small brown envelope in her hand. She waved it back and forth. "Yes?" said Eve, glad of the interruption.

THE PRISON OF POWER: A MAN-MADE TALE

"This was left at the front desk, and it has your name on it," she said sweetly. "Do you want it now or should I put it in your mailbox?" She looked at it. "I noticed that whatever is inside must be important. This little envelope has a self-destruct stamp. It will pulse the contents with a mini EM pulse and kill any data contained inside if it is opened by someone else besides the recipient."

Eve's eyes widened. "I'll take it now," she said, standing to meet the girl halfway. She took the envelope and thanked the girl, then watched the messenger leave. She was probably a student earning some volunteer credits. Eve reached up and closed her office door. Sitting back at her desk, she set the envelope down, then flipped it over. All she could see was her name and a small stamp on the corner. It was an outline of an eye with a padlock in the iris. She had heard of these but never received one before. She lifted it up to her face and looked at it. There was a dull click from the inside. She set it down and saw that the end flap was no longer shut. She picked it up and shook out the contents on her desk. An empty envelope and small data chip bounced on her keypad. She picked it up and glanced at her door. There was no lock. There did not seem to be a need, for it was an unwritten rule to avoid any office with the door closed and to knock if the door was open. She picked up the chip and was about to insert it into her office desktop. She hesitated and remembered the device Mary had given her in the café. She took it from her bag and inserted the chip. A small holo popped up from the device. She set it down and watched. A person's head appeared. It was not a real person, but an avatar. It was incredibly realistic. The holo face smiled and spoke, "Eve. We hope you are comfortable in your new position. Your first task is to look into what happened to Margaret Carver while she was a captive of her abductors. Anything about this group that Fempol has discovered would also be useful. We have intel suggesting that the AMEN group is responsible and that they are trying to infiltrate the government. This is something we must stop using any means possible. As soon as you have something, record it to the other chip using this device. Place it in the included envelope and write 'XPWX' on the front. Drop it in general office mail. Discard this chip as it is single play." The holo disappeared.

Eve sighed. She pulled the chip out of the device and tossed it in the trash. It bounced off the edge of the bin, did a flip in the air, and landed on the floor. It seemed to say, '*I will not be discarded so easily*'. For the first time, she doubted her mission and her affiliation with the Plague Warriors. She still hated all men for what they did to her. She did not see any possibility that they might ever regain their previous status as rulers of the country and the planet. She knew she did not want to ruin her newfound connection with her sister and if she got caught spying, that is exactly what would happen. She would just have to be careful and not take any risks. If the information fell into her hands—well, was not sure what she would do. It would depend on the information. She was no longer an automaton that blindly did what she was told. She would make intelligent decisions before she did whatever anyone asked. She put the new chip and device back into her bag and reread what she had already written on the brief. She glanced up. Someone was just outside her door. She walked to her door and opened it. Dolores Fineman was just walking away. She called out to her, "Ms. Fineman, can I help. Sorry about the closed door." She did not offer any further explanation.

Dolores turned, "Eve, I just wanted to ask you a favor."

"Anything," she smiled.

"I have some family issues. My mother is ill and I have to go back home and look after her for a week or two. I was hoping you might like to be me while I am away. I don't leave for a couple of days. My sister is there right now but has to go home and I will take over. I can show you what is expected from you as the Commissioner's aide. You are a quick study." She smiled. Eve smiled back. "No problem. I will finish up this brief for Nisheeta and you can give me an overview of what you want me to do."

"Perfect."

"Give me 20-minutes and I will come to your office."

Eve looked back at her screen. Her fingers typed as if the pause had been the perfect break to bring it all into focus. The words flowed with ease. She was soon finished. The typing had blocked out the obvious idea that she would soon be in a perfect position to do exactly what the PW had asked her to do. The new job was like a pretty package that held some very nasty spying opportunities. Maybe this was what fate had in store for her. She would be a spy to keep men in their place as opposed to a killer that needed to put them in the grave.

KARIMA
RANI SANYAL

Karima slouched down in the recliner that sat in front of the large entertainment panel covering the far wall of her apartment. She had been given a couple of days away from Karen Chow. She decided to spend the time alone in her apartment. She also decided that she would not answer any calls. She would not put on any clothes that could be described as female. She was going to watch cricket the whole time and eat whatever she fancied. The final tournament of the Indian Premier League was starting, and she intended to binge watch the entire thing. No. That was wrong. Vihaan was going to do these things. Jeeves had warned her about the dangers of shifting her identity back to Vihaan, even for a short period of time.

"You must not compromise Sanyal's identity. I do not recommend you do this," he said with as much disdain as an AI could manage without sounding like his mother.

"I have three days. I have to maintain my sanity as well, and if I do not spend some 'me' time I will go crazy."

"I do not understand," stated the AI flatly.

"I know you do not understand. You are a fucking AI. Do you have a gender?"

"My name is Jeeves. My gender is inferred by my name."

"Well, mine is obviously not."

"Yes, but you have two names."

"That is something I have to deal with. And that is what I am doing. I am dealing with it. Now please leave me alone."

"I am sorry Karima, but I cannot do that."

"Jeeves, listen, for the next three days, my name is Vihaan. If I ask you for anything, you will provide it without commentary. If something comes up like being contacted by my handler, then you may inform me, and I will listen. Otherwise, please, do not bother me. That is, unless you follow cricket. If so, you can comment on anything that is game related."

"I do not follow cricket," he paused, "but I will research the game and the players."

"Great. Maybe we might have something to chat about." Vihaan turned to the screen. "Quiet. The game is about to start."

Two days passed. The apartment smelled like an unwashed human and a giant pot of simmering curry. There were takeout cartons covering every surface. The contracted cleaning crew had been canceled. Vihaan was happy for the first time since he took on this identity. He slept in the giant chair. The time difference demanded he watch games in the middle of the night. He only slept when the score was totally lopsided. He was sound asleep when Jeeves woke him. "Karima. Karima. Your handler would like to speak to you. Karima?" And then louder, "Vihaan. Wake up."

Vihaan stirred and opened his eyes. "What?" he shouted in a very male voice.

"Karima is wanted. Your handler would like to speak with you."

"No video," he said and cleared his voice. "Yes."

"Karima, we have been studying this situation and think that something is about to happen. We ran a number of scenarios and have come to the conclusion that Chow is about to do something soon. We think she is, at the very least, part of the Plague Warriors. She is likely one of the leaders. This group wants to strengthen MARA to the point where the punishments are even stricter. We think they would like to use the death penalty as a deterrent. We don't know what their plan is or who they want to kill with that bomb, so we are taking a wait-and-see stance."

Karima pushed her tangled hair away from her face. "What would you like me to do?" she asked. Her voice came out too low. She continued in a higher pitch. "I am supposed to act as her aide later this week and attend some meetings. That is the next time we will be together unless she wants me sooner for another reason."

We need to get some quality surveillance. We have a monitoring device that we want you to make sure is on Chow's person continually without her knowledge. Do you think you can do that?"

"It will be found. She is constantly scanned."

"This device just listens. It will only transmit in a compressed burst when she is out of the range of scanners. Don't worry. Just do your part and let us look after the rest."

"So, she thinks this kid is walking around with a bomb. We know he is not the target. Someone he knows is the target. Do you think it might be the girl in the hospital? They seem to be very close. Who is she?"

"That is Margaret Carver."

"The Chairwoman's daughter? The one who was kidnapped? That's the girl I met in Quinlan's room?"

"That is her. We do not want anything to happen to her. We are not as concerned with the safety of Smith. He is, however, very important to her. They might be lovers. They are, at the very least, friends."

"Why is she so important?"

"She is one of us."

"So, she is in danger too."

"We do not think so unless they know she is one of us. We have been careful. It is unlikely they have figured out she has been recruited."

"What if Chow tries to set the bomb off and nothing happens?"

"Our analysis of the device suggests that she would have to be able to see when to set it off. It does not have a large blast radius. It is filled with tiny glass beads and just enough explosive to kill anything in a two-meter circle. We will determine who she wants to kill by the location of Smith and the surrounding persons when she attempts to detonate. We will release all our recordings to the Webbies. You will volunteer to give testimony. That will ensure her arrest, putting you in a good position to replace her as Carver's aide.

"What if it doesn't work? What if she finds a scapegoat and says she knew all along what was happening and was trying to capture the perpetrators? What if she blames me? They might start an investigation into me. If they do that, my cover will not hold. One medical examination will tell them that I am not a female. That will lead them to question why I have female nanobots in my bloodstream. If that happens, I am fucked. They will subject me to some of their advanced interrogation methods, and I will spill my guts. They will go after my mother…" Vihaan stopped. The thought of his mother in prison was more than he could bear.

"Relax. We will look after you. Besides, nothing like that will happen. We have a plan 'B'."

"What?"

"A good plan 'B' must be kept a secret, or it will not work. Just do your part and all will be well."

"When do you want this done by?"

"That is up to you. Find out all future meetings and activities that might require Smith's presence and plan accordingly. We suspect this is due to happen in less than a month. The Smith boy is still in the hospital, and it is unlikely it will happen there."

"Where is the listening device?"

"We will get it to you soon. Any more questions?"

"What does it look like?"

"I do not have any idea. Any suggestions?"

Vihaan considered what items that Chow kept on her person or in her bag. He remembered her dumping her bag out after misplacing her key card. She carried a small vibrator with her and had used it at one of her parties. He knew she had used it on a number of occasions. It was remote controlled. She put it in one of her orifices and turned it on as she walked around the sex party. "Make it look like an egg-shaped vibrator with a small remote."

"A what?"

"She is a sex freak. I will tell her I bought her a little present. She will love it. I will make sure she puts it in her bag. Make sure it works as a vibrator as well as a transmitter."

"Is that absolutely necessary?"

"Yes. She will try it out and it had better work."

"Okay. I will comply and have it for you in the next couple of days."

Karima heard the line go dead. The nausea welled up in her. She ran to the bathroom and vomited. She was not sure if it was due to knowing that she finally had a job to do or the fact that she had eaten a couple of containers of curried goat the evening before. In any case, she felt disgusting.

QUINLAN SMITH

Quinlan was excited. His life was about to return to normal. He thought of what he had been offered by the commissioner and updated his definition of normal. If any of it actually came to pass, then his future life would definitely not be normal. There were very few males that had the kinds of rights Davenport had offered him. The last part of her offer was what he most hoped for. *'I can also offer you credits so you can pretty much do whatever you wish...'*. With money, he could get his own apartment near the university and complete his degree. After all that happened, it was something he had not even hoped for, but now it was a real possibility.

He was sitting in the chair beside his hospital bed. He was waiting. He was dressed casually in what he found in his closet. There was also a COM. He turned it on. It was new because it required that he sync with it. He went through the process. There were people in his contact list. He scrolled through and realized he only knew one person and that was Margaret. He guessed she had left it for him. His finger hovered over her name. He was indecisive and dropped his hand. She said she would send a car today. He had been waiting for a number of hours. A tech had come into his room early and she had told him he was free to leave. He had gotten dressed and waited. He had nowhere to go. He had nothing but what was on his back. He had no idea if his study materials had been returned to his room near the university. He did not think he even had a room anymore. It had been months since he had been there. They had probably reallocated it. He picked up the COM again and touched Margaret's name. Her picture filled the small screen. He waited. He could hear the ring back tone. It was followed by a weak ringing coming from the hallway. Margaret stepped into his room. She had her COM in her hand. She smiled when she realized he was the one calling her. She raised her arms and rushed to him. He stood and they hugged.

"Where did you get the COM? I was going to take you to get one today."

"It was in the closet. I thought you left it for me."

"Not me. There was a girl here who left you those clothes. Maybe she left it. Who was she anyway?"

Quinlan shrugged. "I have no idea. Maybe the commissioner sent them. She said she would look after me."

"I don't care. You look great. Have you been released yet?" He nodded. "Good, let's get out of here. This place always gives me the creeps." They left the hospital. Waiting in the parking area was a rather large, black, ominous looking vehicle. Margaret walked toward it. Quinlan paused.

"What is that?"

"It is a secure transport. Ever since my kidnapping, my mother has been paranoid. It cannot be hacked. It has a human driver." She grabbed his arm and pulled him into the vehicle. They did not speak during transport. They sat close together and looked out opposite windows. It was as if they were slowly coming together again and words might get in the way. There was so much to talk about but no place to start, so they sat in silence. They exited the vehicle and walked up to the house. The lights on the walkway were dim in the daylight, but Quinlan remembered the first time he had walked up this path. This time he was not told to stop or that he was being scanned. They entered the house.

"That was easier than when I was here last," he said.

"The protocols have changed. It seems more relaxed, but it is not, believe me. It took at least an hour to scan every part of me so the AI couldn't possibly mistake me for someone else and do something nasty. Mother was able to get your bot ID from the hospital. That and the fact you are with me allowed you to enter without being challenged."

"Is your mother home?" he asked with some apprehension.

Margaret smiled and gently shook her head no. "She is at a conference on the West Coast—won't be back for at least two, possibly four, days. We will be alone."

They entered the house and went straight to Margaret's rooms. Quinlan sat on the same sofa he had when he was there for the math tutorials—that turned out to be something quite different. He felt a mixture of pleasure and foreboding. Things were not the same. Margaret was definitely not the same. She had changed, and it was more than a physical change. He knew he had to talk to her, but he had no idea how to start, so he just sat and waited. She knelt beside him.

"We have to talk," she said. She leaned over and kissed him. Quinlan sat frozen. Her words had hit him hard. When a woman needed to talk, it usually meant that something bad was about to happen. "Look at me. This is important." Quinlan turned toward her. His hands were placed on his thighs. They were in plain sight, as was required. He made no motions that might be interpreted as threatening. He tried to smile, but he was sure it came out more of a grimace in preparation for what was to come. Margaret looked at him. "Please relax. Nothing bad is going to happen. In fact, what I am about to tell you just might come to pass and change the world. Are you okay?"

Quinlan nodded and said, "I am fine." He heard the words come out of his mouth, but he did not feel fine.

"Before I start, you need to promise me that you will never repeat what I am about to share with you." Quinlan nodded again. "You need to swear."

Things were becoming more tense, but Quinlan surprised himself. He was actually relaxing. He felt like he had been transported into a movie. It was all just too surreal to be real. "I swear to never repeat what you are about to tell me." He smiled weakly.

"I am going to tell you what happened to me after I was taken prisoner. First, I need to tell you that it was the most enlightening time of my life. It washed away all the ideas I had grown up with. All that business about the males of our species being less than the female. The idea that males are expendable—that we don't need them—is wrong. All the laws that keep your rights prisoner are wrong. I was taken by AMEN." Quinlan looked at her questioningly. "American Male Equality Nation. It is a group of both men and women that strive to change the laws of this country so that men become equal to women in all ways. I think you were captured by them too, but due to unforeseen events, you were left to die. It was not a deliberate act. The men and women were intending to teach you the ways of AMEN and bring you into our group so you could join with me to fight for change, but they had to flee without warning. You were simply left behind."

"Have you told anyone else?"

"No, only you. If my mother knew the truth, she would probably have me committed. Fempol would launch a full-on attack of AMEN."

"Tell me everything they did to you. I will then tell you everything they did to me. I hope you have not totally flipped to the other side because this group is not as nice as you think. At least not from my experience. I met a few of them and I was lucky to come out alive."

Margaret began with the kidnapping and told Quinlan about the time alone in the cell and all that she was taught. At one point, she started to chant the mantra of the importance of men and women loving each other. She ended with waking up in the transport.

Quinlan started with waking up on a cold concrete floor. He explained that he was taken in by a group that must have belonged to AMEN, but then they tried to kill him by stabbing him. He showed Margaret the scar on his back. That nearly stopped his narrative. She reached out and caressed him and kissed the scar. He turned and kissed her on the mouth, but she pushed him away and good-heartedly demanded he finish the story. He told of his time in the hospital and what Nisheeta Davenport had asked him to do and what he could expect in return. He had agreed to go undercover to try and help Fempol capture the kidnappers. He told her about Clark Bacon and nearly being dumped overboard in the middle of a lake with lead weights on his feet. He told her about the trip on the plane back to the city. He ended with a description of how he felt when he thought he was going to die after being abandoned in the cage.

He sat back and sighed. He was finished. Margaret said, "Take off your shirt and show me the scar again." Quinlan pulled off his shirt and turn his back to her. As he did so, there was a rustling behind him. Before he could turn, Margaret touched his back and wrapped her arms around his naked chest. She pressed herself to him. She had removed her blouse. Quinlan felt her smooth skin against his back. He reached up and held her hands to his chest and sighed. They stayed that way for a long moment. With mutual, yet silent, agreement, they both turned and kissed long and hard. They slid down to the floor, pushing the coffee table aside to make room for what was to follow.

SEAN
KILKENNY

It was early evening. Sean was standing outside of the building where the woman from Davenport's office lived. She said she was going to put in a work order, but she didn't. His plan depended on getting into the Fempol building. He needed her to do what she had promised. Just how he was about to convince her to do it now was still not clear. He was sure he could get into her building, and that was a start. There was nothing to lose as long as his presence at her building did not arouse suspicion. This was the second evening he had stood and watched the comings and goings. He decided that he would put on his pest control overalls with a gas mask dangling from his neck and follow one of the women in when they opened the door. To make it more realistic, he waited until he saw a woman walking toward the entrance. He stepped quickly up to the door and took out his COM. He pretended that he was searching for an access code. The woman approached and stood behind him. He continued to fumble, hoping the woman would assume he was just an incompetent male. It worked.

He turned to her. "I have the code here somewhere. I have a work order to eradicate some vermin in this building. They have been using the garbage chute to move around the building." He continued to fumble.

"Here, let me," said the woman as she stepped in front of him and used her COM to open the door. She rushed past him to the elevator that was about to close. She stepped inside and left Sean standing in the lobby. He proceeded to pretend to scan the lobby for evidence of mice and rats. He even dropped some of the wild rice in the corners to give the appearance of mouse turds. He was waiting for the elevator to arrive back at the lobby so he could travel up to the woman's apartment. He had already pressed the call button. Once it arrived, he stepped inside. He breathed a sigh of relief. It did not require an ID code to use. He pressed the number of the woman's floor and the door closed. It opened on her floor. He was going to knock on every door and ask if anyone had seen any mice in their apartment, but then decided that the fewer witnesses to his presence in the building the better. He went directly to her door, pushed the gas mask up onto his forehead concealing most of his face and knocked. He waited and knocked again. He could hear someone coming to the door. It opened. The woman was standing in front of him dressed in what looked like a bathrobe.

"Yes?" she asked, obviously not recognizing him.

"Excuse me, ma'am I am the pest control officer assigned to this building and there have been reports of some vermin in the building. I am checking in with everyone on this floor. Have you seen any evidence of rats or mice? They usually come out at night and leave their droppings in cupboards and closets as they hunt for food."

"God, this city is becoming infested. Why just last month we had an infestation at work."

"Where is that, ma'am?"

"Work? Oh, Fempol offices downtown."

"Yes, I worked in that building. I was supposed to go back, but never got another work order. Are they still there?"

No idea." She stopped and peered at him. The mention of her workplace and workorders to Pest Control jogged her memory. "Have we met?" she asked and snapped her fingers. Her memory answered her own question. "You were the PCO that I met at Fempol offices."

"Yes, I was," he said and smiled.

She smiled back, and the hand that was holding her robe together at the neck dropped into her pocket. Her robe fell partially open. Sean could see her cleavage and smell her perfumed soap. He stared. "Well, you might as well come in and check." She turned quickly. Sean stared as the ties that held her robe together dropped to the floor and her robe opened completely. He could see nothing from behind her, but the dragging ties filled his mind with an imagined view. She quickly grabbed the ties and pulled her robe closed. She turned and pointed to the kitchen. "That's the kitchen there."

Sean walked three steps toward the kitchen with a few grains of wild rice from his pocket pinched between his fingers. He turned back to her, "May I have your permission to inspect the cupboards, especially the upper ones." He noticed that her robe was not closed so that it overlapped. The two sides were just meeting, which resulted in a line of skin from her neck to between her legs. She walked toward him and didn't seem to notice that the gap opened and closed as she moved, giving him a peek at her nakedness with each step.

"You will need something to stand on. I have a small folding step stool." She opened a tall cupboard and took out the step stool.

Sean took it from her and looked away. He knew what this woman was doing. It was a trap. She was trying to make him react so she could report him. He climbed up and shone his light into the cupboards. He put the rice grains back into his pocket. He turned and looked down. He could see her breasts from the steep angle. She looked right at him but made no moves to cover herself. She stepped forward so her face was right in line with his penis. He knew he was hard and knew that she couldn't help but notice. "Nothing there," he said as he climbed down. "Guess you are one of the lucky ones. Found an infestation in the basement. I will deal with that and hopefully that will be enough." He stepped back. "I would like to get back into the basement where you work to make sure I got them all. Makes less work for me if they don't return." He walked past her and then turned. "Hey, you were going to put in a work order so I could do just that. Any chance you might still do that soon?"

She stood with her robe nearly open. He could not help himself. His eyes scanned down her body. Both her breasts were nearly totally exposed. His eyes stopped at her sex. It was devoid of hair. That surprised him, for the latest style was for women not to shave at all. She was obviously old school. He looked up quickly. He wanted her to agree to send him a work order and then he wanted to get out of there. A pest control officer having sex with a woman in her apartment would almost surely lead to bad things happening. She took a step toward him. He took a step back. "Well, Mr. Pest Control officer, I will put in the work order on one condition." She reached out and put her hand on his shoulder. Her touch was electric and amplified by her breast as it popped clear of the robe.

Sean's eyebrows arched. "Sure," he said. The word came out choked. He knew he wanted to grab her tit and squeeze until she squealed like the sow she was.

"You must come and see me and take me to wherever these mice are hiding. I want to check them out myself. And besides, I have never seen the basement. Sounds mysterious." She leered at him and smiled at her obvious effect on him.

"Sure," he said and walked to the door. He turned, grabbed the handle, and started to pull it closed. His last view was her dropping the robe to the floor, turning away and walking to the living room. Her ass wobbled as she put one foot directly in front of the other. He muttered to himself as he rode the elevator to the ground floor, "Fucking cunt." He pressed his hand to his still hard penis. He punched himself there in an effort to push the images of a woman he could not have, at least have in the way he wanted.

NISHEETA DAVENPORT

Nisheeta leaned back in her chair and closed her eyes. Thoughts of sitting in the sun and reading some trashy novel had become her go-to state whenever she felt stressed. Retirement kept coming up in conversations. At first, she just laughed. *Retirement is a dream* was always the final thought that followed its mention. There was always too much to do. That thought brought a list of tasks she needed to address before the end of the week. She opened her eyes and pushed the chair to its upright position. That seemed to signal a knock at the door. "Yes," she called.

Her aide, Dolores Fineman, entered. "Ma'am, I would like to go over this month's agenda. There are a number of items that need your signature. Is now a good time?"

Nisheeta sighed.

"I can come back later."

"No. Let's get this out of the way. Sit. How is your mother? You were only gone a few days."

"She is fine. It was not as my sister led me to believe. I had visions of her on her deathbed. I think she just wanted me to visit for a few days. My sister is a selfish bitch."

"Families can be trying."

"How was Eve? Did she…"

"Eve was fine, as far as I know. Didn't really have any contact with her. I think she likes it that way. Let's go over the agenda." Fineman placed a tablet in front of her boss and sat opposite with her own tablet at the ready. She started to follow a list of items, describing each as she went. Nisheeta listened and nodded her ascent or shook her head. Fineman was able to read her boss and fill in the blanks.

"This next item is something that I had an idea about. You know that the Justice Department is about to discuss possible amendments to MARA. There is scuttlebutt that it will not get past the committee. I know you would like those amendments to pass in the Ruling Committee, but the amendments are unlikely to get to the floor for discussion."

Nisheeta leaned forward. "That Male Assembly Restrictions Act has put a lot of strain on Fempol personnel, not to mention the prison system. Most of our time is spent making sure the males do not congregate in any public area. It has become silly. I was looking at the arrest reports. A couple of my officers walked into one of the bars that have just popped up in the warehouse district recently. The rules state that no more than three males may congregate in an area less than 100 square meters and the groups must be a minimum of 10 meters apart. This particular bar thinks it is following the letter of the law by painting a sequence of rectangles on the floor around the edge of the warehouse that conforms to the exact minimums. The men can communicate through a sophisticated sound system. They are not breaking the letter of the law, but they are breaking the intent of the law. My officers arrested the whole raft of these assholes, but when they got to court, the case was tossed. That bar is still there, and it will hold at least 100 males. So, what is the point? Dump the law or, at the very least, make it so that it does the job for which it was intended and let us deal with the men that really need our attention instead of having my officers chase after a few men getting together for a beer or two."

"I know how you love politics, but…" Nisheeta waved her hand in dismissal of anything political. "Hear me out. I think we should do a public and well-promoted presentation for that young man that helped get Margaret Carver back."

"What is his name again?"

"Quinlan Smith. You promised him…," she glanced at her tablet, "*protection from any repercussions that might arise and dispensation from common penalties imposed on men* as well as enough credits to live comfortably." She looked up to see Nisheeta frowning. "We can always renege. He cannot hurt us even if he were to take his case to the Webbies. We can just deny, and no one will believe him. After all, what you promised him was a little out of the ordinary to say the least."

"No, we will honor our agreement. He will be given some credits in a lump sum and a monthly stipend." She lifted her finger and wagged it at Fineman. "We will not, under any circumstances, mention the bit about protection. We will honor it, but it must never become public. He cannot be seen by either woman or men to be above the law. I suspect he would never break it, but you never know. There are some women out there who would love to make an example of him by setting him up. We will protect him from that."

"We can have a celebration of Margaret Carver's freedom. We will give her a medal. For bravery or something. We can invite everyone who is anyone in this city. We will do the presentation to Quinlan at the celebration. You can do a speech about how he volunteered to help find and rescue the Carver girl. I think they were friends before. They may also be lovers. Do you want me to find out if they are doing the nasty?"

"No. Leave them alone. The Webbies will do that job for us. I think this just might give those who are pushing for a repeal of MARA some additional ammunition. Here is a man that helped rescue the Commissioner's daughter without any concern for his own safety. He could very well become the poster boy that will give the men more freedom. Don't get me wrong. I do not want men to get the vote. That is beyond the pale. But if they feel less victimized, that will ease the job of Fempol. That would make it worthwhile."

"Maybe we should leak that they are fucking. That might make the voters more sympathetic. Lovers have a tendency to make everyone smile."

"No. We don't want to make it look like we are manipulating the story. It will be better to let it unfold naturally."

"Where should we hold this big shindig?"

"I don't want it to be seen as a part of a government event. I want it separate. So, how about the Fempol ballroom? It is not as large as Government

House, but it will force people together and that will require them to talk to each other. We will serve a full meal with a few appetizers and lots of booze. You can even throw in some of those newly designed…what are they called?"

"You mean 'Happy Tabs'?"

"Yes. Booze and Happy Tabs. Lots of both and a little food will bring people together for a "feel good" event. We might just succeed in getting rid of MARA once and for all. That can be my legacy. All I can pray for is that it is a positive legacy and not viewed as the first step to men getting power back."

"I wouldn't worry about that. Given the time it might take that to happen, men might be extinct. The whole exercise would be moot." She smiled and left the office.

"I'm not sure about that. There are things about men that I kind of like," she whispered to herself, and smiled wistfully.

MARGARET CARVER

Margaret's hand swept out behind her to feel the other side of the bed. She touched a bump and sighed. She opened her eyes and turned over. Quinlan was sleeping soundly. Daylight was shining brightly in the light chimney. She slid her hand under the sheet and touched him. The sex of the night before flooded her mind with its memory. It was delicious. She touched his back lightly, stopping at the stab scar. Her finger explored the line, sweeping back and forth. He moaned and turned on to his stomach. Her hand ran down his back and stopped at the dip of his spine. She ran her finger over the soft patch of hair. He relaxed back into a shallow sleep. Suddenly, she wanted to see his body. She wanted to examine it as she touched. She reached out with her other hand and slowly slipped the sheet down. His bare buttocks came into view, and she literally gasped at the sight. The muscles were relaxed, but their potential to tighten and flex was secreted beneath the pale skin. The potential enticed her hand to reach out. Her fingers did a fairy dance over each cheek. The muscles flexed with each touch as if she was controlling them instead of them reacting to her touch. She stopped and his buttocks relaxed. She leaned over and pressed her wet mouth to his now cool skin. Quinlan moved and turned over. He reached out for her face and drew her to him. Their bodies silently slid together, locked in place by a seemingly eternal kiss. They made love until their bodies demanded food and water.

Margaret pushed down on Quinlan's chest and rolled to the side. "I'm starving. The new maid will make us a breakfast."

She grabbed her COM and sent a note to the maid. She turned to Quinlan. "Food will be here in 30 minutes. You can have the shower first." Quinlan grunted and grabbed the sheet as he stood, wrapping it around himself. As he passed, Margaret reached out and grabbed the trailing sheet in an effort to take it from him and expose his nakedness. He smiled, let go of the sheet, and ran into the bathroom. Margaret laughed. She stood and stared down at her body. She knew she had gained some weight since returning home. Her breasts were bigger. Not as big as before, but definitely bigger. She squeezed them and muttered to herself, "Nice tits." She strained to look at her bum and spoke to it like it was a person. "You look good too, but don't think just because my tits put on a little weight that you need to too." She slapped it. "You must stay just as you are. I will not have a chubby bum ever again."

She heard a voice from the bathroom. "Who are you talking to? Is there someone out there?"

"There is no one here. And by the way, there is a toothbrush and a razor in the drawer. Help yourself."

"Thanks."

Margaret entered the bathroom and stepped into the shower as Quinlan ran a razor over the few bits of stubble that grew on his chin. A short while later, they were sitting on the sofa. There was a soft knock on the door. Margaret leapt up. "Food," she exclaimed. She opened the door, and a woman pushed a cart into the room.

"Miss Margaret, I have a message for you. It came this morning. It is marked important." She held out a brown paper envelope.

"Who is it from?" She turned it from side to side, inspecting the seal. She opened it and pulled out a smaller envelope trimmed in gold and sealed with red wax. Her name was written in a curly font on the front. "This looks formal. Nobody sends out messages like this." She dropped the larger brown envelope. Another small envelope fell to the floor. She reached and picked it up. It was the same as the one addressed to her, but this one had Quinlan

374

Smith on the front.

"Miss Margaret, I suspect they are invitations."

"To what?"

"I am sorry, miss, but I am not privy to that information. Will there be anything else?"

"No. Thanks for breakfast."

"Enjoy. If you need anything else just call." She turned and grinned at Quinlan and closed the door behind her.

"What is it?" asked Quinlan.

"An invitation to something. You got one too. Let's open them together," she said as she dropped to her knees onto the sofa beside him. She kissed his cheek and handed him the envelope with his name on the front. She broke the wax seal and ripped the small envelope open. Quinlan stared at her. His envelope was still clutched in his hand. "Go on. Open yours too. They probably say the same thing, so let's open them together."

Quinlan looked down at the small, gilded envelope with his name on the front. The wax seal caught his attention, and he looked closer. The symbol pressed into it was Fempol initials inset into the World Order of Women logo.

He was careful not to break the wax seal. For all he knew, there might be a rule against defacing it. He slowly removed it and opened the envelope, being very careful not to rip the paper.

"Quinlan!" she shouted. "Just tear it open."

He looked at her. "I have never gotten anything like this before. I really don't want to destroy it." He continued in his careful way and finally opened the envelope. He reached in to pull out the card inside.

"Stop. We have to do this together." She grasped the edge of her card. "On three. One, two, three." They both pulled out the cards at the same time and looked at them. They read:

You are cordially invited to a
Gala Evening

Celebrating the rescue of
Margaret Carver
From her kidnappers.
There will be a special
Presentation to
Mr. Quinlan Smith
For his selfless courage.
He was instrumental
In procuring the freedom
of Miss Carver.

Nisheeta Davenport
High Commissioner
Fempol

This was followed by a location, a date, and a time. "Holy crap," said Quinlan as he slipped the card back into the envelope.

"Great. You will get what she promised. I will make sure of that. If they try to fuck you around, I will haunt my mother until you get your due."

"You knew this was coming?"

"Yes. They spoke to me about it. They want to give me some sort of stupid medal for bravery. I told them they were crazy and to forget it, but my mother…." she lowered her voice, "and the others you now know about, want me to accept it. It is funny because they both said it would be good when I go political."

"Political? What do you mean?"

"Well, if we want to change this government and start to reintegrate the males, we will have to have people sympathetic to our cause in positions of power." She bounced up and down and struck a pose. Quinlan stared at her breasts, bouncing beneath the thin material of her blouse. She noticed him staring. "Do you like my tits?" she asked with a coy smile. "I hope so because I want you to always pay attention to them even when I am the chairwoman."

"The chairwoman?"

"Of course. I intend to go big because I am not going home." She jumped off the sofa and started to eat the breakfast that was laid out before them.

Quinlan just sat and stared into space. His life was about to change again, and he was not sure of his place. He did not like that feeling. Margaret stepped up to him. She had a strawberry in her hand. "Open up, Q." She stuffed the berry into his mouth, kissed him, and continued chatting as she ate.

EVE
RINNE

Eve arrived early. She knew she had to catch up with her own job that she had neglected while Fineman was away. She set up the files that her sister needed in a pile on her desk. She took the top one and began to enter the new data. There was a knock on her open door. She turned to see Fineman standing with her tablet in her hand.

"Can I interrupt?" Fineman asked.

"No problem. What can I do for you?" Eve looked up with a smile. She was really starting to love this job.

"Thanks for the last few days. I am back earlier than I initially thought."

"You are welcome."

"I hope you are not too far behind with your own." She waved the tablet. "I am sorry, but I have a new job I would like you to do. It takes priority over that." She pointed at the pile of files stacked on Eve's desk.

"Whatever you need?"

Dolores stepped up to the desk and tapped her tablet to Eve's. "There is going to be a gala event happening in Fempol ballroom downstairs. Here are some tasks I would like you to take care of. Have you ever organized an event like this?" Eve shook her head. "Well, this is a good time to start. You will have whatever help is required. It is mostly tasks you can delegate as long as you keep everything on track. Find people from the pool to look after the food, the decorations, the music and the bar. There is a list of possible menus. It will be up to you to research the guest list and provide finger food that is safe for everyone to eat. I don't want someone encountering something they are allergic to. You will also be in charge of the invitations. Make sure everyone on the guest list receives one. It is all laid out in the files I just dropped on your device. Any questions?"

"Not yet, but I might after I have explored those files."

"No problem," said Dolores as she left the office.

Eve looked at the list of files dropped on her tablet. She went immediately to the guest list. She glanced up at the door to her office and took out the device given to her by PW and slipped the recording chip into it. She selected a series of files she had just received and copied them over. They were added to at least a dozen files that she had been entrusted with, regarding a series of ongoing cases. She put the chip in the envelope, labeled it XPWX and buzzed the mail girl.

She started to organize the persons required to make the gala come to life. When she had it all in order, she set to research the names on the list. This required a series of permissions from the guests, which took longer than she had anticipated. In fact, most of the guests automatically rejected her inquires. Eve had an idea to make her job simpler and stood and walked to Fineman's office and knocked.

"Yes,"

"Dolores, would it be okay if I sent out a Webbie release about the gala? I think it would really ease my job, determining what the guests cannot eat, if there were some hype. I will make it the event of the month so that everyone who is anyone will want to be on the guest list. I am sure my inquiries will be answered if they think that they might have made the list. What do you think?"

"I think that is brilliant. It will make it a must-attend event." Eve turned to leave. "Eve," she called after, "great job."

Eve left Fineman's office. The blood rushed to her face at the compliment. She felt great. The thought of being a spy for PW started to weigh on her. By the time she sat down, the guilt of betraying her half-sister's trust swelled. Just then, the mail girl knocked on the doorjamb. "You have something for me?" she asked.

Eve looked down at the small envelope filled with Fempol data on her desk. "Sorry—nothing," she said. The girl scrunched up her forehead and gave her a puzzled look. Eve ignored it and the girl left. Eve put the envelope in a drawer and slid it shut. She pushed what she had done out of her mind. Dealing with her decision was not something she wanted to do. She did not know why she did not want to send the data to the PW. Spying was what she had intended to do when she got the job. Things had changed, and that was enough of a reason for now. She began to write the Webbie release, satisfied that PW would find out the same as everyone else.

She proceeded to create the to-do lists for the staff she had been given when she saw movement near her doorway and looked up. Nisheeta was standing in the frame and was about to knock when she noticed Eve staring at her. Eve stood. She was not sure why, as her half-sister had always been someone she disliked. What she really liked was the job. They wanted her to think for herself and not be some sort of automaton. Standing was a way to show that she appreciated the job without having to actually say anything. "Hi," Eve paused, "…Ms. Davenport."

"Oh, for god's sake, Eve. Just call me Nisheeta. We have not stopped being sisters. I feel stupid when you use my full name like that.

"Okay. Sorry."

"You don't have to be sorry. I just dropped by to tell you to make sure you put your own name on the guest list for the Gala. Put me, yourself, and Fineman at a table with the Chairwoman and the two guests of honor. Put us near the front. Don't put anyone else. If you put anyone else, they will try to take over every minute of conversation. Talking to them during the reception will be trying enough without having them spoil my dinner."

Eve smiled. "Okay, sounds good." Then a strange thought entered Eve's mind. It never occurred to her that she would be attending. She blurted, "What will I wear? I don't have anything to wear."

"Oh goodie," said Nisheeta and she clapped her hands together. Eve frowned. Nisheeta rushed on. "Let go shopping together and get new outfits just for this event. Don't worry about money. This is something that is just like work, so the government will pay for it." She stepped into the room. "When do you want to go?" She rushed on. "I will send you a note with the times I am free. You pick." She smiled and left the office.

Eve felt a warmth in her center. It made her think of a time before her parents were killed. She had worshipped her older sister. Maybe now was the time to reconnect. Maybe.

KARIMA
RANI SANYAL

The Webbies were exploding with excitement over the up-coming gala to celebrate the rescue of Margaret Carver. Karima listened to a webcast as she snoozed. Her life had become rather boring. Chow seemed to have lost interest in all things that usually included Karima. She had been relegated to girl Friday. Anything that was a personal requirement of Chow was her job to attend, even to the point of replenishing the woman's liquor cabinet. Today was no different. She glanced at her COM. There were messages from Chow. She wanted Karima to pick up some new lingerie. And to shop for a particular piece of jewelry with a centerpiece of lapis lazuli. It was something that someone had told her was a strong good luck charm.

Karima got dressed and called a ride when her COM buzzed again. She looked at it. There was a flashing red icon in the middle of her screen. It occasionally showed up when Chow wanted something done ASAP. Karima yawned. Chow's emergencies were seldom that. It just meant that she wanted something done immediately. She let it buzz six times and was about to answer it when Jeeves spoke. "Ms. Sanyal. Your handler is—" He was cut off.

A new voice spoke over the COM system. "Your request for a vibrating sex toy as the receiver for Chow was quickly dismissed as not practical. If the woman decided to use it while she was at the gala, the interference could very well ruin any recordings. Instead, they want to set it in a piece of jewelry. Something that she could wear to the Gala. Any Ideas?"

Karima smiled. Their timing was perfect. "She wants me to find a necklace of lapis lazuli. It is a blue stone."

"The research team spent some time on what she had worn to these kinds of events in the past. The final decision was a necklace with a large stone. She tends to the garish. Lapis Lazuli will do perfectly. We will get it to you soon. Your job is to make sure she wears it. Can you do that?"

"I can," said Karima with assurance.

"Good," said her handler.

Jeeves spoke, "Ms. Sanyal, there is another call for you. It is Ms. Chow. Do you wish to take it?"

"Yes, but with voice only." There was a click. She spoke softly, "Yes, Gorgeous?"

"What took you so long?"

"I was in the shower."

"What the fuck is wrong with your AI? Never mind. Have you seen the Webbies? Do you know if I am on it?"

"I'm sorry? Webbies? On what?"

"Oh, for fuck's sake. Do you know if I am on the guest list for the Gala? I had better be. So, do you have any contacts that might have inside info on who is invited? Fempol is putting it on to celebrate the rescue of the Carver girl. That cow Davenport would exclude me just to piss me off."

"I do not know off-hand. Why don't you ask the chairwoman? You are her aide. You have a right to know. Just call up Davenport's office and ask."

"I will not give that woman the satisfaction of knowing that I even care." There was a pause. "You call. You call, but don't let them know you work for me. Can you do that?"

Karima rolled her eyes. "Of course, gorgeous. I'm sure you're on the guest list, but I will call to verify."

"Good. Call and then call me right back."

"Who should I say I am? I can't be me. I will have to be calling for someone with influence."

"Crap. I don't know. You want to move up in this world—well, here is your chance. Just get it done." Chow disconnected.

Karima looked at her COM and shook her head. She called the office of Nisheeta Davenport. The answering system asked and directed her call to the information desk. She requested to speak to someone in charge of upcoming events. A woman answered, "Ms. Davenport's office. Eve Rinne speaking. How may I help you?"

"Hello. My name is Serina Wyland, and I work in the chairwoman's office. We need to know who from this office is on the list of guests for the Gala evening celebrating the rescue of Miss Carver. We need to know who is being invited so we can determine who we might need to add. So can you answer that first part for me?"

"Yes, I think so. The list is yet to be finalized, but I suppose I can tell you if someone is on the list. What names would you like me to check?"

"For starters, Karen Chow, Karima Sanyal," Karima paused. She had to make up at least two more names. "Paula Mitchel and Winifred Holtz."

"Let's see. The only name on the list is the first one. Would you like me to add the other three?"

"Yes, please."

"I will need their addresses so I can send out the formal invitation."

Karima's mind raced. She tapped out her address on her COM. "Send them all to this address. I will be sure to pass them on."

"Great. While I have you, can you tell me if any of these people have any life-threatening allergies?"

"No. None of them do."

"Great. Is there anything else I can do for the chairwoman's office?"

"No thank you. You have been a great help."

Karima quickly called Chow. She answered immediately. "Did you find out?"

"Yes, you were already on the list. I took the liberty of adding myself. I thought you might like the company. We can go together."

"I will need something to wear. So will you. Let's get something that matches. We can go as twins."

Karima rubbed her temple and held back a sigh.

"That's a wonderful idea. I will browse the boutiques."

"I'll join you. I'd hate to miss the fashion show."

Karima breathed, "Don't tease me."

Chow growled.

"I have a little surprise for you. I saw it in a specialty shop the other day and just knew you would like it."

"What is it?" demanded Chow.

"Be patient. It's a surprise." Karima disconnected.

SEAN
KILKENNY

Sean flashed his light around the basement of an older apartment building. There were a number of large motors mounted on the floor. Pipes snaked around them and up the wall. They entered a track and disappeared out of sight. On the floor, he could see a number of sticky traps he had set the previous week. He walked over to the far side of the room and picked up a trap. There were at least a dozen roaches inside. He inspected the area where the trap had been set. There was a water pipe going through the wall near the floor. The packing around the pipe had deteriorated. There were gaps where the roaches had entered. He set his tool bag down, removed a sprayer, and stuck the nozzle into one of the openings around the pipe and sprayed insecticide. He sealed the crack with a putty that could withstand the temperature of the hot water pipe. The other sticky traps were empty. He stood and cracked his back. He had nearly eradicated these vermin from this building. It was a lucrative contract that he attended to when the city allowed him the time. Lately he didn't care and did his private contracts on city time. *Fuck them,* he thought. His COM buzzed. He looked at it and smiled. It was the work order from the woman in the Fempol building. Attached was a schedule of events in the building, allowing him to time his activities when those areas of the building were not being used. "Perfect," he muttered. He grabbed his bag and headed out to his van.

THE PRISON OF POWER: A MAN-MADE TALE

The van was parked in the back alley of the building. He slipped inside and scanned the attachment for the Fempol building. There were the usual meetings. He scanned down, looking for one that Davenport had to attend. There were at least four. There was one with the three-month meeting of all the commissioners. Fempol system had a committee like hierarchy. The committee of commissioners had six members. Davenport was the head of that committee. "That looks fucking perfect," said Sean out loud. He chastised himself. There were ears and eyes everywhere, especially those that detected a male through their bots. He grinned. He could kill the entire committee. "Fuck yeah," he whispered. He proceeded to flip through the remaining items on the schedule. He stopped short when he saw Fempol Gala and its location. It was to be held in the ballroom. That meant there would be a crowd. He flipped his COM and went to the Webbies. He spoke, "Fempol Gala." There were a zillion hits. He chose the first one and read. The opening phrase brought a huge smile to his face: *Everyone who is anyone will be there.* "Holy shit," he said out loud, not caring if he was being surveilled. The movie that played in his mind was filled with raw pleasure. He could get an entire room of government bitches in one fell swoop. There would be a few men present, but that would be too bad for them. They chose to be female slaves. The irony, given his own job, was totally lost on him. He always saw himself as his own man even if he had to kowtow to them.

It was late afternoon, so he headed back to his own tiny apartment. He lay on his bed. He had to think. The first thing that came to mind was how to deliver the poison gas to the room. The second thing was how to keep the bitches in the room to allow the gas to do its job. A plan started forming. He knew the basement space. That was where he had explored the venting that fed fresh air to the meeting rooms on the floors above. There was an actual passageway leading from the room holding the power panels and motors for air circulation to the ballroom. It acted as one of the emergency exits. The stairs that led to this mechanical room could be accessed from the ballroom in case of an emergency.

If he could get into the room in the late afternoon by using the last batch of female nanobot laden blood, he would be able to stay for as long as he wanted. If he didn't have it, the sensors would know he was in the building after hours and security personnel would be dispatched to remove him. With it, he could stay for as long as he wanted. It also had the added benefit of keeping his presence in the building from the security system. A simple alibi could be created by leaving a pint of his own blood circulating in a heated web in his van parked near one of the bot sensors. It would read that he was nowhere near the building. That just left one or two possible witnesses to his presence. Maybe he could entice them to look in on the Gala. There was a lot to think about, but the possibilities were seductively sweet.

BEFORE THE GALA

THE PRISON OF POWER: A MAN-MADE TALE

The Galleria was crowded. Karen Chow was sitting in a small coffee shop. She was waiting. She picked up her COM and touched the screen. The map that appeared showed Karima's location. She was at least ten minutes away. Chow sipped her latte and watched the crowd of people stream by. The shop she wanted to go to first was straight across the corridor. She looked at the window-dressed outfits. They were all a little revealing. She considered going in something better suited for a 25-year-old. Something sexy. She then chastised herself and thought, *This is not some sex party. This is a one-time event. This was the event that everyone wanted to attend. I have to be...*, she paused and searched for the right words, *...beautifully professional and professionally beautiful. Going as a twin with Karima was not a good idea. In fact, it was really stupid. Who would stand out? A middle-aged professional woman or someone as striking as Sanyal. No. I will try to buy Karima something that does not flatter her tall, dark, gorgeous body, if that is at all possible.* Her thoughts shifted. She felt in her purse for the device that she would use to change the course of history. It was a small box that would require her index fingerprint to open. She would open it tomorrow evening and press the small red button on the inside. In one fell swoop, the chairwoman and her daughter, the commissioner, and that little male sycophant would become dust to be brushed aside by the winds of change. She was on her way to the top. She shivered at the possibilities. The best part was the deaths would be blamed on AMEN. The Smith boy had been captured by them and could easily have been brainwashed to do their bidding. Besides, the parts of the explosive had been made to match some of their previous explosives. Constance and Mary had assured her of that. She glanced at her COM. Karima was in the Galleria. She looked up and saw her approaching. She smiled. This was the best Loverboy anyone could imagine. The only scary thing was something had been niggling at her. This woman was becoming more than just a Loverboy. She was becoming important. That was not good. Attachments always seemed to get in the way of climbing to the top. It was power she craved. This would give her a perfect way to take over from the Chairwoman as well as getting rid of Davenport.

"Hello, gorgeous," said Karima as she sat in the chair opposite. "I am looking forward to finding matching outfits."

"Forget about that. We are going to an important event. I am a professional and I must dress as such."

"That is a very good point." She reached into her bag and removed a red kid-leather pouch. She set it on the table.

"What is that?"

"I told you I had a present for you. Well, this is it. I hope you like it. And I hope you will wear it to the Gala." She picked it up and set it in front of Chow.

Chow's face broke open into a smile. It was not her usual way of forcing her face to smile. That was a smile of impending nastiness. Nor was it the smile she painted on her face when they went to sex parties. This was a smile that flooded her eyes with something real. She was reacting naturally for the first time since Karima had known her. "A present?" There was still some incredulity in her voice. She picked up the small satchel and felt it with her fingers. "What is it?"

"Open it."

"It is not some sort of joke, is it?" Her smile nearly reverted to a caustic smirk, but that was soon overcome by the real smile again. She opened the small leather pouch and drew a gold chain slowly out. The blue stone of polished lapis lazuli popped out of the pouch and swung in front of Chow's face like a hypnotist's bauble. It seemed to mesmerize her.

"I thought it would look good on you. Do you like it?"

Karen looked up with the same smile. "It is beautiful. I love it."

"It wasn't as expensive as you deserve, but I wanted to use my own money to buy it for you," Karima said softly, and looked aside, demurely. Her mind was desperately trying to hold on to the pretend emotion. She watched Chow fondle the necklace, and she was sure she had her and could easily manipulate her in the future. Chow got out of her seat and stepped to Karima and kissed her. She looked once more at the necklace and said, "Let's go and see if we can find an outfit to show this off."

"Before we go, I meant to tell you that I put two fake names on the guest list. I figured it couldn't hurt. If you have someone that you want to join us, the two names will get them in. I had the invitations sent to my address. Do you want the names?"

Chow realized that one of her little problems was now solved. She needed to get both Cassandra and Mary into the Gala. "Perfect. I do have someone who has been trying to get invitations. This will do perfectly. You can't have too many people owing you favors. Thank you. I am not sure what I ever did without you. In fact, I have decided to formally make you my aide." Karima smiled and squeezed Chow's hand. She felt that this was not the time to push her for detail.

"Now let's go spend some government money," said Chow.

Dolores stepped into Eve's office without knocking. She was excited. "Sorry for rushing in, but it is time to go shopping. I love going shopping, especially when I am spending someone else's money."

Eve was shuffling some guest invitations. "These will have to go out by courier. They are some last-minute invites requested by the Chairwoman's office."

"Who are they for?"

"Karen Chow and a few of her crew. I don't recognize the names."

"I wish that bitch wasn't attending. She gives me the creeps. You never know what kind of things she is going to try to fuck up. We had to lock her out of a series of interviews with the Smith boy. She wanted him in prison. Who knows what she will try to do to upset his presentation? Where have you got her seated?"

Eve picked up a large seating chart and scanned it. "This was a bitch to set up. There were so many requests for special placement that I finally had to tell everyone that they would be seated wherever the AI decided would be best. It looks like she is near the front on the left-hand side. She is the chief aide to the Chairwoman."

"Can you move her...," she looked at the chart. Her finger pointed to the very back of the room near the fire exit that passed through the mechanical room.

"Are you sure that is a good idea? It might cause problems if she suddenly wants me to change it on the day."

"Fuck her. Put her and her crew there. If there are any problems, just send her my way and I will deal with it. I'll tell her that the sudden addition of three of her people caused the AI to readjust her location. That will send her crazy. Let the AI take the blame. Let's go. Davenport is waiting for us. Just drop those at the front desk and get them to send them out."

The two women met Davenport in the lobby. Davenport's driver picked them up in the front of the building and took them to the local Galleria.

The three women were heading out to their pickup spot. Davenport was standing with her COM. She was calling the vehicle. Dolores and Eve were chatting. They were carrying the parcels they had purchased. Dolores looked back at one of the shops they had just exited. "Look, Eve, that is Chow. I have no idea who the other woman is, but by the look of her, she is a Loverboy. She is too good looking to spend time with that cow without being paid." She grinned.

"How can she afford a Loverboy? That must cost a bundle."

"That is a really good question. That woman would demand a stipend and an apartment. There is no way Chow could afford that on her government salary."

"She must have some other source of funds."

"Interesting point. I am going to do some research on her next week and see if I can connect her to any of those subversive groups with a right-wing agenda. Someone is paying her besides the government."

"They are coming this way." Eve watched the two women walk in their direction and then they turned a corner. She stared. The older woman had a slight limp that she knew she had seen before. She couldn't place it at first, and then she saw two other women approach them from the far end of the corridor. It was Cassandra and Mary. Then it came to her. The café. She had seen this woman walk the same way and had the same hair. Blood blanched from Eve's face. This woman was the person listening to the conversation that occurred at the meeting in the café. She must be PW. Probably high up in the PW. She spoke, "I think I have seen her somewhere before." She immediately regretted her words.

Dolores looked at her. "Where?"

"I don't remember. Maybe I am mistaken."

"You probably are because that woman is really hard to forget." She looked down the hallway at the approaching women who obviously knew Chow. "Have you seen those two women before?" Eve just shook her head.

Davenport turned as she put her COM away. "Our ride is here." They exited the galleria. Chow, in the presence of Cassandra and Mary, filled Eve with fear. She realized that she was actually working for those women. She was working for PW. She was working against the women she was with. She was a spy. It did not feel good.

"Why can't your mother just deposit the money in my account? I gave her all the details. She asked me to choose a place to live. I chose that place near the university, but she rejected it. Margaret, what is going on? I feel like it would be a good idea to just go back and live off my government cheque. I can't stay here anymore."

Margaret knelt on the sofa, facing Quinlan. She reached up and tried to brush his hair aside. It had fallen over his eyes. He pulled back with a flip of his head. "It is the presentation at the Gala. Mother wants it to go perfectly. You will get everything you were promised once that is over. She is a control freak. Everything has to be done her way." She jumped up. "Let's try on your tux."

"My what? What is a tux?"

"A tuxedo, silly. This is a formal occasion. The entire world will be there. The list of guests even includes some of the ambassadors that have embassies in the city."

"How many males will be there?"

Margaret tilted her head to the side and scrunched up her face. "I don't know. It is possible that an aide to one of the ambassadors might be male."

"Are there any male ambassadors?"

"Not in this country. Males from any country that may have even a measure of government power would be disallowed. I suppose that is to avoid any unforeseen incidents with our own male population."

Quinlan pulled one of the sofa cushions over his chest and wrapped his arms around it. "So, I will be the only male at this shindig?" It was a hard statement.

"There will be others. Waiters and such. You won't be the only male in the room," she said, knowing that he would take little satisfaction in her statement.

396

With a scrunched-up face that was soon concealed by the cushion, he screamed, "Fuuuuucckkk." The sound came out like a muffled moan.

Margaret reached up and took the cushion away from his face and placed it in her lap. She stared at him with a stern look. "Quin, this is no longer just about you. This is a beginning, and you are a symbol of the beginning. If a man can be seen by the public as strong, honest, and dedicated…." There was a noise from outside the rooms. Margaret lowered her voice. "….it will make it a lot easier for my mother to get the votes to kill MARA. So, stop being a big baby. She slipped herself into his lap and kissed him. There was a knock on the door. She stood and called out, "Who is it?"

"It's me, darling," her mother called. She entered the room without waiting for an invitation. "How are you two doing?" She did not wait for an answer. She looked at Quinlan. "Have you tried on your outfit yet? I will call the tailor if things don't fit properly. I just used the AI scans so there might be errors." She inspected him. "You might have lost some weight since then." Quinlan was still sitting with the cushion clutched to his chest. She looked back at Margaret. "Is there a problem?" Again, she did not wait for an answer. "This is an important evening. We don't want a scene." She looked at Quinlan expectantly. "Quinlan, is there anything I can do to make you less…," she paused and looked for the correct word that would not make things worse, "…apprehensive."

"He is just a little nervous," said Margaret. Her mother frowned. "Well, wouldn't you be if you had to attend a big ceremony where you were a part of the focus and everyone there was male. Just try to see it from his point of view."

Vivian's tone softened. "I'm sorry. That was a little callous of me." She looked at Quinlan. "You have an opportunity here to change a law that keeps persons of your gender under a kind of house arrest. We will use you as the perfect example that men have accepted their role in our society and there is no need to subjugate them further, for doing so will probably result in some nasty confrontations. I think I have enough votes to, at the very least, to stop the new amendments to MARA from passing. Once that is done, we might get rid of it altogether." She smiled, satisfied that she had convinced him to do what she wanted. "Now put on that new tux and show me what you look like."

THE PRISON OF POWER: A MAN-MADE TALE

Quinlan got up and Margaret grabbed the tux that was hanging from a rack in the corner of the room. She handed it to him and then followed him into the bathroom to change. They did not speak as he dressed. Margaret stood in front of him and tied his tie. Margaret exited the bathroom and stood with her arms out. "Tada," she said with as much fanfare as she could muster. Quinlan walked out of the bathroom and stood before them. Vivian walked up to him and brushed her hands down his lapels. She clapped her hands on his shoulders and said, "Good." She turned and walked to the door. "Margaret, get him a haircut. He looks like one of those homeless men that live in the park. On second thought, I will get someone to come here."

"Yes, Mother," said Margaret. Her words dripped with sarcasm. The door closed, and she stepped up to Quinlan and threw one arm around his neck while the other dropped to his crotch. "You look and feel delicious," she said with a husky lilt. "You just need to relax. Perhaps this will help." She grinned and unzipped his trousers. She slid down to her knees. She took out his erect penis, looked up at him, standing with his mouth open as she stuck out her tongue and licked the end. "Yum," she said, and slipped the end of his penis into her mouth.

Sean lay back on the cot in his hideout. His eyes were closed. A tube snaked out of his left arm and terminated at an almost full blood bag. He needed the blood for his alibi. A full pint being pumped around a web of tubing of his own design could fool any nanobot sensor. With it, he could be in two places at the same time. Sitting on his chest was the bag of Fineman's blood with her (still viable) nanobots. He had taken it out of the freezer that morning. He would have to warm it to at least 30 degrees Celsius. His body would do that. The scale beeped, and he removed the needle from his vein and applied a small bandage. He took his bag of blood and put it in the refrigeration unit. He hung the blood he obtained from Fineman on a pole at the head of the cot. He sat down again, inserted a needle into his right arm, and connected the tube from the hanging bag up to his arm. He lay back and waited as the female bots dripped into his arm. They would make him female as far as Fempol AI was concerned. That would last at least 48-hours before they would no longer be viable. That would be plenty of time. The big gala was tonight, and he was nearly ready.

His bag with his Pest Control uniform draped over it was waiting at the door. The gas was ready. He had even painted the canisters with a logo of the company that supplied him with rodent pheromones, along with a scientific name of the contents. As far as the world was concerned, this was a perfectly legal, organic item in his bag of tricks. He even brought a small fan to ensure that the poison gas could be forced into the air vents.

Later today, he would park his van under a bot sensor in the alley behind an apartment building that had some pest problem. He would enter the building and secretly leave again, avoiding any sensors. He would take a bus to Fempol building. He would enter via the service entrance and set up in the mechanical room. There he would wait until it was time - time to kill as many of the monsters who had stolen his family as he could. If there were a few innocent male casualties, that was just too bad. They were giving their lives for the best of causes.

THE MORNING OF THE GALA

Eve walked into the ballroom. She had spent the entire day organizing and making preparations. Now it was done. She was alone. She scanned the nearly 100 tables set out in a half circle in front of the stage. Each table would hold up to eight guests. Most were no more than four. Groups of two were put together. That had been a real challenge. Finding people who would complement each other was important. There was a large seating plan at the entrance as well an individual diagram that came with the program. This was a tightly kept secret. That was one of the challenges, and Eve felt she had succeeded in putting everyone in a location they would be able to accept. There were a few exceptions. She meandered through the tables, looking at the name cards. She had come to know many of these people vicariously through her research. As she got to the back of the room, she stopped at a table that was just outside the doorway to the prep room on the right and the mechanical room hallway on the left. This was where she had been told by Dolores to seat Karen Chow and the others. She read the names: Ms. K Chow, Ms. S Karima, Ms. P. Mitchel and Ms. W. Holtz. Her mind went back to seeing Chow at the galleria. There were three women with Chow. She knew two of them were Cassandra and Mary. She had never known their full names. The names on the cards must be fake. The third was someone that was a total enigma. Karima Rani Sanyal was a person who seemed to spring full grown from somewhere in Europe or India. Her research was not positive about any of it. She arrived in the city earlier in the year and became Chow's Loverboy/aide maybe both. She shook her head and strode to the entrance. In general, she was happy with everything she had done to prepare. She hoped it was enough.

Sean opened the door from the mechanical room a crack and peered out. The short hallway was empty. There was no one in the part of the room he could see. He tiptoed down the hallway and peeked around the corner. He ducked back quickly at the sight of a woman walking to the large double door entrance. His heart rate jumped. He expected the room to be empty. He had no intention of spending any time in the room, but he wanted to get the lay of the land and to ensure himself that there were air vents near the ceiling evenly spaced. He peeked again and scanned the room. The woman was gone.

He breathed a sigh. Everything was as he expected. The main doors were held open magnetically. If the power was cut, they would automatically close, and the emergency lights would come on. Someone might try to enter the mechanical room to see if they could fix the problem, but he would block the door. They would have to go upstairs and down the dedicated stairway, but by then, the gas would have filled the room and they would all be in various death throes. He smiled and imagined the smell of four hundred some odd women shitting themselves as the gas robbed their muscles of control. He would be wearing a mask and wouldn't have to actually smell anything. To imagine it was gross enough. It was perversely disgusting, but still wonderful. His mind went back to his father and uncle at the arena so long ago. As soon as the images of bouncing bodies entered his mind, he blinked the thoughts away. He went back into the mechanical room to wait.

The woman who sent him the work order was behaving strangely. She sent a message to his COM. She wanted to know when he was going to be in the building. He had not answered. She sent him another message. It was cryptic. It said, *'I see all. I know all. You cannot hide from me.'* Then it occurred to him that she knew he was in the building. He had been very careful. The female nanobots circulating in his bloodstream had allowed him free entry through the service entrance. He came in just before it closed. He watched the guards leave and slipped inside unnoticed. The AI simply saw him as Dolores Fineman.

He began to think it through. *'She must be tracking my COM. She had access to my personnel files. She must have the clearance to lock on to my COM and track my location. She would have a record of that on her COM.'* Now he wanted her to find him. He needed her COM. It must be erased or destroyed. She might come in unexpectedly and make a mess of things. The best way to deal with that was to invite her to come to the mechanical room. He had to do it in a way that didn't make her suspicious. He took out his COM and sent her a note: *I am in the mechanical room. What can I do for you?* He waited for a reply, pretty sure she would just show up. He prepared. He took out the bottle of xenon with a face mask on top. It was the same one he had used on Fineman that day in the park. He set it within easy reach. He heard the door at the top of the stairs open. He stood with his gas mask set on his forehead. The click of her heels on the stairs made him smile. This was going to be fun. He was not going to suffer through the teasing anymore. She would get more than she asked for.

She came into view. She stopped three steps from the bottom and placed both her hands on her hips. "What are you doing here? This is not the best time to be in this room. There is a big gala tonight."

"I know," said Sean. He took a couple of steps toward her and removed his gas mask from his forehead and set it down on his tool bag. "What can I do for you?" he asked.

She walked down the remaining three steps and stood in front of him. She smiled and spoke, "Well, I just wanted to ask you something. Something personal."

"What?"

She smiled coyly. "I was wondering if you like me."

"I hardly know you," responded Sean. He knew where this was going and felt the anticipation of what she might do next.

"I mean, do you like this?" She twirled around and her skirt flared. She reached up and undid the top buttons of her blouse. "The last time we met, remember, in my apartment—you came looking for mouse droppings and found me nearly naked." Sean nodded. "You could easily have had your way with me. Why didn't you? I obviously wanted you to."

"I just figured you were testing me."

"God no." She undid the rest of the buttons on her blouse and lifted her bra so her breasts flopped out. She ran her fingers over them and tweaked her own nipples so they stood erect. "I just want you to fuck me." She stepped closer and whispered huskily. "Do you want to fuck me, Mr. Pest Control Man?" Sean simply nodded.

She grabbed at his crotch. "Take it out. I want to see it."

Sean reached down and undid his trousers. She helped him free his penis.

Suddenly, Sean took control. He reached out and grabbed her breasts and squeezed them. He had never been this hard before. It actually hurt. It was as if his penis was swollen beyond the skin's ability to stretch. His hands went to her shoulders and pushed her down until she was squatting in front of him. He heard a squeak from her, but he did not stop. He pushed his penis into her face. He looked down at her and growled, "Open your mouth." She looked up at him with limpid eyes. "This is what you need. Open your mouth!" This time it was a command, and she opened her mouth slightly. He pushed hard, and his penis slid past her teeth and down her throat. He felt her gag. He held it there and wallowed in the pleasure of his penis deep in her throat. He thrust back and forth until her saliva was smeared on her cheeks. Suddenly, he pulled it out and grabbed her by the hair and pulled her to her feet. He spun her around and pressed her face to a section of the concrete wall. She moaned as he reached up under her skirt. He expected to find underwear of some sort, but she had come down into the mechanical room not wearing any. This fact immediately dispelled any fear that she might try to alert anyone. "Stick out your ass." This was another order. She stepped further away from the wall, hiked up her skirt, and stuck her ass out. Sean plunged into her. He grabbed her hips and attacked her with his penis. She moaned. He was only five strokes in when he began to orgasm. He stopped thrusting and pushed into her as far as he could and held it there until the orgasm subsided. He stepped back. She tried to look over her shoulder at him. She wiggled her bum at him seductively. "I hope you have a little more for me," she said. He ran one hand down one side of her ass and, at the same time, he reached for the bottle of xenon. He pressed himself to her as if he was about to continue with what she wanted. He stepped into her. His newly erect penis entered her and he thrust again. She moaned. He slipped the mask over her mouth and pressed it tight to her face. "This will make you cum harder than you have ever cum before. Breathe deep, baby," he hissed as he increased the power and frequency of his thrusts. She started to struggle. Then, as if she had accepted his lie, she moaned and slowly went limp. This only excited Sean more. He removed the mask covering her face and supported her body from falling by grabbing on to her hips and pressing her face into the wall. He continued to thrust himself into her until he orgasmed. When he released her, she slipped to the floor in a heap.

Sean was breathing hard. His heart was pounding. His eyes were like fire as he looked down at the woman. "Fuck you, bitch." He heard a sound from behind the door to the ballroom. He quickly did up his trousers. He reached into his bag and removed a small tarp that he tossed over the still unconscious woman. He went to the door and listened.

Karen Chow entered the ballroom, followed by Mary. She stopped and looked at the large seating chart. She started to laugh. "Fucking unbelievable."

"What?" asked Mary.

"Look where that bitch seated us. We are practically in the parking lot. Well, the joke is on her." She walked to the back of the room and found the table with her name. She looked up at the hallway that led to the machine room. The hall was about three meters long. She stepped into it. "This is a perfect place to be at the climax of the evening. We will step in here to pretend to make a call." She stepped out of the hallway and looked up above the entrance. An EMERGENCY EXIT sign glowed above the opening. She pointed down the hallway. "Where does that lead?"

"I think it goes into a room with electrical panel and big motors with pumps and stuff and at the far side there is a stairway up to the atrium. I will check out the specs of the building just to be sure."

"After the main event, we will not leave. I have to make an attempt to be the hero, if for no other reason but to dispel any suspicion. Sanyal will be with us. I don't want her to get suspicious. Both you and Cassandra will have to keep your mouths shut."

"No problem," said Mary.

"If this comes off without a hitch, we will be on our way to the chair. If males think MARA is bad now wait until I am in charge. I will assure them a place in history, if anyone can even remember them. Maybe I will tell my great granddaughters that the human race used to be rather primitive until the male chromosome was eradicated." She grinned and looked at Mary's face. The 'xox' scars were particularly red. She reached out to touch them. Mary pulled away and let her hair fall over them. Chow was back to being all business. "Good. Let's go. I have a date with Karima. I need some attention."

Sean waited until the voices stopped. He pulled the tarp back and looked down at the woman. He reached out to her neck and checked her pulse. It was slow but steady. He straightened her body so she was lying on her back. He searched her and found her COM in a leather pouch at her waist. He took it out. He held it up in front of her face and pulled up one of her eyelids. The COM read her iris and beeped. He was in. He looked around until he found any references to Pest Control and erased them. He erased the text entries she had sent to him. He checked the tracking system. It had not been turned on. Obviously, she did not want a record of her escapades. He checked the photo log. There were a number of pictures of men in various stages of undress. He looked at them and left them as they were. He put the COM back into the case on her hip. He looked down at her naked breasts. He was about to tuck them back into her bra when he stopped. He pinched both her nipples between his thumb and forefinger and twisted. When he let go, he watched the blood flow back, changing their color from white to red. He tucked them into the bra and buttoned up her blouse. He lifted her skirt, spread her legs, and looked down at her sex. His semen was oozing out of her. He got a cloth and wiped as much of it away as he could. If they did a check, they would think she had sex before she decided to peek in on the Gala. They would not connect him to her. When they found her, along with all the others, it would appear as if she had stumbled into the mechanical room and died from the poison gas he was about to release. All he needed to do was keep her sedated. He had used up all the benzodiazepine on the Freeman woman. He decided that he should tie her up with something that left no marks. He found some rags in a bucket. They smelled of cleaning fluid; probably paint thinner. He ripped them into strips and tied her hands and feet together. It would not hold her for long, but if she tried to free herself, he would just give her another dose of xenon.

He set to work removing the cleaning cover of the main ventilation pipe leading to the ballroom. It branched out to all the air vents surrounding the ceiling of the room. He blocked out the part of the pipe that led back to the main feed. He did not want his poison gas to be spread throughout the building. He set his canister just inside the pipe. Behind the canister, he placed a small fan. It would push the gas up and into the ballroom. It was heavier than air, so once it reached the vents it would fall. Then they would fall like so many rag dolls. He smiled and stepped back to admire his work. Everything was set. All he had to do now was wait. His eyes fell to the fan. He could not remember testing the fan.

"Crap. It isn't even plugged in," he said as he went to his equipment bag and dragged out an extension cord. He plugged it into the fan and scanned the room for a receptacle. There was one on the wall directly behind the unconscious woman. He went over and nudged her with his boot. She did not react. He reached out, plugged in the extension cord, went to the fan and turned it on. He reached into his pocket for his igniter and lit a small piece of cloth on fire, then blew out the flame. The smoke curled up and was grabbed by some invisible force and sucked away, disappearing up the pipe. He was satisfied that his plans would work. He sat back and rested.

THE GALA

ONE

Margaret stood in front of the bar. She had a half empty glass of champagne in her hand. It was not her first. She was turned away from the crowd of guests entering the ballroom. She wanted to remain incognito for as long as possible. She turned and glanced at the entrance. This was not her first glance. She quietly hissed as she turned back to the bar, "Where the fuck are you, Quinlan?"

"Pardon?" said the bartender. "Can I get you another glass?"

Margaret smiled at him. "No, not yet anyway." She felt a hand on her shoulder. She turned sharply, but her tension ebbed and she smiled. It was Quinlan. "Where have you been? I thought you might not show. This is going to be hard enough without the added stress of doing it alone."

"Sorry," Quinlan said. He glanced over his shoulder and then quickly kissed Margaret's neck. I had to go and get something called a 'BotMod'. Your mother set it up for me. It allows me to get the dispensation Davenport promised. Supposedly, they transmit a 'Do Not Interfere' code to the AI system. I tested it out by going to my old rooms in the university district. I did not get stopped once." He smiled.

"Fantastic." She sipped her champagne and slipped her hand inside his open jacket and squeezed his waist. "Do you want one of these?" She held up her glass.

"What is it?"

"Champagne." He made a face suggesting it might be something he would dislike. "It is just bubbly white wine."

"I have never tasted it before."

"No time like right now." She turned to the bartender. "He will have one of these and I will have another." She gulped down the remaining liquid and set the glass on the bar."

"Yes, ma'am," said the bartender.

He was about to pick up the champagne bottle and pour two glasses when a voice behind Margaret said, "No. No more, young lady." It was Lillian Carver. The bartender nodded and pushed the bottle back into a sink filled with ice. "You can, however, give me a double G&T. These two will have a soda." The bartender poured soda into the champagne glasses.

"Mother—I am eighteen now. I can drink whatever I want."

"You are already tipsy. I need you sharp. Drink later. I understand there are a number of after parties that have invited both you and this young man to attend. Don't think you can go without...," she paused, turned and gestured. Two women dressed in black skirts and jackets stepped forward. Quinlan noticed that they both had small buds in their ears. "This is officer Peters, and this is officer Singe. They will be with you. You might not see them, but I guarantee they will be there if they are needed." She looked at the two officers for an affirmation of her words. They both nodded.

"For fuck's sake, Mother," hissed Margaret.

"Don't argue. It is either that or nothing. You have to consider what we all went through the last time. We will...I will not risk that happening again. Do you understand, young lady?"

Quinlan discreetly brushed his fingers over the back of Margaret's hand. She did not react. She did make a face and sarcastically said, "Yes, mother."

"Good. Now take your drinks over to the table and sit. This shindig is going to start soon." She turned and walked to a door beside the small stage and slipped inside.

Quinlan reached for the soda the bartender had placed on the counter. "Leave those," said Margaret. She walked toward their table but beckoned to one of the male waiters who were offering glasses of champagne to the guests. She picked up two glasses and sat down at the table with a flourish. She handed one to Quinlan and said, "Drink."

Quinlan noticed that the word came out as an order. He followed it and sipped the wine. It was not to his liking, but he did not reject it. She looked at him with expectant eyes. He nodded, "Good." He knew his role in all of this and had fallen back on his training. Compliance was what was expected. He would comply with everything, at least for now. He watched Margaret looking around the room and boldly drinking the champagne. Her new glass was practically gone, and she was once again trying to catch the eye of one of the waiters. He picked up his glass and sipped again.

The room slowly filled. Some of the guests had taken their seats at the tables and others were still milling in small groups. Schmoozing was the word that jumped into Quinlan's mind. One of the matrons often used the word when the boys at the school would gather in groups. He could hear her voice. *'Boys, be aware that schmoozing in groups larger than three is illegal and punishable by the courts. The MAR Act strictly forbids it. It is also for your own protection.'* The last part about it being for males' own protection made no sense to Quinlan, for exactly how that was true was never explained. He glanced around the room and noticed at least a half dozen males in tuxedos that he assumed were actually invited guests, because they sat at the tables and were not part of the service crew. He stared at one and realized they were Sexmen accompanying the women in their household. The thought struck him, *that is what they all think I am*. He rolled the thought over in his mind. *Maybe that is what I am considered to be? I am just Margaret's Sexman.* He wrinkled his face at the idea.

At that moment, he was alone at the table. Margaret had gotten up a number of times to visit some of the other guests. She was presently at a table that was, like theirs, near the front of the room. He looked at the name cards at his own table. Davenport was on one of the cards. The six tent cards indicated where each guest would sit, but no one was seated at the table. He looked up as two women walked over and sat at his table. They both smiled at him. There was no need to introduce oneself, but Quinlan felt he must. "My name is Quinlan," he said, "Quinlan Smith."

The younger of the two women said, "Yes, we know. We are from the Commissioner's office. My name is Dolores, and this is Eve." Eve smiled weakly. They all turned to the stage.

There was some motion from the stage, and Inspector Davenport walked out. She held an empty champagne glass and tapped it. The sound was amplified and filled the room. Everyone turned toward her. "Good evening, ladies," she said and then continued, "and some gentlemen." There was a low rumble from a few of the tables. One woman went so far as to shout, "Let's just call them men." It suggested that those women did not think any male could be considered 'gentle'. Davenport ignored the gibe and continued, "Please, I invite you to take your seats." She waited while the women slowly moved to their respective tables. Lillian Carver slipped into the seat opposite Quinlan, and Margaret sat beside him.

Once everyone was seated, she continued. "Tonight, we are here to celebrate the rescue of a young woman that is well on her way to being a successful and dynamic member of our society. Some of you know how this came about, but I feel I should give you the details—well, as many of the details as security will allow. The young woman in question is none other than Margaret Carver, the daughter of our Chairwoman, Lillian Carver. Margaret, would you please stand up and join me on the stage." Margaret stayed seated until her mother poked and glared at her. She glared daggers as she sipped her champagne defiantly in front of her mother. She set her glass down and slowly stood. The room clapped as Margaret walked onto the stage.

Davenport stuck out her hand and shook Margaret's. She put her arm around her shoulders and continued, "She was taken at the university the day a group of males preparing their bodies to accept an artificial womb were murdered."

There was a shout from the back of the room. "Call them what they are. Sweets." Then from the other side of the room, "Soft Candies."

Davenport continued unfazed, "These men were brutally murdered, and Margaret Carver was taken along with another male student." She went on to tell about the Roma gang that had been hired to kidnap the daughter of the Chairwoman, the suspected group that used the Roma mercenaries to do their dirty work. She talked about the AMEN group as being the main suspects in the kidnapping. She explained the male student's attempt to save Margaret from being taken prisoner, which resulted in his capture and subsequent release.

She went into some detail about the demands of the kidnappers and the plan to capture them and rescue Ms. Carver from their clutches. She stated that all the prisoners who were demanded set free by the kidnappers were re-captured. She did not mention that one of the prisoners had not been recaptured. She did not mention that Quinlan had been a prisoner of the AMEN group more than once, and both times they had nearly killed him. That information had to remain secret. She talked a little about how the boy who was taken with Margaret had agreed to work with Fempol to find and save her. She then focused on Margaret herself and how brave she was to survive at the hands of the hardened male criminals that made up the American Males Equality Nation. She did not mention that the information collected on this group showed that some of the leaders of the group were, in fact, females.

She finished by stating the reason for this Gala Event. She signaled to the wings, and a woman came out with a velvet-lined box holding a medal. She took it from the box and hung it around Margaret's neck. "Congratulations, Margaret Carver. We thank you for your bravery in the face of danger." She looked up at her audience and continued. "Today we celebrate the victory of the females of this great country against those who tried and would continue to try to overturn what we all created together. We will never return to the oppression experienced by women since the beginning of time." She clapped. The audience followed suit as Margaret walked down from the stage. Once settled, Nisheeta Davenport invited Lillian Carver to the stage to say a few words and make a special presentation. The audience clapped as the chairwoman stood and walked to the stage.

TWO

At the rear of the room sat Karen Chow. The other three women chatted about the lack of transparency of Fempol, specifically the Davenport woman. She could not really make out what was happening at the Carver/Davenport table. She needed to be sure that Carver, the Carver girl, and the male sycophant were sitting together before she pushed the button. That was the most important. If Davenport was also there, then that would be gravy. The bomb in the boy's COM was just powerful enough to kill all of them with very limited collateral damage. It would open a lot of doors for her. Taking out the daughter was important, given that she was being groomed to become the chairwoman. The boy didn't matter except as a distraction. She would begin a social media campaign to show he was in on it. He would be the suicide bomber sent by AMEN. Chow was taking no chances. The PW's reasons for killing the Chairwoman were more political than personal. They suspected that she was soft on MARA and they needed someone in power that would follow their agenda.

The bar was just to the side of the stage, and the bartender was in her employ. She would signal when the time was right. The bartender might become a problem later, but that was easily dealt with. When she got the signal, she would send her Loverboy, Karima, up to the bar to fetch her a special brandy. That would keep her out of the way. They would serve dessert after all the bullshit. That is when she would do it. She sipped her wine and let the warmth in her belly swell.

THREE

Lillian Carver stepped on to the stage. Everyone clapped. She held up her hands to stop them and spoke over the dying sound. "I am not the person you should be clapping for. I have the great honor to give a special award to a very special young man." The room was silent. "Yes, I said 'man'." This young man was instrumental in saving the life of my daughter and securing her release." She paused. There was a rumble of conversation. She waited for it to subside. "I am not able to go into the details but suffice it to say that he put himself in harm's way. It was due to his selfless acts that my daughter is free today. He was nearly killed twice: once from a stab wound and once from thirst. He survived both, and it is my proud duty to present him with a onetime cash payment and a lifetime stipend so he can live his life independent of the trials of other men. I also want him to serve as an example of what the males of our species are able to do when given the chance. I want all of you to treat him as you would treat me." There was some scattered clapping and a lot of mumbles and grumbles. No one dared speak out. "I would like to call Quinlan Smith up to receive this pledge from our government. Quinlan."

During the speech, Quinlan had slid down in his chair. He would have liked to disappear entirely. Margaret was clapping and cheering for him. She pushed him to his feet. He slowly walked up to the stage and stood beside Lillian Carver.

"He's a cutie," said one woman.

"He is so young," said another.

"Ladies. Be respectful," warned Carver. She turned to Quinlan and held out her hand. She shook it, turned for the photos she knew were being taken, and handed him a scroll of paper with a gold ribbon surrounding it. "Along with this pledge I would like you to have this." She held up a small pin with the Fempol logo on the front.

She pinned it to the lapel of his tuxedo. "The AI system will always identify you when you are wearing this. It will keep you safe for there are those out there that might wish you harm." She clapped. At first, she was the only one clapping besides Margaret, but a poignant scan of the audience encouraged others to applaud. Soon the room was at its feet, clapping enthusiastically. Quinlan's face had long since turned crimson. He left the stage and returned to his seat beside Margaret. "Thank-you ladies. Dessert will now be served." She returned to her place beside Margaret, Quinlan, Nisheeta, Dolores and Eve.

FOUR

Chow looked at her empty glass of wine and turned to Karima. "Be a dear and get me a glass of brandy—orange brandy—none of that cheap stuff—Grand Marnier." She smiled one of—what Karima called—her false faces. "Make it a triple."

Karima stood up and walked slowly around the tables and up to the bar. She felt eyes on her as her hips swayed. She was good at drawing attention. She heard a series of comments that the speakers did not even try to conceal. As far as most of these women were concerned, she was just a high-class prostitute. She had no status outside of her affiliation with her patron. Still, Karima could not help herself. She smiled, waved and winked her way to the bar. Everyone she passed was, at the very least, appreciative. She stood at the bar and ordered the drink. The bartender looked at her and said, "I will have to go to the storeroom and fetch some."

Karima nodded her assent. Her thoughts went to the bomb that had been removed from Quinlan's COM. She was not privy to what her handler expected would happen when Chow tried to murder him along with the Carvers. There was no bomb. At least, that is what she was told. *Maybe the necklace had been tampered with so Chow blew up herself? Shit. That would make quite the mess. She shook her head, trying to get the image of Chow's head exploding. Would they do that? She decided that they wouldn't, not without telling her. And besides, there wouldn't be room for a recorder and a bomb. She might be close by and become collateral damage. The necklace was just a recorder of sorts. They wanted evidence to use against her. They would get rid of her politically rather than physically.* She breathed and tried to see across the ballroom to their table. She could not make anything out. It was just too far away.

FIVE

Chow watched Karima walk toward the bar. Both Mary and Cassandra also followed her with their eyes.

Mary kissed the air and said, "Wow, is she gorgeous. She must be one pricy piece of ass. How did you land her?" she asked, turning to Chow.

Chow was staring in the direction of the bartender. Karima had not yet arrived at her destination. The bartender waved a bottle of champagne in the air. That was the signal. The Carvers and the Smith boy were all seated eating their dessert. Now was the time. She reached into her bag and removed a small box with a sealed lid. She felt a surge of power that shivered down her spine. She looked around. She did not want anyone to see her actually open the box and push the button, so she stood up. "I am going over there," she said to the other women. "Come, join me." She walked over to the dark hallway with the emergency exit sign glowing amber on the wall above the opening. She stepped down the hallway just far enough so that she could not be seen by anyone in the room. The three women stood with their backs to the wall. They were all excited. Mary's scars were all red, with a mottle of white at the edges. Cassandra's hand had unconsciously slipped down and was pressed against her crotch as if she had to pee badly. Chow's forehead was beaded with sweat. She held the box out and pressed her pinky finger to a slight indentation on the top surface. The box popped open. She smiled, for the box held the proverbial red button. The only thing missing was a small white arrow with the words 'Press Here' embossed on the black surface. "Ready?" she asked. "Shit, I don't give a fuck if you are ready. I'm definitely ready." She held up her finger and pressed the red button. It gave a satisfying click and then nothing.

"What happened?" asked Cassandra.

"Was it silent? Are they dead?" whispered Mary.

"Fuck," said Chow and she pressed the button again. This time, it did not even click. She handed the box to Mary. "What is wrong with it? Was I supposed to do something else? Maybe I was supposed to hold the button down for a count of three or something."

A couple of the guests heard their chatter. One stood up and glanced at the hallway. Cassandra noticed and pushed the other women further down the hall and out of sight.

"I can't see shit. Open the door. There will be light in there. Maybe I can fix it?" hissed Mary.

SIX

Sean heard the word 'dessert' through the door and figured they would soon all be seated. He checked the time on his COM. *They would be a little drunk by now*, he thought. *Time to get the show on the road.* He looked at the woman. She was still and appeared to be unconscious. He had not had to dose her for some time. Maybe she was dead. He turned away, dismissing her completely. He stood in front of the open ventilation pipe. He reached inside and turned on the fan. It whirred and was louder than he had anticipated. The pipes were amplifying the noise it made. *Now is the time. Now I will get my revenge. Fucking cunts deserve everything they get,* he thought. "This is for you, Dad," he hissed as he pulled the gas mask over his face and turned on the valve. The gas hissed. The fan pushed it up the pipe. He smiled and pulled the mask off and set it down in front of the pipe. He stepped over and flipped the switch that would cut the power to the magnetic doors. He heard them close. He flipped another switch that set the electronic locks. No one could leave. He wanted to hear them start to panic, so he stepped over to the door. He was about to put his ear to the door when the fan stopped.

He looked at the hole in the vent pipe. He could see the gas falling out of the pipe instead of being pushed up and into the ballroom. He caught motion from the woman in the corner. She had untied her hands and had pulled out the cord to the fan. Sean leapt over to her and tried to grab the end of the cord and plug it back in to the receptacle. She rolled away from him toward the door. She used both her tied feet to kick the wedge that was stopping the door to the ballroom from opening.

At that instant, the door opened, and three women entered the room. One was staring at a small black box in her hand. She spoke, "Let's see if it has a battery compartment." The other two women looked up and took in the scene of a tied-up woman holding the end of an extension cord while a man was trying to wrest it from her. The man quickly stood and rushed at the three women. He pushed them aside, grabbed the wedge from the floor, and shoved it under the door. The women screamed. The woman tied on the floor, still holding the plug in her hand, yelled, "Stop him. He raped me and tried to kill me."

Sean stepped up to her and kicked her viciously in the belly. She moaned but did not drop the cord. He grabbed the cord and tried to plug it in the wall in an effort to restart the fan. The woman lifted her bound feet and slammed them into his side. He rolled to the floor and stopped near the open vent pipe that was now spewing the gas. It was spreading out over the floor. The three intruders were coughing. The woman in the corner was turning gray and coughing. He was coughing. He had to move through the gas that was billowing out of the hole. He held his breath, ran, and tried to grab his gas mask that was sitting like a bowl under a running tap. He pressed it to his face and sucked in. He gagged and pulled the mask away. His lungs were burning. Suddenly, he vomited and fell to the floor. His eyes were nearly blind. The last thing he saw were the three intruders from the ballroom writhe with him as they died. He could not smell the deaths. The gas had taken that small pleasure away.

420

SEVEN

Karima was standing at the bar. She was waiting for the bartender to return with a bottle of Grand Marnier. She glanced across the large room. It looked like her table was empty. Chow and the others were no longer sitting at the table. She thought she saw them duck into the hallway that led to somewhere else. *Probably a fire exit*, she thought. "Where are they going?" she muttered under her breath.

"Where is who going?" asked the bartender. She was holding up a large bottle of Grand Marnier and looking for approval.

"My boss and her friends seemed to have moved." She looked back at the bartender. "Make it two," she said and watched as the bartender poured the liqueur into large snifters. She picked up one and smelled it. She swirled it and took a sip. It smelled wonderful, but it was very strong. She felt a burning in her throat. She was not used to such a strong drink. She took another sip, hoping it would be just a matter of getting used to it. She was partly right. It did taste better. She turned around and stared at the still empty table. *What on earth were they doing?* She took another sip. The drink tasted better. Her experiences with alcohol were very limited. When she was Vihaan, she had tasted some of her uncle's drink. He had offered it once when he was visiting. She remembered that it tasted vile. His mother had been angry, and she had yelled at her brother for being stupid and ordered him to leave the house.

Thoughts of her mother filled Karima with yearning. She missed her mother. He missed his mother. Whenever Karima thought of home, she ended up confused as to who she was. Home was Vihaan. The world was Karima. She needed to be Vihaan again, if only for a little while and only within the confines of his mother's house. Karima would visit soon. It might take some convincing of her handlers, but they would allow it if she forced the issue. She knew she was much too important for them to disallow this request. She was close to becoming part of this government ruled by women. She was Chow's aide now. She had no place to go but up. Chills ran up her spine. With some careful planning and some judicious manipulation, she very well might become the chief aide to the chairwoman. She knew she would have to embrace her female identity even more. If she got a position like that, she would no longer have to use her body to provide favors for favors. She would not have to fuck anyone in any literal sense, but she suspected that AMEN would want her to get to the top anyway she could. *Perhaps only figurative fucking would be required,* she thought, and smiled to herself. Suddenly, the doors to the ballroom closed. Karima could hear the locks click. Everyone was eating dessert. Only those nearest took note. She was close to one set of doors and stepped up and tried to open them. She could not. They were locked. There was a rumble from the room as more guests noticed they were in lockdown. A number of women stood and walked toward the doors. At least a half dozen of the chairwoman's security contingent were moving from various parts of the ballroom toward the chairwoman. It was as if they had magically appeared, because Karima had not noticed them before this moment. On impulse, Karima moved toward the chairwoman's table. She was closer than any of the security. A moment later she was standing, two glasses of Grand Marnier in hand, in front of the chairwoman with the security personnel closing. "Hello. My name is Karima Sanyal. I am an aide to Ms. Chow. I thought you might like to taste this superb liqueur. The bartender got it especially for you." She lied and set the glass down in front of Lillian Carver.

The first of her security personnel arrived. The woman, dressed in a dark suit, had her hand on what appeared to be a taser device clipped to her waist. Ms. Carver held up her hand and the security woman stepped back. They, once again, seemed to fade to invisibility. "Thank you," said Lillian Carver as she picked up the glass and sipped. "Delicious," she said. "Have you met my daughter?"

"Yes, we met briefly at the hospital. I was delivering a package to this young man." She pointed at Quinlan but held Margaret's gaze. A strange understanding seemed to pass between them. The words they both received at the hospital - '*You will soon have a visitor. It is a perfect opportunity. Introduce yourself. Be cordial and make friends. All will be explained later,*' ran through both of their minds. There were weak smiles all around.

Margaret spoke, "Yes. I remember you. Nice to see you again."

Quinlan stood. It was a reflex. He had been taught that he should stand in this kind of situation. He was about to offer her his seat when he realized there were two free seats. Lillian Carver gestured toward one of the chairs. Karima glanced toward Chow's table. The table was still empty, so Karima decided she would join this table. She looked at Quinlan. "Congratulations on your award," she said and pulled the chair away from the table.

Suddenly, an alarm sounded. All the security officers reappeared and moved to the chairwoman's table. They were no longer hesitant. The persons at the table were escorted toward the stage entrance. To her surprise, Karima was included. They all disappeared out of the ballroom and into an elevator at the back of the stage.

The security room on the admin floor lit up. Gas leak indicators were flashing red and blue. Soon there were a number of Fempol officers in the room. They did not know why the doors had closed, but they decided to err on the side of caution. None of the gas sensors indicated there was a leak in the ballroom proper, so the locks were overridden. There were just too many important people in that ballroom to take any chances. The room was cleared, and the source of the problem was discovered by an officer from the atrium looking down the stairway into the mechanical room. The gas was slowly rising up. They quickly sealed off the room until the personnel with the proper equipment could repair what was initially thought to be a gas leak.

QUINLAN
SMITH

Quinlan sat down in the cafeteria. It was afternoon and his classes were finished. He sipped his coffee. He had grown fond of coffee. It was something he did not have access to in his other life. Now, he was not sure he could get through a day without at least three cups. He looked up at the video screen on the side wall. The Webbies were running a news cycle that never seemed to end. It was following the murders at Fempol Gala that happened three weeks ago. There were stories that delved into Sean Kilkenny's past. He was made out to be a male monster by the conservative right. They were using him as a perfect example of why males should be restricted even more than they presently were.

Interview of Madeline Gerard:
Fempol Commissioner of the South-Eastern States

Interviewer:
Commissioner Gerard, would you say you agree with the MAR Act as it presently stands?
Commissioner Gerard:
In a word: NO. The restriction put on males by this law has obvi-

ously failed to achieve its purpose. The murders at Fempol head office must serve as a warning to all women. This man—this monster—was given freedom to move about the city as a pest control officer. He was actually working for the city. He was working for us. We allowed him access to Fempol offices. We allowed him access to poisons. We gave him our trust. We are to blame for the deaths of these four women, one of whom was an aide to the Chairwoman. The deaths of over four hundred powerful women were averted by the narrowest of margins. Can you imagine the fallout? We must never let something like this happen again.

Interviewer:

How do you propose to ensure that it doesn't?

Commissioner Gerard:

That is very simple. We already have the skeleton in MARA. All we need to do is flesh it out and give it some muscle. There are a number of loopholes that need to be filled. For example, I know of a popular male hangout location that seems to uphold the letter of the law as imposed by MARA but flaunts its dismissal of the intent.

Interviewer:

How does it do that?

Commissioner Gerard:

The hangout serves liquor and houses at least a hundred men. They have kept the men separated by the required distances and deliver drinks by drone. This does not stop them from organizing and recruiting others to rise up against us. They are not technically breaking the law, so the law must be changed.

Interviewer:

Have you heard Chief Davenport's comments?

Commissioner Gerard:

First of all, Chief Commissioner Davenport must be questioned as to her part in this fiasco. Whatever she says has to be thoroughly vetted. After all, she created a male hero and rewarded him. This sets a dangerous precedent.

Quinlan turned from the newscast and gathered his materials. He looked around to see if anyone was watching him. Things seemed to have settled.

He knew he had to keep a very low profile. His relationship with Margaret was strained. She seemed to be much more interested in learning the ropes of government from her mother. Her ideas about giving men more freedom were not as evident as they were before the 'Gala Murders', as the incident was now called. She had said something to him about staying apart until *'things settled down'*. Her words. He did not understand what she meant. Things were never going to settle down for him. They were just going to get worse. He was one of the lucky males who had a small fraction of immunity from any kind of retaliation. At least that is what he chose to think. To think anything else would only make things worse. He chose to behave as he had always behaved. He would work to be what the world expected him to be. If the MAR Act changed, it would not affect him. He did not have any male friends with whom to assemble.

Margaret had also said that her work with one of Chow's aides, Karima something or other, had given her some insight into how to overcome some of the restrictions placed on males. Her mother was starting to see that continued restrictions on the males of the population could only bring about revolution. It was better to get in front of it because it was bound to happen. The pendulum was swinging back, and no amount of legal or illegal restrictions could stop it. Males needed to be given more freedoms, not less. They were intelligent enough to see that women had made the world a better place in only two generations of leadership. How could they not? The US had not lost a single soldier in any conflict for the last 20-plus years. All soldiers were female. All police were female. All government officials were female. All company CEOs were female. This was not going to change in the near future. Change like that was likely impossible. It had taken women too long. It was unlikely men would get any real power back, but what they could get is a good life without the pain of repression. Quinlan would be satisfied with that.

TREATISE

THE PRISON OF POWER: A MAN-MADE TALE

"The Transmogrification of Power from Male to Female in the United States of America: A History"
Addendum: "The Gala Murders - The Impetus for Total Gender Equality/Inequality Polarization" by Simi Timpani Rau
University of Delhi, New Delhi, India
November 2113

The events that occurred at the Fempol ballroom on September 23, 2051 initiated extreme polarization that amplified the differences between American Males Equality Nation (AMEN) and right-wing extremist groups like the Plague Warriors. It was leaked by a number of government officials that AMEN was involved in the attempted gassing of all 400 of the guests. They suggested that the perpetrator, Sean Kilkenny, was under direct orders of AMEN. This was vehemently denied by AMEN. It was subsequently confirmed that he acted alone, but the accusation continued to be used to further the right-wing's political agenda. They pushed the General Committee of the time to pass legislation that would further subjugate the males of the society using this as their main reason.

It was discovered that three of the four women killed in the machine room adjacent to the ballroom when the release of the gas went awry were members of the PW, including Karen Chow. It was further discovered that Karen Chow, the aide to the Chairwoman of the time, was also a high-ranking member of the PW. She was responsible for several of the murders, including the attempted murder of the Chairwoman and the head of Fempol, Nisheeta Davenport. There were a number of claims that she was also instrumental in the executions of the accused rapists eleven years before. This was denied by the right-wing as being lies perpetrated by AMEN. None of the evidence collected over the years has clarified who was really responsible.

The efforts to return males to their previous status in the society of the American States has, as you know, made some strides. It continues to be discussed by those that see male self-determination as important to any modern society, but the argument has lost some of its lustre. It is difficult to maintain the debate that male power would improve what most women see as the best possible society ever conceived. As of the date of this article, wars have become extinct. Most illnesses have been eradicated. Murders are

438

extremely low and almost always occur where men have been allowed to gather in groups. All the societal problems of the past have been greatly reduced. It is called a Regulated Democracy. It is the first form of government in human history to achieve what some have termed "femtopia." Yes, there are some that will argue that it is not democracy at all when a large portion of the society has no say, but perhaps it is the process that matters. It is, perhaps, the beginning of an evolution in humans where gender does not dictate the basis of power. Nature demands that the pendulum slows.

ACKNOWLEDGEMENTS

I am eternally grateful to all those who stuck with me as I wrote this novel. COVID 19 extended its publication. I have concluded that was a good thing. Many more people were able to give me constructive criticism, especially my wife Cheryl Cameron, my editor Vanessa Anderson, and my daughter Lindsay Smith. They gave me valuable feedback and tolerated my tendency to passionately defend my position on, "What would a woman do?"

I thank my friend John Wirtanen who kept me above water when the emotional floods tried to sweep me away.

I thank all the women in my life for providing me the opportunity to gain insight into the female psyche.

ABOUT THE AUTHOR

G MICHAEL SMITH is a retired teacher of Computer Programming, Drama, Math, English, and Theatre. He's written and directed plays for both adults and children. He also writes poetry and novels.

His body of work includes *The Forevers, a YA SciFi series;* *Hijacked,* a middle-grade mystery; an Early-reader Children's Books series including the titles *Lily Liar and the Eleventy Headed Monster, Tiny Tina and the Terrible Trouble,* and forthcoming *Ashley and the Hornets,* as well as a Children's Picture Book titled *The Accidental Adventures of Bernie the Banana Slug.*

Smith resides in Qualicum Beach, Vancouver Island, BC, Canada with his wife, Cheryl, and enjoys spending time with his three adult daughters and three grandchildren. He's also known to enjoy a rigorous game of pickleball, softball, squash, or badminton.

Learn more at gmichaelsmith.com.

The Seven Days of My Creation

Cover photograph:

Lyminge Forest near Canterbury in Southern England, an ancient forest with Bronze Age burial mounds and rare bird species. This photograph was taken after the forest had been saved from destruction by years of protest by local people and over one hundred eco-warriors. The author, who grew up nearby, lived and worked in the forest with the eco-warriors. She describes what happened in this book. (See page 517 and following.)